YOU'RE NEVER THE SAME

BILL BATEMAN

ODYSSEY
BOOKS

Published by Odyssey Books in 2019
www.odysseybooks.com.au

National Library of Australia
Cataloguing-in-Publication entry

Author: Bill Bateman
Title: You're Never the Same / Bill Bateman
ISBN: 978-1925652628 (paperback)
ISBN: 978-1925652635 (ebook)

Cover design by Elijah Toten

For my mate, Stu—the best of men.

1

'Vinny, it's Trisha.'

Dr Vincent Hanrahan was twenty minutes behind and about to call in his next patient. Vince never answered his mobile when he was consulting but he knew this call must be important. His sister wouldn't ring him mid-morning on a weekday just to say hi.

'I'm up home,' she went on, her voice strained. 'Joey's missing. He's not with you, is he?'

'No, Trish. He's not down here. What's the story?'

'He was supposed to come into Horsham on Monday night to spend New Year's Eve with Jane and the kids, but he didn't turn up. So Jane came out to the farm yesterday and found no sign of him and the dogs are still here and Uncle Jack and Aunty Margaret and the neighbours haven't seen him and—'

'Steady on, sis,' Vince said as Trisha's words tumbled out in an urgent torrent. 'He could be anywhere. Maybe he's gone fishing with his mates.'

'He hasn't taken his car, and his camping and fishing gear are all here. The ute's still in the garage.'

Bloody strange. 'Has he finished the harvest already?'

There was a pause and a comment in the background.

'Joey didn't put in a summer crop this year.'

Must've decided to cut his losses, Vince reflected. 'What about his clothes?'

He could hear further conversation.

'Jane says nothing's gone.' Another pause. 'She hasn't heard from him since Christmas Day and he usually rings the kids every night.'

A destabilising wave of nausea passed through Vince's body. 'What about his motorbike, you know, the farm bike?'

He heard a volley of fading footsteps, then the back door banging. Vince pictured Trisha and Jane rushing out to the machinery shed, two hundred metres across the yard.

A few minutes later, Trisha came back on the line. Panting. 'The motorbike's not there, Vinny. It's gone!'

Vince frowned and looked at the appointment list on his computer screen—chockers. Too bad.

'Hang on.'

He picked up his desk phone. 'Lorraine, I'm taking the rest of the day off, maybe the week. I know, I know, so re-book some and see if Shirley or the Prez can see the rest. Can't be helped. Family business. Yeah, I'll let you know.'

Vince hung up and grabbed his mobile. 'I'm on my way.'

He strode out through the crowded waiting room, jumped into his old Volvo, drove down to his modest dwelling in South Warrnambool, and threw a change of underwear and his toothbrush in a bag. He asked his next-door neighbour to look after his dog, filled up Benny's tank at the servo, then headed out of town on the long road north.

For most of the trip, despite the loud distractions of Courtney Barnett and Van Morrison, interspersed with snippets of Test match commentary, Vince's mind oscillated between his little brother's disappearance and his own fall from grace. Both topics unpleasant but inescapable. He had no awareness of passing through all the places on the way but was jolted out of his reverie as he approached Rupanyup, just twenty kilometres from his destination. He glanced at the dashboard clock—two and a half hours had vanished into the hot, dry Wimmera air. Without a trace.

The small town, strung out in a long line either side of the split road, was at once both familiar and strange. Vince was back on home territory, but he wasn't feeling at home. He glanced across instinctively at the pair of towering cement grain silos on the right. His mouth fell open. They now displayed huge monochrome spectral faces—a footballer and a netballer—with a sign underneath saying 'Silo Arts Trail'. *Street art in Runpanyup. Now I've seen everything!*

He continued up the gun barrel-straight road, which was crossed at intervals by red gravel tracks, each sign posted either side with family farm names. Vince recognised them all. It was a featureless terrain, save the straggling rows of eucalypts along the sides of the road, the power lines overhead, and the occasional farmhouse, with its grove of trees and orderly row of rocket-topped steel silos gleaming in the sunshine. The landscape was tabletop flat too, as far as the eye could see, relieved only by the heaped-up dirt edging the dry dams, the attendant impotent windmills, and the distant dark shape of the Grampians to the south. There were none of the undulating hills, majestic tree-lined drives, bluestone fences, and historic homesteads of the Western District properties he had blindly passed on the way up.

Vince glanced around. The beauty of this land was not apparent to the casual observer. He knew that. You had to look deeper. And when you found that beauty, it was bleak and brutal but worth the quest. His father loved the Wimmera. 'This dirt gets into your blood, boys. God's own country.' The family had given Mick a light-plane trip over the district for his seventieth. Vince had joined him on the flight. It was just before harvest—in a good year. The geometric patterns of the farms and the colours of the ripening crops were stunning and otherworldly. Mick had peered out the window at the expansive vista below with a radiant smile and tears pouring down his craggy cheeks.

As he drove on, Vince was struck by the arid and forlorn appearance of the surrounding countryside. As his father used to say, 'Come January, son, it's as dry as a dead dingo's donger round here.' But this was different. The huge sky and distant horizon were recognisable enough, but where were the paddocks full of chest-high stalks, loaded with grain, ripe for the stripping? And where were the headers, those majestic broad-combed beasts that should be rumbling up and down, pouring streams of golden grain into the bins, rows of chaff and yellow stubble in their wake? Instead, the fields were still—dormant or speckled with failed crops.

Vince slowed down as he approached tiny Minyip, a roadside sign proclaiming it to be 'The Home of the Wheat Belt'. His father had regarded that sign as pretentious. Now it just looked ironic. He passed the timber Lutheran church, its tall white spire reaching for the heavens, and stopped at the crossroad in the centre of the town. Twenty years ago, the town had achieved fame for being the setting for the fictional 'Coopers Crossing' in a TV series about the Flying Doctors. But the showbiz buzz of those halcyon days was long gone. Now there was an eerie silence. Little sign of life. No one in the few shops, the farm machinery dealership deserted, and just a few utes outside the pub.

Vince grimaced and followed the Warracknabeal road out into open country. Ten minutes later, he turned into the familiar entrance, the farm gate open and 'Clonmel' emblazoned on the fence in dark green letters. He drove across the cattle grid into the poplar-lined drive, bounced along the corrugations, trailing a cloud of dust behind him, and pulled up outside the family homestead. One of Joey's dogs bounded up as Vince emerged from the car.

'Settle down, Danger,' he said, patting the excited kelpie.

He walked around to the back of the house and was greeted by the diminutive figure of his sister as she opened the ancient flywire door. Trisha's auburn mane was greying and her customary bouncy verve was absent. Even her freckles seemed muted. As children, she was as small as he was big, and they were both carrot-topped, whereas Joey had the dark fineness of their mother.

'Two of you got the Hanrahan hair,' their father remarked. 'Poor buggers.'

Vince ran his hand over his chrome dome. Things had changed. Many things. He and Trisha hugged, sibling style, and he followed her onto the rear porch. Out of habit, he took off his shoes and put them on the wooden rack.

'No sign of him?'

She shook her head. 'Uncle Jack and I have driven all around, asked the neighbours, been into town.' She shrugged, hands forward like a priest at the altar.

'No note or anything?'

She shook her head harder still. 'Nothing.'

'Jane has no idea?'

'No,' Trisha said with a grimace.

'Has she gone back to Horsham?' Vince glanced into the house. Horsham was the big smoke, the capital of the Wimmera.

'Yep, the children were with a sitter.' She waved a hand around. 'Janey told me she couldn't stand even being *in* this house.'

'I didn't know she'd moved out altogether,' Vince replied. 'I thought it was just a trial separation.'

'Like you and Lydia, you mean?'

That's a low blow. He looked around the kitchen, a few new appliances but otherwise the kitchen of his childhood, although his mother would've said the place needed a clean. Vince glanced through to the lounge room—newspapers stacked upon the floor, dirty dishes on the table, and a pile of unopened mail on the mantlepiece. The adjacent family photos and old clock were covered with a film of dust.

'Have you rung the police?'

She sat down, face tight, and balled her hands on the table. 'What do you think? They were here this morning and took statements off Jane and me. They've notified Missing Persons, we've contacted Dad's nursing home, been to the pubs, the golf club, I've rung all Joey's farming friends—not that he's got many. Old school mates and guys from Ag college—ditto. I spoke to his fishing buddies, and we've—'

Vince put his hand up. 'Okay, okay, I get it. I've just arrived and started asking stupid questions. Sorry, sis.'

He and Joey always came to Trisha when they were in trouble and needed her to advocate for them with their parents. Being back home made Vince feel like that little boy again. Except now there was a grown-up problem to solve. And *he* was a grown-up.

Trisha blew her nose into a tissue from a box on the table, got up and lifted the kettle, her eyebrows raised.

'Yeah, that'd be good, thanks.' He looked out the window at the still-blazing sun sinking in the big Wimmera sky. 'I tell you what would be even better—a nice cold beer.'

* * *

Vince drank his tea in silence, the kitchen clock ticking and Danger producing the odd, tired bark from the back door. *Where would Joey have gone? On the motorbike?* He gazed around the kitchen and his mind drifted. The three of them used to be wild farm kids back in the day. Chasing the chooks around, annoying the dogs, riding their bikes up and down the drive, hanging around the old house … *Shit, the old house!*

Down the bottom of the home paddock on the far side of the plantation was the homestead built by Vince's grandfather when he was given a soldier settler's block after the war. His son had built a new place higher up the rise after he married Vince's mother in the sixties, and the original home had become derelict.

'Has anyone been over to the old house?' Vince tried to keep his voice steady.

'Of *course*, Vinny,' Trisha answered, chin in her hands, face drawn. 'We went over and looked everywhere. Nothing there, apart from lots of birds nesting and a few rats.'

Vince pushed his chair back from the table, his mind racing. 'What about the Old Mass Shandrydan?'

She frowned. 'Pop's old caravan? Why would he go there?'

He stood, trying to suppress a rising sense of panic. 'That's where he used to hide. After you went to boarding school.' He headed for the door. 'When he was in strife,' he added over his shoulder.

Vince burst through the flywire door and sprinted along the path, past the front gate and across the paddock, Danger yapping at his heels. There was no grass underfoot, just dust and the odd tussock or thistle. He was breathing hard as he passed the empty dam and rounded the front fence of the old house. As he neared, he slowed to a jog and walked the last few metres toward the ancient wooden caravan, its large iron wheels rusted and crooked.

It was floodlit by the setting sun. Luminous and ominous. 'Pop used to go droving in that,' their father had told them, 'when he'd just started farming and had no money. His old mare, Clover, used to pull it along the roads.'

Despite the heat, Vince shivered with a cold sweat. He felt like he was in a dream. There was the motorbike, parked behind the van. His gut lurched. A loud roaring started in his head as he climbed the rickety steps, waving away a cloud of flies before opening the door.

Joey was sitting at the little built-in table, head backward, jaw a mangled mess, the back of his cranium missing.

Shotgun on the floor.

Blood and brains everywhere.

He was quite dead.

2

The trip home the next day was a lot slower than the drive up. Not that Warrnambool was Vince's home—anything but. On the journey back he noticed everything around him, each farmhouse, the little towns with their railheads and silos, and the slow build of activity as the small communities woke for another day. He focused on all the mundane details of the passing scenery—anything to distract him from the turbulent thoughts in his head and the ache in his heart.

The bottle of water and sandwich Trisha had given him lay untouched on the seat. Zero appetite. Nausea gnawed at his stomach and he was close enough to vomiting. He turned on the radio and listened with intense concentration. Infighting in the federal government, bush fires in Queensland, and Nick Kyrgios misbehaving at the tennis. While he was on the road, Vince could escape reality. For now.

In a trance-like state, he arrived back at the 'Bool, pulled up outside the surgery, and glanced at the time—just before midday. He eased himself out the car, rubbed his stiff back, and pushed open the rear door. The Timor Street Clinic was housed in a once-majestic sandstone home close to the hospital. It had been modified over the years but still displayed some of its former grandeur. Vince's boss, Shirley Tiang, an ebullient sixty-something-year-old Malaysian-Chinese GP, had started the clinic several years before and it now boasted four doctors.

Vince walked straight to Shirley's consulting room and knocked on the door.

'Come in if you're good lookin'.'

She was sitting at her desk—a tiny elfin figure, head bobbing and dangly earrings dancing. Shirley was between patients—good timing.

'The return of the proverbial son,' she said, looking up. 'What's going down, Rooned? Sort out your family stuff?'

Shirley's eclectic combination of Sino strine and malapropisms was acquired growing up in Western Sydney after moving with her family from Kuala Lumpur as a child. She'd borrowed the 'Rooned' moniker from 'We'll all be Rooned, said Hanrahan,' a bush poem she'd encountered at school. '*That* Hanrahan was a miserable cove,' she'd told Vince, 'just like you, eh?' The same author had also penned 'The Old Mass Shandrydan', about a horse-drawn cart used for taking a large country family to church on Sundays, hence the nickname for Leo Hanrahan's abandoned caravan.

Vince flopped down onto the chair on the other side of the desk, damp clothes clinging to his tired body.

Shirley peered at him through her purple, oversize Edna Everage glasses. 'You look like something the dog dragged in, buddy.'

He hadn't shaved for days and was still wearing the same crumpled jeans and polo shirt he'd left in.

'I'll be getting all suited up tomorrow. Got a funeral up country.'

She gave him a Puckish look, eyebrows raised.

'My little brother Joey.' Saying it out loud for the first time, the words stuck in his throat. 'Took his own life.'

Shirley jumped up, her mouth open. 'Jeez, poor beggar! What the deal?'

'Isolated farmer, drought, marriage breakup.' He shrugged. 'You know the stats for rural blokes, Shirl.'

'This was your blood and flesh, no stat.' She came around the desk, arms out for an embrace.

Vince stood and backed away. 'I've just got to tidy up some stuff here, check on the dog, and pick up my suit from the house.'

'Don't worry about this joint,' said Shirley, waving her arm around in a circle. 'I'll check your results and hospital patients, take your times. *Suicide* is serious shit.'

Hearing the word was like a kick in the guts.

3

'That's another one down to El bloody Nino.'

Vince looked up from the grave at the parched, brown paddocks surrounding the cemetery. Dry riverbeds, empty dams, and failed crops. Joey dead at forty-four. Interred back into that same baked earth. Vince looked up to the heavens—the endless, opalescent, cloudless Wimmera sky, the distant horizon, and the huge and fiery sun. Felt more like hell than heaven.

Uncle Jack loosened his tie, tilted back his hat, and gestured across the fence. 'Should be flat out harvesting all round the district, by rights.'

Vince surveyed the landscape. This was supposed to be the centre of the Victorian wheat belt. In better days and better years, he and Joey had worked like men at harvest time. Opening and closing gates, shifting the field bins, and bringing food out to their dad as he drove the header up and down the rows, stripping wheat, barley, and the thick yellow carpets of canola. No air-conditioned cabins with their TVs and computers back then. Hard yakka all round. Then the happy drive into town in the truck to the weighbridge, another source of summer employment for the boys as they got older.

'Was shaping up as a bumper crop this year,' observed Jack. 'But the spring rains never came.'

Vince looked down at his father in his wheelchair at the graveside and put his hand on that thin shoulder. Mick Hanrahan's farming days were long behind him—he could barely control a walking frame these days, let alone a tractor. Vince inspected the puzzled expression on his father's craggy, weather-beaten face. He had no idea where he was. Home was now the dementia wing of the Chatsworth Nursing Home in far-off South Melbourne. His wife was long gone—breast cancer, fifteen years earlier. Now his youngest son was dead too, laid to rest next to his mother and grandparents. Old Mick's demeanour was one of bewilderment rather than sorrow, but Vince wondered whether the gravity of the day had penetrated that dense neural fog, even just a little.

'Three years with no crop,' Uncle Jack went on. He paused again, in the sparse manner of the men Vince had grown up with, and looked down at the coffin.

'Young Joseph won't be the last victim of this drought.'

* * *

The service had been simple and affecting. Mostly family and neighbours. A few words by a generic chaplain at the graveside with Joey's estranged wife and their children, shocked and sobbing at the front, clutching roses in their hands, ready to drop onto the casket. It was a still day, flies everywhere, and a heavy blanket of oppressive heat surrounded the mourners. Vince had no hat or sunglasses and felt like he was melting inside his suit. There'd been no Requiem Mass. No church ceremony at all. *Mum would've been devastated.* He looked at her grave, adjacent to the freshly dug one.

Jane had organised the burial ceremony. Vince rang her after the gruesome discovery. The conversation had been brief. No, she didn't want to come out to the farm, and no, she didn't want a visit from her husband's siblings. Then she'd gone to ground, not answering her phone and refusing to see any of the Hanrahans. Seemed more angry than sad.

Trisha had done all the arrangements for the wake in her usual role of family organiser.

'Joe left strict instructions in his will about the funeral,' she told Vince back at the house as they sat out on the deep front veranda overlooking the bedraggled, once-thriving garden. 'He had no time for the Catholic Church.'

'He wasn't on his Pat Malone there.'

'That's the problem. Joe *was* alone.' She put down her teacup with a clatter. 'When were you last up here to see him?'

Vince paused, memories and guilt flooding into him. 'I used to come up and help him with the harvest. But when the drought started he stopped returning my calls.' He looked out at the brown earth. 'I assumed there wasn't enough crop to strip.'

Trisha turned her tear-stained face to his. *Mum's frown*, thought Vince. Bad portent.

'You could've driven that big BMW up to see him, couldn't you?'

A dagger in the heart. 'Was a bit busy with the practice, and then since … you know, the shit hit the fan for me, I …'

Empty words, he knew. Trisha's look, just like his mum's, told a thousand of them.

'Perhaps it wasn't the drought.' She looked away and motioned toward the arid surrounds. 'After you went to uni, Joey knew he had to come home and help Dad. Maybe his heart wasn't in it.' She shook her head. 'He seemed to lose his way.'

'Is that the sister speaking or the family therapist?'

Trisha turned to face him again, eyes blazing. 'It was obvious to anyone with a shred of empathy, for God's sake!'

Vince nodded; he had no answer.

Trisha stood, walked over to the veranda rail and gazed into the dazzling stillness. After a few minutes' silence, she sat down again, dried her eyes and took a deep, slow breath. 'Your crew not here?'

Another dagger. 'The girls have important VCE summer school subjects.' He paused. 'So I'm told.' He raised his hands. 'They hardly knew Joey.'

She scoffed. 'And whose fault is that?'

Vince shrugged. 'Mine, I guess.'

'And Lydia?'

'OS. Ivan had a conference in Singapore and she couldn't get back in time.'

'Fair enough.'

Trisha headed for the front door. 'I'd better see to Dad and help Aunty Marg with the sandwiches. You should get off your bum and give Uncle Jack a hand with the drinks. That's your forte, isn't it?'

She glanced back over her shoulder. 'Joey really looked up to you, you know.'

Coup de grâce.

* * *

'Uncle Joe would've enjoyed this, mate,' Paddy said as he booted a big torpedo punt down to the trio of shouting boys at the bottom of the paddock, wrestling and rolling in the brown dust.

It was Sunday, and Trisha had gone into town for mass—'Still hanging in, just'—and Vince was having a kick of the footy at the front of the house with her husband Paddy and their three wild lads. They used the two poplars near the dam as goal posts, just like he and Joey used to do all those years ago. *Except the dam had water in it back then.* Vince looked around. *And there used to be grass underfoot.*

Paddy, Trisha, and their brood lived in a terraced cottage in Brunswick. Trisha worked as a family therapist at the nearby community health centre. Vince envied their devotion to each other and their close family unit. *Me and Lids and the girls started out that way,* he reflected. *What the hell happened?*

'Joey told me that you and him used to play kick-to-kick out here all the time when you were little tackers.'

Paddy was tall and wiry and always smiling. He had a ponytail, a sleeve of tats, and an earring, and he and Vince had gotten on well right from the start. When Trisha brought her new boyfriend up to the farm that first Christmas, Vince was just off to uni and Joey was still at school. Paddy, a chippie by trade, had helped with the harvest and replaced a few worn weatherboards on the house.

'Wild-looking bugger,' their father had said. 'Decent enough young bloke all the same.'

Vince jerked himself back to the present. 'Too right, we did,' he answered. 'The old man used to roost it down to us and we'd fly for a specky. I was always bigger, but Joey would fight and fight for that ball. He'd *never* give up.' Vince's heart started pounding and his chest tightened. *Too right. Joey would never give up.*

Detectives from the Ballarat CIB and their forensic examiners had spent most of Friday in that old wooden van, concluded that the cause of death was suicide, and closed the case.

'I think I'll go inside for a spell, Paddy. Bit out of condition.'

* * *

Trisha had volunteered to clean up the house and go into Horsham the next day to see Joey's solicitor. Vince had an early dinner, said his goodbyes, and headed south again. It was a sad farewell too, even for a renowned emotional cripple like himself. With Joey gone and the end of the line of three generations of the family on that land, it was gut-wrenching to drive away from Clonmel, maybe for the last time.

'Lucky the old man's away with the fairies,' he said to the long, straight bitumen strip ahead. 'Joey in the ground and no one running the farm—it would've killed him.'

Vince drove on through the small Wimmera towns. He knew the road well. Every year after harvest, Mick and Mary would pack up the family and head down to Port Fairy. They rented the same small fibro near the caravan park on Griffiths Street each summer. 'Just a change of sink,' Mary would say as she wrangled the children while her husband talked farming and racing in the front bar of the Star of the West Hotel. The boys would play cricket at low tide on the East Beach and assign Mary and Trisha to positions in the outfield amongst the shallows. Little Joey was full of mischief and spirit in those days. Appealed after each delivery, swung the bat like Adam Gilchrist, chased every ball …

As he slowed approaching Ararat, Vince noticed a salty taste in his mouth and realised his cheeks were wet with tears. Trisha's words after the funeral had hit their mark. The last time he had been up to see his brother had been well over a year ago, a few months after he'd been banished to Warrnambool …

'Joey's battling,' Trisha had said on the phone. 'Jane and the kids have been spending more and more time staying with her mum in Horsham.'

Vince had just been smashed by both Lydia and the Medical Board and sent to Coventry. *I'm battling too*, he'd thought, but he reckoned there was a bit of schadenfreude at work there.

'He's become more reclusive and less communicative,' she went on, 'and sounds like he's hitting the bottle.' She paused. 'Alcohol and marriage breakdown—what is it with you Hanrahan boys?'

'Okay, Trish, I'll go up and see him,' he replied, letting the last comment go through to the keeper. 'But it'll be like the blind leading the blind.'

So Vince had driven up for a visit. It soon became apparent that each brother was immersed in his own cocoon of existential suffering. On the first night, Joey put away half a dozen VBs and Vince OD'd on diet Coke and cups of tea, amongst the sporadic conversation about sport. On the Saturday evening after a counter meal at the local pub, he decided to chance his arm.

'So, Joey, what's going on?'

Long pause. Joey stared steadily at his glass. 'How do you mean?'

He looked up, lips compressed in a slant and one eyebrow raised. A familiar expression. Joey had restless brown eyes, a slender but strong body, and was 'tough as a Mallee root', as old Mick used to say. Vince noticed that his little brother's black curly mop was thinning out and turning silver at the temples.

'I don't see Jane and the kids around the place.'

Joey laughed. 'Too isolated. So I hear.' He pointed out the pub window. 'Been a bit dry too, you might've noticed.'

'Must be tough on the financial front.' Vince pulled out his chequebook. 'I'm happy to help you out.'

'You can stick that where the sun don't shine.' Joey picked up his pot, gulped it down, and slammed it back on the table.

'Fair enough,' Vince said after a pause. *Come this far.* 'You seem to be giving the grog a nudge. What about seeing a counsellor?'

Joey laughed again, as before—no smile. 'Shit! Once I start taking advice from you, I might as bloody well give the whole game away.' He got up. 'Time to hit the sack. Best you make an early start tomorrow. Bit hot and dusty for big-shot doctors up here.'

Vince had rung Joey once or twice since then, but found he wasn't up for chitchat so he'd stopped bothering. He'd emailed him that year to arrange to meet down at the MCG for their usual date at the AFL grand final, but received no response. Surprising, he'd thought; the Cats were favourites and Joey was a Geelong fan like him. Even his dogs were named after their players.

Vince had spent the following year trying to save his own professional and personal futures—a temporary reprieve with the first and facing a straight-sets loss with the second. Just keeping his head above water. No time to worry about his little brother.

4

It was close to midnight when Vince arrived back in Warrnambool. He parked Benny on the cracked cement drive, went inside, and switched on the lights. The old farmhouse was like *Home Beautiful* compared to this place. His New Year's resolution to keep the house at least half tidy had already unravelled. *Too bad. It's just a staging post.* He reached out for the broom then shook his head.

'Forget it,' he told his dog Deefer, who looked happy but confused by her master's nocturnal arrival. 'I'll do it tomorrow after work.'

The next morning he was up bright and early. Well, early anyway. Now over two years into his exile, Vince started every day with a run on the beach. Unless there was a good swell, that was. Or he was knackered from a busy night on-call. *Or if my little brother had just topped himself.* Deefer whined and pawed at the back door at first light anyway, so staying in bed wasn't an option. Sleep had eluded him last night. His body was exhausted but his mind was in overdrive—shifting dark tabloids of childhood memories and self-loathing.

He dragged himself out of bed and stood under the shower for ten minutes, struggling to bring himself back to the present. He pulled on some clothes, then swallowed two Weetbix and drained a mug of instant coffee before pouring some pellets into Deefer's bowl. The dog cleaned it up in seconds and trotted to the back door, tail wagging.

Vince glanced at his reflection in the back-door window and a stooped, bald figure with a pale face stared back. 'Who's that old bloke?'

he asked Deefer, then shook himself and straightened his shoulders. He'd always been a big unit—a ruckman's build with small, deep eyes, a crooked nose and, in recent times, a bald pate. Lydia used to say his teeth were his best feature, but his smiling muscles seemed to have weakened over the last few years. *Lack of bloody use.*

'Okay, mate, we'll go for a walk.'

Vince grabbed the lead and they wandered down Fay Street over the Merri River Bridge and cut in past the skate ramp to the path through the bush and onto the beach. It was a beautiful morning and the water looked inviting. There was a nice break with a gentle off-shore breeze. Vince breathed in the salty air, normally a balm for his soul, but the magic wasn't working today. They trudged along the shoreline for a few hundred metres and then headed back to the house.

Time to get back to doctoring. He grabbed his bag and hit the road. Rural general practice was a big come down from his former life as a high-flying obstetrician and gynaecologist in the big league. A text from Shirley had encouraged him to take a few days off, but he knew better.

'Don't let that intense introspection take over, Dr Hanrahan,' his shrink had said. 'It'll do your head in. Keep busy and be in the moment.' *Yada yada yada.*

* * *

Vince walked straight in the back door of the Timor Street Clinic, looking neither left nor right, and marched to his consulting room. He sat down and turned on his computer. There was an immediate knock at the door and the practice manager poked her head in. Early forties, curtains of wavy brown hair, and a no-nonsense demeanour.

'Welcome back, Dr Hanrahan. Sorry for your loss. I blocked out a few spare appointments for today.'

'Thanks, Lorraine.'

Vince brought up his list and scrutinised the names. He was about to beckon the first patient when his door swung wide. *Jesus, now what?* Shirley Tiang waltzed in with a bunch of flowers and sat in the chair opposite his desk. She had on her usual work outfit—a vivid stripy blouse, chunky jewellery, black pants tapering to the ankles, and low-cut leather boots.

'Make yourself at home.'

She sat back and looked around the room. 'You need a painter and docker here, bud. This is like a hospital outpatient cubicle. Needs a bit of colour and movements.' She glanced at the bare walls. 'No family pics, even.'

Vince grimaced. 'My family is shrinking fast.'

'We all thinking of you, cobber.'

'Thank you.' Vince felt his voice break. *What's that about? Thought I was doing okay.*

He hustled Shirley out, took a deep breath, then called in his first customer: a young woman with two kids in tow and one still cooking. Vince knew Tracey Cartwright well. She was the daughter of his neighbour, Carmel Harrington, and he was conscious of that extra obligation. In country practice, he'd come to realise just about every patient ended up being a special case. By the time you excluded friends, relatives, and work colleagues, there were few regular punters left.

Tracey's voice was flat, ditto her appearance. Thin as a stick apart from her distended abdomen, her honey-blond hair was dull and unkempt, her complexion pallid. *Par for the course for a pregnant young mother of two.* But he knew it wasn't just fatigue. Tracey was also sporting a bluish bruise along her right temple and around her eye. *Not for the first time.*

'Looks like you've had a bit of a buster.'

She frowned and put a hand to her face. 'Trod on the rake in the backyard. Happen to anyone.'

Vince shook his head. They both looked across at the boys playing in the toy corner. He leant forward, wrapped a grey cuff around Tracey's skinny upper arm, and spoke softly. 'We both know that's not true. It was Dustin, wasn't it?'

She watched the changing numbers on the blood pressure machine for a few moments before answering. 'He just can't settle since he came back from Iraq. When he gets on the drink, he … he … loses control.' She put her head in her hands. 'I know he still loves me.'

Vince motioned Tracey up onto the examination couch and palpated her belly and listened to the baby's heart with the foetal stethoscope.

'Bit on the small size,' he commented as she retook her seat. 'Heart sounded good though, didn't it?'

Tracey gave an indifferent shrug, pulled out her phone, and started reading her messages.

'Listen to me, Trace. I know he had a tough time over there, but that doesn't give him the right to knock you around.'

A fierce dispute broke out about the contested possession of a red fire truck.

'Stop fighting, you boys,' called Tracey. 'Over here, Toby, and let the doctor have a look at your sore ear.'

Vince could see the shutters come down.

'When Dustin comes in next week for his methadone script, I'll try to get him into a Department of Veterans Affairs PTSD program. In the meantime, I think you should have a talk to your counsellor and maybe the police.'

Tracey shook her head. 'You have *no* bloody idea, Doc. Just have a look in Toby's ear and let me get out of here.' She touched her bruised face again. 'And don't you *dare* tell me mum.'

* * *

The rest of the morning flew past in a rapid procession of sore throats, blood pressure checks, and bad backs. Vince farewelled his last patient, ignored the large pile of repeat script requests and phone messages still sitting in his too-hard basket, and headed for the back door.

'I'll do 'em tomorrow, Lorraine,' he said in the vague direction of the practice manager.

'Heard that before, Dr Hanrahan,' she responded with a mixture of frustration and resignation.

He climbed into his car and headed off through the darkening streets. As he turned into South Warrnambool, he wound down his window and inhaled the familiar tangy breeze. Almost two years he'd been renting the house in Fay Street and had nearly bought the place a few months ago. *Lucky I came to my senses.* Warrnambool had its attractions, but his children were in Melbourne and so was his real career. Not to mention his wife.

Still, he liked living in the unfashionable south part of the town. It was near the beach, the people were genuine, and rents were cheap. Even though Lydia was shacked up with an upmarket plastic surgeon in South Yarra, Vince was still paying the mortgage for the Canterbury house and the twins' school fees.

Number seven was distinguished by metre-wide vertical red and white stripes on its conite front. A previous owner had slapped on the artwork to celebrate the South Warrnambool Snappers last premiership win back in 1991. As a result, the place was known by the locals as the 'Snapper house'.

Vince nosed Benny into the drive and discovered his dog in the front yard chewing on the garden hose. She bounded up to him as he opened the car door and slobbered all over his shirt.

'Settle down, Deefer,' he said. 'How many times do I have to tell you not to eat the bloody … Oh, what's the point?'

Golden retrievers had been very much *de rigueur* in Canterbury, along with Range Rovers and white picket fences. She was a gorgeous dog with a low IQ and an insatiable appetite. Vince gave her some food and took her for a brisk walk. He then bombed a frozen curry in the microwave, ate it over the sink, and fell into bed.

5

'Morning, Vincent.'

Vince started the following day at seven o'clock with his weekly counselling session. The labour-ward catastrophe of three years ago had seen his specialist registration revoked, and he'd been issued with a temporary provisional ticket to work as a GP in an area of need. He was allowed to manage simple obstetric cases under the supervision of a Board-appointment mentor.

'Don't fuck up, Dr Hanrahan,' was the take-home message, 'and stay off the grog, and we might let you back in the team.'

Then after yet *another* maternal death last year in Warrnambool, this time a murder, Vince's long pathway back to resuming his specialist OBGYN practice had grown even longer. Regular therapy was a condition of his provisional registration.

So, here he was, sitting at his kitchen table, mug of coffee in his hand, staring at the smiling face of Dr Myfanwy Williams on his laptop.

'G'day, Myf,' he said. 'How's tricks?'

Dr Williams smiled and nodded. She had a round, flat, freckly face, a halo of curly red hair, shrewd cornflower blue eyes, and a lyrical Welsh lilt in her voice. *It's that accent that does it for me; it's the music, not the words.*

'Fine, thanks. And you?'

'Brilliant, mate. All good here.'

She shook her head and laughed. Vince knew he couldn't put much past her. Myf was one of Melbourne's top psychiatrists and specialised in damaged doctors.

'How are you sleeping?'

'Like a baby.' *A baby with nightmares, flashbacks, and cold sweats.*

She looked unconvinced. 'Is that why you look so fresh in the mornings?'

Vince shrugged.

'And how's work going?'

'Whingeing patients and the worried well, the usual GP menu.'

Myfanwy grinned. 'My, aren't we surly today?'

'I was doing all right last year, Myf, not loving the place, but getting by.' He took a deep breath. 'Then things went arse up again and the Board extended my sentence. So, no, I'm *not* a happy camper.'

'You just have to stick with the program—take the meds, meditate, do the CBT exercises, keep the communication channels open with Lydia and the girls, and—'

Vince zoned out and imagined paddling up and over the swell, cold slap of water in the face and then gunning for a wave, the ocean roaring and foam flying. The intensity of the moment erasing all else—

'Are you listening to me?' Myf's insistent sing-song voice cut into his daydream.

He refocused on the screen. 'Here's the thing. My little brother committed suicide last week.'

She leant into the screen. Demeanour changed, voice softer. 'I'm so sorry to hear that. Was he the farmer?'

Vince felt his eyes moisten again. 'Yeah. Joey. Shotgun.' He gestured to the north. 'Up home.'

'Had he been depressed, having problems, or …?'

Here we go again. 'You've heard it all before. Isolation, rocky marriage, years of drought.'

She frowned. 'Sounds like you almost expected it.'

'That's just it. I *didn't.*' He shook his head. 'Joey was always such a resilient little bugger.'

He stared out the window for a full minute. Dr Williams sat back and waited.

I've got nothing more to say, either.

'Going have to pull the plug. Got to go and heal the sick.'

'I don't think I've helped you much today. You've a lot on your plate.'

'Just listening to your voice is therapeutic for me,' said Vince. 'It's like a private reading of *Under Milk Wood*. Dead sexy.'

The Dylan Thomas classic with the rich, mellifluous voice of Richard Burton narrating was one of his treasures.

He got up. 'See you next week, Myf.'

* * *

Vince shaved, showered, and dressed; his shirt crumpled but clean(ish). He fed the beast, jumped into Benny, and almost backed over his next-door neighbour, Kieran Harrington, who was sweeping the footpath in front of the Snapper house. Kieran, a seventeen-year-old with Down syndrome, was Vince's regular fishing buddy, and his mother Carmel was a one-person local gossip machine.

'Morning, Super K,' said Vince, winding down his window.

'G'day, d-d-d-Dr Vince,' stammered Kieran. 'Mum's coming in to see you later.'

Great, another twenty-minute barrage of confusing symptomatology. Still, better than her usual approach of over the fence consultations on the fly.

After waving goodbye, Vince headed to the local hospital and did a quick ward round—a child with croup, an oldie with pneumonia, and one threatened miscarriage. *Talk about the cutting edge of medicine!* Then he was back in his car, headed down Timor Street, and arrived at the clinic fifteen minutes late. He raced in and dragged in his first punter, then motored through his list, making up the lost time on the way, hopefully getting it right *most* of the time.

Vince's old uncle, who ran a solo practice up in the Mallee, had dubbed GPs as 'Geeps'—small, versatile, all-purpose vehicles. The patients were 'punters', entrusting their health to these 'jacks of all trades'. Always a bet at unknown odds, added Uncle Phonse, himself a fixture in the bookie's ring, with variable outcomes.

After over two years in this Geep game, Vince had developed two golden rules: have a good nose for trouble, and don't drill down too deep. Never mind Shirley Tiang's attempts to educate him in the bio/psycho/social holistic model as espoused by the Royal Australian College of General Practitioners. Vince's approach was much simpler. And quicker. *Blow the RACGP, I just need to stay out of strife and re-join the RANZCOG. ASAP.*

His last patient for the morning was indeed his neighbour Carmel Harrington coming in for a blood pressure check. She was a short, round woman with a bouffant of frizzy grey hair—straight out of a Dickens' novel. Vince braced himself for the usual bruising encounter. Mrs Harrington had diabetes, high blood pressure, and elevated lipids—all out of control like her alarming BMI.

'Mrs H,' he scolded, 'your pressure's way up and you still haven't had that blood test.'

'I don't need no blood tests,' she confided with a knowing smile. 'I can tell when me sugar's up. I feel it in me waters.'

Vince shook his head and printed off her usual script, stood, and handed over another pathology request. 'This time, do it, okay? Who's going to keep me on the straight and narrow if you conk out?'

Mrs Harrington ignored Vince's feeble attempt to wrap up the consultation. 'I've got a lot of worry, Dr Vince. What with Tracey and the boys and the new bub on the way. And Dustin with that PSDT and no work and drinking all the time.'

'I think you mean PTSD,' said Vince.

She shrugged. 'Whatever. But he's got it real bad.'

Vince sat down again, an admission of defeat. When Mrs H got wound up she was unstoppable.

'The government should look after boys like Dustin. He done his bit for the country, fighting the Arabs and that. Them Moslems will take over. I don't know why the Mons lets 'em stay here …'

Vince was aware that Monsignor O'Shannassey, the parish priest, had converted an unused part of the presbytery into transitional housing units for the homeless, mostly asylum seekers and some substance abusing locals. He'd set up a charitable foundation to fund the project.

'The homeless have to sleep somewhere, and the Monsignor giving the refugees a bit of shelter and some food sounds very Christian to me.'

He stood again and edged toward the door, but Mrs Harrington was having none of it.

'The Mons is good-hearted, but they take advantage. It's a crying shame what that Commission has been saying about the priests, bringing up all those old stories and people making things up. Them Jews and Proddies was worse, Dr Vince, but they blame it all on the Catholics.'

The recent federal government Royal Commission into Institutional Child Sexual Abuse had provided Mrs Harrington with much angst. Vince was well aware of her conservative, populist views about everything from refugee policy to marriage equality, which seemed to be informed by the strident opinions of the radio shock jocks he could often hear blaring across the fence in Fay Street.

'Looks like the Catholic Church has done most of it,' said Vince. 'And ruined many young lives. The final report's due in a few months.'

'Anyway,' she said, levering her bulk off the chair at last, 'you look after my Tracey. Dustin's not knocking her around, is he? Used to be gentle as a lamb but he's got all agro since he come back.' She raised a stubby index finger. 'I'll 'ave him if he lays a finger on her.'

Vince opened the door. 'You know I can't discuss Tracey's medical issues with you, Mrs H. I suggest you talk to *her* about that.'

6

'You're looking a bit flash, Sarge,' Vince said as he sat down at Fanny's café for his regular Friday dinner date. 'Going out on the tear with the Lord of the Manor?'

Vince and local policewoman Elena Genovesi had a permanent weekly booking, and despite their two-year friendship they continued to refer to each other as 'Sarge' and 'Doc', even though the former was inaccurate and the latter hackneyed.

The two of them had put the café's owner behind bars after the untimely deaths of two of Vince's patients had threatened to transform his medical career from precarious to terminal. The combination of his professional salvation and a few reds had almost resulted in a more carnal expression of their friendship that night. But not quite. *Just as well—local copper ten years his junior, him a doctor in the town. And married! Still, she'd seemed keen at the time …*

Elena was wearing a tailored black leather jacket over a pretty voile top, her lustrous dark hair pulled back, revealing glittering silver earrings.

She laughed. 'No, nothing to do with Will.'

William Carlisle was her ardent suitor and lived on his family's property thirty minutes north. Vince knew Elena really liked this scion of the Western District squattocracy and couldn't understand what was holding her back.

'I'm going to my nephew's concert after this.'

'Is that Aldo's boy?'

'Yes, Peppi. You're welcome to come. There's a celebration afterward. Mum would love to see you.'

Vince smiled and shook his head. He knew Elena's mother had high hopes for the two of them getting together. Mrs Genovesi had confided to Vince that she was wary of Will Carlisle because he was an Anglican. 'You a good Catholic boy, Vincenzo. *And* a Dottore.' Vince figured old Maria assumed he was single too. Odd that Elena hadn't explained his situation to her mum.

'Thanks, Sarge, think I'll give it a miss.' He paused, then looked up. 'You know how I had to cancel on you last week?'

'Better offer, Doc?'

He swallowed and experienced that familiar chest tightening. 'I had to go up to the farm because my little brother went missing.'

Elena put down her glass, eyebrows raised.

Vince swallowed some water. 'Thing is … well, he … he killed himself.'

She reached across and put her hand on his. Big eyes even bigger. 'My God, you poor thing. Was it … unexpected?'

Vince pulled his hand free. 'What do *you* reckon?'

Elena flushed. 'Stupid thing to say. Forgive me.'

Vince waved her apology away. 'Usual thing. Farmer, drought, failed crops, relationship troubles.' *It was becoming a mantra. Sounded like he was trying to convince himself.*

'And in the Wimmera, no crop means no money,' said Elena. 'We're protected from that.' Her family were dairy farmers near Timboon, which had one of the highest rainfalls in the state.

'Yep. Cropping's a gamble up there. If it doesn't rain, you've wasted the dough you borrowed from the bank to put the crop in. And if you don't do it, you have no income at all.'

'Did he have a family?'

'Yep,' said Vince. 'Wife and two kids.'

'How terrible for them.'

He shook his head. 'I should've seen it coming.'

'I'm sure there was nothing you could've done, Doc.'

'When our mother was dying,' Vince went on, his chest in a vice, 'I promised her I'd look out for him.'

Elena nodded and said nothing.

'Great bloody job I did.'

Vince blew his nose on the paper napkin from the table. 'You know what, I'm sick of discussing it.' He looked up. 'Tell you all about it another day.'

The waiter arrived with their meals—same order every week. Fanny's wasn't chef's hat territory, but the food was passable. Elena selected a glass of Bannockburn pinot noir. *That'd go down well right now.*

'How about *your* week?' asked Vince. He knew the protocol by now. Dr Williams had taught him. Apparently, he'd never asked Lydia that question, took her for granted, and that's why she went wandering. Of course, as he'd explained to Myf, there *were* other reasons …

'Good thanks. I'm a fully-fledged Detective Senior Constable now. I've finished the Detective Training School and I'm officially part of the local CIU.'

Vince raised his drink in a toast. 'Congratulations, Sarge.' They tapped glasses. 'So no more kicking in doors with that other mob?' He knew that while still in uniform she had been attached to an undercover squad.

Elena smiled. She had the whitest teeth, an aquiline Roman nose, and large liquid dark eyes. 'The District Support Group, aka the divorce and separation group. No, I'm out of that now.'

Conversation ceased while they ate. After a few minutes, Vince paused and topped up their water glasses. Sad that this weekly dinner had become a proxy for another family tradition: Friday night Vietnamese with Lids and the twins. *I wonder if that's still happening. Without me.*

'How're your girls, Doc?'

Typical Elena, straight to the point. Quick and lively, as his dad used to say. And that unsettling ability to read his mind.

'Dunno, Sarge. I seem to be out of the loop these days.'

'Are they still all staying with that surgeon?'

After Vince's disgrace two years ago, his wife had imposed a moratorium on the relationship and then discovered a new boyfriend—Ivan Becker, labelled 'Ivan The Tool' by the twins.

So much for 'Let's just have a bit of a time out, Vincent, then see what happens.'

'Yeah, Lydia and the girls are living high on the hog in South Yarra.'

'And Georgina and Tessa are doing year twelve now?'

'Yep. Too busy to come down to see their old dad.'

Vince lapsed into a moody silence and they finished their meals without further discussion. Elena made a couple of attempts to engage him, but to no effect.

Fifteen minutes later they were standing outside the café saying their goodbyes. She moved forward as if to embrace him. Vince leant away and dodged the gesture. *What is it with these women and hugging?*

Elena nodded and stepped back. 'I'm really, really sorry for your loss. Take care of yourself. Sure you don't want to come to Peppi's concert?'

Vince shook his head, gave a desultory wave, and walked off.

Important cricket to watch on the box. Plus, I've got my own family, haven't I?

He climbed into his car and headed home. Benny was a late-eighties, mission brown, Volvo station wagon. A West Warrnambool car yard special. Back in the day, he'd piloted a sleek, black 5 Series BMW from hospital to hospital in his role as baby catcher of choice to the posh young breeders of the Eastern suburbs. That was until a combination of alcohol and a bad judgment call had brought it all tumbling down. Now Lydia had the Beemer and the house, and he ended up with Benny and the dog.

Vince headed south down the main street. It was just after eight-thirty, a breezy summer evening, and the shops were still open. The eateries were full and there was raucous laughter blasting from the open doorway of the pub on the corner. *Glad someone's having a good time.* He turned down across the railway line into South Warrnambool and pulled up in the drive of the Snapper house, the red stripes on the front walls fading into the gathering gloom.

Deefer greeted him with a barrage of excited barking and jumped up onto the car door.

'Settle down,' said Vince, extricating himself. He swung open the back door, dumped his bag, grabbed a box from the kitchen, and filled up her bowl. 'We'll go for a run in the morning.' The grateful dog cleaned up the food in record time, followed him into the house, and curled herself up on the floor.

Vince collapsed on his ancient, lumpy sofa and turned on the box. A West Indian player had just hit a six in a Big Bash League match, sparking a burst of ear-splitting music and the frenzied gyrations of dancing girls. Shaking his head, he switched over to *House of Cards* and fell into a miserable trance at the depressing Machiavellian antics of the protagonists.

'What a pack of immoral bastards,' he told Deefer. 'Nearly as bad as our mob in Canberra!'

Just as he was about to go to bed, his phone played its usual refrain, *'We are Geelong, the greatest team of all, we are Geelong'* to the tune of the Toreador Song from *Carmen*. Vince was tempted to ignore the call until Trisha's name flashed on the screen.

'G'day, sis.'

There was a pause. 'I'm okay, thanks for asking. Spent all Monday with Joey's lawyer, then the rest of the week cleaning the house. Paddy returned Dad to the home on Tuesday and drove back to the farm to pick me up today. Fun time all round.'

'Sorry, Trish, I *do* appreciate it. You're a—'

'Save it, Vinny. Let me tell you about Joey's estate. The solicitor said he had only a small debt on the farm.'

'That surprises me,' said Vince. 'Shelling out to the two of us cost him a fair whack. I would've thought he'd be still way in the red. Especially with the drought.'

Joey had bought out his siblings' share of the property after their father had hung up his boots—a common but often divisive farm succession strategy.

'He'd stopped sowing grain,' Trisha continued, 'but had been growing intensive winter crops—legumes and lentils—and he'd put a fair bit into super during the good years.'

'He also had a few of those wind turbines, didn't he?'

The state government had licensed a company to manufacture wind turbines in Horsham and Joey had signed up to host some on his farm.

'Over thirty,' she said. 'And they bring in about five thousand a year each.'

'Good for him,' said Vince. 'Does Jane plan to put a manager on or sell the place?'

'It's already on the market.'

'The end of an era. No more Hanrahans at Clonmel.' *If one particular Hanrahan had spent more time there, things might've turned out differently.*

'So Jane and the kids will be okay,' said Trisha, 'financially at least.'

'That's a relief.' Vince paused. 'So why the hell did he …?'

'Who knows? Jane said he'd been seeing a counsellor in Horsham. Maybe it was not wanting to be on the land, maybe the marriage breakup, maybe the drinking …'

'I'm not in a strong position to comment, Trish, but those last two sound more like symptoms than causes.' Deefer was scratching at the back door, so Vince let her out. 'What about old-fashioned endogenous depression, you know, chemical, and coming from within? We both see a lot of that.'

'Except there's no family history and it came on so quickly,' Trisha said after a pause. 'More a reactive pattern.'

'Reactive to what?"

'Jane would be the best person to ask about that. Anyway,' she added, 'enough psychological speculation. I need to get on with my own life, start back at work and organise the kids for kinder and school and stuff.'

'Yeah,' responded Vince. 'Life goes on.' *Such as it is.*

7

The next morning Vince pulled on his footy shorts, nearest t-shirt and old trainers, and he and Deefer headed out for a run. Myf Williams had reminded him to keep up the exercise. 'It's good for your head as well as your body.'

They trotted up through the breakwater car park and turned onto the walking path. 'Tide's in, too hard running on that sloping soft sand,' he said, after looking at the beach. 'Let's stay on the track.'

He put on his shades and pulled down his cap—a bid for anonymity. The last thing he needed was impromptu al fresco consultations. After ten metres of progress, Deefer squatted and deposited a large turd in the middle of the path.

'Good on you,' said Vince, his left arm having been almost pulled out of its socket. He considered leaving the offending dump where it was, but there were witnesses, so he grabbed a plastic bag from the nearby container and binned it. They continued on past the front of the café next to the sailing club and along the path as it wound amongst the scrub above the main beach. There was a decent two-metre swell and an off-shore wind, resulting in some good sets coming in. 'Might have a crack later, Deef.'

The track then led them up a slow steady incline and Vince started to puff as they approached the Hopkins River lookout. They paused at the top and he glanced at the stately river as it wound its way toward Deakin University, a few kilometres down river, then started the run home and took in the view on the descent, with the Southern Ocean stretched out ahead, the salty wind in their faces and the surf crashing down below. As the waves rolled in, carrying an array of grommets and longboarders into shore, Vince found himself wiping tears from his eyes.

Joey had been a much better surfer than him. Lithe and light and a goofy footer, he would be on his feet in seconds, swaying along the face of the waves like a ballet dancer.

'Joey's got the build for this game, son,' old Mick used to say. 'You're better off sticking to footy.'

* * *

After a shower, a read of the paper and a quick lunch, Vince went off to the South Warrnambool footy ground. It was the Snappers first day back training and the coach, Mark 'Big' Brody, wanted to talk to him about some rehab plans for players coming back from off-season surgeries. As usual for January, the players were red-faced, sweating, and complaining.

'Been in too good a paddock over the festive season, by the looks,' Vince said as they leant over the boundary fence.

'I'll soon whip 'em back into shape.'

'Long as you don't kill any in the process, Brodes.'

The coach laughed. 'Best thing about this time of the year,' he added. 'So far we're undefeated.'

Mark, a plumber, was the brother-in-law of Vince's neighbour, Mrs Harrington. Vince had inherited the entire extended family as patients, courtesy of her recommendations. Brodes, a former Snappers full back and on-field enforcer, had put on a lot of condition since his playing days, and at fifty-three was fast racking up heart attack risk factors. He had a crew cut, a red square face, and no neck to speak of.

They looked on as a young rookie threw himself into the training drills like a kamikaze fighter. Vince was transported back to Minyip, leaning on the fence alongside his father, watching the young Joey playing junior football. 'He goes in hard, the determined little bugger. Comes of trying to keep up with you.'

Vince found the football club a sanctuary from his own demons, but not today. He took a deep breath, excused himself on the pretext of an urgent call, and headed home.

* * *

He found Deefer snoozing next to her kennel and discovered a plastic container on his kitchen table with an attached note.

'Bit of shepherd's pie for your tea, Doctor Vince. Kieran fed the dog and took her for a walk down the river.'

'Mrs H and Super K, you are legends,' Vince said out loud.

He bunged the container in the microwave and unplugged his mobile from the charger. There was a series of messages and missed calls on the screen.

First was a text from his old school friend, Father Luke Kelly, reminding him about a thirty-year school reunion up at St Bernard's in Ballarat. Luke was an assistant priest to Monsignor O'Shannassey.

Re next Saturday. Want a ride? Leaving @ 11

He tapped a reply. *Not my thing Kel. Enjoy.*

Next was a series of missed calls from his wife.

'Vincent, Lydia here. Give me a ring.'

'Vincent … pick up.' Voice annoyed and insistent.

'Answer your bloody phone. It's Georgina, she's in trouble!' Now impatient and angry.

In trouble, thought Vince, what does that even mean? He was well used to these 'urgent' calls from Lydia. His fatherly advice was only sought when there was a crisis. Otherwise, he was a husband and father in absentia.

He shook his head and tapped the return call code.

'Vincent, about time! Why don't you answer your phone?'

'Hi to you too, Lids,' he answered. 'I'm fine, thanks. And you?'

She snorted in reply.

Vince put his mobile on speaker, then put the kettle on. 'Pity you couldn't make it to Joey's funeral.'

Her voice softened. 'We … we couldn't get back in time from Singapore. I'm sorry about that.'

Vince grunted. *Doesn't sound like you tried too hard.*

'What with the drought and everything, farmers seem to be particularly susceptible to—'

'Knocking themselves off.' *Still finishing her sentences. Old habits …* 'Thing is,' he continued, 'Joey had no financial worries and the farm was going well. I just don't get it.' He shook his head. 'We must be missing something.'

'Like what?'

'Wish I knew.'

Lydia paused. 'How is Jane going?'

Vince shrugged. 'Dunno. Since the funeral, she won't take my calls. I need to talk to her.'

'Seems strange.'

The whole thing's strange.

'Thanks for the flowers, Lids.'

'Least I could do. Ivan was upset too.'

'And how is dear Ivan? Say hi from me.'

Lydia snorted again. 'Ivan's worried about Georgina. And so am I.'

'What is it this time?' Vince said. 'Forget to empty the dishwasher? Late with an essay?'

'It's no laughing matter, Vincent. Everything's a joke with you.'

He tossed a teabag into his Go Cats mug and sat down. 'Oh yeah, all fun and games here. Ever hear the one about the bloke who got kicked in the arse, then the love of his life left him for a plastic surgeon? Talk about a laugh!'

There was a pause. 'Ivan and I are just friends. He's been very kind to me and the girls, since your … your … *you* know.'

Vince poured some hot water into his mug. *Oh, I* know *all right.*

'So, what's the deal?'

Another pause. 'Georgina's been caught at school with marijuana.'

He pushed the tea away and picked up his phone. 'What!'

'She claims one of the other girls gave it to her, but the principal called me, and … and they are going to ex*pel* her.'

'They can't do that. She's a good kid, just a bit of rebel, that's all.'

'I'm worried sick. I want you to come down here and speak to Dr Robinson. Ivan says Georgina will end up with the riff-raff down at the

Warrnambool High School!'

'Is that right, Lids?' said Vince. 'A—it's *none* of Ivan's business. And B—the local school here is *better* than that princess factory anyway!'

8

Monday morning, Vince hit the ground running. 'Just a quickie this morning, Deef,' he said, staggering out the back door with the dog's lead. 'Places to go, mate. People to see.' He and the eager Deefer did a fast walk down the street and onto the coastal track and checked out the surf.

They headed home and Vince swallowed a coffee and a muffin of indeterminate age, then jumped in the shower. Minutes later he was gunning Benny up to the hospital. After a rapid-fire ward round, quick hi to a toddler with gastro in the children's ward—'*If he's drinking and piddling by lunchtime, take out the drip*'—and brief enquiries of a few postnatal patients on the mid-floor—'*Sprogs feeding and the mum's not bleeding? Home tomorrow*'—he appeared at the clinic early. For a change.

He strode in the back door, feigning deafness to the appeals of the receptionists, vanished into his consulting room and closed the door. Then he took the desk phone off the hook, turned on his computer, and commenced the assault on his backlog of paperwork. A minute later he was interrupted by a loud knock.

'I'm not here,' he called out. 'Go away.'

The door opened and Shirley Tiang materialised in front of his desk with hands on hips and a broad smile. 'What's going on, you the teacher pet or what?'

Vince didn't look up. 'I'm just being a good boy and doing my homework.'

'Jeez, cobber, you are the bees nuts.'

Vince laughed. 'The bee's *knees*, Shirl, and the duck's *nuts*.'

'That's what I said.' She looked at her watch. 'Time for our tutorial, Rooned.'

As part of his provisional registration, Vince had weekly educational sessions with Shirley, who sent regular reports back to the Medical Board on his progress.

He groaned. 'I don't need to learn any more about eczema and piles. By next year I'll be back at the Royal Women's and my specialist practice. Just tell the Gestapo I'm all over it.'

Shirley sat and put a book on the desk. *Cardiovascular Screening in General Practice.*

Vince shook his head.

'If I tell them you're a slack bum,' she said, 'they'll pull the pins altogether. So, listen up.'

After the thirty-minute tutorial, the waiting room was full and the patients were champing at the bit.

'Time to roll and rock, Rooned,' said Shirley as she stood. 'You still got a lot to learn.'

Ain't that the truth.

* * *

He brought up his waiting room list and called in the first punter. 'Dustin Cartwright.'

The young man came in, took a seat, gaze locked to the floor. Shaven head, pale narrow face, twitchy and agitated. 'Bout fucken time, Doc. Haven't got all day.'

'Busy, eh Dusty?' said Vince. 'Got a bit on have you, mate?'

Dustin tensed and clenched his hands to fists. Then he sat back and stared with red eyes at a point over Vince's shoulder. 'Just get on with it.' Tight mouth and staccato speech.

'I've got your Department of Veteran's Affairs application form for Total and Permanent Incapacity here,' said Vince, opening a large envelope. Eighteen bloody pages! 'Bit young to go for TPI, aren't you, Dusty?'

Dustin sprang to his feet and leant forward on the desk, his face inches from Vince's, a snarl twisting his features. 'Youse just don't get it. I got completely fucked up over there! Now I'm good for nothin'!' He held that position for thirty seconds, then collapsed back in the chair, chin on his chest.

Vince nodded and looked at the first page. 'So, what can you tell me about your health?'

Dustin sat forward and slammed his fists on the desk. 'It's this fucken PTSD! Youse *know* that. No sleep, flashbacks, palpitations, can't breathe, and crap concentration.'

Hmmm, sounds familiar.

Vince got busy with his pen. 'Alcohol or other substances?'

'What do ya reckon? Only way I can get to sleep. Few Bundys and a cone or two.' He looked back at the floor. 'Seein you won't give me them Xanaxs no more.'

'Okay,' said Vince, ticking boxes. 'Next is "Family and Relationships".'

Dustin shook his head. 'The kids do me head in with their bloody noise! And relationships ...' He sat back and laughed. Crazily. 'Twenty-nine and can hardly get it up. Funny, eh?'

Vince said nothing to this and completed the form. 'I'll send this off to the DVA, mate. See what happens.' He tossed the envelope to one side and looked straight at the young man, now slumped back in the seat like a collapsed balloon.

'Tracey reckons you have a bit of trouble with anger management.'

Dustin sat bolt upright again. 'I just lose it sometimes.' He pointed to the form. 'All that stress, Doc.'

Vince leant forward. 'If I thought you were knocking her around, I would have to tell the coppers.'

'Yeah, and they'd lock me up. Bloke who served his country. While all them ragheads and refugees get new houses and free TVs and shit.' He rolled up his sleeves and pointed one shaking finger at Vince's chest. 'Time we reclaimed our country back again!'

Vince glanced at Dustin's heavily tattooed arms, which featured the Australian flag and 'Tracey', as well as a Swastika and obvious needle tracks.

'No woman deserves to be belted. PTSD or not.' This time Vince did the finger pointing. 'Don't forget that, mate. Or I'll act on it.'

Dustin shook his head. Thin lips compressed. Feet tapping on the floor.

'How long since you've seen that DVA counsellor?'

Another bitter laugh followed by a head shake. 'Just another know-all chick with short hair and big earrings. No bloody help to me.' He got up and headed for the door. 'Never been to the Red Zone, has she?'

* * *

That night Vince stayed late at the clinic and emptied his too-hard basket, then put a call through to Jane, which went through to her message bank. Again.

'There you go, boss,' he said to Shirley on his way out. '*Both* desktops tidy. Aren't I just the duck's knees now?'

He drove home through the dark streets, picking up some dinner from Noodles-R-Us on the way. Deefer greeted him with a volley of excited barking as he pulled in. Vince fed and watered her while he drained a Coke and cleaned up his 'Deluxe Singapore Pack'.

The dog pawed at the back door until Vince came out with the lead and they set off down the road and onto the beach. He took off his shoes and socks and walked on the cold sand, picking his way through the seaweed. Deefer ran around, chasing nothing in particular. Vince sat on the edge of the breakwater and gazed over the heaving dark ocean, across the crescent-shaped Lady Bay up through the fringe of Norfolk pines to the flickering road and house lights beyond. All was quiet, save for the lapping waves. His mind slowed and stilled.

'Sometimes Warrnambool's a bit of all right, Deef,' he told the dog sitting at his side. 'You don't get this in Canterbury.'

* * *

Back home, Vince conducted a five-minute tidy up—more so he could find a place to sit on the couch than out of any notion of good housekeeping.

He fired up his laptop and sent off an email to Georgie—third for the day—looked on Facebook, Instagram, and Twitter and messaged her repeatedly, but got no response. He sank into a frustrated torpor on the couch and nodded off, then was wakened nearly an hour later by his singing mobile.

'Hi, Georgie, what's up?'

'You were looking for me, Dad?' Voice flat and distant.

'I understand from Mum that you've got yourself into strife at school.'

Silence for a full minute. Then muffled tears.

'Look, sweetie, I know it's hard for you guys—year twelve and me being down here. But your mum really wants what's best for you.'

'What's best for *her*, you mean! She's embarrassed, that's all. Bad for her image.'

Not far off the truth there. 'So, George, I have to ask. Have you been smoking weed?'

Another silence. 'No, well yes. I mean, once or twice, max. But the stuff they found at school wasn't mine, I swear. Stupid Meg bloody Bonham stashed it in my locker.'

Not a really convincing answer. 'Well, you and I need to discuss that issue ASAP. But the bottom line is: do you want to stay at the school or not?'

More sobs followed by another pause. 'I'm just over my teachers at the moment. And some of the girls. But our crew has a real shot this year. And I'm gunning two of my subjects. And, obviously, there's Tess. Plus, where could I even go? I'm a semester in. But the Gollum wants to kick me out and Mum is—'

'Whoa, whoa there, George,' said Vince. 'I'm coming down Friday to see if I can convince the principal to keep you on. If that's what you want. Then I'll catch up with you girls for dinner and maybe a movie.'

'We're heading down to Portsea to Ivan's house straight after school. So have to be another time, okay?'

That'd be right!

'Thanks, Dad. I have to get moving, I'm going to Jonno's to discuss some Lit stuff. Sorry about Uncle Joey.'

'Call ended,' appeared on Vince's phone. Well, that's that. Apparently. And who was Jonno anyway?

He got up and threw his mobile on the table.

I'll never get these years back.

* * *

The week disappeared in a cavalcade of whingeing punters. 'I don't think I've seen a sick person for months,' Vince told Shirley on the way out the door on Thursday night.

'Coughs, colds, and sore holes, eh, Rooned,' she replied. 'At least they pay the bills.'

He laughed. 'But it's all so trivial.'

Shirley frowned and put her head to one side. A sure sign of an impending rocket.

'If I do an STI swab *every* time I do a cervical screen and treat the positive ones, I will *prevent* a heap of pelvic infections. Isn't that more better than a fanny mechanic like you *operate* on those chicks to unblock their tube when they can't get preggers later?'

Vince shrugged.

'See? I rest on my case. GP is more sexy than specialist.'

'I'd *much* rather be the guy in the operating room.'

She pouted and threw her hands in the air.

'Anyway,' he went on, 'I'm going to Melbourne early tomorrow, so can you look after my hospital patients till Monday? More family business.' He handed over a list.

'Sure, bud. Aunty Shirley's babysitting service at your disposals.'

9

'We have a very strong policy on drugs at CLC,' said Dr Ruth Robinson, aka 'the Gollum', peering over her large leather-inlaid walnut desk. 'This ice epidemic is especially worrying.'

Sure Madam Headmistress, thought Vince. He bet there was ecstasy and cocaine floating around the hallowed grounds, but crystal meth would be a bit low rent for her Eastern suburbs darlings.

Dr Robinson had pale pop-out eyes, a plastic smile, and a sinuous body but none of the wheedling obsequiousness of the Tolkien character. In fact, she was direct and sledge-hammer blunt. Anyway, *Vince* was the one doing the pleading.

Benny's gearbox had blown up during the week, so he'd caught the early train to Melbourne, then a suburban connection and walked the kilometre from the station to the imposing redbrick edifice that was the Canterbury Ladies College. During his enforced holiday from driving three years ago, Vince had become an expert public transport user and a regular Uber patron. This, after a decade of piloting a succession of large German cars from labour ward to labour ward. Or even to the local shop to get the milk.

He and Georgie were sitting on the other side of the Gollum's desk. 'Just look contrite,' he'd told his daughter before entering. 'I'll do the talking.'

'She is really, really sorry, Dr Robinson,' he said in his most charming voice. 'Aren't you, Georgina?' Georgie nodded, her face pale and eyes tear-filled. 'Life has been difficult for the girls, since I … well, since their mother and I …'

The Gollum raised her permanently arched eyebrows ever higher. 'Understood, Dr Hanrahan. But that's no excuse for the possession of illicit substances,' she gestured out the window, 'on CLC property.' She leant forward, a serpentine and intimidating figure. 'Georgina will have to leave the college by the end of next week.'

'What about the Head of the Schoolgirls on the long weekend?' asked Georgie, silent up to now. They both looked at her—tall and freckled with the Hanrahan red mane tied tightly behind her ears and a badge with a pair of crossed oars on her blazer. Vince knew that this regatta was the ultimate prize in schoolgirl rowing.

Vince sensed an opportunity. He jumped to his feet. 'CLC hasn't won the senior eights for ages, yes?'

The Gollum nodded.

'But this year, you're the favourites and Georgie's the stroke.' He pointed at the honour board of interschool champion sports teams on the wall. 'CLC prestige on the line.'

She paused. 'I'm sure Georgina can still participate in the regatta.'

Vince pounced. 'Surely not if she'd been expelled! What if word got out to the other schools?'

The Gollum stared hard at Georgie, then looked out the window across the pristine lawns toward the imposing chapel, eyes popping. *Needs her thyroid function checked.*

'Dr Hanrahan,' she said eventually, 'perhaps you'd better sit down.'

A few minutes later, Vince was speeding back into town courtesy of an Audi four-wheel drive, a blonde toothy lady at the wheel. 'Just a bit of pin money, Doctor,' she told him. 'I'm *very* selective with my clientele.'

She dropped Vince in Lygon Street and he had a late lunch at Tiamo's, an old haunt of his and Lydia's in their student days. He chose the same seafood risotto dish as back then, but instead of a tempting glass of Chianti Classico, he made do with mineral water, followed by a double espresso and tiramisu. *Why not?*

He then rode the tram to Brunswick, where he was staying at Trisha's for the night. Paddy and the boys were playing cricket in the back yard and Vince joined in the game. The associated noise was deafening.

'*Howzat!*'

'*Not out*, ya dickhead, I didn't even touch it!'

'You nicked it. *Didn't* he, Uncle Bins?'

When the boys were little, 'Uncle Bins' and 'Aunty Lids' were the closest they got to Vince and Lydia's names, and those sobriquets had stuck. Paddy referred to the family as the 'BinLids' back then and teased the twins about their red hair during family Christmases up on the farm.

'Yeah, Liam,' said Vince. 'I reckon he was out.'

He watched the boys and their father tumble about, laughing and shouting, while Trisha looked on with a smile.

That's one happy family unit out of three siblings.

After stumps were declared, Paddy fired up the BBQ and Vince was given the task of feeding the boys some sausages. This was accompanied by frequent skirmishes and a brief but disastrous tomato sauce squirting war.

'Vinny,' said Trisha, coming out with some salads, 'you're supposed to be in charge here. Looks like World War Three! Wipe your hands, boys, and say hello to Aunty Jane.'

Joey's widow walked down the steps, air-kissed Vince and embraced the boys. Vince hadn't seen her since the funeral. Her mass of blond curls had been trimmed back to a wavy bob and her olive-skinned face had acquired some deep lines, changing her appearance from chiselled to haggard. She sat down next to Vince and crossed her tanned, muscular legs. Vince knew she'd been a champion athlete in her time and had completed a triathlon the previous year.

'Get this into ya, Janey,' said Paddy, handing her a glass of sparkling. 'I'll organise bath-time while Trish cooks the spuds. Watch that fish on the barbie, mate,' he added on his way back inside.

'What brings you to the big city, Jane?' Vince asked after a pause.

'Got an in-service at the Royal Melbourne,' she replied. 'Wound healing.' She lit a cigarette and inhaled deeply. 'Ironic, eh?'

'Back on the smokes?'

She met his eyes. 'That's right, *Doctor*.'

'Fair enough,' said Vince. 'How are the kids?'

'Well as can be expected. They're up home with Mum. Jack's in grade four at Horsham Primary and Maisie's in year seven. She's boarding at Ballarat Grammar now.'

Vince chuckled. 'The Anglicans, eh? Mum would turn in her grave.'

Jane inhaled heavily, paused, and blew out a stream of smoke above Vince's head. 'That's what Joseph wanted. He hated the Catholic Church.'

Hate! That's a strong word.

Vince drained his Coke and took a deep breath. *Now or never.* 'So if it wasn't the drought, what was it?'

She stubbed out her cigarette butt and lit another. Vince topped up her glass.

'You're right, it wasn't the drought. Joseph had drought-proofed the place by preserving the stubble and sowing intensive winter crops.' She looked at Vince in the gathering gloom. 'You weren't the only one with brains, you know.'

He swallowed hard. 'Was it that he felt obligated to come home to the farm after I went off to uni?'

She laughed. 'Well, he would've liked a choice in it, but he loved the land. Joseph was a born farmer.'

Vince nodded.

'He was very involved in the local community until the last few months—the football club, the CFA, the silo art project. Even joined the Minyip Philosophical Society.'

'That sounds like an oxymoron,' Vince said with a sceptical smile.

'A local academic, Homer Reith, has been running philosophy classes there for years.' Jane took a deep draw on her cigarette and slowly exhaled a plume of smoke. 'There's more to Minyip than meets the eye.'

Vince shrugged, hands out. 'So …?'

'Joseph had been depressed for years.' Jane nodded at Vince and then toward the house. 'None of you seemed to pick up on it.'

He paused. *Might as well be hanged for a sheep as a lamb.*

'Was it his drinking or the … you know, the relationship?'

'Oh my God, talk about the pot calling the kettle black!' Jane stood, eyes flashing. 'Things weren't great between us in recent years and he certainly drank too much, but …' she struck her chest with her fist, 'he had a hurt *deep* inside. A thing from his past. Way back.' She sat down, cheeks awash with tears. 'And I couldn't fix it.'

Something from his past. What's that about?

The back door burst open, shattering the awkward silence, and a blast of yellow light lit up the yard. Trisha appeared, apron on, holding a tray.

'Vinny, that snapper's not burning, is it?'

* * *

Next morning, after an uproarious family breakfast, Jane went off to her course and Paddy and the boys headed to a working bee at the primary school. Trisha and Vince tidied up, then sat down for a cup of tea.

'I'm off to work shortly. What are you up to today?'

'Dunno, Trish.'

'Catching up with the girls?'

He shook his head. 'Gone to Portsea for the weekend with Lydia and Ivan.'

They exchanged glances. Vince looked out into the back yard. 'Jane reckons Joey was fine with life on the farm. But she said he was depressed due to some problem from his past.'

Trisha frowned and pursed her lips. 'Joey didn't really *have* a past. Went off to school then Ag college, married the childhood sweetheart, and started farming. Had kids, played golf, and went fishing. Grew crops.' She put her hands out, palms up.

'I don't get it either. Such a happy kid.'

Trisha shrugged, stood, and picked up her bag. 'I have to go.'

Vince laughed. '*More* family therapy, you poor thing!'

She grinned and fished out her car keys. 'Stay as long as you like.'

He walked her to the door. 'Thanks for last night. Enjoyed it. Good to catch up with Janey, too. I'll go and see Dad, then head back to the 'Bool. Say thanks to Paddy and hooroo to the boys.'

The house felt quiet when Vince shut the door behind his sister. A clock was ticking somewhere and there was faint traffic noise from the front. He sat at the table and spread out the *Saturday Age* but couldn't engage with any of the news, so he packed up his gear, trammed it into the city, and jumped on the light rail to South Melbourne.

His father had been a resident of the Chatsworth Nursing Home for three years and Vince was well overdue for a visit. He hopped off the tram and walked up the road, opposite the Albert Park Lake. Workmen were putting up barricades for the looming Grand Prix motor race; a few swans watched from the water with disdainful expressions. It was a warm midsummer's day and the men were sweating and breathing hard.

Vince looked on for a minute, then walked up the steps to the front door. He found old Mick in the day room staring into space and pulled up a chair, putting a box of his father's favourite chocolates on the side table. Mick's ruddy face was a patchwork quilt of scars left over from numerous skin cancer removals over the years.

'Hi, Dad. How are you going?'

Mick turned his head and stared at Vince. Didn't seem to be much going on behind those blue eyes. A few minutes passed and he put his hand on Vince's arm and his mouth slowly opened.

'Vinny,' he murmured, voice hoarse and halting.

Vince leant forward. 'Yes, Dad, it's me.'

'Young Joey's coming down with you to Ballarat this year. Mary's fretting.' His grip tightened. 'Look after him.'

Mick fell back, seemingly exhausted from the effort of producing so many words. *First time in years. Something must have gotten through after all.*

'I will, for sure.' Vince felt his voice catching. 'Tell Mum not to worry.'

Mick nodded and returned to his silent world. Vince sat for a while, his heart pounding, then blew his nose and said goodbye.

When he got outside, he caught the light rail into Southern Cross station and looked at the departures board. No Warrnambool train till six-twenty. *Shit! Don't want to wait here all day. Nothing for me in Melbourne.* He noticed the next departure was to Ballarat in two minutes. Vince raced to the platform, swiped on his MYKI card and just made it. He dumped his bag and collapsed in the seat. As the train pulled out he sent a text.

G'day Kel. On the 11.30 from Melbourne. Pick me up at Ballarat station.

10

'Check out the roses, Kookaburra,' said Vince. 'It's like the home straight at Flemington on Melbourne Cup day.'

Vince and Father Luke Kelly walked through the large and familiar wrought-iron front gates and down the imposing drive past a long line of rose bushes.

Luke was short, with a permanent smile, the bluest of eyes and a shock of blond hair, now shot with grey. He laughed often and loudly and had been dubbed 'Kookaburra' by the football coach at school. Like Vince he was forty-six, but unlike Vince he was regarded as an absolute cutie by the Catholic matrons of Warrnambool.

He smiled and nodded. 'They've spruced the place up a bit since our days.'

Vince had been sent off to board at St Bernard's in year seven and Joey joined him three years later. The Christian brothers ruled with a formidable combination of rote learning and corporal punishment. Vince enjoyed his time, all the same. He was big enough to look after himself and was a good football player, which was a guarantee of popularity in an all-boys' school.

Vince had met the young Luke Kelly on his first day in the boarding house and they'd become instant friends. Luke was also a farmer's son and was a fearless, lightning-fast rover. They were a great combination on the football field and featured in two premierships with the First Eighteen. After school, they went in very different directions—Vince to Melbourne University to study medicine and Luke out to the seminary at Clayton. After his ordination, the newly minted Father Luke went overseas for further study and they'd lost touch until Vince's arrival in Warrnambool.

They strolled on down the drive, then noticed a sizeable group of men gathered next to the statue of St Bernard outside the chapel and walked over to join them. There was an outbreak of mutual recognitions, handshaking, and general bonhomie.

'Heard you weren't coming, Vince,' said one of his classmates.

'Thought I better make sure you old blokes were still alive, Tony.'

The event started with an obligatory mass, although almost half elected to stay out in the weak Ballarat sunshine and chew the fat. Vince was inclined to join the abstainers but followed Luke into the tall, forbidding chapel, replete with memories—few of them good.

'It's still so cold in here, even in the summer,' Luke murmured as they knelt in front of the heavy wooden pews.

'It's all right for you,' Vince responded, looking around. 'This is foreign territory to me these days.' The austere, intimidating décor made Vince feel like that apprehensive eleven-year-old all over again.

After mass, they all set off behind the vice principal, an impossibly young-looking man with a salesman's smile, for a tour of the school.

'You lay blokes running the show now, Justin?' asked a machinery dealer from the Mallee. 'Where are the brothers?'

'All gone, Tim, just a couple of retired ones over in the big house.' He nodded to the large brick building on the other side of the drive.

'Gone, but not forgotten, eh?'

One man, a builder from up country, who looked like he'd seen better days, snorted. 'There's a couple of 'em that *I'll* never forget.'

Nods all round. 'Where's your other mate from Mildura, Keith?' said Vince. 'You know, Curly Connell?'

Keith shook his head. 'You wouldn't get Curly here. His little brother copped it from that paedo bastard Delaney.'

Vince frowned. 'I don't remember a Brother Delaney.'

'He wasn't one of the frères. He was a priest, chaplain to the junior school. You wouldn't have had much to do with him.'

'Fair enough,' said Vince.

'Young Billy never got over it. Hit the grog, left his missus, got on drugs.'

'That's terrible,' said Vince. 'Poor kid.'

They walked on past the new performing arts centre, which drew a few whistles of appreciation.

'Bit different to when we were here,' commented one of the men.

The tour finished with a dinner in the refurbished dining hall and a series of anecdotes from various old boys about hijinks back in the day. A cackle of mirth followed each one. The vice principal finished with a speech extolling the facilities, academic achievements, and vision for the future.

'Forget that stuff, Justin,' said one, a stock agent and former full forward. 'Are we still winning the *footy*?'

There was a chorus of laughter and clapping, followed by a raucous rendition of the school war cry.

'They're just wanting us to send our sons here,' commented the guy sitting next to Vince, a local businessman with a large brood. 'It's just a big ad.'

'Any of yours here, Gaz?' Garry Murphy was from a prominent Ballarat Catholic family. Generations of St Bernard's boys.

'No, they are all at Grammar. Pam wouldn't hear of it. Not after what happened to her brother. The Church needs to clean up its act, starting from the top. Like the bishops and priests who just moved those paedophiles around.'

'Some of those old buggers are still about too,' added Keith.

Vince looked around the table. Other conversations had stopped and everyone was listening. 'But they weren't all at it,' he said. 'There were some good guys amongst them, and a lot of great teachers too.'

This was met with a general murmur of approval. 'Must have been,' Murphy said with a grin, 'if they got you into medicine.'

Vince gave him a cuff across the ear. 'Thanks, mate.'

One of the others, a softly spoken accountant from Geelong, sat forward. 'Must make it hard for guys like you, Kookaburra.'

Vince looked across the table at his friend. He'd been quiet all afternoon. Bad memories of St Bernard's? Hardly, Vince surmised. Luke was school captain and excelled at everything.

'Just got to get on with things, Simmo,' responded Luke. 'It is what it is.'

'Hey boys,' Vince said after a few minutes awkward silence, 'remember the time Rotten Rod made that big speech in English.'

There was a chorus of laughter. 'I'd never heard you say so many words in a row till that day, Rotten,' said Garry Murphy.

Rodney Walsh sat back with his trademark broad smile. 'No big deal. Brother Tancredi said I had to make a speech, so I did.'

'Give it to us again,' Vince urged, and there was an outbreak of banging on the table and a chant of 'Rotten, Rotten, Rotten …'

'Jeez,' said Rodney, 'how old are you blokes? All I said was "one year Beulah Footy Club didn't have enough players, so we joined up with Hopetoun and formed the Southern Mallee Giants."'

'Then you just sort of grinned and sat down!' said Murph.

Guffawing broke out all round.

'And that was the whole bloody speech!' added Vince.

* * *

The day ended with a rolling parade of old photographs projected on the dining room wall. Everyone went quiet. *Combination of nostalgia and a few red wines,* thought Vince, cradling his mineral water. There was the occasional outbreak of laughter and ragging of individuals as old sporting teams, cadet corps, and groups of pimply boys moved through.

He smiled as he recognised himself in the premiership-winning First Eighteen—skinny legs, red hair trimmed into short back and sides. Next was a faded image of Luke Kelly winning the cross country, followed by a formal picture of a group of prefects receiving their badges, then a shot of three figures standing in front of the brothers' house. Vince sat up. It was Joey, Joey's friend Terry Cleary, and the smiling figure of a youngish priest in the middle, an arm around each boy and a cheesy smile on his face.

'Shit!' shouted Vince. The chatter stopped and everyone looked at him. '*Now* I remember. *That's* Father Delaney. Joey and Terry were both altar boys.' He paused. 'And Joey was his favourite.'

* * *

The drive home from Ballarat was a quiet affair. Luke said little and Vince had troubling thoughts racing through his mind. It was close to ten when they pulled into the Snapper house driveway.

Vince grabbed his bag from the back seat. 'Thanks Kel,' he said. 'I'm glad I went.'

'Good to catch up with the guys,' said Luke.

'Yeah.' Vince nodded and closed the car door.

Luke pulled away and Vince went round the back. He tiptoed past the sleeping Deefer, went inside, and found a note on the table.

'We fed the dog and there is pumpkin soup in the fridge.'

Thank you, Mrs H. He bombed the soup and sat down, but soon found he had no appetite and after a few minutes staring into the steaming yellow brew, he stood, pulled off his clothes, and fell into bed. He went out like a light but awoke again in the early hours, haunted by nightmares.

But instead of lacerating images of dead women in labour wards, he was visited by the young Joey Hanrahan in his new St Bernard's uniform and his mother's tearful words: 'Look after him, Vinny. I'm counting on you.'

11

'Vincent,' said Myf Williams, peering from the laptop, 'you look awful.'

Vince had struggled through Monday on autopilot and then had a reprise of the previous night's terrors. He glanced at his reflection in the screen—pale, unshaven, face blank.

'Just a touch of insomnia.'

She looked worried. 'You haven't been drinking?'

Vince shook his head. *But I came very close last night.*

'Still on the meds?'

He nodded. *Well, most of the time.*

'Meditating?'

'Yep. Sort of.'

'Not sliding again, are you?'

Vince shrugged. 'What is this, Myf, twenty questions? Oh, shut *up*, Deefer!' He ducked off camera to feed the howling dog.

He returned to find Dr Williams with raised eyebrows. 'It's my job to ask questions. My concern is your mental health. I know you are angry with the Board's approach and frustrated by your isolation, but—'

'That's not the half of it,' he said, sitting down again. 'You know that school reunion I told you about?'

She nodded.

'So I went after all.'

'See some old friends?'

He laughed. Tense and bitter. 'What I saw was a picture of my brother Joey when he was an altar boy. With the chaplain.'

Myf sat forward. 'I guess that was distressing for you. So soon after—'

Vince looked away. 'It was Father Delaney, the priest who's been charged with all those … those sexual assaults on the St Bernard's boys.'

Dr Williams paused for a minute. 'You don't want to jump to conclusions. Just because they were photographed together doesn't necessarily mean—'

'Wish I could believe that.' Vince leant into the camera. 'I was too busy playing football and being a big-shot prefect, didn't take any notice of what Joey was doing.'

'You can't blame yourself.'

'I remember him going down to the priests' holiday house with the other altar boys.' He threw his hands up. 'We trusted those guys. Should've fucking *known* what was going on—'

'Vincent,' Myf interrupted. A softer tone. 'Joe never told you he was being molested, did he? Maybe you're overreacting here.'

Vince got up and started circling the kitchen. He was in what Lydia called his 'Kerouac vibe'—a cascading stream of consciousness with words gushing out on top of each other.

'No, no, NO! It all makes sense to me now. Joey started out confident and happy. He got married, had a family, ran the farm and did okay for a while, but that abuse shit always catches up eventually. *You* know that, Myf. And they have a really high suicide rate, and—'

'But you said it was the isolation and the drought that triggered your brother's depression.'

Vince shrugged. 'I was stabbing in the dark before.' He pointed at his face. 'But that picture hit me right between the eyes.'

Myf frowned. 'As human beings, we look for someone to blame when things go wrong. You know this anger may lead you to a dark place again. Let it go. Okay?'

Vince sat down again and stared at the floor. A deflated balloon.

'*Okay*?' Face close to the camera. Querying look.

He looked up. 'Sure, Myf, whatever.'

* * *

Next morning Vince caught a cab to the garage to pick up Benny.

'Replaced the gearbox,' said the mechanic, 'and I done a service.'

'Good as new?'

He smiled. 'Wouldn't say that. Too many Ks on the clock, the head gasket's nearly rooted, and the body's full of rust.'

'Sounds like me, Serge,' said Vince.

He struggled through the day's consulting, going through the motions, but his mind a million miles away from the issues—real or imagined—of the patients as they came through. When he got home, he fed Deefer, trotted her around the block, then bunged a supermarket frozen lasagne into the microwave, even though the label on the packet informed him it was 'best before' last week. *No wonder it was cheap.*

While it was cooking, Vince opened a Coke and cranked up his laptop. 'Maybe you can't change the past,' he informed Deefer, 'but you can find out what really happened.'

He Googled 'Father Gerald Delaney' and 'Royal Commission'. Seemed no less than twenty-six complainants had come forward with allegations of sexual abuse against him. Delaney had been the junior school chaplain at St Bernard's in the eighties, having been moved on from a parish in Swan Hill after complaints of inappropriate behaviour with minors.

'So they send him to minister to teenage boys at a boarding school, eh Deef? Unbelievable!'

Vince discovered that Father Delaney's time at St Bernard's had come to a sudden halt halfway through his third year. 'Surprise, surprise!' After that he was moved in rapid succession to Stawell, then Portland, and eventually stood down after an eighteen-month spell in Corio. Along the way, complaints had mounted but no charges had been laid until he was caught sodomising an eleven-year-old boy in the bathroom of the family home, where he'd been dispensing last rights to the lad's dying grandfather in the next room.

'All *right*,' said Vince, slamming his laptop closed. 'I've heard just about *enough* about that prick.' He dragged out the lasagne and binned it. His appetite had vanished.

He flopped on the couch, turned on the box, flashed through the stations and turned if off again, then fished out his mobile and dialled Jane's number.

'Jane Schultz.' Back to her maiden name already, Vince noted.

'G'day, Janey.'

'Hi, Vinny, what can I do for you?'

Vince took a deep breath. 'Feel free to tell me to mind my own business, but I want to ask you some questions about Joey.'

She paused. 'Like *what* exactly?'

'You told me on the weekend he was really hurting inside, something from his past.'

'I really don't want to discuss—'

'Just tell me this. Please. Did he ever talk about bad stuff happening to him at St Bernard's?'

She laughed. A grim sound. 'Like missing out on the First Eighteen and not being a prefect like his big brother?'

Ouch!

'I mean, being … fiddled with by the brothers or priests.'

Complete silence for a full minute. 'Joseph had nightmares, mood swings, and depression.'

Another pause.

'*You* join the dots, golden boy.'

* * *

Thursday evening found Vince at the Snapper's ground for training. Again he found himself leaning over the boundary fence with Big Brodes. They watched as the players did their drills. The coach nodded toward one youngster as he bounded past them.

'Nat Hayes. Gunna be a champ. Fast as buggery, can take a mark and got a terrific tank. Boys call him "Fifey".'

Vince nodded. Nat Fife was a star footballer from Freemantle.

'If he's that good, surely the AFL will snap him up.'

The big man emitted a low rumble, which Vince recognised as Brode's version of a chuckle. 'He's just started his apprenticeship with me *and* he's got the hots for Chook Parker's girl.' He grinned. 'Fifey's not goin' anywhere.'

They watched as the lad leapt sideways for a mark. He clutched the ball to his chest and fell awkwardly, his right foot planted and his knee twisting sideways—more than knees were made to twist. Especially young knees with immature soft tissue support. Vince and Brodes raced out onto the ground. Nat was lying on his back, clutching his leg and moaning.

'Just hang on, mate,' Vince said as he palpated the offending joint. He leant on the boy's foot and gently pulled the lower part of his leg forward. It was alarmingly loose, as if there was no anterior cruciate ligament there at all. He stood and looked at the coach.

'ACL gone?' murmured Brian.

'Have to wait for the scan,' he whispered, 'but looks like he'll need a reconstruction.' He looked at Brodes. 'Should be okay for next season.'

'They're never as good, them onballers, after a reco,' the coach said as they walked off the ground. 'Somethin like that happens when you're young, you're never the same.'

* * *

Vince drove home, fried up a couple of eggs, and collapsed in front of the box. He couldn't engage with the news so he put on an old DVD of *The Bridge* and after fifteen minutes lost interest. He sat on his lumpy old couch and looked around the room—guitar neglected in the corner, a pile of books gathering dust, and his running gear still on the floor from last week.

'Hell, Deef,' he informed the dozing dog, 'to paraphrase the great George Costanza, this isn't a life.' As he walked off to his bedroom, his mobile burst into song, 'Lydia Hanrahan' appearing on the cracked screen.

'Hi, Lids.'

'Hello, Vincent.' Conciliatory tone.

'Something on your mind?'

'Just wanted to thank you for speaking up for Georgina. She tells me you schmoozed Doctor Robinson.'

Vince laughed. 'I can be quite the charmer when I've a mind to. Remember?'

A pause. 'That was all a long time ago, Vincent.'

'Still got it, Lids.'

'Moving right along,' she continued, 'the Head of the School Girls is next weekend and the twins are both in the Senior Eight.'

'Wouldn't miss it for quids.'

'Ivan can't go, because he has golf and—'

'Shame.'

'—I will be coming down with the Browns and the Donovans.'

Vince winked at Deefer and raised an imaginary glass. 'Spiffing.'

'That's just it,' she went on. 'I don't want you to embarrass the girls.'

'Or *you.*'

'Exactly. So wear decent clothes and don't insult anyone.'

He laughed. 'Don't worry, Lids, I can play the game. It'll be just like old times. See you down at the river.'

* * *

Next morning Vince woke just after six, groped under his bed for his laptop, dragged himself into a half-sitting position, and resumed his Googling. During his fitful slumber, he'd realised that he needed to dig some more. He was convinced that Joey's death was a result of his treatment at the hands of Father Delaney, who was already in jail and, after the plethora of new charges, was likely to stay there until he died.

'And that'll be too good for him,' he muttered. 'But why didn't the Church defrock him and hand him over to the coppers?'

Vince trawled through the transcripts of the Royal Commission and the media reports about the appearance of Cardinal Patrick Evans, a priest around the Ballarat area in those dark days, by video link from a hotel in Rome. He combed through the testimony of the late Bishop Carroll, the senior cleric when the worst paedophile priests were around the diocese. It was clear that instead of reporting these offenders to the police, those responsible had merely moved them from parish to parish. Not only that, but they'd attempted to avoid responsibility by blaming each other for turning a blind eye.

'Bastards!' Vince shouted at the peeling, seventies'-style wallpaper in his bedroom. 'We can't let them get away with it!'

The dog started scratching the back door and Vince looked at the clock. Almost eight-thirty! He leapt out of bed, shed his boxers, jumped in the shower, pulled on some clothes, filled Deef's bowl, then went and fired up Benny.

'Sorry, mate,' he called out the window, 'walk tonight, okay?'

* * *

'Hi, Doc,' Elena said, her voice warm and welcoming. 'You're looking a bit ordinary. Busy week?'

Vince had missed last week's rendezvous with Elena and didn't feel like going this time. After starting his Friday half an hour behind he'd played catch up all day and it was after seven when he finally walked out the surgery door. Elena was in situ by the time he arrived at Fanny's.

He nodded and slumped in the chair opposite. 'No different to any other.'

'Well, what then?'

Jesus! What do you reckon?

'I'm sure your brother's loss is still weighing down hard on you.'

He sat forward. 'I already have a counsellor, Sarge, so stop with the therapy, okay?'

She looked away and sipped on her wine. Seemed to know when to back off—one of the things Vince liked about her. They ordered their meals and sat in silence.

'How are the Cats going in the pre-season comp?' Elena ventured after a few minutes.

'Dunno.'

She displayed her trademark Mona Lisa smile. 'Not like you, Doc.'

Vince took a deep breath. 'I went down to Melbourne last Friday. Georgie's been playing up at school and I had to plead her case with the principal.' Best not to mention the exact nature of the misdemeanour to a copper.

Elena raised her eyebrows. 'How did that go?'

Vince paused as a tattooed and bearded young waiter served their entrees. 'Okay,' he said. 'They aren't going to kick her out. Not yet anyway.'

He speared some fried calamari and washed it down with mineral water.

Elena made a start on her sardines and looked up. 'So, that's all good?'

Vince shook his head. 'It's all *bad* really. Just one crisis averted, that's all.' He looked up. 'I feel like my family is slipping away from me.'

He lapsed back into moody silence. The rest of his starter lay untouched. Elena continued with her dish and said nothing. Vince realised she avoided commenting on his family life as a matter of principle. That was another thing he liked about her. Odd, he thought, glancing at her across the table, the list was growing. He frowned; *that's enough of that*!

'Seen Will lately?'

'No, but I'm going down to Brae to have lunch with his mother on Sunday.'

Brae was a hatted, destination restaurant near Birregurra. It had been a favourite of Vince and Lydia's in happier days.

'Sounds serious,' he said with a low whistle. 'Lady Bracknell must be thawing a bit, is she?'

On a previous Friday night, Elena had described her first encounter with Will's mother, who lived in Barwon Heads. Mrs Carlisle had given her the impression that an Italian dairy farmer's daughter was not an appropriate consort for her son and heir. Vince had then dubbed the old lady 'Lady Bracknell' after the domineering matron in *The Importance of Being Earnest*.

Elena shrugged and made no further comment.

'Good luck with *that*.'

Still nothing.

He guessed she was feeling intimidated by that Western District 'born to rule' thing. At least the Wimmera was more egalitarian; good farmers up there had been able to prosper regardless. Like his father. And Joey ...

He shook his head again and Elena responded with an expectant look.

'Just wait, Sarge. There's steak knives too.' Vince took a gulp of his water and noticed his hand was shaking. 'Next day I went to a school reunion up in Ballarat with Kookaburra.'

'Kookaburra?'

'Father Kelly. He laughs a lot. Unlike me.'

'Got it.'

Vince went on, palms sweaty and chest tight. 'I saw a photograph of my little brother and … and a school chaplain. Gerald Delaney.'

'Isn't that the priest who molested all those boys back in the seventies and eighties?'

Vince nodded.

'And you think that he …?'

He nodded again. 'And *I* was supposed to be watching out for Joey.'

'That priest has been defrocked,' said Elena, 'and he's already been locked up. After these new charges, he'll do life.'

'That's not the point!' exclaimed Vince. 'It was the cover-up by those in authority, instead of telling you coppers. Those old bishops and priests—*they* need to be held to account!'

Elena leant forward and touched Vince's hand. 'That won't bring your brother back, Doc.'

He pulled his hand away. 'I *know* that. But those holier than thou buggers got away with it, that's what's burning me up.'

Silence fell as the waiter cleared away their plates.

'When the Royal Commission began,' Vince said after a pause, 'I didn't give a shit.' He looked into his glass. 'Now it's personal.'

12

After farewelling Elena outside Fanny's, Vince headed home. He turned on the TV and spent five minutes watching the Fifth Test against the touring English team. 'Low care factor,' he told the dozing dog.

He switched off the TV, evicted Deefer, and fell into bed. Somnolent with emotional fatigue, he fell into a deep sleep. After what seemed like a few minutes, his phone started singing its familiar refrain. He was shocked to see it was just after three am.

'Hanrahan.'

'Colleen from the mid-floor, Doctor.' An only too-familiar voice. 'It's Tracey Cartwright. Multi three. She's got a high head and type one dips.'

Don't like the sound of that. 'What's her cervix doing?' said Vince, now wide awake.

'She was seven centimetres when she hit the place ten minutes ago. Hopefully, she'll crack on.'

'On the way.'

A surge of adrenaline dragged Vince out of bed. *Type one dips!* He turned on the light and dragged on jeans and windcheater, scooped up his car keys and hit the road. *Can't afford any more obstetric mishaps.* He sped through the dark streets.

Five minutes later he burst into the labour ward and went straight over to the paper strip pumping out of the machine attached to the foetal monitor strapped to Tracey's heaving abdomen. There were deep drops in the baby's heart rate during contractions, but the decelerations also persisted after the contractions—'type two dips'—a sure sign of foetal distress. He pulled on a glove and examined Tracey as she moaned and groaned on the bed.

Vince's searching fingers palpated the top of the baby's head and he located the diamond shaped soft anterior fontanelle. Instead of being down and forward, it was on top and back—a posterior position. *Bugger!* When he removed his hand, the fluid on his glove was stained brown, *another* sign the baby was battling, then looked up at Tracey. Dustin, at her side, was ashen-faced and seemed to be breathing even faster than his partner.

'Good news and bad news, guys. You're almost fully dilated, Trace, but the baby is distressed and a bit stuck. We need to get him or her out quickly.'

Tracey nodded, then moaned as the next contraction started, morphing into a full-blooded scream as it peaked, her sweaty face red and straining.

'Don't push, lovey,' said Colleen. 'Just breathe the pain away. Like this.' She put her face in front of Tracey's and puffed in and out as if she was the one in labour.

'The baby is upside down,' Vince added during the next lull. 'Like a square peg in a round hole. So I need to use forceps to rotate the head.'

Colleen got busy, attaching vertical metal poles to the end of the bed and laying out a large white pack on a trolley. She and Vince lifted Tracey's legs and attached them to the poles with canvas stirrups. Vince leant forward, grasped Tracey's hips and dragged her bottom to the end of the bed, pushing her legs wide.

Dustin grabbed Vince by the arm and got in his face. 'Why don't youse do a bloody Caesarean?'

'Too late for that.'

His grip tightened. 'If you hurt her, Doc, I'll fucken hurt you.'

Vince shook Dustin off and pushed him away.

One of the midwives, Marge Simpkins, a burly farmer's wife, dragged him up to the head of the bed. 'Dusty, you're way out of line. Shut up and hold your wife's hand.'

Colleen nodded toward the beeping machine. The foetal heart had dipped right down as before, but this time was not picking up at all.

Vince's own heart rate rocketed as he drained Tracey's bladder with a catheter, did a quick nerve block with local anaesthetic, and picked up one of the gleaming forceps blades.

'I can't hack this,' said Dustin, and he bolted for the door. *You and me both*, thought Vince, now breathing hard himself. High head, posterior position and a distressed baby—a recipe for disaster. *Another disaster.*

He eased both blades on, gently manipulated the handles, then nodded to the midwife.

'Listen, sweetheart,' said Colleen, her hand palpating Tracey's abdomen. 'Here's the next contraction. Just give me a big push and you'll have your baby.'

Vince pulled the forceps handles together. Even though he'd done thousands of forceps deliveries, a Kielland's rotation could be hazardous and he knew that, given his precarious professional status, the Medical Board would decapitate him if things went belly up.

Too bad, no choice. With his heart in his mouth as he steadied his stance, he rotated the handles, cut a big episiotomy, and started a slow steady pull as Tracey pushed and screamed.

For a minute there was a stalemate and Vince started sweating like he was on a big run. Suddenly he felt things move and out came the baby's head—the right way up. *Thank God!* He removed the forceps, completed the delivery, and watched as the greasy white creature let out a cry and turned pink.

Vince's hands were shaking as he stitched up the episiotomy. *What's wrong with you, Hanrahan? You've been doing this stuff for twenty years.*

Mrs Harrington, resplendent in a purple dressing gown and ugg boots, burst in, kissed Tracey, and pounced on her new granddaughter.

'I knew Dr Vince would look after you, Trace.'

Vince grimaced. 'Otherwise, I would have had you to deal with, eh Mrs H?'

She nodded. 'And you haven't seen me fired up.'

'It's a scary thing, Doc,' Tracey added with a weak laugh.

Not as scary as the Medical Board.

* * *

Vince went through to the nurse's station to enter the birth details into the computer. Colleen Maloney was sitting at the desk, doing paperwork.

'Why don't you leave that till tomorrow?' she suggested. 'Might as well go back to bed and get some shut-eye.'

'I'm a dot every "I" and cross every "T" man, Col,' he answered. *These days.*

'While I've got you're here,' she said, 'I'm chair of the Parish Social Justice Group and I'm looking for a speaker for our meeting next Wednesday.'

Vince grimaced. 'I'm not too keen on the Church. This child sex abuse stuff has moved me from indifferent to hostile.'

'Fair enough, but the topic is indigenous inclusiveness. Zero religiosity.'

'Can't see how I could contribute, anyway.' Vince completed his data entry and signed out. 'Not my scene.'

'I thought you could tell us about your experience in Aboriginal health.'

He cursed himself for telling Colleen about the six months he'd spent as a remote-area obstetric registrar as part of his specialist training. Flying to indigenous communities across the Kimberley and providing antenatal care and gynaecological treatment wasn't as glamorous as she believed. But perhaps …

'Does the Monsignor go to those Social Justice meetings?'

Colleen nodded. 'He set up the group and is very supportive.'

Vince thought for a minute. 'Well, I might just come along.'

Wouldn't mind a chat with the Mons. He might've been in Ballarat himself back in those dark days.

13

Vince woke the next morning in a cold sweat, chest tight and palpitating. It took several minutes for him to engage with reality.

It had been after four o'clock by the time he'd gotten to bed. Then his hyper-aroused nervous system had kept him awake for a further hour. *High forceps rotation—big risk and no safety net. Dodged a bullet.*

When he had dropped off, he was revisited by an old nightmare, a re-run of the funerals of a young woman and her baby back in Melbourne three years ago.

He rolled out of bed, put the kettle on, and opened the back door. Deefer bounded up, seeking both food and company. Vince gave her a pat and a tickle and filled up her bowl, then looked out at the day. It was sunny—blue sky and very still.

'Great day for a surf, mate.'

Deefer kept on munching, and Vince went inside and glanced at the calendar on the back of the kitchen door. 'Oh *no*. Great day for a rowing regatta too!'

He showered, then started dragging clothes out of his wardrobe and throwing them on the bed. 'What am I supposed to wear, Deef?' He pulled on some crumpled cream chinos, a passable shirt and gave his old RM Williams boots a wipe with yesterday's jocks. He looked in the cracked mirror leaning against his bedroom wall. His girth seemed to have grown and his eyes looked sunken and dark in his large, lined face.

Vince pushed his shoulders back and sucked in his stomach. 'Looking good, my man.' He grabbed his old straw hat, ducked next door and rang the bell. Kieran appeared straight away, wearing his customary big smile, his mother close behind.

'H-h-hi, Doc. Can we go fishing t-t-today?'

'Sorry, Super K, maybe tomorrow. I've got to go down to Geelong to watch my twins row in the school girls' championships. Can you look after Deefer for me?'

'Give me them clothes,' said Mrs H, shaking her head. 'They want pressing. They'll be all dressed up posh at that rowing. Kieran, grab your dad's old FJ sports jacket. It'll fit Dr Vince nice.'

Vince knew that Mrs Harrington's husband had died years before, leaving her to bring up Tracey and Kieran, plus another five children in between.

'Thanks, Mrs H, but I've got to get—'

She squinted at him and beckoned with one hand. 'Hand 'em over, Dr Vince. By the time you have a shave, they'll be ready.'

* * *

Two hours later Vince rolled into Geelong. He gave a nod of appreciation as he passed Kardinia Park, home of the mighty Cats, and drove around to the banks of the Barwon River. There was an alarming number of cars, mostly large four-wheel drives and sleek imported sedans parked in every available spot. He squeezed Benny next to a silver Jaguar, avoiding scraping the gleaming duco. Almost.

Grabbing his hat and sunnies, Vince walked along the riverbank past the row of school tents, each emblazoned with appropriate colours and school crests, until he arrived at the Canterbury Ladies College group. Sitting on a rug under a market umbrella on an adjacent patch of grass were Lydia and her party.

'Ciao, Vincenzo,' said a bejewelled ash blonde in pink polo top and white shorts, revealing suspiciously bronzed legs, brandishing a glass of wine. 'Have some bubbly, darling.'

'G'day, Jen,' said Vince. 'Long time, no see.'

She drained her glass, stood, and gave Vince a hug. 'Well, you just *disappeared*, sweetie. Here one minute, gone the next!' She shrieked with laughter and the rest of the party fell about at this witicism.

This is going to be a really long day.

He dutifully kissed the proffered female cheeks and shook hands with the men—resplendent in blazers and Panama hats, some wearing rowing-club ties.

'How is Warragul?' asked Caroline Donovan, another friend from his former life.

'Don't know,' said Vince. 'I live in *Warrnambool*.'

She giggled. 'Silly me.'

'Bit too much fizz, Caro,' said her husband, an old cycling mate of Vince's. 'You're getting tipsy.'

'Just in time,' said Lydia, offering Vince an orange juice and a spot on the rug. 'The senior eights are the next event. CLC is the leading school so far.'

He nodded. 'Where are the twins?'

She pointed up the river. 'Walking to the start with the rest of the crew. You just missed them.'

Vince scrambled to his feet. He could see Georgie and Tessa up ahead, amongst a gaggle of gangly girls in their light-blue zooties.

'Hey, girls,' he called, 'wait up!'

The twins looked embarrassed as he caught up with them.

'We have to keep going, Dad,' said Tessa. 'The race starts in a few minutes.'

'Where did you get that jacket, Bins?' asked Georgina. 'You look like a weird country bumpkin.'

They gave him a casual wave and sped up to join the others. 'Break a leg, team,' he called after them, eliciting a twitter of giggling from the group.

Vince re-joined the others, mixed feelings in his heart—proud of his girls but conscious of his detached status in their lives. He resumed his seat and listened to the chatter. Renovations, overseas holidays, and VCE expectations seemed to be the dominant themes. *What's new?*

'How do you think Geelong will go this year, Vince?' asked one of the revellers, a tall man with a shock of curly hair and a friendly smile, who had been Vince's anaesthetist at the Royal Women's Hospital.

'Not too bad, Thommo,' replied Vince. 'Garry Ablett's back but depends on injuries, I guess. What about the Pies?'

Thommo laughed. 'Probably finish about ninth, as usual.'

'How's the gassing caper going?'

'Same old,' he replied, sipping on a glass of red. 'I miss our Thursday operating lists though.'

'Those were the days.'

'When are you coming back to the big city?'

Vince shook his head. 'Don't know. Hopefully next year.'

Thommo raised his glass in a toast. 'Sooner the better.'

Lydia handed Vince a tasty pulled-pork slider and another juice and they sat back in the sunshine. Her dark, straight hair was pinned up under a large light-blue hat and she was wearing a beautiful, floaty print dress. *Like a Monet painting.* She asked him about Jane and her children and enquired after his father and they chatted about her job and the twins. *Just like old times.* The sun was high in the sky, bouncing off the water, and Vince felt his taut muscles loosening and his agitated mind quieting. He joined in other conversations with the old gang and began to relax. *I could do this.*

After a few minutes, he excused himself, walked behind the tents toward the toilets, and ran straight into a short, dapper man sporting a dazzling smile under a crisp white boater.

'Afternoon, Vincent,' he said, extending his right hand, a bottle of Billecart-Salmon champagne in his left. 'Ivan Becker.'

I know who you are, you bastard. 'Thought you were golfing.'

'Finished early, as it turned out, so came straight from the eighteenth green down to the river.' He was still wearing his Royal Melbourne polo and golf trousers. 'Thought I'd surprise everyone.'

Ivan wandered over to Lydia's throng and joined the revelry. There was a fresh outbreak of kissing and handshaking and Caro shrieked again and handed the new arrival a brimming glass. Lydia looked over at Vince and shrugged her familiar 'what can you do?' pose.

Vince frowned in response and strode back up the river toward his car. The dream was over. *Surplus to requirements.* He fished in his pocket for the keys, then noticed that Benny was blocked in by a large black Range Rover. *That'd be right!*

Just then a voice boomed from an overhead speaker. 'The Senior Eights are in the starter's hands.'

Vince swore, looked around, and headed up onto a footbridge overlooking the finishing line. The four crews in the final appeared in the distance, moving toward him in that typical stuttering but powerful fashion, as the rowers moved forward and slid back after the catch, propelling their shells onward. The roar of the crowd drowned out the commentator's call and the cox's instructions as the finish line beckoned. CLC were half a length behind the leaders, their long-time nemesis Pemberley Hall. Vince noticed Georgie pick up the rate in the stroke seat and the other girls responded, pulling level with fifteen metres to go, then hitting the finish line, victors by a canvas!

Vince's heart swelled with pride and he leapt in the air and let out a whoop, almost knocking over an elderly lady standing nearby. He ran along the bridge and back down to the riverbank and watched the excited CLC girls as they disembarked, screaming with joy, and tossed the reluctant cox back into the water.

Vince gave the twins a big hug. 'Girls, I am *so* proud of you,' he told them, his face streaming with tears. 'You are both dead-set champs!'

'Thanks, Bins,' said Georgie, giving him a kiss.

'We'll see you at the dinner,' added Tessa.

Just then Vince noticed the gaggle of excited supporters, led by an ebullient Ivan, running up the riverside path.

'I've got to head back to the 'Bool,' he lied, moving away. 'On-call. Sorry.' He retreated into the trees and headed back to his car, now unobstructed, and made his escape.

Vince turned Benny back onto the Princes Highway, gripping the steering wheel like a vice, and headed west. As he picked up speed, he shouted at the windscreen. 'You coward, Hanrahan!'

* * *

He arrived back in Warrnambool to find Deefer dozing in the late afternoon sun, last week's dirty clothes washed and ironed, and a freshly cooked beef casserole in the fridge. He went next door straight away and knocked loudly.

Mrs Harrington, wiping her hands on her apron, came to the door. 'Welcome back, Doctor Vince. How did your girls go in the rowing?'

'They won the big race, Mrs H.'

'Isn't that grand?' she said, face beaming.

'Yeah, it was terrific, but never mind that. Just wanted to thank you for doing my laundry and for that casserole. You're spoiling me.'

Mrs Harrington crossed her arms across her ample bosom. 'Just being neighbourly. It's how I was brought up.'

'Well, thanks anyway,' said Vince. 'How are Tracey and the baby?'

'Real good. Margie Simpkins told me you done a miracle to get young Skylah out safe and sound.'

His gut lurched. 'Wouldn't quite say that. How's Dustin?'

Mrs Harrington frowned. 'You never know what he's gunna do.'

'H-h-hello, Dr Vince.' Kieran appeared at the door, along with another young man Vince didn't know.

'Thanks for looking after Deefer, Super K. What about we go fishing on Wednesday arvo?'

It was Kieran's turn to beam. 'N-n-no worries.'

'Who's your mate?'

'He's me c-c-cousin. Same age as m-m-me.'

'Introduce him properly, Kieran,' his mother interrupted. 'This is Travis, Dr Vince. Geraldine's boy.'

'G'day, Travis,' said Vince, extending his hand.

The thin-faced, pimply young man, with a large black ring occupying most of one earlobe, stared at the ground and proffered a limp, cold paw.

'Geraldine and Mark don't have no room at their place out at Dennington,' Mrs Harrington said with a theatrical eye roll. '*Apparently*. So Trav is stopping with us for a while.' She dropped her voice to a loud whisper, no doubt audible to Travis. 'He was studyin' for a priest.' She moved closer with a wink and conspiratorial tone. 'He's been in trouble, like. Drugs and that.'

'What are you doing now?' asked Vince, turning to Travis.

He shrugged in reply. *Wouldn't have made much of a priest.*

Mrs Harrington made a circling movement next to her head with her index finger. 'Speak up, Travis. Dr Vince is just being friendly.'

'Yes,' added Kieran, 'he's a t-t-top bloke.'

'Don't really know,' Travis said after a pause. 'Might look for some work around here and maybe do a course at Deakin.'

Mrs Harrington patted him on the head. 'You could even meet a nice girl out at the uni, eh Trav?'

The young man shrugged and looked away.

'Anyway,' said Mrs Harrington, raising her eyebrows, 'we're off to mass.'

'I'll leave you to it,' said Vince, and he headed back across his arid front lawn. A few minutes later he noticed Mrs H backing the little Datsun out, Kieran waving from the passenger seat. No sign of Travis.

'Probably had a gutful of the Church,' Vince told Deefer as he shut the front gate. *Join the club.*

Vince heated the casserole and made a big dent in it while watching back episodes of *The West Wing*. When he was feeling glum, the familiar faces and narrative soothed his nerves. Pure escapism. Sometimes he felt closer to the various characters of these TV shows than to people in real life. *That can't be good.*

Halfway through series three, his mobile burst into song—it was a FaceTime call and the giggling twins appeared on the screen.

'Am I looking at the two best rowers in Australasia?'

'You bet,' said Georgie. 'We kicked Pemberly's butt—'

'Pity you couldn't make the dinner,' interrupted Tessa. 'It was really cool—'

'Except the Gollum kissed us both—'

'And said we were both a credit to the school—'

Dr Robinson's changed her tune.

'She said the crew was awesome, then spelled it out like "oarsome".'

'Very droll,' said Vince.

'But no one laughed—'

'Awkward.'

'Except Ivan The Tool—'

'He cacked himself—'

Why am I not surprised?

'Great sense of humour, that ITT.'

They both made faces, Georgie putting her finger in her mouth and affecting a gag.

'Hope you didn't have to work too hard when you got back to War-rnie, Bins.'

Vince looked around his dishevelled lounge room. Empty DVD cases, chip packets, and Coke cans all around. 'Flat out, guys.'

Tessa peered into the screen, frowning. 'That room looks like a tip, Dad. What's going on?'

'Just about to do a bit of a cleanup.'

'Make sure you do,' added Georgie. 'You're not a dero.'

Vince saluted the screen. 'Message received, Captain.'

'We have to go, Dad. Thanks for coming to the river today.'

'Later, Bins.'

'Bye girls, congratulations. See you at the Tokyo Olympics.'

Vince sat back in the surrounding debris and looked around. The Snapper house was a far cry from the forty-eight square renovated Italianate villa in Canterbury—a metaphor for his life. Deefer nuzzled up to him.

'A different world, mate,' Vince told her, 'not that you care.'

He turned on the box and looked at the late news. The usual array of international strife, squabbles in Canberra, and various sports reports. Vince started to nod off, then through his stupor noticed Monsignor O'Shannassey on the screen and turned up the volume.

'*… Parish priest in Warrnambool for almost fifteen years. He was in the Ballarat diocese when these atrocities occurred and gave evidence at the Royal Commission last year that he had no role in the moving of suspect priests around the region. When asked today about the Commission's Interim Report on the Ballarat Diocese, the Monsignor responded "The bishop and senior priests were derelict in their duties".*'

'Truer words never spoken, Deef.'

* * *

He staggered off to work the next morning and proceeded to do what Geeps do.

'It's like shearing sheep, Rooned,' Shirley explained at the start. 'You just boot the shorn one down the race and pull the next one out of the pen.'

His heart was heavy and mind unfocused, but as the week unfolded he lost himself in the relentless rhythm of viral infections, back pain, and antenatal visits. On Wednesday evening he farewelled the last punter for the day, and as he started to pack up, his desk phone rang.

'It's Professor McKenzie,' said Lorraine. 'He says it's urgent.'

Little Lachie—that'd be right!

The Medical Board had appointed Professor Lachlan McKenzie from the Royal Women's Hospital to supervise him from afar. It didn't help that the two of them had done their specialist training together and back then Vince had treated the young Lachie, a nerdy try-hard, with disdain. It seemed the memory still rankled.

'Say I'm busy.'

'I've told him that three times today. He's on line two.'

Vince took a deep breath. 'Okay.' He picked up the phone. Silence. 'The little bugger must have hung up,' he said. 'What a pit—'

'Vincent,' the professor cut in. 'I understand you performed a potentially hazardous Kielland's rotation without consulting me, and—'

Bad news travels fast.

'No choice, Lachlan. Fully dilated and a distressed baby with a posterior position. What would you expect me to—'

'Be that as it may, Vincent,' interrupted McKenzie, voice terse. 'But you are one labour-ward mistake away from deregistration. I don't need to remind you that your professional future is at *my* discretion.'

Vince paused and took another deep breath. As Shirley put it: 'Little Lachie's got you by the ball, Rooned.'

'Sorry, mate, won't happen again.'

'You must anticipate these complicated cases and refer them on in a timely fashion.'

What bullshit! Little Lachie knows these things can just appear out of nowhere. However, Shirley was right—Vince could feel Lachie's hands on his testicles. Squeezing.

'Will do, Lachlan. Depend on it.'

There was a pause on the line. *He's trying to figure out whether I'm sincere or being a smart arse.* Self-awareness was never Little Lachie's strong point.

'I'll expect a full written account, Vincent,' he replied. 'Then I will report back to the Board with a recommendation. You are already on thin—'

'Ice. Yeah, I know that.' Vince now felt like his balls were in a vice. 'Lovely to chat, Professor. Got to go. Bye.'

Vince shook his head, sucked in a quick breath, and tried to expel the air slowly, just like Myf had taught him. One … two … then it all came out in a sudden rush. *I can never get the hang of that technique.* After checking his results, he wrote a couple of scripts, shut off his computer, walked outside, and hopped into Benny.

He headed off through the darkening streets, Professor Lachlan McKenzie's words ringing in his ears. After decades of being a 'top notcher', as old Mick would say, in the Obs and Gynae world, it was galling to have his competency questioned by such a man, a B-grader at best—only a professor because he was a champion arselicker. And a vindictive, small-minded prick. Vince's anticipated return to his former status seemed to be as remote as ever. *Let alone my status as husband and father.*

He smacked the steering wheel. *Fuck!* And then there was Joey's suicide and that bastard Delaney! *Double fuck!* Vince frowned and looked out the window at the passing shops and businesses, doors closed and windows black. Except one. He turned into the well-lit entrance of a drive-through bottleshop and slowed as he approached the service counter. A young man stepped forward as Vince lowered the passenger window and eyed off the wine shelf.

'Hi Doc,' he said. 'Never seen you here before. What'll you have?'

Vince paused, then shook his head. 'Nothing, Sam. Changed my mind.'

14

As he pulled up at the Snapper house, Vince's mobile burst into song. He looked at the number. 'The mid-floor,' he told the steering wheel. 'The one call you can't ignore.'

'Hanrahan.'

'Hi, Vince, it's Colleen Maloney. You still okay for tonight?'

'Tonight, Col?' *I know I've been distracted, but surely I would remember making a date with a midwife.*

'The Parish Social Justice group. Eight o'clock in the church hall. You're the guest speaker. Remember?'

Oh, yes, that. Forgotten all about it. Just what I need, a close encounter with the Catholic Church.

'Course I remember. Aboriginal health, yeah?'

'That's right, just an account of your experiences up there.'

And a chance to chew the Monsignor's ear.

'No worries,' said Vince. 'Any food?'

She laughed. 'There will be supper—sandwiches, slices, and chockie biscuits, courtesy of the Social Justice members. And a cuppa. Can't offer you a drink though.'

* * *

An hour later Vince was again on the road. He'd fed and watered Deefer and downed a tin of baked beans, just in case the Social Justice sangers ran out. Even brushed his teeth and washed his face. *Must be that Catholic guilt thing about cleansing your soul—Mum would've been proud of me.*

He headed up Lava Street and pulled up outside the hall, which was opposite the church with a bitumen car park in between. He decided not to drive through the bluestone entrance and found a spot for Benny on the road outside—better for a quick getaway. Dusk was falling and the spire of the Sacred Heart Church looked eerily otherworldly as it reached to the clouded heavens. *What am I doing here?*

Vince skirted around to the front of the hall, took a deep breath, and walked in. Colleen and a young man he recognised as one of the hospital IT guys were sitting behind a desk, welcoming and registering the attendees. Colleen smiled as she stood.

'Hi, Vince. You know Nigel.' She stuck a name tag on the front of Vince's shirt. 'He'll be helping you with your talk.'

'Do you have a memory stick with your slides, Doctor? Or have you emailed your presentation to us already?' Vince knew Nigel was a dedicated tech head. He had short hair, an eyebrow piercing, and a Ned Kelly beard. *A hipster in the 'Bool! What next?*

Vince tapped his temple. 'It's all on my hard drive up here, Nige.'

The room was full and Vince recognised almost everyone. There were the usual uber-Catholic ladies and a rainbow coalition of greenies, earnest social worker types, representatives from the local Aboriginal cooperative, and a few other hangers-on, presumably after a free feed. Colleen led Vince over to a table out the front, where the Monsignor was already seated, and with a loud clap of her hands called the meeting to order.

'Welcome, everyone, to the Sacred Heart Social Justice group. Our topic this month is Indigenous Disadvantage and we are fortunate to have Dr Vincent Hanrahan as our guest speaker. He will talk about his experiences as a medical volunteer in the Kimberley. First, I will invite Monsignor O'Shannassey to lead us in an opening prayer.'

Vince looked across at Colleen with a frown. *So much for no religion being involved. Next thing there'll be happy clapping!*

'Thank you, Colleen,' said the Mons, getting to his feet. He stood out the front with his the tips of his fingers together, head bowed. 'We pray to God to help us in our discussion and may we learn from each other in a spirit of mutual respect and regret for the suffering of our indigenous brothers and sisters. Amen.'

Fair enough. Sounds like the Mons is *one of the good guys.*

'Thank you, Monsignor,' said Colleen, 'who is himself a long-time champion of social justice.' She turned to Vince. 'Now, let's hear from Dr Hanrahan.'

Vince stood and prepared to do his thing. What with presentations to Rotary clubs, high schools, and medical students, not to mention numerous dinner-party conversations, he must have given this talk a zillion times. People loved it. They thought he was a saint, living in the outback, helping the disadvantaged Aboriginal women up in remote communities. And all out of the goodness of his own heart. What a hero! In the past he'd lapped it up, his already inflated ego filling to bursting point.

But that was Before. This was Now. *Time to stop bullshitting.*

'Thanks for your kind introduction, Col, but I think you may have gilded the lily a little. I wasn't a volunteer. My work in the Kimberley was part of my training and I was well paid.'

Colleen nodded, her freckles fading into a blush.

Vince went on to describe the obstetric challenges facing indigenous women, the high rates of diabetes, kidney disease, premature labour, low-birth-weight babies, and infant mortality rates much higher than the white population.

'These stats are what you find in third world countries,' he added, 'but this is in our own backyard.'

'Why is that, Doctor?' asked a teacher from one of the secondary schools, sporting short grey hair, dangling earrings, and a black and white Palestinian-style scarf. 'Is it due to white colonial dispossession?'

'*Grog*,' said Vince. 'And smoking, bad diets, diabetes, overcrowding, domestic violence, isolation, and lack of access to medical facilities.' He looked around. 'Any more questions?'

The audience looked stunned and fell silent.

A young man of Middle-Eastern appearance stood up from the back row. 'Where is the compassion in the government of this country? Hazaras who escape genocide in Afghanistan are locked up on

Manus Island like criminals.' He pointed at Monsignor O'Shannassey. 'You Catholics talk of social justice, but—'

'Aisif is staying in one of our emergency housing units,' said Colleen, leaping to her feet, 'and is very welcome here. However, we are discussing indigenous issues tonight, Aisif, so perhaps it might be better if you …'

The youth muttered something under his breath and marched out of the hall, eyes flashing and hands clenched. Colleen shut the door after him and took a deep breath.

'It must have been a great hardship for you, Dr Hanrahan,' she said after a few minutes, 'living in those difficult conditions.'

Vince laughed. 'Most of the time I stayed in a swish resort in Broome. I was flown to most of the remote communities, usually back in time for a swim and a cold beer.' He raised an open hand in a mock toast. 'Occasionally, I went out on the road with a small mobile gynae operating set up—in a brand new Land Cruiser with a driver.' He paused and winked. '*Looxury*. But the remote-area nurses and the docs in the East Kimberley,' he went on, 'they *really* do it hard.'

Colleen looked around, trying to drum up more interest, but Vince's sardonic tone seemed to have extinguished the crowd's curiosity.

'How can we help these poor people, Doctor?' asked one of the older ladies, eventually. She was one of Vince's patients and a parish stalwart.

Vince shook his head. 'Don't know, Dolores,' he responded. 'All we white fellas seem to do is make things worse. We need to listen to the communities and the people on the ground.'

'Well, I know what I'm going to do about it,' she said. 'I'm going to *pray* for those poor little black children.'

Vince grimaced, but there was a general murmur of agreement. Colleen stood, thanked Vince, and called the meeting to a close. Within minutes the trestle tables on the sides of the hall were laden with sandwiches, slices, and biscuits. Someone offered Vince a cup of tea and he grabbed a plate and tucked in.

'I gather you don't believe in the power of prayer, Dr Hanrahan.'

Monsignor O'Shannassey was also holding a loaded plate and looking at Vince with a quizzical expression. He'd consulted Vince from time to time about a blood disorder and his gout, but they'd avoided discussion of the Divine.

'No offence, Monsignor, but I'm a bit out of practice with praying these days.' He nodded toward the vaulted wooden ceiling. 'If God's up there, I reckon he would get a hell of a shock if I started petitioning now.'

The Monsignor chuckled. 'The stray lamb is always welcome back to the fold.'

Enough of this religious bonhomie! 'Matter of fact,' said Vince, drawing the priest to one side. 'I was wanting to ask you something.'

O'Shannassey raised his bushy eyebrows. He bore a close resemblance to former prime minister John Howard, but with the bloated, liverish face of a hard drinker.

'I understand you were a priest in Ballarat in the eighties,' said Vince.

The Monsignor nodded.

'My little brother was at a boarder at St Bernard's back then and I think he was abused by Father Delaney.'

The Monsignor put his hand on Vince's arm. 'I heard what happened, Doctor. I'm sorry for your loss.'

Vince pulled his arm away. 'What I want to know is, why didn't the bishop and the other senior priests report Delaney to the police? They knew what he was up to and they just kept moving him around!'

O'Shannassey shook his head. 'It was a long time ago and I can't remember any discussion about Father Delaney at the time. I hardly knew the man. I was parish priest at St Monica's in Sebastopol and not privy to such matters. It was only the bishop and the other members of the College of Consultors who decided these things.'

'But according to the Royal Commission, there were *many* paedophile priests in the Ballarat diocese. The bishop and his henchmen must have known about it!'

'Sadly, the bishop's memory is failing—'

'Convenient, isn't it?' interrupted Vince. 'Shades of Allan Bond.'

O'Shannassey put down his teacup and gestured with his hands outstretched like he was giving a sermon. 'The Church hierarchy let down generations of children and their families and we clergy are all to blame.' He tapped his chest with his right hand. '*Mea culpa, mea culpa, mea maxima culpa.* All we can do is pray to God for forgiveness.'

Vince dumped his half-eaten sandwich and headed for the door. He strode across the car park and looked at the dark church—a heavy black edifice against the night sky.

'You sanctimonious hypocrites!' he shouted at the imposing bluestone structure, and then got into his car, put his head on the steering wheel, and wept.

15

'I want you to check her out,' said Tracey Cartwright, her face white and drawn, almost nodding off as she sat back in the chair, head against the wall. 'Her head looks funny.'

Vince had come to work the next day eager for the distracting effect of the routine slog of general practice. Skylah, now ten days old, was his first patient.

'How's she feeding?' he asked.

Tracey shrugged. She had on a shapeless black top, tracksuit bottoms, and ugg boots. *Not quite the yummy mummy look I used to see in the Eastern suburbs.*

'She's on the bottle now. I got sick of her hangin' off me boob.'

Vince frowned and gestured to the two boys playing in the corner. 'But you breastfed these two okay, didn't you?'

'Yeah, I had plenty of milk but I got sick of her cryin' all the time.' She avoided Vince's gaze. 'It was stressin' me out.' Tracey gestured behind her. 'And I got them troublemakers to worry about as well.'

There was a loud crash near the toy box and the toddler burst into tears. 'JAYDEN,' Tracey screamed, 'share that truck with your brother or I'll give you a big smack. One … two … THREE!'

Vince waited for peace to be restored before continuing. 'It must be handy having Dustin home to help out with the boys.'

Tracey gave an audible sniff. 'You're jokin', Doc. He can't stand bein' around the kids. Bad for his nerves, he reckons.'

'What about your mum? I'm sure she'd be happy to help.'

'She's flat out lookin' after Kieran,' said Tracey, voice flat and fatigued. 'I love my brother to bits, but he's like a baby himself.' She pointed at the pram. 'At least now this one's on the bottle, Mum can mind her and the boys when Kieran goes to work.'

Vince knew how proud Kieran was of his part-time job sorting donated goods for the Salvos.

'Let's have a look at her.'

Tracey picked up the sleeping baby from her pram—at arm's length, as if she was a doll—put her on the examination couch, and resumed her seat.

'Is she putting on weight and weeing and pooing okay?' Vince asked as he undressed Skylah, causing her to wake and open her eyes.

Tracey nodded. 'Spose. The health nurse reckons her percentages is down or something. Gotta get her weighed again next week.'

Vince looked at the *Maternal and Child Health* book. Skylah had been 2670g at birth, just under the twenty-fifth percentile, and had dropped to the twentieth at her last weigh. The same with her head circumference—it was now on the fifteenth percentile.

Vince stripped the baby and examined her from top to tail. Apart from being a bit scrawny and not the prettiest sprog he'd seen, she seemed okay. He pointed to the swelling over one side of her skull. 'That's what we call a cephalhaematoma, just bruising from the forceps. It'll go away soon.'

Tracey nodded.

'She's going well,' he added. 'You're doing a great job.'

Tracey made no effort to come over and attend to Skylah, so Vince made a start.

'You got another nappy?' he said. 'This one's dirty.'

She shook her head, so Vince went out to the treatment room where they had an emergency supply, and did the helpless male thing. He and Rita, the clinic nurse, who had a mane of white hair and a gentle smile, returned to find pandemonium had broken out. The boys were screaming and pounding each other with toy trucks and cars, and the baby, still on the couch, had started crying too. Tracey was engrossed in her phone, oblivious to the furore.

Rita cleaned up and redressed Skylah, then picked her up, soothed her, and passed her to her mother who, frowning with annoyance, pocketed her mobile, put the sobbing baby in the pusher, and stood.

'Stop that racket, you boys, or Dr Vince will give you a belting!'

Vince grimaced. 'Not the *best* impression to give them, Trace.'

Tracey shook her head, gathered up the boys, gave the pusher a shove, and headed for the door.

'She's fine,' said Vince. 'It's really hard work looking after a new baby and other kids too. Let me know if her weight doesn't pick up and sing out if you need any more advice.'

Tracey slammed the door behind her.

* * *

Vince powered on through the day, got to the end of his list, and headed home. He was busting to go for a surf—the ocean always cleared his head. The surf report on his phone told him conditions were good. It was still light as he headed down to South Warrnambool and Deefer greeted him with typical enthusiasm. After giving her a pat, Vince went inside, peeled off his clothes, and pulled on his old steamer wetsuit. Minutes later, he and Deef were standing on the sand hill at the Flume, his favourite surfing spot, looking out to sea.

'Beauty, Deef,' he said. 'Nice swell and an off-shore breeze.'

He dragged his battered nine-foot mini Malibu off Benny's roof racks and trotted down to the sand, Deefer in hot pursuit. There were lots of surfers out, so plenty of other dogs for her to play with on the beach. Vince had noticed that most local surfers had the same sort of dogs—medium-sized, brown, thinnish, and patient. Deef, being large, golden, bulky, and *im*patient, stood out from the canine crowd.

Vince paddled out through the surf and revelled in the salty wetness of the waves as he rode over them. He sat up on his board, waiting his turn—dropping in on another surfer's wave was a cardinal sin—and looked back at the shore. It was a clear evening and he scanned the panorama of Lady Bay from Ritchie's Point in the east across to the breakwater in the west, with the sea-saw fringe of Norfolk pines in between. He turned his board around and looked out across the vast

Southern Ocean to the horizon and up to the huge blue canopy above. *How good is this?*

A big wave gathered in front of Vince and he was closest to the break. He wheeled around and started paddling. The surge of water picked him up. One, two, three more paddles and he sprang to his feet. For an instant, he was king of the world, but the face of the wave was too steep, his board nosedived, and he wiped-out spectacularly. He tumbled under the churning water then came to the foaming surface, the leg rope tugging his ankle as the big board bounced and skated on the surf. Vince swore, pulled the board in, climbed back on top, and lay there panting.

'You okay?' called a grinning, curly mopped grommet paddling past on his pointy-nosed shortboard. 'Might need to call a doctor.'

* * *

After an hour in the surf, Vince jumped on a final wave, but lacking the stamina to stand he bodyboarded into the shallows. He took off his leg rope, slid his board back in its cover, pulled down his wetsuit zip, and towelled off. Exhausted but content.

He knew he was too big to be a good surfer. Well over six feet tall with a ruckman's build, heavy across the hips. 'With an arse like yours, Vinny,' his father used to say, 'you should be knocking a few blokes over when you go for the ball.'

Vince gazed into the distance. 'Look at him, son,' old Mick said as they stood watching Joey surf the Passage in Port Fairy. 'He's a natural.' Vince turned to answer his father and realised he was standing alone on the beach. Thirty years later.

He shook his head and looked out to sea; the sun was setting and the air was getting colder. Vince shivered and pulled the towel around his shoulders, still lost in the past. He recognised Travis, Mrs Harrington's nephew, trudging through the soft sand in front of him. Time to break the spell.

'Hey, Travis,' he called. 'Good day for it.'

Travis gave a brief smile and a half wave.

Vince beckoned to him with a raise of his head. The young man came over and stared at an area near Vince's feet. Vince noticed some vivid tattoos on his pale arms and legs—artistic designs more than bad boy declamations.

'You a surfer, Travis?' said Vince, motioning out to the waves.

'Me?' He blushed and shook his head. 'No, but I … I used to play a bit of tennis … before I went away to the …' His voice trailed off.

'Ah, yes,' said Vince, 'the *seminary*. Your aunt told me it didn't work out. Lost your vocation did you, mate?'

He nodded. 'Bad things happened there … I had to leave.'

Doesn't sound good.

'What have you been doing since then?'

The young man resumed his study of the sand. After a few minutes, he took a deep breath. 'I was smoking a lot of dope … and started hearing voices and had a breakdown. Got put in hospital for a few months.'

Schizophrenia or drug-induced psychosis, maybe.

He looked at Vince for the first time. 'But I'm better now, don't need those injections anymore. Using natural therapies.'

Heard that before.

'My … my boyfriend says those psychiatric drugs can damage your mind,' he added in a low voice.

So much for Mrs H's plan to find him a nice girl.

Travis glanced at his watch. 'I have to go. Aunty Carmel will have my tea ready.' He strode off along the beach toward the Hopkins River.

'Hey, Trav,' called Vince, 'you're going the wrong way.'

By the time Vince took Deefer for a quick run up and down the beach and carried his board up to the car park, it was close to seven. He opened the tailgate, peeled off his wetsuit, wrapped a towel around his waist, then took off his speedos and threw them into a plastic tub in the boot. He pulled on a pair of shorts under his towel the way surfers do all over the world.

'Don't want to scare any passing women, eh Deef.'

He drove back along Merri Street past the war memorial statue, which from the side resembled a masturbating figure, aka 'the dirty angel', and headed back to South Warrnambool. When he got home, Vince dumped his wet gear in the laundry sink, fed Deefer, and jumped in the shower. Tonight, it was his turn to host the month's jam session.

After his shower, Vince walked back through the kitchen, which, even he noticed, was in urgent need of cleaning up. The Snapper house had two reasonable rooms at the front but then fell away to a makeshift rear lean-to, containing the bathroom, tiny laundry, and kitchen. Vince wheeled the rubbish bin to the back door and tossed in the detritus of his last week's dining—sundry takeaway containers and Coke bottles—then washed all the piled up dishes and gave the floor a cursory sweep. *That'll do,* he thought. *It's only Kookaburra and St Charlie, after all.*

No sooner had Vince put the broom away than there was a knock at the door and he opened it to reveal Luke Kelly with a guitar in one hand and a six-pack of Coopers under his arm, along with Charlie McNamee bearing two large pizza boxes.

'Evening guys,' said Vince. 'Come in and take the weight off.'

Charlie was the local Drug and Alcohol physician, a diminutive figure, his face obscured by a grizzly grey beard, above which his small brown eyes sparkled. He was a tidy little man and always smiling, despite the inherent challenges of his job, and was loved by the other medicos in town for taking on this difficult work. Hence 'St Charlie'.

Luke put down his cargo and walked toward Vince with his arms outstretched. 'Just wanted to say sorry about Joey's passing.'

Vince stepped back and dodged the impending man hug. 'The Mons told me,' Luke continued. 'Why didn't you say something?'

Charlie looked puzzled.

'My little brother took his own life a few weeks ago,' said Vince.

'I'm so sorry to hear that,' said Charlie. 'Had he been depressed?'

Vince shook his head. 'Sick of talking about it.' He picked up the pizzas. 'Let's get this show on the road.'

Vince and Luke played guitars, with Charlie on the blues harmonica. Sometimes Charlie's wife added some much needed vocal support, especially when the gig was at their place.

Vince hadn't touched his guitar for the first year or so after his forced move to Warrnambool and was a reluctant participant, even though Myfanwy Williams had told him it was important for him to do something creative as part of his stress-management strategy.

The three of them had similar tastes in music—acoustic roots and blues and, despite himself, Vince enjoyed the sessions. *Better than sitting in the dark watching reruns of Breaking Bad.* However, he still bailed more often than not.

Charlie and Luke followed Vince into the living room and looked for somewhere to sit amongst the piles of books, CDs, and DVDs. Vince put some Dylan on his turntable, passed cold beers to the visitors, grabbed three plates from the kitchen and a mineral water for himself, and they all tucked in.

'Blow it,' said Charlie, glancing at the screen as his phone beeped. 'The hospital. Sorry guys.' He stepped into the kitchen to take the call.

'Kookaburra,' said Vince, wiping cheese off his chin. 'What sort of bloke is the Monsignor?'

Luke took a long sip on his beer. 'Old Dennis is a bit all over the place, but he's okay I suppose. Why do you ask?'

'Dennis!' exclaimed Vince, ignoring the question. 'I didn't realise monsignors even had Christian names!'

Luke smiled.

'He was a priest in the Ballarat diocese,' Vince continued, 'when all that paedophilia was going on.'

'That was a *very* bad time for the Church.'

Vince frowned. 'And an even worse time for Catholic children.'

'You know what I mean.'

'The Mons told me he knew nothing about what that Delaney bastard was up to.' Vince sat forward. 'But there would have been talk amongst the priests. *Surely* he would've known what was happening.'

Luke shrugged, put down his pizza, and placed his hands on his knees. 'There was a culture of secrecy,' he said. Voice hard and edgy. He pointed toward the cracked ceiling. 'From the then Father Patrick Evans, now cardinal, to the bishop,' he turned his finger toward the seagrass matting on the floor, 'all the way down to priests like Dennis.'

Vince nodded. 'Sounds like the three wise monkeys—hear no evil, see no evil, speak no evil.'

He drained a glass of mineral water, another question on his lips. *Never asked Kookaburra this before.*

'Did *you* know about it?'

Luke looked up at Vince. 'After my ordination, I went to the US to do my Masters in Theology at Berkeley, then onto Peru with the Columbans. So I wasn't around.' He paused. 'But I heard rumours.'

'So why didn't the Church do something about it?'

Luke shook his head, his customary youthful grin replaced by a dark frown. 'Bad decisions were made by bad men.'

Charlie came back in, pocketing his phone. 'Sorry about that. Another ice user causing trouble in the ED,' he said. 'What's new?'

He sat, sipped a beer, and started on his pizza. Vince and Luke got out their guitars and tuned up. Vince shook the tension out of his shoulders and began a twelve-bar blues strum. Luke picked out a melody over the top.

'Is that in E?' said Charlie, wiping his hands and face with a tissue. He fished out the appropriate harmonica from his pocket and joined in. As always, Vince was comforted by the familiar sequence and the inevitable turn around at the end of each twelve-bar sequence and he lost himself in the hypnotic progression. Charlie's harp wailed away in the background, adding some muted melodic colour. Luke, however, usually a gentle finger picker, attacked his steel guitar strings with a vengeful plectrum, filling Vince's living room with loud metallic notes.

16

'A re those empty beer bottles I can see on your kitchen table, Vincent?'

Vince was cradling a coffee, gazing at his computer screen. He'd slept well for a change. Always did on those nights.

'Yeah, Myf,' he replied, 'got it in one. Six in total. Coopers. The pale ale, you'll be interested to hear, not the sparkling one.'

'So …' she added, looking worried.

'So, nothing,' he said, moving his laptop cam around. 'See, three bottles of mineral water too. San Pellegrino,' he added, 'if you're wondering.'

'You're not drinking again, are you, Vincent?'

'Not me, Myf. Just my bandmates having a few beers. I was on the soft stuff.' He laughed. 'Sad, isn't it?'

Dr Williams' frown faded and she sat back. 'I'm pleased you're playing your guitar again.' She smiled. 'Good therapy.'

'S'pose,' he conceded.

'How are Father Kelly and the other doctor going?'

'Okay,' said Vince. 'Saint Charlie is flat out. APU.' He paused. 'Kookaburra seems angry about the way the Church has handled the sexual abuse stuff.' He swallowed a mouth full of lukewarm tea. 'I hadn't realised how much it was affecting him.'

'I guess he feels let down,' said Myf. 'Must be disillusioning for the good priests.'

'Sickening all round.' Vince leant toward the screen. 'I want to find out for sure whether Delaney abused my brother. And who was protecting the bad ones back then.'

'You need to deal with your own grief and move on.'

'Not so easy,' responded Vince. 'There's something I didn't tell you.' He looked away, chest pounding.

'Take your time.'

'Joey came to my room in the senior boarding house one night during his first year at St Bernard's.' Vince swallowed hard. 'He told me he didn't want to go down to Apollo Bay for the altar boy weekends anymore. Said he wanted to head home instead.'

'What did you say?'

'I had important exams coming up. And the footy finals. I told him I didn't have time to worry about such trivial crap. Said he would be letting Mum down if he didn't go.' Dr Williams winced. 'I told him not to be such a wimp.'

She nodded.

Vince glanced at the screen. 'He was crying, Myf.' He tapped his chest with a clenched fist. 'And I sent him away.'

'You weren't to know what was going on, Vincent,' she said, her round face looming large.

He shrugged.

'And you can't assuage personal guilt, justified or not, by trying to displace it onto the world outside. It won't make you feel any better.'

'Shit happens, eh?' Vince frowned and looked at the floor. 'Maybe you're right.' He took a quick breath, let it out slowly, and stared out his tiny kitchen window at the large liquid amber tree in the backyard.

'How are the twins?' asked Myf.

More shit happening.

'Who knows?' said Vince. 'Haven't heard from them since the regatta.'

'I guess they're pre-occupied with their studies.'

Vince snorted. 'Flat out being over-indulged private-school princesses with their embarrassment of a father banished from the kingdom.'

She laughed. 'A certain amount of self-centredness is usual for adolescents.'

He shrugged again and resumed his inspection of the tree.

Dr Williams glanced at a document in front of her. 'I hear you've been performing complicated obstetrics procedures,' she said, 'contrary to the conditions of your provisional registration.'

'*Bloody hell*,' said Vince, honing in on the screen again. 'How did you hear about—'

'The Board advises me about any professional issues so I can better monitor your progress psychologically.'

Vince jumped to his feet. 'I've had a gutful of being *monitored*. Little Lachie is leading a conspiracy against me.' He pointed at the screen. 'And I'm starting to think *you're* part of it!'

He logged out, slammed his laptop shut, and stormed out the back door. Deefer jumped up from her post-prandial snooze and looked up with an expectant expression.

'I have to move on, Deef,' said Vince, clipping the leash onto her collar. 'Apparently.' They walked up the drive and headed for the beach track. 'Even though I have no bloody idea where I'm going!'

* * *

After doing a whirlwind ward round, Vince arrived at the clinic at five past nine. Lorraine pointed at the clock and waved her finger to him as he raced into his room. *I know, I know, should get here earlier for paperwork and calls. Guess what? Too bad.*

He collapsed in his chair and surveyed the waiting list screen—packed with the usual array of Geep punters. There was an odd comfort in the increasing familiarity of it all.

After the morning session, he ducked out and grabbed a sandwich and a coffee from the bakery. Vince often ate his lunch at Cannon Hill, which provided elevated views across Lake Pertobe and out to sea, with his car windows down and Classic FM as a soundtrack, but today he headed straight back to the clinic to attack his mounting pile of paperwork. As he made a start, his mobile started singing. *Never a minute's peace!*

'Hanrahan,' he said, mouth full of ham and cheese.

'Hi, Vinny, it's Jane.'

'G'day,' he replied. 'Long time, no hear. How are you?'

'Oh, you know. Okay.'

'And the kids?'

'Maisie's enjoying boarding school and Jack's a budding football champ.' She paused. 'They miss their father.'

'We all do.'

Vince detected a distant snort. 'Anyway,' she went on, 'I'm coming down your way next Saturday for a study weekend. I'm doing a post-grad diploma in wound healing at Deakin and we have an on-campus component every semester.'

'You're welcome to stay. It's hardly five star, but—'

'Oh, no thanks,' she cut in. 'I'm booked into the Mid City Motel with my colleague from the Wimmera Base. I thought we could catch up on the Saturday evening. Want to talk to you about something.'

'Likewise,' said Vince. 'What about we meet at the Pavilion Café?'

'Is that at the yacht club, near the breakwater?'

'Got it in one.'

'All right,' she said. 'See you there around six. Bye.'

* * *

He called in his first patient for the afternoon—Aisif Hamid, a newie. As he sat down, Vince recognised him as the young man who had disrupted the Social Justice meeting last week.

'G'day, Aisif,' he said, putting out his hand. 'I'm Vince. I understand you live in one of the Sacred Heart emergency housing units?'

The boy nodded. 'I do, sir. And I am very grateful.'

'Where are you from?'

'I am a Hazara, from eastern Afghanistan.'

Vince nodded. His grasp of the geopolitics of that area was shaky. 'So what can I do for you?'

Aisif rolled up one trouser leg to reveal a chronic, deep, weeping wound on his shin.

'That doesn't look too good,' said Vince. 'What happened?'

'I fled with my father when the Pushtun Taliban were killing us, because we are Shia and an ethnic minority. I was climbing over a tin fence and I cut my leg.' He paused. 'The rest of our family was murdered.'

You poor kid. 'When did all that happen?'

'Almost one year ago.' Aisif swallowed. 'We went to Pakistan, then Indonesia, and got on a boat from West Timor. Then we landed on Christmas Island and were taken to Nauru.'

Vince whistled as he studied the wound. 'I reckon you've got an infection in the bone there, mate. You need to see an orthopaedic surgeon and have intensive treatment in hospital.' He looked at the young man. 'Are you at school?'

Aisif's dark eyes filled with tears. 'I am in year twelve at Emmanuel College. I am on a bridging visa and allowed to attend school. I was sponsored by a local group. I want to study medicine and become a doctor.'

'What about your dad?'

'My father has no visa, sir.' Tears spilled onto his cheeks. 'He is still on Nauru. They want to send him back to Afghanistan. The Australian government say it is safe there now. But it is not, sir. Not for Hazaras. As soon as he gets there they will capture him, he will be killed, he—'

'Hang on a sec,' said Vince. 'I'm a doctor, not a politician. Have you spoken to the local MP or Monsignor O'Shannassey?'

'The politician says it is out of his hands, says it is government policy. I have written to your prime minister. No answer.' Aisif became agitated, struggling to stay seated. 'That old priest said he will do something, but he hasn't. He comes around, saying he will speak to this one or that one, but nothing happens!'

Vince put his hand up. 'Okay, first things first. What about we see if we can get this leg fixed?'

He took Aisif through to the treatment room. The nurse was tidying up after vaccinating a baby.

'Rita,' said Vince, 'can you swab Aisif's wound and put a dressing on it? I'll start him on antis and arrange some imaging. I reckon he's got osteomyelitis.' He shrugged. 'Bit out of my league.'

Rita was the widow of his running and surfing buddy, Allan Findlay, who'd been murdered last year during an episode that had threatened to ruin Vince—personally and professionally. They'd shared a passion for poetry, Bob Dylan, and the Geelong Football Club, as well as co-hosting a weekly program on the local FM radio station. Allan had been the closest thing Vince had to a local mate. Apart from Elena.

Vince went back to his room and glanced at the computer screen. 'Damn,' he told his desk, 'half an hour behind and *three* waiting.' He called in the next punter, Pauline Murphy, a single woman in her early fifties. Also the practice manager's sister. *Blow it!*

'Sorry to keep you waiting, Pauline.'

'Can't be helped,' she said, sitting down. 'Many people sicker than me.' Pauline was short and freckly with a sweet smile and shy demeanour. 'I just need a repeat script for the HRT, then you can get on with more important things.'

Vince looked at her file. She was overdue for her cervical screen, mammography, and bone density scan. *Groan!* After he'd done all that and had a discussion about her mother's cataracts, his morning schedule was a trainwreck.

He took a breath, powered on through the list, and spent lunchtime making a series of phone calls regarding Aisif. First, he rang his friend, Dr Danny Nguyen, a consultant physician and old medical school classmate, and filled him in about the boy's leg wound.

'Okay, Ox,' said Danny, using Vince's old college nickname, 'do his lab work, take blood cultures, get an MRI, let Patal know, and send him into ED. I'll see him tonight.'

By the time Vince organised the tests and arranged for the local orthopaedic surgeon to catch up with Aisif in hospital, his first afternoon patient was chafing at the bit. When he emerged from the clinic at the end of the day, darkness had fallen and the town was asleep.

* * *

That night Vince fed the dog, swallowed an omelette that tasted like rubber, and collapsed on the couch. An hour later his musical mobile stirred him from his stupor.

'Ivan The Terrible says we need to study harder—' said Tessa.

'Omigod, we study *all* the time—' added Georgie.

Really George?

'Or we'll end up stacking supermarket shelves—'

'Or on the dole—'

'What *is* the dole?'

'Mum wants us to do the Easter term break in Warrnie.'

I bet she does.

'Less distractions, she says, than Melbourne—'

'So she and Ivan can go skiing in Japan, more like.'

Of course.

'Can we, Bins?'

'Pretty please?'

Ambushed!

'Okay, girls, but you will have to study by yourselves. I can't afford to take any time off.' *Not with those CLC fees to pay.* 'And when exactly is this?'

'In two weeks,' said Tessa. 'Do you have Internet coverage down there?'

'Yeah,' he said, 'we've even got electricity and hot running water.'

'*Crazy*,' responded Georgie. 'Let's invite PC Genovesi around one night for dinner.'

'Yeah,' added Tessa, 'champagne and candlelight and—'

'Who knows what might happen!'

The girls had struck up a friendship with Elena over the last two years and seemed keen on bringing Vince and her together. While Vince was fond of his weekly dinner buddy, he knew his life was messy enough without a dalliance with a younger woman. Anyway, he was still married to Lydia. *Wasn't he?*

'We'll see about that.' He had a thought. 'Might be best if I take you out to the Deakin Uni library in the mornings and you can get the bus home in the evenings. No room for studying at my place.'

'Cool. We can hang with those cute marine biology students.'

'On *second* thought,' said Vince, 'maybe the town library. Not many hot guys there. Mostly pensioners.'

After the phonecall, Vince looked around the Snapper house. 'It's barely adequate for one man and a dog,' he told Deefer, 'let alone those two as well.'

He could see he would need to conduct a major decluttering and cleaning exercise. Plus some refurbishing.

And soon.

17

'Where can you get cheap furniture around here, Shirl?' Vince asked on his way out of the surgery on the following Friday evening. He was a man on a mission.

'Plenty of those bargain homeware stores out on the highway,' she replied. 'No buggers ever in them.'

Elena had rung him in the morning to say she wouldn't be a starter for dinner that night. 'Will and I are going to a dinner party at his neighbour's property. Pip and Sally Laidlaw.'

'Sounds dead posh,' said Vince. 'Make sure you use the right cutlery and don't tell any dirty jokes.'

That night he dined alone at their usual table at Fanny's, reading a Henning Mankel crime story while he ate his prawn pasta, studiously avoiding eye contact with the other customers.

The next day he headed out early to the Homemaker's Centre, part of the shopping strip on the road into Warrnambool. There was a bewildering array of furniture establishments, as far as Vince could see, all flogging the same stuff. He walked into the first one and gave his credit card a hammering, then drove across the road to Bunnings and bought two sausages from the Rotary fundraising BBQ out the front. When he got home, he backed Benny up to the front door, opened the tailgate, and dragged out boxes of ancient crockery and cutlery, pots and pans and pieces of broken-down furniture, then headed for the local waste-transfer station.

Vince had never realised that the tip was a social hub, but when he pulled up he encountered a bunch of old punters who were keen for a chat. *Looks like these blokes spent all day out here, looking for treasure, shooting the breeze, and hiding from their wives.* By the time he pulled the old bed frames off the roof racks, emptied Benny's boot, tossed the rubbish in the appropriate skips, and discussed important matters of state with the resident Greek chorus, the morning had vanished.

He came back to find the Snapper house spick and span, Mrs Harrington, Kieran, and the ubiquitous Travis standing out the back, packing up their cleaning gear.

'Thanks, Mrs H,' said Vince. ' I didn't expect you guys to do that.'

'Dr Vince,' she responded with a quizzical frown, 'you couldn't expect them girls of yours to stay there the way it was, now, could you?'

'O-once you took all that stuff out, the house was r-r-real dirty,' added Kieran.

Vince nodded. 'Well, I do appreciate it.'

'That's what neighbours are for. Anyway, you look after Tracey and all of us, so this is our way of paying you back.' She pointed at her nephew. 'Even Travis helped out, didn't you, love?'

'Yes, yes, I helped,' said Travis, pausing as if listening to something, then went back next door, muttering all the way.

'He's not using drugs again, is he, Mrs H?' asked Vince.

'Dunno, but he's carrying on real strange. He's supposed to be seeing that counsellor at the clinic down the hospital, but he won't go no more.'

'Better bring him into the clinic to see Dr Menzies.' *Best if I keep out of it.* 'I'll give him a heads-up.'

Vince fished a card out of his wallet and handed it over. 'If you are really concerned about Travis any time, ring the CAT team.'

* * *

There was a loud hammering at the front door. Vince said his goodbyes to the Harringtons and they headed home along the side path. He went through the house and opened the front door to reveal two burly men and a 'Happy Furniture' truck. Within minutes they'd deposited their cargo—long cardboard packages, numerous boxes and several cartons of kitchenware, towels, and sheets—on the front lawn of the Snapper house.

'Where's the beds and couches?' said Vince.

The main guy pointed at the pile of large flat-top boxes. 'There, Doc.' He handed Vince an Allen key. 'Nothin to it,' he said, provoking a guffaw from his mate.

'You're joking,' said Vince, shaking his head. 'There's a slab in it, guys, if you put all this stuff together.' They looked doubtful. 'And two large pizzas,' he added.

'Done,' said the boss man. 'Make sure it's VB. Cold. And Fanny's' specials.'

'With double cheese,' added his offsider.

* * *

Vince spent the afternoon putting all his purchases away, restocking the kitchen, and making up the beds. He looked around and surveyed his handiwork. 'Not quite Monmeath Avenue,' he told Deefer, 'but who needs all those antiques anyway?' Vince and Lydia's house in Canterbury, complete with swimming pool and tennis court, had been packed with lovely furniture they'd collected. In happier times.

He flung himself down on the new couch, felt an alarming sagging under his bum, and found he was almost sitting on the floor.

'Hell,' he exclaimed after inspecting the flimsy strapping on the underside, 'this stuff must be built for jockeys!'

Deefer went to the back door and started pawing and whining. Vince dragged himself up, grabbed the lead, and they headed off up Fay Street to the boardwalk and then onto the beach. He sat on a bollard in front of the yacht club while the dog got involved in the fruitless task of chasing seagulls. Vince glanced around. The ocean was choppy, no surfers out, and the wind was whipping the sand up as young families of beachgoers pulled down their sun shelters, packed up bags with wet towels and buckets and spades, and called out to their dispersed progeny to return to HQ. Voices tired and exasperated.

Guys, Vince was tempted to tell these annoyed parents, *this is as good as life gets. Enjoy it!*

He looked behind. A few early diners were sitting out on the café deck above his head.

'Damn,' he said out loud, looking at his watch. Almost six. *'Jane!'*

He called Deefer and they headed home. After feeding the confused dog and taking a quick shower, he ran back down through the breakwater car park, up the steps, and found his sister-in-law sitting at a side table, monitoring her phone, empty wine glass, half full ashtray, and a platter of finger food in front of her.

'Hi Janey,' said Vince, giving her a peck on the cheek and sliding into the chair opposite. 'Sorry I'm late. Got caught up.'

'Same old, same old.' She waved her hand in a dismissive gesture. *Fair call.*

'How is the conference going?'

'Good thanks. It's not a very sexy subject but there's a lot to learn about wound healing.'

'Yeah, it seems to change all the time.'

She smiled. 'Doctors are a bit slow to engage with the changes.'

Vince ordered a sparkling water from a passing waitress. 'So "if a wound's wet, dry it and if it's dry, wet it" doesn't cut it anymore?'

'We *have* moved on a touch since then.' Jane held up a cigarette and lighter and raised her eyebrows in quizzical arches.

'Go for it,' said Vince. *Not the time for a sermon on the evils of smoking.*

Jane drew on her cigarette and exhaled off to the side. 'Help yourself to some nibbles,' she said. 'My shout.'

Her peach-coloured top and orange earrings set off her olive skin and ash-blond hair, which now featured a purple flash down onto the fringe. Vince noticed the furrowed lines on her face and the tense and jerky movements as she played with her lighter and took quick puffs on her cigarette. *Used to be so chilled. Seems like a different person.*

'Don't mind if I do,' responded Vince. 'Didn't get around to lunch today.'

Jane ordered another wine and they sat in silence for a few minutes looking out to sea. The beach was deserted, the sun was setting, and the ocean looked like a heavy grey blanket.

'How are those gorgeous twins?' asked Jane.

'Busy being gorgeous in South Yarra,' Vince responded.

She raised her eyebrows again, but Vince let that gesture go through to the keeper. Another pause.

He leant forward. 'You said you wanted to talk to me about something?'

She drained her glass and met his gaze. 'Joseph took his own life due to PTSD and depression resulting from sexual abuse when he was at St Bernard's.' She sat back and put her hands flat on the table, palms down.

'I saw a picture of him with that Father Delaney,' said Vince. 'You could be right there.'

'Oh,' she said, 'I *know* I'm right.'

Vince swallowed, mouth dry and hands sweaty. 'I should've realised. I … I let him down.'

'We *all* let him down.' She took a deep breath. 'Something we have to live with.'

They both looked out into the darkening sky. A full minute passed.

'I've joined Broken Rites,' said Jane, turning to look at Vince again.

'Which is?'

'A research and advocacy group that looks into cover-ups by the Church about child sex abuse.' Jane began to fidget with her lighter again. The wind picked up and she shivered and pulled her jacket up around her shoulders. 'We have detailed information about what went on back then.'

'But they've locked the bloke up,' Vince said with a shrug. 'And I hope they throw away the key.'

Jane stared at the table. 'So that's the end of it, is it?' She stifled a sob. 'Build a bridge and get over it, eh?'

Vince put his hand on her shoulder. 'I understand how you feel, but—'

'Do you, golden boy?' She laughed, the sound tense and tight. '*Do* you?'

'Okay, I *don't* understand how you feel,' Vince conceded.

'And you know what?' she said, pushing his hand away. 'For fifteen years I listened to Joseph call out in the night.' She picked up her cigarette. 'Believe me, it *wasn't* Delaney.' A jet of smoke passed by Vince's left ear. 'There were a lot of them around at that time.' She looked him in the eye. 'But I'm after just *one*.'

Vince nodded slowly. A familiar feeling of nausea washed over him. 'Who was it?'

Jane sat back. 'Watch this space.'

They both looked out to sea, the white tops of the breaking waves still visible in the fading light.

'What about those senior priests who were supposed to be in charge?' Vince said, pushing the nibbles plate across to Jane. 'Like Evans and the bishop?'

'*And* O'Shannassey.' Voice quiet, but deliberate.

'The Mons was just a spear carrier,' said Vince, frowning. 'He wasn't in a position of authority.'

Jane leant in again, her face inches from Vince's. 'The College of Consultors for the Ballarat diocese were responsible for shuffling those criminals from parish to parish. Monsignor O'Shannassey was a member.'

Vince shook his head. 'That's not true, I asked him.'

'Want to bet?'

She pulled a sheaf of transcripts out of her bag and slapped them on the table. 'We've found some secret documents that had been hidden by the Church.' Jane drew her index finger across the blue scarf encircling her throat. 'O'Shannassey was in it right up to his neck. There were *five* calling the shots.' She held up one hand and ticked off her fingers. 'Two are dead, the bishop's memory's gone,' she raised her eyebrows, 'and Evans is untouchable. Friends in high places.' Her thumb remained aloft.

'So that just leaves the Mons,' Vince said after a pause. 'Hard to believe he'd have turned a blind eye. He's so big on social justice.'

'Justice!'

Jane stubbed out her cigarette so hard it disintegrated in the ashtray. 'I just want *justice* for my husband.' Eyes blazing. 'The father of my children.' She stood and grabbed her bag. '*That's* all.'

18

Vince slept in the next morning. That's to say, he got up late. And only then because of Deefer's insistent scratching at the back door. A ghostly image of the young Joey Hanrahan in front of the brothers' house at St Bernard's, with the beaming Father Delaney and a circle of faceless, blacked-robed men standing around them, had haunted him all night long.

He stumbled out of bed, pushed open the back door, squinted in the morning sunshine, and filled up Deefer's bowl. She cleaned her breakfast up in two minutes of manic swallowing, chased it with a few giant gulps of water, burped, then lapsed into a contented torpor.

'Gee,' said Vince, watching from the back step, 'if only my needs were so easily met.'

After a shower, Vince and Deefer took off to the beach. It was a beautiful morning and there was a good swell, but Vince didn't feel like surfing. He watched the happy dog run up and down the beach, chasing the frisbee and dropping it at Vince's feet, tongue out and panting.

As usual for a Sunday, they ended up at a corner table at the surf club café, away from the crowd and facing the ocean. Deefer lapped some water and Vince ordered his usual café latte and bacon and eggs. He leafed through the papers; nothing sparked his interest. Ditto, his breakfast.

'Not in the mood, Deef,' he said, getting up. 'Let's head home, eh? Better tidy up before those girls arrive.'

Vince was looking forward to seeing Georgie and Tessa, but such was his isolation—geographically and personally—that it was like awaiting the visit of strangers. He and Deefer walked home and just as he picked up the mop, his phone started singing.

'Hi, Lids,' he said, 'how are you?'

'Fine thanks, Vincent. And you?'

'Hunky dorey down here. My wife and kids living with another bloke and the Medical Board on my case.'

There was a pause.

'Did you do something wrong again?'

Vince snorted. 'Don't overdo the wifely support there. If you really want to know, I did something *right*—a very difficult rotation in an obstructed labour with type two decelerations.' He dropped the mop on the kitchen floor. 'Mother and baby well and the doctor sent to the sin bin.'

'Aren't you supposed to refer those complicated cases back to the—'

'The baby would've died in the ambulance somewhere between Panmure and Terang,' Vince cut in. 'And the mother would've bled out at about Camperdown.'

Another pause.

'How are Jane and the children going?'

'Good. Janey's down here for a conference. Kids are doing okay. Maisie's going well at Ballarat Grammar and Jack's off there next year.'

'What about Jane herself?'

'She's getting on with things and her work is going well, but …' He paused. *Why not?* 'Lids, Joey killed himself because he was … molested by a priest back at St Bernard's. Nothing to do with the farm.'

Vince heard her suck in a sudden breath.

'Oh, Vincent,' she said, voice softer. 'I'm so sorry. He'd never said anything to you or Trisha?'

'No, but I should've figured it out. I missed the signs.'

'I'm sure that's not true—'

'There was a bunch of paedophiles operating in the Ballarat diocese back then,' Vince went on, struggling to control his anger, 'and Broken Rights have uncovered a massive cover-up involving the top brass and our local parish priest.' *I'll be having a deep and meaningful with*

O'Shannassey first chance I get! He turned down the volume. 'But Jane is chasing down the … the one who abused Joey.'

'Maybe it would be better if the girls don't come to Warrnambool after all. You seem to have a lot going on.'

What's new?

'Come on, don't do that to me.' Vince took some slow breaths and looked around the refurbished Snapper house. 'All is in readiness for the royal visit. So you and dear Ivan go ahead and get on the piste in Japan.'

'But—'

'Knock yourselves out.'

'All right then. They'll be on tonight's train.'

'I'll be there.'

'Vincent, I'm really sorry about Joey, but you mustn't blame yourself.'

Jesus!

'Bye, Lids.'

* * *

'Okay,' Vince said to the snoozing dog. 'Time to get moving.' He put down his phone and opened his tiny pantry. 'A tin of tomatoes, a can of tuna, and an old packet of pasta. All out of date, like me.' He pulled over his bin and tipped the lot in, then opened the fridge and discovered an ancient pot of hummus dip and a half-eaten supermarket BBQ chicken, vintage last Thursday. 'Out they go, too.'

After giving the old fridge a cursory wipe down with a grimy tea towel, Vince drove to the supermarket to load up on provisions. After Jane's hand grenade, he was busting to scrutinise the Broken Rights documents and links she'd given him, but he needed to put all that to one side. For now.

He strode up to the trolley bay and yanked on the nearest handle. Wouldn't budge. 'It's chained to the next one,' he muttered. 'What's that about?'

'Let me help you, Doc.' Elena Genovesi leant over, put a coin in the slot, and released the lock. 'Simple.' She pushed the trolley toward him and released another for herself. 'Painful watching you.'

'Thanks,' said Vince. 'These places give me the heebie-jeebies.'

'Necessary evil, I'm afraid.' Elena was wearing sports gear, her wiry but shapely body encased in tight black skins. Practical but sexy. With some reluctance, Vince forced his attention back onto the task at hand.

'You'll know, Sarge. The twins are coming down for the week. What do sixteen-year-old girls eat?'

She laughed. 'No idea. Not much, probably. I only know what thirty-six-year-old girls eat.'

'Yeah, but you *used* to be a teenage chick. And they're vegos like you.'

Elena pointed to the fresh produce section. 'Looks like the place to start.'

'I only know where the milk, bread, and frozen dinners are,' said Vince. 'All these other aisles are a mystery to me.'

Elena shook her head and loaded him up with brown rice, fish, yoghurt, fruit, and vegetables.

'What's this stuff?' he asked as she tossed in some extras.

'Quinoa and kale. Superfoods.'

Vince laughed. 'Never heard of either of 'em.'

'Tessa will know what to do with them.'

'Ooh, look, it's Dr Vince and that nice police lady,' interjected a passing young woman with a knowing smile, 'doing their shopping. Show him your tummy, Dwayne. See, that rash is nearly gone.'

Elena and Vince exchanged a wry glance. 'Just smile and move on,' Vince murmured.

'More grist to the gossip mill,' added Elena.

'Speaking of gossip,' Vince said as they reached the end of the aisle. 'How did the big lunch with Lady Bracknell go?

'Good, thanks. Janet Carlisle is a very interesting person. She asked me a lot about policing and she's learning Italian. She's even been to the town in Sicily where my nonna grew up.' Elena nodded. 'I enjoyed it.'

'Who'd of thunk?' replied Vince. 'And what of the dinner party with the young Romeo?'

She paused and frowned. 'That's a story for another day.'

'In the immortal words of the Bard,' said Vince. 'The course of love never did run smooth.'

Elena raised her eyebrows and steered him toward the toiletries section. 'You have any of these things at the Snapper house?'

'Maybe, Sarge. There's a bit left in the toothpaste tube. Might be a bit low on dunny paper.'

Another head shake. She added body wash, shampoo, conditioner, tissues, toilet paper, and air-freshener sticks.

'My work here is done.' She pointed to the checkout. 'Next you take it over to young Cheryl and pay for it.'

Vince summoned her closer. 'Can I ask you something?'

'I do have shopping of my own to do,' Elena responded, pointing at her empty trolley and studying the list on her phone.

'Won't take a minute.'

He looked around to make sure they weren't being overheard. 'If a priest covered up child sex abuse thirty years ago, can the Royal Commission charge him and put him in the dock?'

Elena frowned. 'Not really supermarket conversation, Doc.' She dropped her voice. 'The Royal Commission doesn't lay charges, it makes recommendations, which have already resulted in over one hundred prosecutions.'

Vince nodded.

'However, covering up the sexual abuse of children is a crime.' She stared him straight in the eye. 'And it should be reported to the police.'

* * *

Vince pushed aside some of the flotsam and jetsam in Benny's cavernous boot—a pair of damp boardshorts, a stethoscope, and an old bag of potting mix—and loaded in his groceries. He then turned down Liebig Street to find the main street blocked off by a large procession moving slowly down the middle of the road.

'Jeepers,' he said out loud. 'Demos in the 'Bool, what next?'

Vince turned onto Koroit Street, took another route south, and found Timor Street blocked off as well. He parked and lowered his side window. A large crowd had already gathered on a grassed area at the side of the art gallery in front of a makeshift stage. An overhead banner proclaimed 'Palm Sunday Walk for Justice for Refugees.'

Palm Sunday. That's right, the last Sunday before Easter. The start of Holy Week.

In an instant he was back at the old church in Minyip, he and Joey swordfighting with their palms. Joey was too quick for him, even at that irreverent game. Vince put his hand up to his right ear. It still seemed to be burning from the cuff their father had given him that hot Wimmera day, while their mother's lips moved in silent prayer. 'Not that all that praying stopped her from getting crook,' Mick had said over her grave many years later.

'Come and join us, Dr Hanrahan!' Colleen Maloney's loud voice woke Vince from his reverie. He looked up, startled, eyes brimming, and got out of the car.

The procession had finished and the marchers were assembled in front of the stage. A group of Sudanese women in colourful traditional dress were playing drums, singing, and swaying in time and the mood of the crowd was both defiant and festive. Monsignor O'Shannassey was standing on the stage, flanked by refugee community leaders, who were dressed in sober dark suits with crisp white shirts.

'Rent a crowd, eh Doc?' One of Vince's patients, a retired farmer from Mortlake, came over and leant on Benny next to him.

'Pretty harmless, Duncan,' Vince responded. 'Look like locals to me.'

The man waved a dismissive hand. '*Do*-gooders,' he added with heavy emphasis.

The music stopped and a local Gunditjamara Aboriginal elder gave a welcome to country with a smoking ceremony at the foot of the stage. The crowd watched the fragrant spirals from the burning eucalyptus leaves trail up into the sky, then the Mons stepped forward. As he tapped the microphone, a mob of men dressed in denims and motorcycle leathers and faces covered in masks came running up Liebig Street from the opposite direction, waving the Australian flag and chanting 'go back where you came from' over and over. They charged into the crowd and started pushing them back up the road.

'Look out,' said Duncan, 'here's trouble.'

Vince pulled out his mobile and punched in Elena's number.

'Now what is it?' she said impatiently. 'Did you forget the milk or—'

'There's a big barney down in front of the art gallery, Sarge. Better get some uniforms down here.'

Some of the demonstrators pushed back against the attackers, who carried a banner proclaiming them to be 'Patriots of Australia', and an ugly skirmish developed. A woman started screaming as she was manhandled, and the crowd panicked and dispersed, most retreating. Vince and Duncan ran over and tried to separate the opposing groups, but were buffeted to and fro amid the pandemonium.

Minutes later, the unmistakable sound of police sirens pierced the uproar and two squad cars pulled up, discharging several officers, who corralled the Patriots and forced them back. Next to Vince, a thin dreadlocked man with a Ho Chi Minh beard grappled with one of the attackers and managed to rip off his clown mask, revealing a heavily tattooed neck and a pallid face, twisted with fury.

It was Dustin Cartwright.

19

Vince walked into his small kitchen, arms full of supermarket bags. There was nowhere to store his groceries, so he parked some on top of the fridge and the rest on the floor. Lydia was sending the girls with a packed dinner for the trip, so that was one less thing to worry about. He looked at his watch: half an hour to go before the train.

He bombed a frozen meat lover's pizza in the microwave, filled up the perpetually hungry Deefer's bowl, then sat back, ate his dinner, washed it down with a Coke, and emitted a large fart.

'S'pose I'll have to lift my game when the girls are here, Deef,' he informed the sleeping dog. 'No flatulence, eh?'

Vince showered and put on a clean shirt before firing up Benny and heading off. It was a lovely autumn evening, a slight chill in the air. He wound down the window and felt the gentle sea breeze as he turned right into the Norfolk pine-lined Merri Street and pulled up at the station with a few minutes to spare. As usual, the twins were travelling first class—'Can't have them in with the hoi polloi, Vincent'—and were last to get off.

Vince was again shocked to see how grown up they looked. Children no longer. Confident young women, more like.

'Hola, Bins!' shouted Georgie, voice loud and raucous as usual. She dropped her luggage and gave him a hug.

'Thanks for picking us up, Dad,' Tessa added with a kiss to his cheek, her shy smile a reminder of the young Joey.

Back at the Snapper house, Vince carried in their bags and showed off his new furniture and décor.

'Wow, what's this, a whole house reveal?' asked Georgie, looking around.

'Good job,' said Tessa.

The girls unpacked and the three of them settled in for a night of *Seinfeld* reruns, interspersed with stories about school and the twins' lives in Melbourne. Vince could feel his mood lifting. Better than a whole year of psychotherapy, he reflected as they all went off to bed.

* * *

Monday morning, Vince dropped the twins off at the city library on the way to work.

'There's free wifi here, girls, and separate walled cubicles, so no excuses, okay? Your mother will kill me if you don't get some study done, so heads down and bums up.' He pulled out his wallet. 'Here's thirty dollars for lunch at the café around the corner. Pick you up at six.'

Vince did a U-turn back up the main drag, turned left into Koroit Street, and headed to the hospital to do his rounds. Aisif Hamid was in the orthopaedic ward, leg in plaster and an IV pumping a cocktail of antibiotics into his veins. He was sitting up, open textbooks all over his bed and his attention focused on a laptop.

'Hey, Aisif,' said Vince. 'How's it going?'

The boy looked up. 'Very difficult to be in hospital and missing school, Dr Hanrahan. But boss surgeon says one more week then home, and then nurses come and give drugs each day.' He pointed to the cannula in his arm.

Vince picked up the chart at the end of the bed and noted that Aisif's temperature and pulse rate were now normal. 'Looking good,' he said. 'You'll soon be out kicking goals again.'

Aisif smiled again. 'I feel much better, Doctor. Can concentrate on my studies now.' His brow darkened. 'But the Monsignor comes to visit. Give blessing. I don't want blessing.'

'Don't worry,' said Vince. 'That's his job. Just nod and smile.'

The boy sat up and a book slid to the floor. 'I won't smile.'

Vince raised his eyebrows. 'Monsignor O'Shannassey is funding your education, mate. And he does a lot to help refugees.'

Aisif looked out the window, shaking his head.

Vince replaced Aisif's chart. 'Okay. Tell the nurses not to let him in.'

He headed back to the clinic, navigated the packed waiting room, and summoned the first patient. It was Mark Brody, the Snapper's coach. Vince was fond of Big Brodes and they'd become good friends. He dumped his bag, turned on his computer, and spent fifteen minutes explaining why an obese middle-aged man, whose father had died of a heart attack at forty-five, needed to stop smoking, drink less, lose weight, and exercise more.

'I'm always down the footy club, Doc. *That's* exercise.'

Vince laughed. 'Yeah, leaning on the fence, shouting at people and shifting witch's hats around. If you don't lift your game, you're going to wake up one day looking at that lid.'

'Bit late then.' Brodes chuckled. 'What about gettin' a few of them stents in me ticker?'

Vince shook his head. As Shirley Tiang told him on his first day at the clinic, 'Behaviour change, champ, that's the big challenge for Geeps.' Vince knew about behaviour change. *Threat of immediate deregistration did it for me. The sword of Damocles.*

'Nothing against plumbers, Brodes, but unblocking your pipes doesn't cure the problem, just stops the chest pains. For the time being.' He handed over a pathology slip for repeat cholesterol, and referrals to a dietician and the hospital smoking-cessation clinic. 'Prevention's the go.'

Mark nodded. 'Fair enough.'

'The cancer sticks are the biggie,' said Vince, giving him a script for Champix, a smoking-cessation drug. 'Have something with you as a distraction, like nuts or fruit. Something else to do with your hands.'

'Like them worry beads the Turks have.'

'That's the sort of thing,' Vince replied. 'How's young Travis going?' he asked as Brodes picked up the paperwork.

The big man's habitual grin faded to a dark frown, like a squall blowing in off the ocean. 'Battling. He don't want to have much to do with me.'

'Why's that?' asked Vince.

Brodes paused, arms crossed, his big head still but small eyes darting from side to side. 'Trav was all right till he went to that seminary.' He pointed to his temple with a stubby finger. 'Them priests messed with his head.'

He pulled a grimy copy of the *Warrnambool Observer* out of his back pocket and pointed at a picture of Monsignor O'Shannassey leading the Palm Sunday march. 'Specially that one.'

'But the Mons wasn't at the seminary, he was here at Sacred Heart.'

'The rector fella down there was away for a few months last year and that bastard was filling in for him.'

'But your wife is the housekeeper for the Monsignor.'

The big man frowned and shook his newspaper. 'Oh yeah, Geraldine reckons the sun shines outta the bloke's clacker.'

Those holy rays are fading fast.

* * *

Vince hustled out his last patient, sat back in his chair, took a deep breath, and glanced at the time. Ten past six. He turned off his computer and addressed the pile of paperwork on his desk.

'No chance,' he said, getting up. 'Tonight I have a family waiting for me.'

As he headed for the door, his desk phone burst into sound. 'What?' he said, voice impatient and manner brusque.

'Settle down, Dr Hanrahan,' said Lorraine. 'It's just your old pal Professor McKenzie wanting a heart-to-heart.'

That little Hitler. Last person I want to speak to! However, as Shirley said, 'Lachie Mac can drop you right in the shits, buddy. Gotta suck up him.'

'G'day, Lachlan, what can I do you for?'

'Evening, Vincent.' Measured, oily tone. Like a politician. 'I need to inform you that after your recent obstetric … *adventure*, the Board have decided to extend your suspension from specialist practice to at least the end of next year.' He paused. 'Subject to review at that time.'

Vince jumped to his feet. 'But I was supposed to regain my specialist registration this year! What the hell do you think—'

'I'm just the messenger,' McKenzie cut in. 'The Board has the authority in these matters.'

Vince shook his head. *Lachie's own fingerprints are all over this!*

'Any right of appeal, Professor?'

'No, the Board's decision is final.'

Shit!

'Any questions, Vincent?'

Vince terminated the call and marched round to Shirley's room. She was making notes on her computer and motioned for him to sit. He looked around and was struck by the contrast with his own room— flowers and family photos on her desk and her husband's colourful modern artworks on the walls.

She finished her typing and looked up. 'What's up, cobber?'

'My sentence has been extended by the Board to at least another year because of that Keilland's I did.' Vince waved his arm around the room. 'Looks like I'll be playing the country Geep for a while yet.'

Shirley nodded, earrings bouncing and clattering. 'Sound like good news to me, champ.'

Vince gave a wry smile. He knew it was hard to get doctors in the bush, even broken-down specialists like him. 'Due respects, Shirl. When I get my ticket back, you won't see me for dust.'

She tilted her head in her customary Puckish gesture, arms out and the palms of her hands facing the ceiling. 'Heard that story about the medical student and the forceps?'

Vince nodded. *But I'm about to hear it again.*

'The examiner's holding the fake pelvis,' said Shirley, 'and the student puts the forceps blades on the pretend baby's head and starts pulling, then his feet slip and the pelvis, baby, and forceps all fall on the floor.' She paused, struggling to contain her mirth. 'The examiner picks up one of the blades … and … says—'

'Now hit the father with this,' Vince completed, 'and you'll have killed the whole bloody family!'

Shirley burst into a volley of wild laughter, her thin body shaking.

Vince shook his head. 'That story dates back to when Adam was a boy.'

'A goodie but an oldie.' She recovered and mopped her eyes with a tissue. 'Speaking of the old salad servers, I saw that sprog this morning, bud. *And* the father.' She frowned. 'He's a piece of works.'

'PTSD from Iraq.' He mimed a syringe squirt in his arm.

'Funny-looking kid.'

Vince laughed. 'Funny-looking parents.'

'Still got the lump on the scone from the forceps.'

'You know those cephalhematomas can last for weeks.'

A concerned look creased her brow. '*I* know that, Rooned, but you got to explain that stuff to parents. The father angry, reckon baby bit slow and head too small.'

'That kid is fine.' Vince stood. 'I've got more to worry about than the shape of Dustin Cartwright's baby's head.' He headed for the door. 'And so has he.'

* * *

The rest of the week shot past at record pace. Vince would drop the girls at the library in the morning, do his thing at the clinic, then pick them up in the evening and grab some takeaway or Tessa would cook up something back at the Snapper house. Then they would settle in for some old favourite reruns of *Mad Men*, with much giggling and blocks of chocolate. However, Vince was aware that the days were ticking past. *Then back to remote parenting.*

On Thursday evening he pulled up in front of the library to find no sign of the twins, who were supposed to be waiting outside. He parked and wandered in. Vince had spent a lot of time there when he first came to town. It was warmer and more inviting than the small flat he'd rented on the highway. He would hole up in a corner and read the papers, avoiding reality for an hour or two. That's until random patients started sidling up to him seeking freebie consultations, virtually disrobing in the process.

He looked in all the cubicles, around the open area where the desks and computers were, and up and down the book aisles. No sign of them. One of the librarians was tidying up and starting to switch off the lights.

'Hey, Alison,' said Vince, 'those girls of mine here?'

'No, they left a while ago.' The girl frowned. 'They were making a lot of noise. I had to ask them to go.'

'Sorry about that,' said Vince. 'I'll make sure it doesn't happen tomorrow.'

'We aren't open tomorrow. It's Good Friday.'

Vince walked out, grabbed his phone and punched in a number.

'Hi Bins,' Georgie answered with a giggle. 'You probably don't even know where we are.'

Vince could hear chatter and laughter in the background. 'What the hell?'

'We're just across the road, we can see you,' added Tessa. 'Wave, Dad.'

He looked back up Liebig Street at the Whaler's Inn on the far corner. 'Girls, tell me you're not at the pub.'

'We're here with Trav, our new bestie. We met him at the libe. He's the nephew of that old lady who lives next door to you. Say hi to Dad, Travel.'

Bloody Hell! 'Girls, Travis is not quite right in the head, he's—'

'I've just got one word for you, Bins,' said Georgie. 'Speaker phone!'

There was a fresh burst of giggling.

'Listen to me. I want you to get right out of there. Now! Head around the corner into Timor and I will pick you up in front of the ice-creamery.'

Vince jumped into Benny, turned left in front of the performing arts centre, did a U-turn, and pulled up outside Seaside Cones—engine running, lips compressed, and fists choking the steering wheel. After five long minutes, the girls appeared, waving back up the street.

'Later, Travel!'

'Good luck with your quest!'

They jumped in and Vince took off, laying a trail of rubber on the road.

'Whoa, Bins,' said Georgie. 'You hoon!'

'Girls, you are supposed to be studying, not hanging around in a pub with a lunatic!'

'Trav is way cool,' said Tessa. 'He's on a quest to learn about spiritualism and astral travelling—'

'That's why we call him Travel—'

'Get it?'

'And we were just drinking Coke—'

'He says organised religion is dead—'

'And he can help us with our assignment.'

Vince pulled over and screeched to a halt. 'One,' he said, ticking off on his fingers, 'you are not old enough to be in a pub. Two, Travis Brody is fifteen years older than you. Three, he is *not* a person I want you hanging around with.' He stared at them. 'Do I make myself clear?'

Georgie pouted. 'What happened to "time you spent more time with real people, girls. There is a world outside Canterbury Ladies College and South Yarra, you know"?'

Vince paused. *Fair cop.* 'Travis is a troubled soul, George. He has … issues. I can't say any more, but trust me on this. Okay?'

He started Benny up again and headed off down Timor Street, across the railway line into South Warrnambool. It was a clear, crisp autumn evening and the streets were darkening as they pulled up at the Snapper house. Deefer greeted them with an excited bark.

'Good girl,' said Tessa, giving her a pat.

The girls walked through to the front of the house and returned with bags of groceries.

'Where did that stuff come from?' said Vince.

'You heard of home delivery, Bins?' said Georgie.

'We'll feed Deefer,' said Tessa, 'then you guys can go for a walk while we make dinner.'

A few minutes later, Vince and the dog headed down McDonald Street across the Merri River Bridge and down onto the boardwalk in front of the yacht club café. They walked out onto the breakwater, where a few optimistic fishermen were dangling lines off the side.

'Any luck?' Vince said to a slim, dark-haired young man with a Snappers beanie, who was sitting on a camp chair, complete with a stubbie and a smoke.

'Not yet,' he said with a grin, then waved his free hand around the pier, dark water and fading sunset, 'but either way, I reckon I'm miles ahead.'

Vince had a flashback to him and Joey fishing in the river mouth at

Port Fairy. Dad was at the pub. Mum and Trisha were walking on the beach. It was the summer before Joey went off to St Bernard's and they were talking quietly, waiting for their lines to tighten …

Deefer pulled on the lead and gave a loud bark, which broke into Vince's musing. He felt a sudden cold chill and snapped back to the present, a lump in his throat and an ache in his heart.

* * *

Vince returned to the house to find Elena Genovesi, resplendent in a clingy sapphire-blue dress, standing in the kitchen, sipping white wine and chatting to the girls. All three were laughing and enjoying the moment.

He kissed Elena's cheek, accepted a mineral water, and sat down on one side of his tiny kitchen table, neatly set with a tablecloth and napkins. She sat opposite him and Georgie brought over three platters of colourful, exotic food.

'Run out of chops, did they, George?'

'You'll have to ask the chefs, I'm just the waitress.'

'That's roasted cauliflower and hazelnut salad,' said Tessa, pointing at the dishes in turn. 'This is quinoa and pomegranate, and that one's roasted aubergine with garlic and lemon, courtesy of the PC.'

'Thanks to all concerned,' said Vince.

'Well done, girls,' added Elena.

The twins perched on the old kitchen stools and they all loaded up their plates and started eating. The accompanying conversation centred on food, school, fashion, and music, and Georgie had them in stitches with impersonations of various teachers.

Vince sat back in his chair. 'De-licious. I don't think I've eaten stuff like this before.'

'You *have*, Bins,' said Tessa. 'Mum used to make,' she paused, 'I mean, *makes* the quinoa one. Don't you remember the food we had when we all went to Nobi, that Ottolenghi restaurant in Soho, for your fortieth birthday?'

'Oh, yes, of course. It was the night we saw *The Book of Mormon*.'

'That was *soo* funny,' said Tessa.

'And Mum said the toilets at Nobi were the poshest she'd ever been in—'

'You said "a dunny's still just a dunny"—'

'Mum giggled so much, she sprayed champagne all over your face!'

The three of them were now roaring with laughter. Elena cleared the table and put the dishes in the sink.

'Then we went on the London Eye the next day,' said Vince.

'And rode those bikes around Hyde Park—'

'Mum said she saw Kate Middleton walking out of Kensington Palace pushing a pram—'

'As *if!*'

'Didn't I drive us down to Cornwall that weekend?'

Tessa nodded. 'Just so Mum could see that *Doc Martin* village.'

Georgie made a face. 'It took *soo* long.'

'And it rained and rained.'

'Wasn't that when we had fish and chips with those squashy peas?'

'That's right,' Tessa said with an excited grin. 'And Mum said that *Alice in Wonderland* thing—'

'No wise fish would go anywhere—' Vince added in a theatrical voice.

'Without a porpoise!' shouted Georgie, and they all fell about giggling again.

'I'll leave you to your reminiscences,' said Elena, standing in the doorway.

They looked around and Vince jumped to his feet. 'Stay there, Doc, I'll find my own way out.'

She picked up her coat and bag and headed for the front door. 'Thanks for the dinner, girls.'

20

Two days later, Vince found himself putting the twins on the Saturday evening train. Back to reality.

'Thanks for the week, Dad,' said Tessa.

'It was a blast,' added Georgie. '*So* good hanging with Deefer and PC Genovesi.'

'Glad you enjoyed it, girls. Hopefully you got some work done.'

'We're all over it, Bins.'

There was a piercing blast as the train pulled in.

Tessa put her hand on Vince's shoulder. 'We're really sorry about Uncle Joey, but you need to look after yourself better.'

Georgie nodded. 'You're turning into a stress head.' *Is it that obvious?* 'You need to relax more and—'

'You can get home delivered whole food dinners in the 'Bool now—'

'We put the app on your phone, so—'

'No more pizzas—'

'Or fries—'

'Keep up the meditation stuff—'

'And be nice to the PC.'

Vince saluted. 'Message received.' He carried their bags across the platform. 'Study hard, girls, it'll be over before you know it,' he said as they climbed into the first class carriage. 'Say hi to Mum.'

'Any message for Ivan?' Georgie asked with a grin.

Vince laughed, shook his head, and trotted next to the train as it pulled out, pumping his arms, imitating a steam locomotive—an old family joke.

The girls pulled down the window as they sped up.

'Bye, Bins.'

'Thanks, Dad.'

* * *

The Snapper house seemed cold, empty, and miserable. Vince always felt gutted when the girls left. Even Deefer looked sad.

'It's not that bad down here in Warrnambool,' he said as he filled her bowl and topped up her water. 'But I'm just marking time.'

He went back inside, flopped on the couch, and opened his laptop, which the girls had commandeered for the week. The inevitable list of new emails appeared and he scrolled down, binning spam and unwanted messages as he went. He noticed one from Jane, dated Tuesday and opened it.

Hi Vinny,

Wanted to let you know that Broken Rites have found more information re the Ballarat diocese.

As I told you, we have accessed files that had been hidden by the Archdiocese, which prove that Fr Dennis O'Shannassey was a member of the College of Consultors. We have now discovered that he was personally responsible for the decision to move Delaney from parish to parish, despite numerous complaints about his behaviour.

The lying old bugger!

We have also found a written complaint by Mr Terrence O'Leary of Cressy that was sent to the bishop in 1997, which states that a Ballarat priest, he referred to only as 'Dirty Dennis', took the altar boys from St Bernard's for weekends to the priests' house at Apollo Bay, and repeatedly sexually abused him and the other boys. Apparently, the bishop has no memory of receiving this letter.

Mr O'Leary died of a drug overdose in 2009.

Shit!

Joseph was an altar boy that year, Terry O'Leary was his best friend, Monsignor O'Shannassey's 'Christian' name is Dennis, and he was in charge of the altar boys. Your brother had terrible nightmares all our married life and used to repeatedly scream out, 'Piss off, Dirty Dennis! Leave me alone!' Joseph never talked about it much, but he did tell me there was only one man who abused him, it happened at 'the Bay', and he did it over and over again.

I have contacted the Monsignor but he refuses to see me. He'll see you though. Before I pass this information onto the police, I want you to show him the attached copy of O'Leary's letter. O'Shannassey needs to admit what he did, own it, and face the consequences.

If you don't do this ASAP, I will come down there on Sunday and take matters into my own hands.

Jane.

Fuck!

Vince grabbed his phone and hit Jane's number. No answer. He swore again, left a message and sent a text. Next, he rang the presbytery.

'Sacred Heart. Can I help you?'

It was Geraldine Brody, the housekeeper.

'Dr Vince Hanrahan here. I want to talk to the Monsignor.'

'Anything I can help you with?'

'Tell him it's about Terrence O'Leary.'

'He's at the church, Doctor, Stations of the Cross.'

'What about tomorrow?'

She laughed. 'No chance, it's Holy Saturday. He has meetings in the morning, the service at West Warrnambool in the afternoon, and the Passion in the evening. Is it urgent?'

You bet! 'It's crucial that I talk to him this weekend.'

She paused. 'He could spare a few minutes after mass on Sunday before he goes out to Koroit for his Easter lunch.'

'What time?'

'I'll put you down for twelve-thirty here in the sitting room. The Mons might like to have a glass of wine with you.'

I doubt it, not after he hears what I have to say. I doubt it very much.

21

Vince couldn't remember the last time he'd been in church. Voluntarily that was—not for weddings and funerals. He didn't even darken those big wooden doors for Christmas, but he always came to mass around December the twelfth for his mum's anniversary. His dad used to come along too, before the Alzheimer's set in. Vince liked to bring the girls as well, but last time they were in Bali with their mother and 'Ivan The Tool'. Turned out Ivan was a rich tool too, so there were lots of expensive holidays.

He looked around the old building, the expansive central nave, the fluted grey stone columns, the vaulted timber ceilings, and the carved wooden Stations of the Cross on the sidewalls, alternating with sunlit, stained-glass windows. There was a large crucifix shrouded in purple on the right wall and the choir stalls on the left. The Paschal candle burned brightly in front of the elevated altar, separating the congregation from the priestly domain—*a metaphor for all that's wrong with the contemporary Church.*

'Hey, Doc, don't see you here too often,' said an overweight potato grower from Killarney, who took up half the pew in front. 'Maybe you'd better line up for confession while you're at it,' he added with a chuckle.

'Haven't been to confession for years, Damian,' Vince responded. 'I hate to think what the penance would be if I went now.'

'Just about a full Rosary, don't ya reckon?'

Vince looked at the congregation; the place was half full, with a preponderance of over-sixties. 'I'm one of the youngest here,' he whispered. 'Where's all the kids?'

'They won't come these days and no one's makin' 'em. It's all that abuse stuff startin' to stick.'

Sacred Heart was an imposing bluestone structure on a hill in the middle of town, with a large double-storey balconied presbytery next door. Vince could imagine that back in the glory days the church would have been packed for Sunday morning mass, given the strong Irish Catholic presence in the district, but things had changed. To her dying day, his mother Mary had dismissed the talk about paedophile priests as being Protestant and media scuttlebutt, but since then the scales had fallen from the eyes of even the most fervent believer. The government's Royal Commission was nearly finished, and brothers and priests were being charged and imprisoned.

Vince glanced at his watch: five past eleven. 'Aren't we supposed to have bounced the ball already?'

'Bloody oath. The old Mons is usually halfway through the mass by now. He musta slept in.'

'Does he always say this Easter Sunday mass?'

'Yair. Lukey Kelly will be over at Our Lady's out in East Warrnambool doing the ten-thirty. They don't have no priest of their own anymore.' Damian nodded his huge head back to the foyer. 'Look at 'em, all dressed up and nowhere to go.'

The readers and altar boys were waiting like a bridal party at the entrance, and a group of church elders were in deep conversation next to the closed door of the sacristy, the small room where the priests put on their robes before mass.

'Look out,' said Damian, 'they've sent Frankie over to the presbytery to find him. Old Dennis must have a hangover.'

Vince recognised the elegant, suited figure of Francis Doyle, a local lawyer, as he walked resolutely out the back door.

'Is Frank Doyle the grand poobah at Sacred Heart, Damo?'

'Yair, he's the chairman of the parish council, Doc. Frankie's a real big noise.'

Vince looked up toward the altar and recognised the commanding figure of Colleen Maloney off to the left, sitting at an electronic organ and whispering to the members of the small orchestra—a violinist, cello player, and a flautist. Colleen was almost six feet tall, her flaming red hair—released from the tight knot she wore at work—cascading onto her shoulders, and a regal, if insouciant, bearing. Several people sat on short angled pews behind the organ, presumably the choir. Everyone seemed to be in a state of suspended animation, waiting for the entry of the Great Man. Vince looked again at the time: quarter past.

He felt a sudden tap on the shoulder and turned to find Frank Doyle leaning down toward his ear. 'Dr Hanrahan,' he said, voice low but tone urgent. 'I need you to come over to the presbytery. Something's happened to the Monsignor.'

Vince stood and followed Frank out the back of the church, down the broad stone steps, across the churchyard, and into the dark interior of the large, forbidding building. It wasn't the first time he'd been there. Luke Kelly was the only other resident and Vince had dined with him once or twice. He'd also done a call to the big house to see Monsignor O'Shannassey when he'd had a bad flu last winter.

Frank took him through the large hallway, along a corridor, and then stopped outside an open door. Old Frank's pretty cool in a crisis, Vince reflected, must be pushing seventy-five. Mr Doyle looked the epitome of the respectable country solicitor—tall and dignified with carefully groomed white hair, his youthful unlined pink face without even the hint of a whisker. *That'll be due to the hormone therapy he's on for his prostate cancer, aka chemical castration.*

'He's in there, Dr Hanrahan.'

Vince entered the small room. There was a filing cabinet on one side and a large cross on the wall. Monsignor O'Shannassey was sitting at a desk below a small window, dressed in a white shirt and dark trousers, a pair of gleaming black shoes near the door. His body was slumped forward and his head was turned to the side on the flat wooden surface. A heavy set of rosary beads was wound tightly around his neck and his large, bloated tongue was lolling from the slack, open mouth.

'What do you think, Doctor?' Frank Doyle asked in his considered, legal voice as Vince undertook a perfunctory examination.

'Well,' said Vince, 'absent pulse, no respirations, pupils fixed and dilated … I reckon that makes him deceased,' Vince touched the Monsignor's purple brow, 'and has been for some time. Too late for any resuscitation attempt.'

'I thought as much,' responded Frank. 'I took the liberty of phoning the ambulance and police.'

'Fair enough.'

They both looked at the motionless figure at the desk. Vince felt devoid of any emotional response—he wasn't sure whether this was the numbing effect of his job or because of his alleged personal empathy deficit. *Alleged by Lydia.* His eyes were drawn to the heavy wooden necklace around the priest's swollen neck.

'You know,' he said, 'every night before bed, Mum used to summon us all for a decade of the rosary and she had a set of beads just like those. We'd all kneel in a line and my brother used to drop farts and blame them on me.'

Frank Doyle frowned and pursed his lips.

'Most of the time it ended in a flogging from the old man,' Vince went on. 'I've had no time for rosary beads ever since.' *Or praying.*

There was the sound of heavy vehicles pulling up just outside the presbytery, and seconds later two paramedics appeared at the door, followed by two police: Elena Genovesi and a young constable.

'Hi guys,' said Vince. 'What's this—two by two, like Noah's ark?'

Mr Doyle fired off a disapproving glance at Vince and motioned the visitors into the small room.

'What's the story, Doc?' asked one of the paramedics.

Vince shrugged and gestured toward Mr Doyle.

'Monsignor O'Shannassey failed to appear in church for the eleven o'clock mass, so I came over to investigate. I knocked, but there was no answer. Father Kelly is saying mass out at Our Lady's in East Warrnambool and I understand the housekeeper, Mrs Brody, doesn't prepare the priests' breakfast on Sunday mornings.'

'They have to get their own brekkie these days,' interjected Vince. 'Sign of the times.'

'Be that as it may,' said Frank. 'So I came in to find—'

'The front door was unlocked, Mr Doyle?' interrupted Elena.

'Frank kicked it in, Sarge, what do you reckon?'

'Dr Hanrahan,' she responded, a frown appearing above her large, dark eyes, 'I'm sure Mr Doyle can answer for himself.'

The solicitor glowered at Vince—another silent rebuke. 'It *was* locked, Detective Sergeant, but I have a key. I entered to find the parlour empty, and no one answered my call, so I came here through to the Monsignor's study. The door was ajar … and …' He fell silent and looked at the figure in front of them.

'Someone's obviously strangled him,' said Vince.

He lifted the Monsignor's lifeless head to reveal the fingers of both hands trapped under the taut wooden ligature. 'The usual desperate attempt to avoid asphyxiation.'

'Just don't touch anything, thank you, Doctor.' Elena's voice was authoritative and compelling. 'This is now a crime scene,' she added, nodding to the eager young policeman, whose eyes were popping out of his head. 'Get the equipment from the car, Constable.'

Probably his first murder. A bit like an obstetrician's first dead baby. *Or dead mother.*

* * *

'What's going on?' Luke Kelly's insistent voice ripped Vince back to the present. 'Did someone collapse during the service?'

Luke's blue Subaru was now in the carport outside the presbytery and he was striding toward Vince and Frank standing at the front door next to the ambulance and the police car.

'Something's happened, Father,' said Frank. He motioned Luke into the presbytery entrance. 'You can't enter the house at present. The police are in there.'

Luke looked puzzled. 'What do you mean, something's happened?'

Frank put his hand on Luke's shoulder. 'Monsignor O'Shannassey is deceased.' He dropped his voice. 'And it looks like foul play.'

Luke's eyes widened and his mouth dropped open. He pointed toward the church. 'But … but, what …?'

'The congregation is waiting, Father,' said Frank. 'Should I tell them the service is cancelled or …'

Luke looked back at the presbytery and grimaced. 'No, no. I better go over and say the mass.'

* * *

Vince drove away from the church, head spinning. He'd lost all interest in going back inside. O'Shannassey murdered! Just when he was going to make the old bugger squirm! The enormity of what he'd just witnessed hit him hard as he passed along the empty streets, blue sky overhead and a stiff sea breeze. He guessed the locals were gathering in houses all over town for a big Easter feast with their families. *Lucky them!* Easter Sunday, a time to celebrate the resurrection. A time for forgiveness. Vince wound through South Warrnambool and pulled up at the Snappper house. There was no forgiveness in *his* heart.

Deefer danced up to him and demanded a pat. Vince tossed an old tennis ball around the yard and the dog ran about in a noisy frenzy. He then went inside, put the kettle on, and sat to ponder the events of the morning. A few minutes later there was a thunderous knocking at the front door and Vince walked through to find Kieran Harrington on the porch.

'H-h-happy Easter, Dr Vince.'

'Happy Easter, Super K.'

'M-M-Mum said will you come in for dinner? She's cooked a leg of l-l-lamb.'

'Tell her thanks,' Vince replied, 'but I'm flat out with work so I'll have to give it a miss.' *Lying on Easter Sunday—probably a mortal sin.*

Kieran nodded and headed home.

Vince grabbed Deefer's lead. 'Better look busy,' he told the eager dog. 'We'll go for a walk before hitting the couch again.'

He pulled out his phone and punched in Jane's number. Still no answer.

'It's Vinny,' he said. 'Where are you? Ring me back ASAP.'

As soon as he pocketed his mobile, it started to ring. *Okay, Jane and I have some serious talking to do.*

'Hi, Bins!'

'G'day, Georgie. How's it going down there at Chez Becker?'

Vince had learned from Lydia that she and the twins were going to Ivan's house in Portsea for Easter.

'Prince Ger-*ard* ate a massive chocolate rabbit and spewed everywhere. It was gross!'

Gerard was Ivan's precocious twelve-year-old son who lived with his mother in Sydney and spent occasional holidays with his father. The royal nickname had been Vince's creation.

'Happy Easter, Dad,' said Tessa. 'Did you get any eggs?'

Vince laughed. 'Don't think the Easter bunny could find me down here.'

'The bunny *sooo* came, Bins. Have a look in your front yard.'

Vince walked through the Snapper house into the modest garden in the front and found six gaudily wrapped chocolate eggs stashed in obvious locations.

'Thank you, bunnies.'

'The head rabbits had to subcontract the job to a local distributor,' said Tessa.

Kieran, thought Vince.

'Don't eat them all at once,' said Georgie.

'What are you doing for Easter lunch?' asked Tessa.

'I've been invited to the Harringtons next door,' Vince replied as he grabbed Deefer's lead and headed for the door. *Well, I have.*

'Awesome! Say hi to Super K for us.'

'And Travel.'

'And Mrs H.'

'Bye, Bins!'

22

The next day Vince pushed open the door of the post mortem room and observed the slight body of Monsignor O'Shannassey lying on the slab. 'G'day, Ilsa.'

Sarah Bell, the pathologist, was an old medical school classmate and they'd had a brief dope- and poetry-fuelled relationship way back in fifth year. He and Sarah had re-met when he started his sentence in Warrnambool. They'd been fans of *Casablanca* back in the day and often defaulted to their old pet names from that movie.

Vince looked around the room. He felt uncomfortable in the clinical, austere surroundings of Sarah's professional domain. 'You're welcome to this stuff,' he said. 'I prefer my patients to have a pulse.'

'Hi, Ricky,' she responded. 'Each to her own.'

Sarah had finished the autopsy and was tidying up. She was tall and willowy, long golden tresses now replaced by a silver bob.

'Cause of death, acute asphyxiation. Strangulation with a tight ligature.'

He nodded. 'How were his coronary arteries?'

She looked at her notes. 'Widespread atheroma and hypertensive changes. Fatty liver too.'

'No surprises there. He had elevated cholesterol and blood pressure.'

'Too much good living over the years,' she responded, glancing at Vince. 'I guess priests are entitled to a few vices.'

Yeah, but you have the draw the line somewhere.

'He's also got an abrasion to his face,' said Sarah, pointing at the Monsignor's left cheek.

'Recent?'

'No more than a day old.'

'Probably happened at the same time as the murder.'

'I'd be looking for a *strong* killer,' said Sarah, snapping off her gloves. 'It'd be hard work strangling someone with rosary beads.'

'He was pretty frail,' Vince observed. 'Bad arthritis and chronic leukaemia.'

She shed her gown and they both looked at the pallid body on the table. 'Poor man.'

Vince felt nothing.

I'm only sorry because we won't get our day in court and the mongrel won't get to rot in jail.

* * *

Vince headed home, his thoughts and emotions locked in a duel—the finality of this resolution versus the yearning for retribution. It was a fine day, still some warmth in the air but a fluky breeze and dark clouds to the west. Shirley was on-call for the public holiday so he had the afternoon to himself.

He flopped on the couch, left another message for Jane, and turned on the box—wall to wall sport. The semi-finals of the Stawell gift were on, the Rip Curl Pro at Bells Beach was coming up, and the Cats were playing the Hawks in their traditional Easter Monday opening clash at the Melbourne Cricket Ground.

He and Joey had always met at the 'G' for that big match. They would watch the first half from their seats then retire to the bar, shoulder to shoulder with other country blokes. Vince would be in the thick of it, full of beer and bullshit. Joey would be off to one side, listening and grinning gently. Vince sighed; those were the days …

He shook himself and jumped up. 'Come on, Deefer. Let's get out of here. Fancy a drive?'

They travelled west on the Princes Highway and turned off down Mahoney's lane, passed the sprawling antique shop, and drove to the

Killarney beach. The wind was now strong and gusty, the tide was out, and big waves were crashing across the rocks and whipping up a salty spray. Families were milling around the tents in the campsite overlooking the ocean and a few fishermen were trying their luck, but Vince kept his head down and spoke to no one. He threw the frisbee for Deefer to fetch, over and over—each time she dropped it back at his feet, panting with an expectant look. Then they went for a long walk on the soft sand until both were spent.

* * *

Dusk was falling as Vince steered Benny back into the drive at Fay Street. He opened the tailgate and the dozy Deefer shook herself and jumped out. No sooner had Vince gone inside the house than there was loud tap at the door. He opened it to find Mrs Harrington bearing a tray with a large foil-covered plate.

'Just some leftover lamb and vegies from yesterday, Dr Vince. And a bit of gravy too.'

'Thanks, Mrs H,' said Vince. 'You're spoiling me.'

'I know you don't eat real proper, all them takeaways and that. You should know better.'

Vince put his hands up in mock surrender. 'Guilty as charged.' *I'll start following the twins' advice. Soon.*

Mrs Harrington pushed past him along the narrow hallway, placed the tray on the kitchen table, wiped her hands on her ubiquitous floral apron and sat down. *Uh-oh. Here we go.* Vince took the other seat.

She put her hand up to her mouth in her usual conspiratorial way. 'Wasn't it terrible about the Mons?' she said in a trademark loud whisper. 'Our Geraldine is beside herself.'

'It would have been a big shock for her,' said Vince.

'She's been housekeeping for him for over ten years,' she went on, 'and for young Father Kelly now, into the bargain.'

Vince detected a disapproving note in that last comment. He knew Mrs H didn't believe in priests wearing jeans, surfing, and playing the guitar.

'If you ask me,' she continued, 'it would have been one of them refugees. Arabs don't hold with the Church. The Mons never should have let 'em live in the old school.'

'That a bit harsh, Mrs H,' said Vince. 'You'd think they'd be grateful to him.'

Mrs Harrington sniffed and looked unconvinced. 'They could be terrorists or anything. You wouldn't know.' She put her hand up again and resumed her loud whisper. 'Geraldine reckons they are crook on the government for not letting all their families come here too.' She raised her eyes and looked heavenward. 'Maybe they blamed the Mons.'

O'Shannassey was to blame for a lot of things, but not that one.

He stood in a vain attempt to finish the conversation, but Mrs Harrington was having none of it.

'Or it could have been one of them druggies, you know those no-hopers he looks after … I mean, *used* to look after.'

Vince walked toward the hall entrance. 'Best to leave it to the police, Mrs H.'

'And another thing,' added Mrs Harrington, staying put and craning her head around. 'Geraldine said nothing was stolen, but the Mons' vestments all had rips slashed through them. And he's been getting hate threats in the computer.' She nodded as she stood. 'Like I told Kieran, we shouldn't be letting 'em in. Now look what's happened.'

* * *

Vince fed Deefer, heated the lamb in the microwave, and settled down in front of the TV. He couldn't remember the last time he'd eaten a roast and he cleaned it all up, including the half dozen potatoes.

'Better go for a run tomorrow,' he advised Deefer, then laid back to give his digestive system a fighting chance and nodded off. After ten minutes, '*We are Geelong …*' jolted him awake. *Hope it's not the hospital.* He looked at the name on the screen and sat up.

'Hi Janey, I've been trying to get onto you.'

'Hello, Vinny.' Voice quiet and reserved. 'Mobile coverage is patchy up here.'

Not that *bloody patchy.* 'I had the girls staying last week and I only got your message Saturday. Sickening stuff.'

'Yes, it's the smoking gun we were after,' said Jane. 'But I've just seen on the news that O'Shannessey's dead anyway.'

'That's right, yesterday morning.'

'Did you show him the letter?'

Vince shook his head at the phone. 'No, no chance. I was going to talk to him after mass.'

She sighed. 'Too late now.'

Vince paused. 'You said in your message you were going to come down and front him yourself.'

'Couldn't get away, with Easter and the kids and everything.' Her turn to pause. 'Anyway, you were the man on the spot.'

Ouch!

'Was it his heart?'

Vince stopped and thought for a minute; may as well tell her. 'This is confidential, but it looks like someone murdered him.'

Jane laughed. Strained and teetering on hysterical. 'Well, like Joseph used to say, what goes around comes around.'

'Can't argue with that.'

'Still would've liked to see him in the dock.'

'Too right. But at least we get some closure. For Joey's sake.'

That bitter laugh again. 'Closure! I'm never going to get closure.'

23

'Standing room only,' Vince said to Lorraine as he surveyed the waiting room.

'The day after a public holiday is always like this,' she said. 'Monday and Tuesday rolled into one.'

He nodded. 'The punters sit on their ailments over the long weekend, then all want to be seen first thing.'

His last patient for the morning session was Skylah Cartwright, due for her two-month vaccinations. Dustin was there too. First time he'd fronted up with the kids.

'She don't look right,' he said as Tracey undressed the sleeping baby. 'Her head's all flat at the back.' He pointed his finger at Vince. 'Musta been them fucken forceps.'

Vince examined Skylah, now awake and screaming. She wasn't going to win any beautiful baby contests. 'That's called positional pla-giocephaly, mate. Lots of bubs get it. It's just because we nurse them on their backs to reduce the risk of Sudden Infant Death Syndrome.' He pointed to the area of concern. 'It'll come good.'

'But she's got this weird cry,' said Tracey, 'different to what the boys done. And the health nurse still reckons her head's too small.'

Vince looked at the measurements in Skylah's health record. Her weight and length were still on the twenty-fifth percentile but her head circumference was now below the tenth.

'It's just swings and roundabouts, guys,' said Vince. 'As long as her head circumference doesn't drop down any more percentiles.'

Tracey picked up the now crying baby and redressed her.

'We'll go through to the treatment room now,' he went on, 'and Rita will give Skylah her shots. I'll check her again at her next vaccination at four months.'

Dustin stood and eyeballed Vince. 'Tracey and her mum reckon you're a saint, Doc,' he said, 'but I'm gunna take Skylah to Dr Isaacs. I got a referral off that quack Paras from the other clinic.'

Natalie Isaacs was the local paediatrician, well known to Vince. She was a good clinician, diligent and risk-averse. They had crossed swords in the past about her insistence that newborn babies *never* be given formula feeds. 'It increases the risk of food allergy, asthma, and eczema' versus 'the sprogs have to be given *some* tucker if the mother's milk hasn't come in.' They'd agreed to disagree.

Dustin pointed at Vince again. 'You might'a damaged her brain. I'm gunna talk to a lawyer.'

* * *

After they left Vince sat at his desk, mind racing and heart belting. *What is it with these palpitations?* Hadn't he done everything by the book that night? He was almost certain Skylah had suffered no trauma or hypoxia. *Almost.*

Just then his desk phone rang. 'Get your bum in here, Rooned. It's powwow and chowwow time.'

He headed off to the back room to find the weekly practice meeting well underway. He grabbed a sandwich, found a seat, and then lost himself in his own thoughts as Lynne ran through the agenda.

'Sad about Monsignor O'Shannassey, Vince,' the Prez said after the last item had been dealt with. 'I heard you were there.'

'That's right,' said Vince, jolted from his daydream. 'I was minding my own business in the congregation and got caught up in the whole thing.'

'Wonder the Holy Ghost didn't hit the place with lightning at the shocks of you being there, Rooned.'

'It *was* Easter Sunday.'

'I see in the *Observer* that Elena Genovesi is leading the investigation,' said Rita.

'Yeah,' responded Vince, 'the coppers are a bit excited.'

'Dr Hanrahan will be very happy to help the police with their enquiries,' Shirley exclaimed with a lewd wink. 'That detective chick is Vince's squeezer.'

'Shirley, you know that's not true,' replied Vince. 'Elena and I are just friends. Platonic as it could be.'

'Bit of a shock for Father Kelly,' said the Prez. 'He's an old school friend of yours, isn't he?'

'Yeah, Kookaburra was my rover in the 1989 St Bernard's premiership team.' He grabbed another sandwich. 'Kicked three in the granny against Ballarat College.'

'You would've been a fearsome sight in the ruck, Vince. How tall are you?'

'About six-four in the old. But I was eleven stone wringing wet back then.' He pointed to his head. 'With a mop of red hair.'

Vince had gained a few kilos since those halcyon days and lost all his hair along the way. *Most of it went in one go when the shit hit the fan one night back in Melbourne.*

'Who would want to kill the Monsignor?' asked the Prez. 'Wasn't he one of the good guys?'

Vince shrugged but passed no comment. *No point going into that stuff here.*

'I barely knew the man, apart from professionally.'

Shirley laughed. 'His profession or yours?'

'*Mine*. I certainly had no need for *his* professional services.'

'You're a lapsed black sheep?'

'You bet.'

After completing her agenda, Lorraine called the meeting to a finish and they all went their separate ways. Vince found himself walking out with Rita Findlay.

'How's it going, Rit?' he asked. 'What did you do for Easter?'

Rita still lived in the family home, a large Victorian sandstone on Merri Crescent. She and Allan didn't have any children and it must have been a lonely existence. Vince called in from time to time and her husband's ghost seemed to still be present amongst the paintings, travel mementos, and golf trophies. He'd left a big hole.

'Went to my brother's house in Port Fairy for the weekend,' she said. 'Just a quiet time with his daughter and grandchildren.'

'Remember last Easter, when we all went camping and canoeing on the Glenelg river? Allan was in vintage form. I don't think I've ever laughed so much.'

'Oh yes, Vincenzo, I remember.' Rita's eyes brimmed with tears. *You unfeeling bastard, Hanrahan!*

Allan and Rita had spent a few years living in Italy while Allan was doing his PhD and embracing the *dolce vita*, and they loved all things Italian, hence the Vincenzo moniker. Their generous hospitality and legendary dinner parties had kept Vince sane during his early, lonely months in Warrnambool.

As Rita dabbed her eyes and fought to regain her composure, Vince made a mental note to visit her more often.

* * *

'How was your week, Sarge?' Vince said, serving himself a glass of sparkling water. *I'll get in first with the magic question for a change.* He and Elena were sitting in their usual booth at the rear of Fanny's, away from the prying locals.

'Fine, thanks,' she replied, pausing to sip her wine. 'Dominated by the murder investigation. What about you?'

'All over the place. The girls went back on the train Saturday, then O'Shannassey died, and I've been flat out ever since. Got some ongoing hassles with the Medical Board simmering away too.'

Elena raised her eyebrows.

'I'm sure it will sort itself out.' Vince paused. 'One way or another.' He drained his glass. 'And there's something else I've got to tell you.' He leant in. 'Jane—Joey's wife—mailed me last week that her Broken Rites group have information that the Mons was guilty of shuffling around those paedophile priests back in Ballarat.'

'Was that when Joe was at boarding school?'

'Too right.' He dropped his voice. 'They also have evidence that he—' he stopped and swallowed '—interfered with Joey when he was an altar boy.' He slumped back, exhausted, in a lather of sweat. He hadn't said that out loud before. It really hit hard. A visceral jolt.

'You didn't think to tell me about that a bit sooner?' asked Elena. 'Like before Sunday?'

Vince shrugged and put his hands out, palms up. 'I only found out about it Friday. Been a bit busy since then.'

'I *see*,' she said. 'Has Broken Rights passed this information on to our people?'

Vince shook his head. 'Jane wanted me to confront him with it before that. I was going to see him on Sunday.' He paused. 'After mass.'

'But someone else got there first.'

A young waiter came along and served their entrees, bruschetta for her and chicken kebabs for him. 'Evening, Doc Hanrahan,' the young man said as he put the plates down. 'Me cough's nearly gone, throat's still a bit sore but.'

Vince and Elena sat in silence for a few minutes as they tackled their food. He hadn't had time for lunch and was famished.

'How's the investigation going, Chief?' Vince asked after some refuelling. He waved his arms around the booth. This was to enforce a Maxwell Smart style 'Cone of Silence', meaning they both understood any police or medical matter they discussed was strictly confidential. A running joke between them, but crucial in a small community.

'Too early to say. Still doing what we do. Dr Bell reckons the time of death to be some time after ten.'

Vince nodded. 'He was still warmish when I examined him.'

'No one saw the Monsignor that morning. Father Kelly left early to say the mass at Our Lady's and the housekeeper had the day off.'

Vince picked up his last kebab. 'O'Shannassey was a polarising figure,' he went on. 'People either loved him or loathed him.' He pointed at his own chest. 'I started out indifferent and ended up in the second group.'

'Understandable.'

Vince lowered his voice. 'Have you spoken to Geraldine Brody about some emails the Mons received and looked at the state of his vestments?'

Elena frowned and tilted her head to one side. The equivalent of anyone else saying 'What the *fuck*?'

'How did you hear about those things?'

Vince winked and touched the side of his nose. 'I must protect my sources.'

Elena smiled. 'I can guess where that intel came from.' She looked around again and leant forward. 'The vestment slashing suggests a religious motive. There were no fingerprints. The messages were hate mail about the Catholic Church and threats that if the Monsignor continued harbouring asylum seekers, there would be unspecified retribution.'

'Retribution all right,' said Vince. 'Anything about child sexual abuse?'

She shook her head. 'No, nothing. Our IT people are working on the sources of those emails,' she went on. 'But looks like they're local.'

'Could be just a nutter or someone with a grudge,' said Vince. *No shortage of the latter.*

'We have one lead,' Elena continued, lowering her voice. 'Father Kelly said a woman came to see Monsignor O'Shannassey at around ten o'clock, just as he was leaving to go do the earlier mass at Our Lady's.'

'Young? Old?'

'In between, he thought.'

'Probably one of the church ladies with her knickers in a twist about the liturgy.'

'Not from around here, was his impression.'

Vince shrugged.

Elena paused and frowned. 'Your sister-in-law wasn't down this way for Easter, was she?'

'No, Sarge. She was up in Horsham with her kids and mother.'

They both sat back as their main courses arrived and chatted about lighter topics for the rest of the evening. By nine-thirty, they had finished their coffees, paid the bill, and were standing in the street outside the restaurant. It was a dark, but fine autumn night. They watched the passing parade of Friday-night shoppers and kids out on the town for a few minutes, then Vince gave Elena a brotherly peck on the cheek.

'I know it won't bring Joey back,' he said. 'But I'm glad the old bastard is dead.'

24

Vince was on-call for the weekend. His Saturday morning ward round took well over an hour, and he was already late when he fronted at the surgery. His first patient was Aisif Hamid.

'G'day,' Vince said as the boy limped in and took a seat. 'When did you get home?'

'The surgeon doctor discharged me on Monday.' He pointed to the bunged off IV line in his wrist. 'The nurses have been coming to give the drugs and dress the leg.'

He handed over his hospital discharge summary and Vince read through it quickly. Mr Widjeratne wanted him to check Aisif's wound and temperature.

'Did you see that the Monsignor died?'

Aisif nodded. 'Sorry and not sorry.'

Vince laughed inwardly, then had a sudden thought. 'Do you have access to a computer?'

'Yes, Dr Hanrahan. Laptop from school. Look up Internet for study and send emails to my father.'

Wonder if that included messages to O'Shannassey?

'Okay,' said Vince. 'Let's go through to the treatment room and I'll have a look at this leg of yours.'

Rita took down the dressing, revealing a pink wound with no surrounding redness. 'Looks to be granulating nicely.'

'Too right,' said Vince.

She applied a new dressing and arranged a follow-up review.

Aisif bowed. 'Thank you, Sister and Doctor. See you on Friday.'

After he left, Vince punched some notes into the treatment room computer while Rita tidied up.

'Forgot to tell you I saw Joe's wife over at Port Fairy on Easter Saturday night,' she said. 'Guess you guys got together with all your children.'

'No, I was here on my own.' Vince frowned. 'Janey was up in Horsham with her family. It must have been someone who looked like her. You wouldn't have seen her for a while.'

Rita shook her head. 'Jane's been doing the wound care course at Deakin with me, Vincenzo. I'm sure it was her. She walked past the restaurant where my brother and I were having dinner. I went out to say hi but she'd disappeared.'

'That's *very* weird,' said Vince.

* * *

The rest of the weekend flew past at a cracking pace—a blur of house calls, sick toddlers, and injured footballers. It was Sunday night before Vince got a chance to take a breath and allow his mental ruminating to come to the surface. He sat on the beach while Deefer tore up and down, and let his mind off the leash too.

He didn't really care who'd killed the Mons. 'Good riddance,' he informed the dog as she presented a cuttlefish to Vince and shook her wet, sandy coat on him. 'But what was Janey doing in Port Fairy?'

After they got back to the house, Vince fed Deefer and feasted on reheated noodles left over from the previous night, washed down with mineral water. He'd stopped buying Coke. *Got to start somewhere.* Then he sat back on the couch and, for the fifth time this weekend, phoned Jane. This time she picked up.

'Vinny,' she said, 'will you *stop* calling me?'

He took a deep breath. 'Rita Findlay saw you in Port Fairy last Saturday night.'

She paused. 'It was a last-minute thing. No biggie. My sister and family were coming to Port, so I decided to bring the kids down to spend time with their cousins.'

'But you told me on Monday night you spent Easter at home.'

She answered quickly. 'I don't need to justify my every movement to you Hanrahans.'

'Agreed,' he responded. 'But why lie to me?'

She laughed, this time a hard and dismissive sound. 'You didn't help me when I needed you. Don't call again.'

* * *

Next morning, Vince found himself peering at the smiling face of Dr Myfanwy Williams.

'Sorry I unloaded on you last time, Myf. I feel like I'm under the microscope. Turning paranoid in my old age.'

'No offence taken. Are you keeping out of trouble, Vincent?'

'Trying to. But trouble's got a way of finding me.'

'How so?'

'That baby I pulled out with the forceps is not kicking on so well and the father is talking legal action.'

A shadow passed across Dr Williams' sparkling features. 'Does he have a case?'

'No he doesn't … well, he might,' Vince said with a sigh. 'Who knows?'

She paused, frowning. 'Have you been in touch with your medical defence people?'

He shook his head, conscious of a sudden feeling of nausea. 'Not yet. The less I have to do with them the better.'

Myf moved in closer. 'They are there to help you.'

'Let's change the subject.'

'I see on the news that Monsignor O'Shannassey passed away on the weekend.'

'Yep,' said Vince. 'Someone killed him. Saved me the effort.'

'You mustn't talk like that. Your mouth will get you into trouble one day.'

'Like it hasn't already?' Vince laughed. 'Here's the thing.' He leant into the screen. 'Joey's wife and her Broken Rites group found out that O'Shannassey was complicit in moving those dodgy priests around and … and …' He swallowed hard. 'And that he abused Joey himself.'

Dr Williams' hazel-coloured eyes widened and her brow creased. 'Oh Vincent. How terrible!'

'There's plenty of people who'd be happy to see the back of that prick.' Vince took a swig of his tepid instant coffee. 'But if I tell the coppers that Janey had such a compelling motive and was in the area even though she told me she wasn't ...' He paused. 'She'll be a suspect.'

'You mustn't withhold information from the police,' Myf said quietly. 'Your whole career is imperilled as it is. You can't afford—'

'Really, Myf?' he cut in. 'Geez, you're on the ball. Guess that's why you're on the big bucks. Bye.'

Vince shut down his laptop and looked at the time. 'Almost eight,' he said out loud. 'Better get moving.'

After a quick shower and quicker bowl of cereal, he fed Deefer and piffed an old tennis ball around the back yard for a few minutes to give her some exercise. He jumped in the car and barrelled off to the surgery to find he was already twenty minutes behind. After working the weekend, his in-tray was overflowing with results to follow up and phone calls to return, but he pushed all that to one side and launched into his morning list.

No sooner had he seen his first patient than his mobile started singing. *'We-ee play the game as it should be played ...'* He moaned out loud. *Now what?*

'Vincent Hanrahan, at your disposal twenty-four-seven.'

'Settle down, Doc,' said Elena, unperturbed. 'Fancy a run on the beach tonight?'

Can't say I don't need the exercise. 'Righto, Sarge.'

'Meet you at the breakwater at six-thirty.'

'Done.'

* * *

At the end of the morning session, Vince ducked into the café next door to get some lunch. 'Pie and sauce and a lartay coming up,' said Jerry, the cheerful owner. He leant over the counter. 'By the way, me bum's still itchy. That cream done no good.'

Great, an impromptu consultation. 'I better have another look.'

Jerry glanced around and started to loosen his belt.

Vince put his hand up. 'Not here, mate!' He nodded toward the clinic. 'Make an appointment.'

He looked at the food on offer. Time to lift my game, he thought. 'Forget the pie and coffee. Better give me that nori roll, the one with the brown rice. And a green juice.'

Jerry made up Vince's order with a grin. 'S'pose you gotta set the right example, eh Doc?' He gave his rear end a scratch. 'See ya soon next door.'

Back at the clinic, Vince went through his emails while he ate his lunch. *Blah, blah, blah*, he thought as the various specialists' reports and pathology results flashed past, then a letter from Medical Practitioners' Board of Australia pulled him up. Fast.

Dear Dr Hanrahan,

We have received a complaint from Mr Dustin Cartwright about your handling of the birth of his daughter, Skylah, in February this year. He claims she suffered brain damage during the delivery and as a result has failed to thrive, has a small head, and is behind in her milestones. Mr Cartwright is having the baby assessed by a paediatrician and plans to initiate legal action regarding this matter. Professor Lachlan McKenzie will be in contact with you to discuss the ramifications of this complaint. We suggest you contact your MDO as a matter of urgency.'

BUGGER!

Vince took a deep breath, forwarded the letter to the Medical Defence Organisation, had a quick chat with the claims manager, then struggled through his afternoon list.

* * *

He arrived at the car park next to the yacht club at six forty-five and sidled Benny in next to the familiar white Mazda SUV. Elena was sitting inside the car scrutinising her iPad. He jumped out and tapped on the passenger side window.

'Hey, Sarge,' he said, pointing to his watch, 'you going to sit in there all day?'

She shook her head and got out of the car. 'Don't tell me, held up at the office.'

'Something like that.'

They did some stretches on the boardwalk, then trotted down onto the sand.

The sun was sinking fast and the beach was deserted, but the tide was out and there was a wide expanse of sand stretching off around the crescent-shaped Lady Bay. They set off at a brisk pace and ran in silence apart from their rhythmic breathing and the water lapping. After passing the surf club, they ascended onto the track behind the dunes and continued up to Point Ritchie and paused for a break. They looked out to sea and watched the last glow of the sun sink behind the breakwater and then down in front to the Hopkins River mouth.

'Never mind Machu Picchu and the Taj Mahal,' Vince said after a few minutes when his breathing had slowed enough for him to talk. 'This is my all-time favourite view.'

'Yeah,' replied Elena, 'it's not bad.'

'You're hard to please, Sarge. S'pose you think Uluru's just an okay sort of a rock.'

She shrugged and smiled, transforming her face in a way that made Vince's heart skip a beat.

'I guess you're even underwhelmed by Tallangadeet?'

'No. That place is seriously impressive.'

Tallangadeet was the Carlisle property and consisted of five thousand acres of prime grazing country. Vince had seen the place when Mrs Carlisle had opened it up to the public as a fundraiser for the local hospital. The homestead was a blue stone mansion with deep verandas and surrounded by a magnificent park-style garden. Vince had learned from a farming mate that most of the original fifteen thousand acres had been sold off to Chinese investors to fund old Robert 'Bobbo' Carlisle's gambling debts. The grandeur of the property was in stark contrast to the modest Genovesi dairy farm down near Timboon—worlds apart.

'How did you meet young squire Will?'

'His wife was killed five years ago on her way into town. Cleaned up by a truck on the highway. I was the first uniform on the scene and had to go back to Tallangadeet and tell him what had happened.'

'I never knew that,' Vince said with a shudder.

'She was just pregnant with their first child. We kept in touch.' Elena stared out at the ocean for a moment, then took a breath and turned her head to face him. 'I had a chat with Father Kelly this morning.'

Vince's respiratory rate started to speed up again. 'Been meaning to give Kookaburra a ring myself. How's he doing?'

'Still shocked, I think,' said Elena, 'but he gave me a description of the woman he saw visiting the Monsignor that Sunday morning.'

'So … she's your main suspect?'

'Let's just say she's a person of interest to us.' She glanced into the darkness. 'She had the opportunity. When we find her, we'll look for a motive.'

'Was it someone familiar to him?'

'He reckoned he knew her from somewhere but couldn't place her. Early forties. Leather jacket and jeans. Athletic build. Around my height. Greying blond hair with a purple streak at the front.'

Vince felt a sudden lurch in his stomach.

'Ring any bells, Doc?'

Really should tell her. 'Nope.' A shiver passed through his body. 'Tell you what though, it's getting a bit fresh up here—we better make tracks.'

They set off back down the beach, ran in silence through the darkness until they reached the car park, and went their different ways.

∗ ∗ ∗

It was after seven when Vince got home. He fed Deefer, jumped in the shower, shoved a frozen beef stroganoff dinner in the microwave, and collapsed on the couch.

'Not too much beef in this crap,' he told the dog as he forked up some of the brown gooey mass on his plate. *Yuck! Maybe I should look at that healthy whole food app.* As he cast the meal to one side, his mobile started singing.

'G'day, Trish.'

'Evening, Vinny,' she said. 'How goes the battle, brother?'

'Fair to middling,' he said. 'How's life in the fast lane?'

She laughed. 'Same old. Kids, work—work, kids.'

'What's that wild man Paddy up to?'

'Doing renos for hard to please inner-city professionals.'

'Long as they're good payers,' said Vince. 'What about those urban terrorists?'

'Fine thanks. Fighting, playing footy, and turning their mother's hair grey. And your girls?'

'Had them down here before Easter,' he replied. 'I really enjoyed it, but they are growing up so fast, and … and …' his voice faltered, 'they're turning into strangers.'

'I'm sure that's not true,' said Trisha. 'You need to get yourself down here more often and stay involved in their lives.'

'Thing is, Warrnambool's getting to be almost home now. I feel like a fish out of water in Melbourne.'

'But aren't you moving back here when you've done your time?'

Vince laughed. Bitter more than amused. 'That's the plan, sis.' *Assuming I don't get struck off altogether!*

'You know it's Dad's eightieth on Sunday, right?'

Shit, is it? 'Yeah, course I know.'

'I'm going to bring him home here for a slap-up lunch—roast beef, his favourite. I want you and your girls to be there.' She paused. 'Lydia's welcome too.'

'But Dad won't even know what's going on.'

'*So?* I'm determined to keep this family together, Vinny.' Steely voice. 'What's left of it.'

25

Next morning Vince went straight to Shirley's consulting room. She was on the phone and motioned for him to sit. He dropped the letter from the Board on her desk and flopped into the patient chair.

'Well, Cheryl,' she said, 'you just gotta take cranberries juice and drink more water to stop these UTIs. And after horizontal folk dancing,' she added with a cackle, 'have a slash before you shut eyes.'

Shirley listened to the reply and rolled her eyes as she read the letter, then hung up.

'Jeepers, Rooned. You in the deep doggy doo. I told you she was an FKL.'

Vince laughed in spite of himself. 'FLK, Shirl. "Funny-Looking Kid".' This politically incorrect acronym was commonly used in the obstetric and paediatric worlds he used to inhabit to describe newborns of odd appearance.

'Whatevs,' Shirley responded with a shrug.

'Pete Paras referred the babe to Natalie Isaacs,' said Vince. 'She confirmed Skylah had microcephaly and delayed milestones and is arranging bloods and an MRI.'

'How did you get that report if you weren't the referring doc?'

'I just rang up Gloria at Nat's office and asked for it. She and I are old mates.'

Shirley shook her head. 'You a bad boy, cutting off corners all the time.'

Vince pointed at the letter. 'This could turn into serious shit. I've got to know what's going on.'

'Let's wait till the MRI, champ. There's bulk other causes for small head than birth injury.' She paused. 'But maybe ring up your medical defence mob just in case.'

All roads lead to Rome.

* * *

He got home that night to find a container of freshly cooked vegetable soup on his kitchen table, along with some grated cheese and a bread roll. *As least Mrs H hasn't turned against me.* He heated it up, sat at his tiny table, and gulped it down in five minutes flat. After washing out the container, he walked around to his neighbour's back door and knocked loudly. Kieran came to the door.

'Hi, Dr Vince. C-c-can we go fishing this weekend?'

'G'day, Super K. I've got footy on Saturday, then I should go down to Melbourne for my dad's birthday. Sorry, mate.'

Mrs Harrington appeared in the hallway.

'Thanks for the food, Mrs H,' said Vince. 'It was delicious.'

'No trouble,' she said, wiping her hands on her apron. 'I hear Dustin's been getting stuck into you. I told Tracey that you wouldn't have done nothing wrong.' She nodded barely perceptibly toward Kieran. 'Things don't always turn out right with babies. Nobody's fault.'

'I guess they're both worried about Skylah. It's understandable.'

She rubbed her thumb and index finger together. 'Dustin's just after a quick buck. Never done a day's work in his life.'

'Do you reckon he'd knock the kids around, Mrs H? Or the baby?'

Mrs Harrington gave a brief shake of her head and the shutters came down. 'Night. Make sure you go to your dad's birthday.' She pointed a pudgy index finger at his chest. 'Family's everything.'

* * *

Vince settled in for a night on the couch and picked up a novel. Sarah Bell was in a local book club and passed the books onto Vince after each meeting. In the old days, he and Sarah had a shared love of literature, but Vince had become addicted to TV series and staring at the wall and his reading had waned. He opened the current book, a new Ian McEwan—one of his favourite authors, but also flicked on *The Bureau*, a series the twins had given him. Neither claimed his attention and fifteen minutes later he woke to his singing mobile.

'G'day, Kookaburra.' He turned down the TV and picked up the book that had slid off his lap.

'Evening, Vince. Hope I'm not interrupting anything.'

'Not at all. How are things?'

'Not too bad. Bit busy with Dennis gone. Sorry I didn't make it to the band practice.'

'We cancelled it. I couldn't get there either. Can't they send another priest to help you out?'

Luke laughed. 'Not likely. Vocations have dried up.'

'Can't say I'm surprised.'

There was a pause. 'A woman came to see the Mons that Sunday morning, Vince.'

'So I heard.'

'She didn't want to give me her name but said she had an appointment with him.'

'Go on.'

Another pause. 'I think it was Joe's wife Jane.'

'Can't imagine what Jane would be doing there,' said Vince.

'The thing is, I asked her why she wanted to see the Mons.'

'Yeah?'

'And she told me that Dennis had been part of the Church's cover-up of paedophile priests.'

'Uh huh,' said Vince.

Vince heard a nervous swallow. 'She said she had proof that Dennis had molested boys from St Bernard's. And that she'd sent a letter about it to the bishop.'

'Anything else?'

'She told me that's why her husband had killed himself.' He paused again. 'It was then I realised who she was.'

Looks like the cat's well and truly out of the bag.

'Okay,' said Vince. 'It *was* Jane. She'd told me all of that too.'

'I was so angry!' said Luke, raising his voice. 'I broke bread with that man every day for the last five years!'

There followed a full minute of silence. Vince could imagine his friend's emotional and spiritual turmoil.

'Have you told Elena Genovesi it was Jane?'

'Not yet.'

Luke paused again. 'But you know I'll have to.'

* * *

Saturday afternoon found Vince at the Reid Oval, home ground of the Snapper's archrivals, Warrnambool. It was always a grudge match and today was no exception. At half-time, the Snappers were seventeen points behind and kicking into a strong breeze in the last quarter. So far there had been no injuries and Vince's medical skills had not been required.

Big Brody summoned him over as they walked off after the three-quarter huddle, during which Brody had exhorted the players to 'kick some bloody goals and knock these fucken peacocks over!'

'You're earning your pay easy today, Doc,' he remarked.

Brody pointed toward a forlorn track-suited figure talking to some of the players. 'When's Maxxy gunna be ready to play again?'

Max Saunders was a talented young indigenous footballer from Framlingham, a former Aboriginal mission settlement twenty kilometres out of Warrnambool on the Hopkins River. He'd kicked over sixty goals last season and Vince knew the coach regarded him as a potential match winner.

'You know hamstrings take a long time,' said Vince. 'It's not even a month yet.'

'Fair enough. Bloody hard without a full forward. And he's a ripping young bloke.'

They reached the boundary and sat in the coach's dugout.

'Have they worked out who killed O'Shannassey yet?'

Vince shook his head. 'Don't think so.'

'Blokes would'a been lining up.'

'Keep your voice down, Brodes, or someone will be pointing the finger at you.'

The big man laughed. 'Don't worry, Doc. It wasn't me.' He nodded toward his team, now dispersing into their positions. 'I was at the recovery session that Sunday after the practice match the day before.' He shook his head. 'That's when Maxxy did his hammie. Just doin' some sprints on the boundary.'

'So you missed Easter Sunday mass?' asked Vince.

The coach shrugged.

'You're a Mick, aren't you?'

Brody laughed again. '*Used* to be.' He gestured at the players. 'These blokes are my religion nowadays.'

* * *

The last quarter revival failed to materialise for the hapless Snappers and they went down by five goals. Vince went to the rooms to see if he was needed. He noticed Travis Brody talking to the stand-in full forward, who had kicked a total of two points. Travis's eyes were flashing and arms waving. Looked like he was attempting to explain where he felt the player had gone wrong.

'Leave the poor bloke be,' said Brody, leading Travis away. 'You don't know what you're talking about, son. This is no place for the likes of you.' He pointed at his temple, rolled his eyes, and patted the glum player on the back. 'Just ignore him,' he added. 'That's what I do.'

Vince looked at a couple of sprained joints and a bruised rib or two, then went out and jumped into the waiting Benny. He'd packed the car in the morning to ensure a quick getaway, but it was still almost dark by the time he hit the Melbourne road and yellow lights were twinkling in the houses along the way.

He turned on the car radio to discover Geelong had been pipped at the post by three points against Richmond at the MCG and was shocked to discover that he really didn't care. In the good old days, he and Joey would've have analysed the game to the nth degree. *Not anymore.*

He put on a Springsteen CD and maxed the volume. Anything to avoid thinking about Skylah Cartwright or Jane Schultz. *Or Joey Hanrahan.*

It was almost nine-thirty when Vince pulled over and parked in front of Trisha and Paddy's Brunswick terrace. The boys were in bed and there was a lamb tagine bubbling on the stove. Vince embraced them both, drained a glass of sparkling water, and sat in front of the fire, nibbling on the delicious mezze plate Paddy had prepared. Trisha put on the couscous, then sat down on her husband's knee and gave him a kiss. Cosy domestic bliss. In the background, Paul Kelly was singing 'I've been careless, I lost my tenderness ...'

No tenderness in my life these days. It's all hard edges.

* * *

Sunday morning Vince and Paddy took the boys off to footy. They all played for the local junior club, the oldest two in the under tens and the youngest in the under eights. They had to travel over to Camberwell and it was after eleven when they returned.

'So much for being home early,' Trisha said as she opened the door. 'You better get that Weber fired up, Patrick. I just got a call from Janey—she's coming after all.'

Vince's phone beeped in his pocket. He pulled it out: a message from Lydia. 'Lydia's on her way too, sis,' he said, 'and the girls.'

'Bit of notice would've been good,' replied Trisha. 'But Dad will be pleased to see them all.' She glanced at the time. 'Nearly eleven-thirty. You better go and pick him up. Harry, you go with Uncle Vinny. Noah and Liam—in the shower. Paddy, get that beef on and I'll do some more vegies.'

'Looking forward to seeing your cousins, Harry?' Vince asked as they headed over to South Melbourne.

'S'pose,' said Harry. 'We see them pretty often anyway. Their mum and dad bring them over to our place.' He frowned. 'Are you their dad too, Uncle Bins?'

'I'm their *only* dad, mate. That other man is just their mother's boy-friend.'

Shit, he thought as they pulled up outside the nursing home, *I'm getting photoshopped out of the family!*

Old Mick looked bewildered but happy to come for a drive, and they arrived back in Brunswick to find the party in full swing. Paddy was pouring drinks, Lydia and Jane were chatting away in the back yard, Tessa was helping Trisha make a salad, and Georgie was teaching her cousins some dance moves in the hallway. Paddy gave Mick a light beer and they all broke into a rousing 'Happy Birthday', then sat down to lunch.

The afternoon passed in a blur of chatter and laughter. Vince tried to corner Jane, who no longer had the purple streak in her hair, but there was always someone else around. She seemed to be avoiding him. By four o'clock Mick was starting to look weary and Trisha suggested Vince take him back.

'Least we've got a designated driver these days,' she said with a laugh, sipping on her wine.

'Why don't you come for the drive, Jane?' said Vince, sensing his chance.

Mick fell asleep on the way back and the staff brought out a wheelchair to convey him back to his room. Vince and Jane returned to the car and sat in silence for a few minutes, looking at the swans strolling across the road to Albert Park Lake.

'A woman came to visit the Monsignor just before ten that morning,' Vince said after a while. He turned his head and looked at her. 'Was that you?'

'Lots of women in Warrnambool. What makes you think it was me?'

Time to stop pussyfooting around. 'Not with your hair and your … your motivation. Anyway, Luke Kelly recognised you. And he'll be telling the coppers.'

She paused, then nodded. 'I thought he might've figured it out.'

They both watched as a column of cyclists circled around Lakeside Drive.

Got to ask the question. 'Did you kill O'Shannassey?'

'Part of me would've liked to.' She turned to face him. 'But no, I didn't. I just wanted to make him *own* his crime.'

Hope the coppers accept that version of events. 'So what happened?'

She sat in silence for a few minutes, then took a deep breath and slowly let it out. 'O'Shannassey had refused to take my calls. And you,' she glanced at Vince, 'hadn't responded to my email, so I decided to ambush him. I drove across from Port and went to the presbytery. Father Kelly was on his way out and I said I had an appointment with the Monsignor.' She looked out at the lake. 'I explained what it was about, even showed him O'Leary's letter. He let me in and I went through to the office.' She swallowed. 'O'Shannassey was sitting at his desk writing some notes.'

She paused and took another deep breath. 'I told him who I was and slapped the letter down on his desk. He got up and smiled at me. "You're barking up the wrong tree, Mrs Hanrahan," he said. "I remember this O'Leary, a nice boy. But he's mistaken. I wasn't at those altar-boy weekends. I delegated that task to one of my brother priests. His name has slipped my mind." He picked up the letter and thrust it back at me. "I don't respond to scurrilous myth-making. If you don't cease this harassment, you'll be hearing from my lawyers. Now, if you'll excuse me," he said, "I need to finish my homily."'

Jane put her head into her hands and started sobbing.

'Did you believe him?' asked Vince.

'*Course* not. I told him he was lying and that we were coming after him and we were going to press charges and—' She slumped back in the seat like a deflated balloon.

'So you read him the riot act and left him to it.'

She nodded.

'How long were you there?'

'Fifteen minutes all up. I was back in Port Fairy by ten-thirty.'

They sat in silence for a few minutes, then Vince fired up Benny's engine, dropped Jane at the station and headed back to Brunswick. He got there to find the birthday lunch had broken up. Lydia and the girls were on the front porch making their farewells, Trisha and Paddy at the door and the boys rushing around their cousins madly.

'Nice of you to drop by,' Lydia said with a frown.

'Took the scenic route, did you, Vinny?' asked Trisha.

'You missed my Persian love cake, Bins,' said Tessa, disappointment evident in her voice.

'Not to mention the washing up,' added Paddy.

'Sorry guys,' said Vince. 'Just had to sort out a few things with Jane.'

'You know what?' Lydia said as she and the girls walked out the gate. 'Time you let the past go,' she nodded toward the twins, 'and focused on the here and now.'

Vince stood out on the road long after the sleek Merc had vanished up the street, then trudged into the house. Trisha and Paddy were tidying up. He volunteered to shower the boys and get them ready for bed.

'Bit late for you to be heading to the 'Bool now,' said Trisha. 'You'd better stay here and make an early start.'

'I don't have to go back till the afternoon. Got a couple of meetings in town in the morning.'

He helped her fold down the sofa and make it up as a spare bed.

'What's up with Janey?' she said. 'Apart from the obvious.'

Vince tossed the pillows on the couch. 'She's involved with Broken Rights, an organisation who try to track down those paedophile clerics and get them charged. She's hell-bent on finding out who abused Joey.' *Mightn't let on that she'd actually found him.* 'She wants her day in court.'

'But surely it was more of a systemic Church issue than just a single perpetrator,' said Trisha, placing a doona on top. 'It was the cover-up and lack of compassion that really needs exposing.'

Vince nodded. 'For sure. And they are working on that too. But Joey implied to Jane there was the one particular priest who … damaged him, and she feels she needs to confront that bastard.'

Trisha shrugged. 'It may not be possible to do that. It was a long time ago.' She looked at him. 'And it's not your job to chase after this person, Vincent. You need to concentrate on your own back yard.'

So I hear.

They said their goodnights, and as he lay there in the dark a question kept rotating around on his mental carousel.

Was Jane telling the truth?

* * *

In what seemed like seconds later, Vince was woken up by the raucous sounds of his three nephews preparing to jump on him.

'Get up, Uncle Bins, it's a school day, lazy bum!' He glanced at the kitchen clock as he wrestled with the boys. Seven-forty-five.

'Noah, Harry, and Liam, leave Uncle Vinny alone and sit up for breakfast!'

After an hour of organised pandemonium, the house fell silent again—the boys off to school and both parents to work. Vince stripped the sofa bed, tidied up the kitchen, and had a shower. His freshly pressed shirt and trousers were hanging in the bathroom and after a quick breakfast he found himself blinking in the autumn sunshine at the tram stop with a cacophony of Monday-morning city sounds as a backdrop.

I don't miss this, he thought as he wedged himself into the packed tram, all the other passengers avoiding his gaze or absorbed in their mobile phones.

* * *

His first appointment was with the claims manager at his MDO. Bridget Ryan had been at the Victorian Medical Defence Agency for many years and had been a contemporary of Vince and Lydia's back in university.

'Morning, Vincent,' she said, shaking his hand. 'We meet again.'

He looked around the office. 'This place is getting way too familiar to me.'

She smiled and opened the file in front of her. A fat file, Vince noted.

'And this case is across two jurisdictions,' she said, 'just like the previous one.'

Last year one of Vince's patients had died in labour and the VMDA had been responsible for the antenatal care, which had been conducted in his rooms, and the Victorian Managed Insurance Authority for the actual labour because it occurred in a public hospital.

'Just trying to keep you on your toes.'

'At least the *first* one was in a private hospital. That made it much simpler from a litigation viewpoint.'

'I don't actually plan these things.' Vince pointed at the file. 'What say we get on with it.'

'Okay,' said Bridget. 'First of all, have you received any correspondence from any lawyers regarding this matter?'

Vince shook his head.

'That's a good sign.' She pulled out a document. 'We were able to get a copy of Dr Isaac's letter.'

'I've read it,' said Vince. 'Be fair to say Nat is not my biggest fan. I tend to push the paeds around a bit.'

Bridget raised her well-groomed eyebrows. 'Clearly. The key issue,' she went on, 'is whether this baby's problems are connected to your management of the labour.'

He nodded.

'I see from your statement that you felt it was too late for a C Section and there was no choice but to proceed with this Keilland's forceps rotation due to a persistent posterior position and foetal distress.'

He nodded again.

'Playing the devil's advocate, how long since you had performed such a procedure?'

Vince cast his mind back. 'Back before I got in strife with the college, Bridg. Be two years. But I've done stacks of Kielland's in the past.'

'And was the labour being monitored adequately?'

He snorted. 'Tracey was already in late second stage when she arrived. The girls barely had time to do her obs and put her on the CTG.'

Bridget raised her eyebrows.

'A cardiotocograph, which monitors the foetal heart and the woman's contractions.'

'And what was that showing?'

'Foetal distress,' said Vince. 'Meaning, time to get that baby delivered. ASAP.'

'And the bruising on her head?'

'Usual outcome with a forceps rotation.'

She studied the file for a few more minutes. 'Dr Isaacs states that a lack of oxygen during the difficult birth may have caused the small head and developmental delay.'

Vince stood, hands clenched. 'That bub would've *died* if I hadn't pulled her out!' He jabbed a finger at the report on Bridget's desk. 'There are lots of other possible causes for her problems.'

'Such as?'

He sat down again and ticked off the fingers of one hand. 'Infection during pregnancy, chromosomal abnormalities, premature fusion of the skull sutures, maternal drug and alcohol use, etc, etc.'

Bridget paused, then looked across at Vince. 'We'll have to wait for Dr Isaac's full report. Then we will seek an independent paediatric opinion ourselves. Let's hope you're right and one of those other possibilities comes through.'

Vince shrugged.

'Otherwise, with your record … we may not be able to defend you.'

* * *

Vince walked out onto Elizabeth Street. It was a chilly day, but he was perspiring freely. He walked across to Bourke Street and stepped onto the tram. Next stop was the Royal College of Obstetricians and Gynaecologists headquarters in East Melbourne.

Vince's *bete noir*, Professor Lachlan McKenzie, sat at his expansive desk and looked at Vince over the top of his half-moon glasses.

'We have the report from Dr Isaacs and have sought an expert opinion from Professor Jobling as well. We are still waiting on the results of the baby's MRI scan, chromosomal array, and other lab work.'

Jim 'Jobs' Jobling was head of neonatal paediatrics at the Royal Women's Hospital and an old sparring partner of Vince's. *Pity I wasn't kinder to him in the old days.* Obstetricians were supposed to give paediatricians a heads-up early in a complicated labour so they could be prepared for a potential urgent call to resuscitate a flat baby. Or they could wait till the last minute, then click their imperious fingers. Vince had been in the second camp.

'This threat of legal action puts the Medical Board in an awkward position. Damned awkward,' added McKenzie, adjusting his spotted bow tie.

'Sorry about that, mate,' said Vince. 'My main aim in life is to ensure the Board sleep well at night.'

McKenzie narrowed his eyes and frowned. 'You need to take this seriously, Vincent.'

'Really?' said Vince. 'You could knock me over with a feather.'

'The Board has decided you should be banned from managing all obstetric cases until this, um, *matter* is resolved.'

'That's just churlish!' exclaimed Vince, slapping his hands on the desk. 'I'm no use to Shirley Tiang if I can't—'

'*And*,' McKenzie cut in, 'if you're found guilty of professional negligence, mismanaging Mrs Cartwright's labour resulting in birth hypoxia for the infant,' he took off his glasses and gave them a polish with a crisply folded handkerchief, 'your registration to practice any sort of medicine may be in jeopardy.'

Vince jumped to his feet. 'What a load of crap! You know as well as I do that the best-conducted labours don't always produce perfect babies. We're dealing with biology here!'

'You know that I will always advocate for you,' said McKenzie, replacing his glasses. 'But the members of the Board are running out of patience.'

Vince shook his head and walked out, got into the empty lift, and pressed the door shut. 'Fuck, fuck, FUCK!' he shouted as the door reopened and a startled looking young office girl joined him.

He trammed it back out to Brunswick, unlocked his car, and headed out of town. As he sped down the Princes Highway, his heart was thumping and his mind was spinning. He felt like he was also speeding away from his old life, his family, and his career.

Permanently.

26

The rest of the week passed in a blur. Vince had only half his mind on the job, just doing what he had to do. After his last patient on Friday evening, he shut the door, took a deep breath and put his head in his hands. The relief of getting through to the weekend was washed away by a tsunami of anxiety.

He picked up his phone. 'Hey, Shirl, are you finished?'

'Dusted and done, champ. Time for a bucket of sav blancs and fishy pho.'

'Sounds delicious,' said Vince. 'I didn't know you did Vietnamese.'

'Gareth is cooking, Rooned. It's therapy for him after treating crazies all week.'

'Good for him,' he responded. 'On another matter, I went to see Lachie McKenzie on Monday.'

'You still in the poo?'

'Too right.' He paused. 'And they've banned me from the labour ward.'

Shirley produced a long, low whistle. 'Me and the Prez are going to struggle with all these mids,' she said. 'Tasman not allowed to do 'em cos she's a trainee. Might have to get another soldier.'

'What are you saying?'

'Put this way, bud. If that little McKenzie doesn't let you back in the labour ward soon, I'll have to look otherwhere.'

Shit, if Shirley dumps me, I'm really screwed. I better pull the boots back on and get back in the game. 'Do you mind reading over Tracey

Cartwright's file with me for a minute? Want to make sure I did all the right things.'

Minutes later Shirley was sitting alongside him. He brought up Tracey's medical record and they looked at his notes from her first antenatal visit.

Vince had documented that he'd advised Tracey to avoid soft cheeses, raw fish, and processed meats; advised her to not smoke or drink; and recommended extra folate and iodine. He'd also done an antenatal depression screen and discussed appropriate exercise.

'Good job. Bring up her first heap of tests.'

Tracey's antenatal lab work showed her routine antenatal blood tests were normal and she'd been immune to rubella, chicken pox, and other viruses.

'What you do CMV serology for?' said Shirley, pointing at the screen. 'No vaccine for that germ. Just makes the girls worry if they not immune.'

Vince nodded. 'I reckon it's still best to know, then you can advise them how to avoid contact with cytomegalovirus during the pregnancy—you know, careful hand washing, avoiding body fluids from little kids, etc.'

'Anyways, you got a baseline,' she responded with a shrug. 'If her CMV level's gone up then she must have been exposed to that bugger during the pregnancy, which could explain this sprog's issues.' She nodded, earrings jangling, and clapped her hands. 'Then back on the baby roster for Rooned!'

'Settle down, Shirl. That's a really long shot.'

They looked at the rest of Tracey's antenatal record in silence. Her first-trimester screening test for foetal abnormalities, ultrasound scans, and routine test for gestational diabetes were all in order.

'Looks like no sign of any maternal infections during the pregnancy, champ, and I see she was GBS negative.'

Vince had taken the usual thirty-seven-week vaginal swab for the Group B Streptococcus, a potential cause of severe infection in the newborn.

'You did all the right stuff,' said Shirley, getting up. 'Maybe Tracey got on the grogs.'

He laughed. 'I doubt it. Her mum would've made sure that didn't happen.' Vince knew Mrs Harrington's husband had been a champion drinker, which had resulted in his early demise just after Kieran's birth.

* * *

That night Vince arrived at Fanny's early. He sat down and ordered a mineral water and a glass of Mornington Peninsula Pinot Noir, then picked up the wine glass, swirled the crimson contents and inhaled the fruity aroma. Maybe just one sip—

'Evening, Doc. I believe that's my drink you've got there.'

Elena moved the glass to her side of the table, put her hand on Vince's shoulder, then bent down and gave him a kiss on the cheek. The pliant softness of her lips against his evening stubble gave him a fleeting frisson of warmth and reassurance. More maternal than romantic.

'How's your week been, Doc?' said Elena, taking her seat. She was looking gorgeous in a pretty, white lacy top and a chunky blue necklace, her casual appearance leavened with a business-like manner.

Vince frowned. 'Not so good.' He nodded in the direction of the clinic. 'Trooble down mill,' he added in a faux Lancashire accent.

She raised her eyebrows.

'You don't want to know.'

Elena sipped her wine. 'Frank Doyle came in to see me today.'

'I'd have thought Frankie was more into wills than crime,' said Vince.

'Mr Doyle's the chair of the Monsignor's All God's Children foundation and he told me there were irregularities in the financials,' said Elena. 'Pauline Murphy alerted him to the issue.'

'I didn't know Pauline was involved with the foundation.'

'She's the treasurer.'

'Makes sense,' said Vince. 'She's an accountant.'

Elena leant in. 'The Monsignor had been making unexplained withdrawals from the foundation's bank account and it was struggling to pay the bills.'

'Putting his fingers in the till, eh?' said Vince. 'The old fox.'

'More a case of not keeping track of expenses, according to Pauline.

Seems the Monsignor didn't bother writing stuff down. He was a control freak though—no one else was authorised to access the accounts.'

Vince shook his head. 'I couldn't care less about the old prick's bookkeeping. It's his moral hypocrisy that sticks in my craw.'

They both sat back and silence fell.

After a few minutes, Elena picked up her glass, put it down again, and looked at Vince straight in the eye. She waved up the Cone of Silence.

'We've identified the woman with the purple streak in her hair.'

'Uh huh.'

'A Ms Jane Schultz. From Horsham.' She paused. '*Your* sister-in-law.'

Vince nodded.

'Father Kelly recognised her. Eventually. Did you know she was in town?'

He took a deep breath. 'I didn't know at the time, Sarge. I found out later.'

She frowned. 'I'm wondering why you didn't tell me.'

'Just needed to speak to her first.'

'And?'

'What is this, Elena, an interrogation?'

'Wouldn't want to think you were hiding anything.'

Vince drained his water glass in one gulp. 'Jane went to see O'Shannassey to confront him about abusing Joey. But he was alive and kicking when she left.' He spread his hands out across the table. 'Lay down, misere.'

Elena paused as the waiter brought their entrees, then sat forward. 'So she told me. But she had the opportunity and a strong motive,' she said. '*And* we found her prints on the crucifix attached to the rosary beads.'

'How the hell did you ...?' Vince half stood up. 'You mean you've been to see her without telling me?'

'Keep your voice down, Doc. There's a lot you haven't been telling me, too, by the way. I drove up to Horsham on Wednesday and interviewed Jane at the local police station.'

'Bloody hell!' said Vince. 'You haven't arrested her?'

Elena put her finger up to her lips. 'Just gathering information, that's all.' She paused. 'As far as we know, Jane Shultz was the last person to see the Monsignor. So she remains a person of interest.'

Vince picked up his fork and chased the chilli prawns around the plate. He nibbled on one but lost interest and pushed the food away, his mind spinning. He knew Jane was devastated and vengeful, but surely she *couldn't* have and *wouldn't* have killed O'Shannassey! She was strong enough, with all that athletics training, but she would've had to have taken leave of her senses to murder the bastard.

He swallowed some water and glanced at the part in Elena's glistening black hair as she bent over her food and fought to suppress his indignation. *Just doing her job, I guess.*

They finished their meals in virtual silence, confining themselves to occasional banal comments about the weather and the change in the colour of the tablecloths at Fanny's. *Like strangers*, thought Vince as they said their goodbyes thirty minutes later and went their separate ways.

* * *

Vince woke Sunday morning to the sound of rain drumming on the roof and leaking in through the ancient corrugated iron above the flimsy rear lean-to of the Snapper house. He'd tossed and turned during the early part of the night, images of babies with small heads competing with visions of his sister-in-law in jail.

The precipitation had started the day before and had lasted all through the match between the Snappers and Cobden at South's home ground. The visitors had got home by a point. After Vince had sympathised with Mark Brody, examined a twisted ankle, and put some sutures into the ruckman's head, he'd headed home to dry out.

Deefer was whining at the back door. Vince let her in and she proceeded to plant her four feet and shake her wet and dirty coat all over the kitchen floor.

'Not there, you *stupid* dog!' shouted Vince. He pushed her outside and gave her some breakfast. 'Stay in the carport and dry out.' She barked in response. 'No, *no* walk.' He pointed at the sky. 'Can't you see it's raining?'

He went inside and collapsed on the couch. *Where do you get off, you cruel dickhead, taking it all out on a dumb animal?* Of all the possible guilty parties that had been swirling around in Vince's nocturnal theorising, Deefer wasn't even on the long list.

The rest of the day he spent dozing on the couch, a replay of *The Last Night of the Proms* on TV. When he and Lydia were living in London a lifetime ago, they'd attended the live performance. The annual telecast subsequently became a perennial family favourite. Despite the predictable music and the eccentric Union Jack and teddy bear waving Hooroo Henrys and Henriettas, they all enjoyed every minute of it. They laughed when the formidable buxom Wagnerian soprano strode out, shed tears to *Jerusalem*, and bobbed up and down during the sailors' hornpipe. The whole thing offended Vince's Irish heritage, but he was willing to set that aside for the spectacle and the familial bonding. This time there was no one on the couch but him, and another tradition seemed to have disappeared. He was starting to wonder what his future would be without this precious shared history.

The sudden sound of thunderous knocking the front door aroused Vince from his slumbering soiree.

'D-D-Doctor Vince,' called out Kieran, walking straight into the house. 'M-M-Mum says can you come? Travis is on the r-r-roof!'

'Hang on,' said Vince, getting to his feet and putting on his shoes. He grabbed his raincoat and followed Kieran into the next-door front yard. Mrs Harrington was standing in the rain, wearing an enormous puffer jacket and looking up onto the roof of her house, where Travis—naked, apart from his Doc Martens—was attempting to dismantle the TV aerial.

'Is your tele on the blink, Mrs H?' asked Vince.

'No, no, he says it's talking to him and he wants to bust it.' Mrs Harrington threw her hands in the air. 'Travis,' she shouted at the pale manic figure up above. 'You'll catch your death. Come inside to the fire.'

'Hop down, mate,' called Vince. 'It's a bit slippery up there.'

'Never!' Travis shouted in response, wrestling with the metal rods and poles. 'Not until I've destroyed this evil communications empire! The Vatican are trying to control our thoughts!'

Vince shook his head and pulled out his phone. 'Go on inside, Carmel,' he said. 'I'll see what I can do.'

It took the combined forces of the paramedics, the fire brigade, the police, and the CAT team almost an hour to coax Travis down. He was still railing against the world in general and the Catholic Church in particular as they wrapped him in a blanket and put him in the back of the ambulance to cart him off to the hospital for assessment.

Mrs Harrington emerged from the front door and watched them drive away. 'Where are they taking him? I don't want him to get into trouble. He don't mean no harm.'

'They'll transfer him to the Lewana Clinic, the acute psych ward. He'll have to be admitted involuntarily and get sorted out. Shirley Tiang's husband will look after him.'

'I better ring Geraldine.'

Vince noticed the Cartwright boys standing behind her and giggling.

'I could see his dick,' said Toby.

'Ya couldn't,' replied Jayden. 'It's even smaller than yours.'

'Get back inside, you boys,' said Mrs Harrington. 'Come in yourself, Dr Vince, and I'll make us all a nice cuppa.'

Vince walked through to the kitchen to find Tracey sitting at the table, cigarette in one hand and a wine glass in the other, baby Skylah howling in a cot in the corner.

'Come to Granny,' said Mrs Harrington, snatching up the infant. 'I've told you about that smoking and drinking, Tracey.' She kissed Skylah. 'If not for yourself then for your baby, for heaven's sake!'

'Mind your own business,' said Tracey. 'I gotta lot of stress, all right?'

Mrs H shook her head, raised her eyebrows at Vince, and continued to soothe the baby. Vince walked over and glanced at her. Skylah's head was certainly small, her eyes were close together and there was something unusual about her upper lip. A distant bell rang in Vince's medical student past. *What does that mean?*

'Leave her alone,' hissed Tracey. 'You're not her doctor no more.'

Vince put his hands up and stepped back. 'I might take a raincheck on the tea after all, Mrs H.'

'That's f-f-funny,' Kieran said with a giggle. 'Dr Vince is going to check on the rain.' He pointed out the window at the downpour. 'But you c-c-can see it from here.'

Vince walked out with Mrs H, Kieran close behind.

He nodded back into the house. 'Trace give the grog a bit of a hiding, does she, Carmel?'

She frowned and paused.

'Drinks like a f-f—' Kieran put in.

'That's enough from you, mister,' said Mrs H, shutting the door. 'Thanks for your help, Dr Vince.'

* * *

Vince returned home, changed out of his wet clothes, had a shower, and resumed his position on the couch. The *Proms* had finished, so he flicked through the TV channels, picked up the McEwan novel, and scanned the paper, but nothing grabbed him.

Instead he made his third attempt for the weekend to ring Jane.

'Hello, Vinny.'

He pulled himself into a sitting position. 'G'day, Jane. Did you get my messages?'

'Been busy. What's up?'

'Detective Sergeant Genovesi tells me she came up to speak with you.'

'She did.'

Vince paused. 'She told me your fingerprints were on the crucifix attached to those rosary beads.'

'So I gather.'

'How can you explain that?'

Her tone changed from passive aggressive to overt aggressive. 'I've had it with all these questions!' she said. 'What's it to you?'

Vince shook his head. 'The optics are really bad here, Janey. You had a motive, the opportunity, and your prints are on the murder weapon. You were the last person to see the man, for God's sake!'

She was silent for a full minute. 'When O'Shannassey told me I was mistaken, I got really angry,' she said, tone now quiet and considered. 'I saw those rosary beads hanging on a hook on the wall. I grabbed the crucifix and swung the beads around and hit him on the face.' She paused. 'Then I dropped them on the floor, turned around, walked out, and drove away.'

'Okay,' he said after a cautious pause, weighing up Jane's answer. 'But you've been lying all along. How do I know you're telling the truth now?'

'I don't care if you believe me or not.' Voice clipped and cold.

'I *want* to believe you, but you're making it really hard.'

'Don't worry, your pal Elena Genovesi said the same thing. Along with, "Hand over your passport and report to the police station every day".' She chuckled down the phone.

'Doesn't sound like a laughing matter to me,' said Vince.

'Listen to this, it's a crack up. It *wasn't* O'Shannassey who abused Joey at all.'

'What!'

Jane blew her nose. 'I spoke to Terry O'Leary's brother during the week. I should've talked to him earlier. He told me that "Dirty Dennis" was Father *Ambrose* Dennis, a younger priest from the cathedral who used take the boys down to Apollo Bay. O'Shannassey's nickname was "DOS" and he wasn't at those altar-boy weekends.'

'So what he told you was true,' said Vince.

'Yes, as it's turned out. The Mons was still guilty of covering up those crimes, but he didn't deserve what happened to him.'

'What's become of this Dirty Dennis?' asked Vince. 'I don't even remember him.'

'Disappeared off the face of the Earth.'

27

Vince sat in front of his laptop and watched Dr Myf Williams materialise from the silver screen.

'Morning, Vincent.'

'Hi, Myf. How's it going?'

'Good thanks. And you?'

He rubbed the stubble on his chin. 'Unlike the curate's egg,' he said, 'things for me are bad all the way through.'

'I understand from the Board that you're facing possible legal action about alleged negligent management of that labour.'

Vince jerked up from his customary slouch. 'You seem to hear about these things almost before I do.' He leant into the screen. 'I did *nothing* wrong that night; in fact, I saved that baby's life. There was no prolonged ischaemia and no brain injury from the forceps. It's a beat up!'

'How can you be so sure?'

Vince slumped back in his kitchen chair. 'Truth is, I can't.' He paused. 'Unless the paed's report exonerates me or I can find another cause for the baby's problems, I could be in big trouble.'

She nodded. 'Best to leave all that to the experts, Vincent. My concern is the state of your mental health.'

'You mean like, do I have low mood, severe anxiety, and insomnia?' He leant in again. 'Yes, yes, and yes.'

'Are you taking your meds and practising the mindfulness meditation?'

'Constantly.'

She looked unconvinced.

'When I'm not trying to keep my sister-in-law out of jail, that is.'

She frowned. 'Is this regarding the death of that priest?'

'Turns out the Monsignor wasn't fiddling around with my brother after all, but Jane believed he was. And the coppers have her in the gun.'

Myf's freckly face, with its halo of red curls, loomed up close. 'Vincent, listen to me. You can't be a vigilante crime solver here. If Jane's guilty she will have to face the consequences. You must let the police handle that and focus on things you *can* control. Same with the issue about this baby.' She pointed straight at the screen with her index finger. 'Wait until that report, and be advised by your MDO claims manager and lawyers. Don't take matters into your own hands.'

Vince shrugged and put out his arms, palms upward as if to say 'who, me?'

'I *know* you,' Myf added. She jabbed again at the screen. 'So, meditate and take your tablets—'

'That sounds strangely familiar—'

'And, most importantly, no *self*-medication.'

* * *

Vince jumped in the shower, dressed, shovelled down some stale cereal, did a quick ward round, and arrived at the clinic at ten to nine—for an eight-thirty start.

He stormed into his room to find Shirley and Lorraine seated there.

'No rush, Rooned,' said Shirley, pointing at the clock on the wall. 'Tasman has seen your first patient. Chick got sick of waiting.'

'*Tamsyn*,' said Lorraine.

'That's what I said.'

'And Dr Tiang has cleaned out your inbox,' added Lorraine. 'Repeat scripts, results, follow-ups and all.'

'Thanks, Shirl.'

She pointed at him from behind his desk. 'You need to lift your game, cobber.' In her other hand was a letter, which she brandished at him. 'Pistol Pete has requested the notes of the Cartwright family. Looks like they sack you.'

Dr Pete Paras was a partner in the GP clinic on the other side of town and Shirley's bitter rival. He'd been the main local GP obstetrician until Vince arrived and knocked him off his perch.

'Damn!' said Vince. 'I wanted to have a good look at that baby. I reckon she's got features of Foetal Alcohol Syndrome.'

'It's called Foetal Alcohol Spectrum Disorder these days. Get with the programs.'

'That'd be right,' said Vince. 'Everything's on a spectrum now.'

'Anyways,' Shirley continued, 'Pistol won't help you. He stick the daggers in. He don't forget and forgive.'

Once word had got around that Vince was a specialist obstetrician, many of Dr Paras's pregnant punters had jumped ship, despite Vince's legendary grumpiness.

He nodded and took a seat.

Lorraine held up an envelope. 'There's a letter for you from the Medical Board too. It's been sitting in your in-tray for days.'

Vince grabbed it, ripped it open, perused the single sheet, and passed it to Shirley.

'Interim report,' she said, then scanned the page. 'Looks like they exclude chromosomal abnormality and craniosynostosis—'

Lorraine frowned.

'Premature fusion of the skull sutures,' Vince translated.

'Still waiting on the TORCH bloods,' added Shirley.

'Toxoplasmosis, rubella, cytomegalovirus, and herpes. Potential mother-to-baby viruses,' Vince said for Lorraine's benefit.

'And the radiologists at the Royal Children's can't agree about the MRI. One say birth hypoxia, one say he dunno.' Shirley looked up. 'Final report in six weeks.'

She glanced at Lorraine and looked back at Vince. 'Anyways bud, the Board want my assessment about you.'

Shirley and Lorraine got up and Shirley did the head on one side thing.

Here's trouble.

'So pull your fingers out, head up and bum down.' She paused, leant over the desk, and pointed at him. 'Or I give bad mark and your whole career in the dunny.'

Vince shut the door behind them and sat behind his desk, head in his hands. He took three slow breaths and was about to call in the first patient when his mobile rang—Elena.

'Yep.'

'What are your plans for lunch today?' Direct and to the point. APU.

'Depends how virtuous I'm feeling by then, Sarge. Either some green stuff or a pie and sauce. Same venue either way—at my desk.'

She laughed. 'What about you meet me around one at Cannon Hill and I'll bring something in between those two extremes?'

With Shirley's words ringing in his ears, Vince glanced at his morning list—busy, busy, busy. He shrugged. *Blow it. Why not?*

'It's a date.'

28

It was a blowy, cold autumn day and the grey sea in the distance was studded with white horses. The breakwater, just visible in the far distance across the Lady Bay, was vanishing into the gloom. Vince pulled in next to the only other car, a police vehicle, hopped out of Benny, and slid into the other car's passenger's seat.

'G'day, Sarge,' he said. 'Bit formal in the cop car. You here on official business?'

'Always on duty in my game, Doc,' Elena answered with her characteristic enigmatic smile. 'Bit like yours.'

She handed over a paper napkin, a toasted roast beef and horseradish panini, and a steaming coffee.

They ate in silence for a few minutes, watching the ocean fade away as the car windows misted up. Soon the world outside disappeared and they were cocooned inside the vehicle.

'Thanks,' said Vince, wiping his hands and face with the napkin. 'That really hit the spot, but I'm sure we're not just here to fill our bellies and take in the non-existent view.'

Elena picked up a laptop from the backseat and turned it on. 'Want to show you some emails.' She passed it over to Vince.

He looked at the screen and started reading.

Dear Monsignor,

My husband, Joseph Hanrahan, was a boarder at St Bernard's in Ballarat. He was abused repeatedly by a Catholic priest and took his own life earlier this year. Broken Rights have proof that you not only protected these criminals but also were a perpetrator. You are responsible for the death of my husband.

Vince looked up.

'Scroll down, Doc, there's two more.'

I don't think you understand the situation—read the attached letter. FYI, Broken Rites is not 'a misguided bunch of fanatics', but a victim support group undertaking serious research. Deadly serious. We'll keep lifting rocks till we find all you spiders. Your denial is meaningless. Your refusal to meet me is a massive mistake. And, yes, thanks for asking, we have excellent legal advice. We are preparing a brief for the police and the Royal Commission. And the media.

Vince looked at the last one.

Threatening me with legal action is laughable. We have a QC on our team and we're on the side of the angels. You can't hide behind that collar forever. I'm heading down there to front you in your coward's castle. You'll get what's coming to you. Prepare yourself, Monsignor. I'll come like a thief in the night …

Vince passed the laptop back and stared at the foggy windscreen, his heart banging and chest tightening. *Better get an ECG. I'll have a bloody infarct the way I'm going.*

'Did you know about these threats?' Elena asked after a few minutes.

'No.' He pointed at the computer. 'But I get it that this all looks bad for Janey.'

'You're right on that one,' said Elena. 'Along with her Sunday morning visit and fingerprints on the murder weapon.' She looked across at Vince. '*Very* bad.'

'She didn't mean she was going kill him,' he responded. 'She just wanted him to own up to what he'd done. Janey wouldn't *murder* anyone.'

'You're hardly an objective commentator about that.'

Fair call.

Elena turned to face him. 'Why did you go to church that morning, Doc?' she asked. 'You told me you'd given that away years ago.'

He shrugged. 'I was to see the Mons afterward, so I thought I might as well roll up for the whole shebang.'

'What time did you get there?'

'Just before eleven. Why do you ask?'

Elena looked ahead for a few seconds and then turned around again with an expectant look.

'Just a minute,' said Vince. *I can see where this is going.* 'I was putting a plaster on a kid's arm prior to that. Check with the ED!'

'I will,' she responded. 'You had just learned that the Monsignor had abused you brother, so—'

Vince sat forward and slapped his hands on the dashboard. 'For fuck's sake, Elena! Do you think I would lie about something like that?'

'I believe you.' She paused. 'But I *will* follow it up.'

'BE. MY. GUEST!'

Vince lapsed into a moody silence and then let out a long sigh. *She was only doing her job.*

'Anyway, Sarge,' he went on, 'we've all been pissing in the wind. O'Shannassey didn't abuse Joey after all. The Broken Rights mob made a blue and Jane jumped to the wrong conclusion.'

'You *sure* about that?'

Vince nodded.

She paused again and then pointed to the laptop. 'The fact remains that on the day the Monsignor died, Jane believed that he *had* abused her husband. *And* had emailed that information to you.'

They sat in silence.

'Someone else must've come in and done it after she left,' Vince said after a minute.

'Such as …?'

'Any of a whole bunch of people who didn't like O'Shannassey,' he replied with a shrug.

'We've been examining the All God's Children foundation financials,' said Elena. 'It wasn't just slack bookkeeping. Looks like the Monsignor *was* siphoning off most of the profits.'

'So much for him being a big hero caring for the homeless. What was he doing with the cash?'

'Don't know,' she said. 'Pauline Murphy suspected he was putting it on the horses.'

'A very Catholic vice.' He pointed at the laptop. 'Any more emails?'

She shook her head. 'But there's a series of very strange text messages from a Travis Brody, who is the son of the priests' housekeeper, Geraldine Brody.'

'And nephew of Carmel Harrington.'

'Also an ex-seminarian.'

'Plus a bit nuts,' added Vince. 'One way or another.'

'Fair to say he's not a fan of the Catholic Church or the Monsignor.'

Vince snorted. 'He's not Robinson Crusoe there.'

'He threatened to burn the church down,' said Elena.

Vince read the messages and grimaced. There was a clear and chilling message behind Travis's chaotic ramblings—Monsignor O'Shannassey's days were numbered.

Elena scrolled down the screen on her laptop.

'There's also some Islamophobic texts from Dustin Cartwright, a former soldier who—'

'Has PTSD and an ice habit as well as a penchant for domestic violence.'

'Also a member of the Aussie Patriots,' Elena added.

And is suing me for malpractice.

'Mr Cartwright wrote that the Monsignor should be hung for treason.'

'Charming,' Vince responded, looking at the texts. 'This stuff is straight from the White Australia playbook.'

'There were also some worrying posts on the parish Facebook page from a Aisif Hamid.'

Vince nodded. 'Aisif's an Afghan refugee in the Sacred Heart emergency housing. He's got … had a grudge against O'Shannassey too.'

'So I noticed,' said Elena, bringing up the page. 'He claims the Monsignor should be silenced.'

Could the slaughter of your family, a hazardous voyage, and mandatory detention poison your mind to the point of murder?

Vince stared straight ahead at the dashboard. 'How did all these people access the Mon's phone number and email, and the parish Facebook account?' he asked after a few minutes of puzzled musing.

'That information is all on the church website, a habit we discourage.'

'I keep forgetting you're a computer whiz, Sarge.' Elena had been completing her Masters in IT and Policing when they'd first met and Vince knew she wanted to take that further. 'You heard back about that job you told me about—the one with the new federal government terrorism task force?'

Elena shook her head.

'Don't suppose the Lord of the Manor wants his paramour up in Canberra tracking down international terrorists when she should be down here making scones.'

'For now,' she ignored the barb and looked across at Vince, 'I'm one hundred percent focused on solving a local crime.' She paused. 'Jane had a strong motive, bluffed her way into the presbytery, and threatened the Monsignor. He was found dead thirty minutes after she says she left him.' She looked at Vince, eyebrows raised.

'Just hang on, Sarge,' said Vince, gesturing toward the laptop. 'What about those other guys?'

'Naturally, we've interviewed them. And they all have alibis.' She started ticking off her fingers. 'Aisif Hamid was in hospital, Travis Brody's mother says he was at her sister's house watching TV with his cousin, and Dustin Cartwright spent the weekend with his father in Melbourne.'

'But you need to make sure—'

'*And* I'm checking them all out thoroughly.' She gestured toward the Victoria Police badge on her jacket. 'That's my job.'

* * *

Vince drove back to work with his head spinning and threw himself into the afternoon session, trying to shut out the turbulence in his mind and nausea in his belly. His last patient turned out to be Aisif, who limped in and sat down.

'G'day, mate. How's it going?'

'Good, thank you, Doctor. Leg healing well.' He pulled up his trousers and exposed the wound.

Vince had a look, then whistled. 'Looks great. No swelling or redness.'

'Mr Wijdernatne very pleased. No more operations. Just need prescription for more antibiotics.'

Vince printed off the script and signed it. 'How're the studies going, mate?'

'Good, but I also need you to sign this VCE Special Consideration form, if you would be so kind. I missed some study tasks when I was in hospital.'

'No problems,' said Vince. 'Listen, Aisif. I understand you've been posting on the Sacred Heart Facebook page.'

Aisif nodded and blushed. 'Is true. I have no problem with the parish community. They have supported me very much.' He frowned. 'But the Monsignor priest, he is … was a bad man.'

Time to sort this out. 'So you've said before, but what do you mean by that? Was he touching you inappropriately or something?'

'Nothing like that.'

'You might as well tell me, Aisif. He's dead now.'

'He was all the time proselytising. Saying I should follow his God. I told him that Allah is the one true God and Mohammad is his messenger. He said I should renounce Islam and become a Roman Catholic.' The young man stopped and fought to control his emotions. 'I told him I could not do this and he said he would cause the parish to stop funding my schooling.' He put his head in his hands. 'Then I could never become a doctor,' he added, sobbing, 'and bring my father to this country.'

Vince patted the boy on the shoulder and handed him a tissue. 'Bad idea to put that stuff up on the parish website. Better to take the issue up with the parish council.'

'Facebook and social media can be easy to make mistake.' He looked up. 'Won't do again.'

Vince nodded. 'So you were still in the hospital on the Sunday morning the Monsignor was killed?'

'Yes, sir.'

'Must have been boring, hanging around and waiting for your antibiotic doses.'

He shook his head. 'The surgeon doctor said I must stay that day and elevate my leg and I could be discharged next day. Just did my books.'

'Fair enough.' *Sounds convincing.*

Vince finished filling out the form in silence, then handed it back along with the prescription. 'See you later. Good luck with the studies.'

Aisif stood up. 'Cats are winning,' he said with a smile as he walked to the door. 'Garry Ablett is back.'

'That's the way, I'll turn you into an Australian yet.' Vince winked. 'A fair dinkum, Geelong-supporting, Muslim-Aussie doctor.'

* * *

At the end of the day, Vince jumped into Benny and headed for Mac's Snacks on the main drag. He knew there was no food at the Snapper house and he was too tired to go to the supermarket. And he'd banned himself from takeaways.

This unpretentious family-run café had been going for decades and was a local institution, especially for the surrounding farming community. Vince ordered the roast of the day and settled himself at a table at the back. He sipped on a juice and pulled out a pen and paper.

Looked like the coppers had shut their book on the case, so it was time for him to start detecting. It couldn't be Janey, could it? *Could it?*

Vince shook his head. *Doesn't bear thinking about.* Okay, it must have been someone else. And he'd better find out *who* before they charge her with murder.

He drew up a list of suspects. Next to the list he added columns for motive and opportunity. First name was Travis Brody. Okay. Motive, well—

'*At home or far away*' burst out of his pocket and interrupted his theorising. He grabbed his phone and glanced at the screen.

'Evening, Georgie.'

'Yo, Bins, what's going on?'

'Not much. How's every little thing?'

'Same old. School sucks, Mum's a witch, and Ivan's a tool.'

'Don't listen to her, Dad. It's not that bad.' A burst of background laughter. 'Except for the last bit.'

'Hi, Tessa—double trouble. What's going down, guys?'

'It's year twelve careers night next week, Bins, and—'

'Tess put your name down to talk about—'

'Being a doctor and specialising in—'

'Ladies' bits—'

'*Gross!*'

Vince frowned at his phone. 'Listen, team, I'm not actually working as an obstetrics and gynaecology specialist just now. I've been red-carded and I'm serving my suspension.'

'Yeah but, no but, yeah but—'

'You still da man, right, Bins?'

I don't know what I am!

'You better cross me off that list, Tess. I'm in a spot of bother with the Medical Board, okay? Best if I'm not parading around as a big-shot consultant for the moment.'

'But when you finish up in the 'Bool, Dad, you'll come back to Melbourne and return to your old job, won't you?'

Heart sink. 'I hope so, just got to sort out a few things first.'

'And you're still coming to the Fathers and Daughters camp, Bins?'

'Remind me about that again, girls?'

'It's the weekend after next—'

'In the Grampians.'

'Wherever that is.' Vince glanced at the calendar on his phone.

'Don't tell us you didn't get the memo, Bins.'

'We've reminded you about a zillion times.'

He looked up the weekend in question—local footy *and* on-call. That's going to take some fast-talking. 'Course I'll be there. See you then.'

Vince's roast pork arrived, complete with apple sauce, roast potatoes, carrots, parsnips, and beans. He draped a napkin on his lap, picked up his knife and fork, looked at the loaded plate, ate one bean, then put down the cutlery and pushed the food away. His appetite had plummeted like his mood.

He made a mental note to re-jig that weekend, took a deep breath, picked up his pen, and made another start on his list.

Travis Brody:

- Motive—bad experience at the seminary? Involving the Mons? Psychotic.
- Opportunity—nil because was next door with Kieran while

Mrs H went to mass. (NB: why was Kieran at home?) Travis's mother works at presbytery, he knows the layout.

 Aisif Hamid:

- Motive—hostile with Mon's attempts to convert him and put his parish scholarship at risk. Damaged by his dreadful experience as an asylum seeker.
- Opportunity—nil because was in hospital. (Easy to check that out.)

Dustin Cartwright:

- Motive—strenuously opposed to the Monsignor's support of asylum seekers. Member of right-wing extremist group.
- Opportunity—nil because was in Melbourne. (Ditto.)

Vince shook his head. *Anyway, how could any of them have gained access to the house?*

He paused, his pen poised above the paper. *Who else? A sudden mental flash. What about Luke Kelly? Jane had told him that the Mons was a paedophile. That made him very angry. Angry enough to kill his boss and housemate? Crazy thought! No opportunity because he was on the road to Our Lady's. But wait, after he let Jane in, couldn't he have gone to his car in the priests' garage, erupted with fury, re-entered the presbytery after she left, committed the murder, and then driven off?*

Too many questions. Need some answers.

What about the Church itself? Jane sent the letter to the bishop as well. Maybe they couldn't afford for such a prominent priest to be prosecuted and feared he might take a few big names with him ... even crazier, but ...

'Have you finished your dinner, Dr Hanrahan?'

The voice of the smiling waitress broke into Vince's theorising and brought him back to reality.

'Yeah. Thanks, Raylene,' he said, handing over his loaded plate. 'Not hungry tonight. Tell Mac not to take it personally.'

29

'And that's our little family,' the night Nurse Unit manager concluded as the meeting broke up. Her staff grabbed their coats and bags and headed off down the dark corridors, and the new nurses spread through the ward and started about their tasks.

Vince had arrived in the general medical ward to find the nightshift nurses just finishing their hand-over to the morning staff.

'Morning, Doctor,' said the morning shift manager, Ingrid—a jolly, experienced senior nurse, well known to Vince. She glanced up at the patient board. 'You've got no one here.'

'Just wanted to follow something up, Ingrid,' said Vince. 'Were you working on Easter Sunday?'

She nodded. 'Sure was.'

'Remember the Afghan boy, Aasif Hamid?'

'Yep. He's a sweetie. Better manners than my lot, I'll tell you that.'

'Was he still here that day?'

Ingrid studied the computer in the nurse's station, flicking back a few screens. 'Yeah, Aasif was in the ward. He was discharged the following day.' She looked up. 'I remember now. We gave him his IV antis at nine and Mr Widgeratne let him go out on leave for the morning.' She chuckled. 'I told him to have an Easter egg for me.'

Well, well, well. So much for Aisif's alibi!

'Do you know what he was planning to do?'

Ingrid shook her head. 'No idea. He was back by midday for his next dose.' She glanced at the computer screen on her desk and stood. 'I'd better move, I've got a ward to run.'

Clever kid was just buttering me up with that footy stuff to put me off the scent. And he had a very strong motive.

* * *

Next stop was Pathology. Vince called in every week to review histology slides with Sarah Bell. This morning's session was short. Two specimens to look at and nothing contentious. One mole with no sign of melanoma in the sections and another skin lesion that turned out to be a basal cell carcinoma—a type of localised skin cancer.

'And both completely excised with good margins,' said Sarah, turning off the microscope and getting up.

'Just a question,' said Vince. 'Can you differentiate changes due to interrupted blood supply from the effects of maternal alcohol abuse on a neonate's brain at autopsy?'

She sat down again. 'Certainly. The histological appearances are completely different. In fact, ischaemic changes are often obvious macroscopically.'

'You mean by just looking at the brain before you make sections.' He pointed at the microscope.

'That's right.'

'Do you reckon the difference should be apparent on an MRI?'

She smiled. 'I'd have thought so, but you're asking the wrong person.'

Vince nodded and headed for the door. 'Thanks, Sarah.'

'Remember our date for Friday night,' she said.

Vince looked at her blankly.

'The MTC is bringing down *Hamlet*. It's part of our PAC season.'

Jeez, I'd forgotten that one. Every year Sarah organised a joint subscription for the local Performing Arts Centre.

'Sure, see you then,' said Vince, walking out of the lab and into the adjacent Medical Imaging department.

'What brings you to the nerve centre of the universe?' A lean man with a shock of dark hair, a prominent nose, and a receding chin greeted Vince at the door.

'Well, if it's not Dominic Lonergan himself, at all, at all,' said Vince. 'Top of the morning to ye.'

The Head of Radiology mimed a knee thrust to Vince's groin. 'Enough of your racist rambling, you antipodean convict. Even your Aussie cricketers are cheats.'

'Just wanting to discuss an MRI,' said Vince. 'Name of Skylah Cartwright.'

Dr Lonergan sat at a computer and brought up some images. 'Ah, yes. *That* baby. Requested by Natalie Isaacs.' He looked up. 'Are you the treating GP?'

Vince nodded.

'Either young Skylah is a celebrity or there's medico-legal issues here,' said Dominic. 'The paediatric MRI gurus in Melbourne can't get enough of these pictures.'

'Your report was a bit inconclusive.'

'Is that right?' The radiologist frowned and gestured at the monitor. 'Want to have a go?'

'Not my caper, Dom.' Vince sat and looked at the screen. 'There's some question of birth hypoxia and trauma due to forceps or later abuse.' He pointed at the images. 'Does it look like injury or ischaemia?'

'No evidence of trauma, either during birth or after. Some subtle diffusion restriction and signal changes, which *could* mean intrapartum lack of blood supply.'

'Foetal Alcohol Syn … I mean, Spectrum Disorder?'

'Yes and no.' He highlighted one of the images with a laser pointer. 'There's some lack of mid-brain development, but not pathognomonic of FASD.' He looked at Vince. 'It's just like my golf swing—all in the timing. Serial studies would clarify things, but I understand the parents won't allow that.' He shrugged. 'Probably can't afford it.'

Vince stood. 'Or maybe they don't want to know the answer.'

He glanced at his watch, bade Dom farewell, then hurried through to the rear of the hospital to Charlie McNamee's detox unit. One of the dedicated drug and alcohol nurses, aka 'Charlie's Angels', was in the office, scrolling through results on the computer.

'The boss around, Anouk? Just wanted to check we're catching up tonight.'

'No, Doctor. He's down at WRAD.' Charlie had set up the Western Region Alcohol and Other Drug centre several years ago, where he ran comprehensive day programs and a needle exchange. The office was off-site in Merri Street.

Vince glanced at the screen. 'Do you store all your clients' results in that system?'

'Sure do. In-patients and out-patients.'

'What sort of stuff?'

'Progressive levels for our patients on the new hep-C treatments, liver function tests, blood alcohols—'

'Can you look up some results for one of my patients?'

Anouk shook her head. 'It's password protected and confidential.' She looked up. 'Even from you.'

Damn. Love to know if Tracey Cartwright had any blood-alcohol levels in there.

'Tell Charlie I'll see him tonight. He can contact me if I've got the date wrong.'

'Will do.'

* * *

Vince drove to the clinic, opened his list, and narrowed his focus. He couldn't afford to give cause for Shirley to mark him down with the Board—that would be immediate professional hari-kiri. *As opposed to this death by a thousand cuts.* At last lunchtime arrived, and he grabbed a falafel and salad wrap from a nearby café and ate it on the short drive to Sacred Heart. He parked out on Koroit Street and looked at the majestic spire reaching up into the clouds. *It's a house of cards.* Vince got out of the car and walked across the bitumen car park to the presbytery. He brushed some crumbs from his jumper and knocked on the tall timber door.

After a few minutes, it swung open to reveal a small, round replica of Carmel Harrington, albeit with more dark hair mixed into the grey curls.

'Hello, Dr Vince. Father Kelly's not here. He's out burying old Matt Donalds.'

'It's actually you that I came to see, Mrs Brody,' said Vince.

A sudden frown creased her features and she clutched her hands to her ample bosom. 'Nothin's happened to Trav, has it, Doctor?' she said. 'Or Mark?'

'No, no, nothing like that. Just wanting to touch base about Travis.'

'Well, you'd better come in,' she said, turning back into the dark building.

Vince followed her through the vast front parlour with its faded carpet, heavy furniture, and an imposing painting of Jesus with his bleeding heart hung over the mantelpiece, then along a corridor to the kitchen.

'Sorry to barge in uninvited,' said Vince. 'Hope I'm not keeping you from your work.'

She gestured around the empty house. 'There's not as much to do, since … since the Monsignor …'

'Understood,' said Vince.

'Cuppa, Doctor?'

'Thanks, Mrs Brody. White with no sugar.'

She put the kettle on and they both sat down.

'You must miss the Mons.'

She nodded, but said nothing. Probably too grief-stricken to trust her emotions.

'He was well loved by the parish,' he added.

Mrs Brody offered Vince a hobnob biscuit and poured the tea. He noticed her hands shaking and she slopped a little into the saucer. 'Well, he weren't no saint, all the same.'

'They say no man is a hero to his valet,' said Vince, sipping his tea.

She looked blank, obviously unused to his obscure literary references.

'I suppose you got to see the great man, warts and all.'

She shrugged and offered him another biscuit. *It's really hit her hard. She must have been very fond of the old rascal.*

'Travis seems much more settled now, don't you think?'

Mrs Brody put her head down. 'S'pose so. I don't like seein' him in that … with all those mad folk.' She paused. 'Poor beggars.'

'Dr Jones feels he's much more stable on the new medication and should be ready for discharge soon.'

She frowned, tears in her eyes. 'Mark won't let him come back home.'

'So he'll go to Carmel's?'

'S'pose.'

'It's very important that he has those injections every fortnight and keeps in touch with his case manager.'

'Dr Jones says he's got schizophrenia. A chemical imbalance in the brain, he says.' Mrs Brody pulled out a piece of paper from her apron pocket. 'Managed with pharmacotherapy and psychotherapy,' she read, then looked up. 'Whatever that is.'

'That means counselling and drug treatment,' said Vince. 'The good news is that now we know what the problem is, he can be treated and live a normal life. The modern drugs and other therapies are really effective.'

She put her cup down with a rattle. 'Mark reckons it's drugs what caused it. After Trav left the seminary he started smoking that marijuana all the time, sent him crazy.'

Vince shrugged. 'Some people have a leaning toward schizophrenia and they take drugs to help them cope. But the drugs can make the illness come to the surface sooner than it was going to. Chicken and egg thing.'

'Trav told Dr Jones it was him that slashed the Monsignor's vestments.' Mrs Brody's eyes filled with tears. 'Apparently he went over to the vestry Holy Saturday morning.' She glanced at her hands. 'He done it with my good sewing scissors.'

Vince nodded. *That's one mystery solved.*

'The priests down there didn't help him when he started hearing them voices. Just told him to pray more.' She dropped her head again. 'And Mark reckons they turned him into a ... a homosexual.' She started to sob and pulled a handkerchief from her apron pocket.

'Gay people are born that way, Mrs Brody,' Vince said gently, patting her heaving shoulders. 'No one turns them into homosexuals.'

She blew her nose, stood, and put the kettle on again.

'More tea, Doctor?'

Looks like that subject's closed.

Vince glanced through the open door on the other side of the kitchen. It led into the Monsignor's office. He could see the chair where

O'Shannassey had been sitting when his dead body had been discovered.

'Bit of a rabbit warren this place, isn't it?' he said. 'You have to go all the way from the front door down the hall, past the parlour, around the corner, then through the kitchen to get to the Mons's office.'

'Or,' she said, gesturing toward the office, 'you can get in there straight off the car park.'

Vince got up and looked into the office. There was a small door on the far wall.

'Was that door usually locked too?'

'Too right, but the priests often leave it unsnibbed so they can take the short cut over yonder,' she nodded in the direction of the church, 'and not worry about bringing the front door key.' She pointed to an old-fashioned key on the table.

'Who else had that key?'

'The two Fathers and meself.'

'I see,' said Vince. 'What about Frank Doyle?'

'Him too,' she added. 'The chairman of the parish council always has a key so he can get into the parish office to look at the accounts and one thing and another.'

'How did Frank and the Mons get on?'

Mrs Brody's voice changed to a loud whisper. *Must run in the family.*

'Not the best. The Monsignor didn't like paperwork and that Mr Doyle is very particular.' She looked around and further dropped her voice. 'They used to fight something shocking.'

Vince thought fast. *Surely Frank Doyle, pillar of the Church and guardian of the law, wouldn't strangle a priest because of his slack bookkeeping?*

He pushed that thought away and had a sip of his tea. 'And you weren't here that morning, Mrs Brody?'

She shook her head. 'I leave out their breakfast things of a Sunday and come in after the eleven o'clock mass to put their dinner on.' She looked round the kitchen. 'The Mons always liked a roast and all that.'

'Except on Easter Sunday.'

'That's right. The Monsignor always goes … went out to the Conheadys at Koroit. Old Pat is his cousin. And young Father Luke was going up to his family at Noorat.'

'So you had the whole day off, eh,' said Vince. 'Well deserved, I'm sure.'

She laughed. 'No fear. Had to cook round home.'

'Brodes would've given you a hand, wouldn't he?'

'You're joking! Mark's always at the Snappers of a Sunday morning.' She raised her eyebrows. 'Just an excuse for drinking beer and talking to his mates.'

'Did you have your whole crew there?'

'Just the six. One of the girls is over in London and me other boys was at their in-laws.'

'What about Travis?' asked Vince.

Mrs Brody paused and blew her nose. 'He was down at Carmel's, watching TV with Kieran.' She sniffed. 'He had his Easter dinner there too.'

30

Vince drove back through the town, his mental engine revving even more than Benny's, and arrived back at work on the tick of two o'clock. He called in his first patient and made himself take an interest in the anxious young woman with her headaches. As he was escorting her to the door, his desk phone jangled.

'Yep?'

'It's Rita, Vincenzo. Sorry to interrupt you but I've got Aisif around here for a wound dressing. Do you want to come and have a look?'

You bet! He headed around to the treatment room. Aisif was up on the couch with his wound exposed.

'Looking good,' said Vince. 'Probably doesn't need any more dressing, eh Rit?'

She nodded. 'I agree, it's almost healed. You can always come back if you have any concerns, Aisif.'

Vince jerked his thumb toward the door. 'Just duck back to my room for a sec.'

As they walked back through the waiting room, Vince noticed that Aisif was now not limping at all.

'You told me you were still in hospital on Easter Sunday.'

'That is correct.'

'It *isn't* correct. The Nurse Unit manager told me you were out on leave for the morning.'

The boy looked away.

'So where were you?'

No response.

Vince waited for a minute or two. 'Listen, Aisif. Monsignor O'Shannassey was murdered that morning.' He pointed at the boy's chest. 'You hated him.' He raised his hands in a quizzical gesture. 'So …?'

Aisif took a deep breath. 'I was at the home of Brooke Hay, a student from my class.'

'Is that Jumbo's daughter?'

'Yes.'

'From the meatworks?'

He nodded. 'We were studying chemistry. SAC is coming soon.' He glanced at the floor. 'Parents were away. Brooke stayed home for studies.'

'Studying anything else apart from chemistry, were you, mate?'

'I am very ashamed. And frightened you will tell parents. Brooke will be punished.' He frowned. 'In my country, she would be stoned.'

'We've given stoning away here,' said Vince. 'But I'd keep out of Jumbo's way if he ever gets wind of this. Get Brooke to give me a call.'

The boy's eyes widened.

'Don't worry, I'm not going to tell anyone. But seeing as you lied to me, I just want to check out your story. Might have a little chat to the young lady about the birds and the bees, too, while I'm at it.'

Vince shook his head as Aisif left, then brought up his list and noticed that Carmel Harrington was his next patient. He felt she'd been avoiding him lately, not being her usual chatty self. And she'd been keeping Kieran away too. He called her in.

'How are things, Mrs H?'

'All right, Dr Vince,' she said. 'Just need me prescriptions, that's all.'

'Okay,' he responded, looking at her file. 'I better check your blood pressure. You haven't had those lab tests yet, have you?'

'Too busy for all that. What with Kieran and Travis and Tracey and her baby.' She spread her hands out in front of her. 'I'm flat out.'

'Even more important for you take care of yourself,' said Vince, pulling out his oversize BP cuff. 'Who's going look after them all if you fall over?'

She shrugged.

'How's Tracey going with the baby?'

'Trace's battling …' Mrs Harrington paused for a few seconds, then went on. 'She's doing all right, what with one thing and another, thank you, Doctor.' She sat back and pursed her lips.

'Did she keep drinking during the pregnancy, Mrs H?'

No response.

Looks like blood's thicker than water. Vince wrapped the cuff on her large upper arm. 'Kieran implied that she did.' He noted her blood pressure reading.

Mrs Harrington frowned and sat forward. 'That boy needs to mind his own business.' She put her hand out. 'I'm not here to talk about Tracey. Just give me them prescriptions, thank you.'

Vince printed out and signed the scripts and pushed them across the desk. 'Your BPs up a bit.'

'Can't say I'm surprised,' Mrs Harrington said as she started to get up.

'Mrs H, did Travis go to Easter Sunday mass with you?'

'No, he never,' she said with a puzzled look. 'Travis don't go to church no more.'

'And Kieran was home?'

'That's right. He was still crook with that flu you was treating him for.'

Vince nodded; Kieran had been in to see him during that week with bronchitis.

'Travis's mother said he spent all morning at your place with Kieran,' he said.

'Geraldine said that, did she?' Mrs Harrington sat down again and pursed her lips.

'You don't sound convinced.'

She leant back and folded her arms across her ample bosom. '*Family* business,' she responded, staring Vince down.

Interesting. Need to do more digging but I'll get nothing more from Mrs H today.

'When did you get back from church, Mrs H?'

'Woulda been close to twelve-thirty by the time Father Kelly finished the mass, after the Mons … you know.'

'Sure.'

'Travis had his Easter dinner with me and Kieran and Tracey and the kids.' She dropped her voice to a whisper. 'His father wouldn't even let his own son home for Easter Sunday.' She put her hand up to her mouth, as if she might be overheard. 'Mark's ashamed of him, being a bit disturbed and a failed priest and that.' She pursed her lips. 'And that man calls himself a Christian.'

'And where was Dustin that day?'

'He went down to Melbourne Saturday arvo.'

'Easter with the family?'

She shook her head. 'His family's all broke up. His mother's passed and his sister's over in the mines in WA. Dustin was supposed to be stopping at his dad's.' She paused and mimicked a repetitive drinking gesture. 'But he really went down there with his mates to protest against that ecu … eco … whatever it's called. You know, the big Easter service in that square opposite Flinders Street.'

'Ecumenical?' offered Vince.

'That's it. Catholics and Proddies and Jews and Muslims and that. All in together.' She leant forward again. 'Dusty's against it, see. He reckons we should kick them Mussies out.' She frowned. 'Maybe he's right. But at Easter time, he shouda been home looking after his own family.'

Loose alibi. Maybe Dustin *was* in Warrnambool after all.

Mrs Harrington sighed, stood up, and pointed at her arm. 'No wonder me pressure's up.'

* * *

Vince got through the rest of his list and went through his mail. There was a familiar buff envelope with AHPRA on the back. He ripped it open.

Dear Dr Hanrahan,

The Medical Board is still considering the matter of Skylah Cartwright. Maternal blood testing has shown no evidence of viral infection during the pregnancy. The chromosomal array was normal, excluding genetic causes.

Expert opinion from a neonatal radiologist is that while there was no definitive evidence of ischaemic changes on the MRI, the abnormalities found are not typical of any alternative aetiology. Dr Formosa finds no sign of brain injury suggesting physical abuse of the baby.

Professor Jobling feels that the baby's clinical features are consistent with Foetal Alcohol Spectrum Disorder, but that birth hypoxia is more likely, especially in a delivery involving forceps rotation. We hope to conclude this matter by the end of next month. While this investigation is ongoing your conditional registration for General Practice in Warrnambool, excluding maternity cases, remains in place.

Yours sincerely,

Dr Simon Rutherford, Chair

Cc Ms Bridget Ryan, VMDA.

Handwritten across the bottom of the letter was: *Realistically, unless you can provide evidence of excessive maternal alcohol consumption during the pregnancy, your medical registration is on the line.*

Warmest,

Lachlan McKenzie.

Vince tossed the letter into his desk drawer and shut it with a loud bang. 'Out of sight, out of mind!'

He turned off his computer and walked toward the door.

'Dr Hanrahan,' Lorraine called from her office. 'I think Mum might have a UTI. Would you mind calling round to see her on your way home?'

'Sure.' *Can't say no to the practice manager.*

Minutes later Vince pulled up outside the house in Lava Street. The old lady lived in the original family home with her other daughter.

'Come in, Doctor,' said Mrs Murphy, greeting him at the front door. 'The kettle's on and I've made a batch of those pumpkin scones you like.' House visits to elderly females involved this established ritual.

After two cups of tea and three scones, Vince pulled out his bag, queried Mrs Murphy about her symptoms, and accepted a large jam jar containing a small amount of urine, which he dipstick-tested on the spot.

'You have an infection, all right,' he said. 'I'll drop off a script to your pharmacist and Pauline can pick up the antibiotics on her way home.'

'Lorraine will do it. Pauline generally goes to the pokies after work,' she said with a frown. 'You'll want to wash your hands, Doctor,' she insisted, steering Vince into the tiny bathroom. 'I've left out a clean towel.'

He arrived home ten minutes later and was greeted by an excited dog.

'At least you still love me,' said Vince, giving her a rub and a pat, 'don't you, Deef?' He fed her and they headed off for a walk around the block.

At the roundabout at the top of the street, they encountered Kieran walking the opposite way.

'Hi, Dr Vince.' Kieran put his hand up for a high-five, then bent down and ruffled Deefer's neck.

'On your way home?'

'Yes. Just f-f-finished work.'

'Hey, Super K,' said Vince. 'Remember that Easter Sunday when you were home with bronchitis?'

Kieran nodded.

'Your cousin Travis was there too, yeah?'

He nodded again.

'Did he spend the whole morning with you?'

Kieran looked back at his house and leant in toward Vince. 'H-h-he went off in the bus,' he said, using his mother's loud whispering technique, 'and came b-b-back again at lunchtime.' He put his finger up to his mouth and shook his head. 'Shoosh,' he added as he walked on and turned into number nine.

Interesting, very interesting.

Vince rushed Deefer around the block, then grabbed his guitar, jumped in the car, and headed for Aldo's Pizzas. *Sure, it's takeaway, but special circumstances.*

'Here you are, Doc,' said the ever-cheery proprietor. 'One Margherita, one Garden Veggie, and one Aldo's special. To go.'

'Bellissimo,' responded Vince, handing over his credit card and scooping up the warm boxes. 'How's your mum?'

'You know her, mate. Complain, complain, complain,' said Aldo, waving the card away. 'She reckon you the best doctor in the town and you look after her good.' He waved at the pizzas. 'This one's on the house.'

'That's not how it works, Aldo. I'm just doing my job.'

'And I'm doin' my job too. Enjoy!'

Vince drove east along Raglan Parade—the long row of tall Norfolk pines splitting the divided thoroughfare. He turned right after the old Fletcher Jones factory, crossed the Hopkins River bridge, headed up Riverview Terrace, and pulled up outside Charlie McNamee's house.

Charlie's wife Annie, a music teacher with a toothy grin, her blond hair in pigtails and a cluster of small children at her feet, opened the door.

'Horsey ride, Bince,' screamed one small McNamee. Vince handed over the pizzas and spent the next fifteen minutes ferrying the young brood around the house on his back, accompanied by hysterical screams as he bucked the odd one off along the way.

'Okay, you lot,' said Annie, 'time for bed. Bince has to sing some songs with Daddy and Father Luke.'

Vince had initiated this horseriding game the first time he visited the McNamees and it had become an unavoidable tradition. He said goodnight to the children and walked through to the sunken lounge room overlooking the river. Charlie and Luke Kelly sat there chatting and enjoying a beer.

'Grab a pew,' said Charlie, standing up and handing him a mineral water. 'We'll get these rascals to bed, then I'll locate some plates and we can get stuck into that health food.'

Vince walked through and glanced out the floor-to-ceiling windows at the twinkling lights on the other side of the Hopkins River.

'G'day, Kookaburra,' he said, sinking into a deep armchair. 'How're you going?'

'Same old, Ox. You?'

'The Medical Board is threatening to cut me off at the knees.'

'How come?' asked Luke. 'I thought you just had to see out your time and then you'd be back in business.'

'I was walking a tight rope already and now I'm facing a litigation charge that threatens to finish me off.' Vince drew his finger across his throat.

Luke frowned. 'That's no good. Anything I can do?'

Vince shook his head. 'No thanks. I've got to sort it out myself. Or else I'll soon be out of a job.'

He put down his glass and leant over. *No time like the present.*

'There's another thing I'm trying to figure out. What time did you let Jane into the presbytery that day?'

'About ten to ten, on my way off to Our Lady's.'

'For ten-thirty mass?'

Luke nodded. 'That's right.'

'The way you drive,' said Vince, keeping the tone light and jocular, 'you'd have been half an hour early.'

'I promised to take Communion to Remy on the way,' Luke said with a frown, 'so I needed a bit of extra time. Why do you ask?'

Remy Dauba was a patient of Vince's, housebound with late-stage disseminated bowel cancer. He lived in East Warrnambool near the church.

Fair enough, Vince thought with a sense of relief. *I didn't want it to be Luke.* Should be easy to confirm. 'Just wanting to clarify the time scale.'

'Shouldn't you leave that to the experts?' said Luke. 'You're not a detective, you're a doctor.'

And barely even that. Vince shrugged. 'The coppers have got Jane in the frame and I know she didn't do it.'

'Are you sure? She looked furious that day.'

'Absolut … well, *almost*.' *Always that nagging doubt.* 'And I need to find out who did,' he added. 'Otherwise, they'll lock her up.' He dropped his voice. 'That stuff she told you implicating O'Shannassey was a balls-up. Janey and Broken Rights didn't do their homework properly. It wasn't the Mons who abused Joey.'

Luke sat up. 'I am really, *really* pleased to hear that, Vince. But how did they get it so wrong?'

'Long story. Case of mistaken identity.'

Luke relaxed back in his chair, drained his glass, and looked at the window, shaking his head. 'This is *exactly* how we all get tarred with the same brush.'

Vince glanced at the fishermen out on the river below them. He decided to throw another line in.

'Jane sent a copy of that letter to the Archdiocese. This might sound crazy, but do you reckon the Church might have gotten rid of the Mons to limit the damage? Save some of the furniture?'

Luke laughed. '"Who will rid me of this turbulent priest?" eh?' *Man*

For All Seasons was just a play, Vince. You're letting your imagination run away with you.' He looked out the window again. 'The bishops have a lot to answer for,' he added, 'but murdering monsignors is not their style.'

Vince nodded. 'It seemed a bit fanciful, even to me.' He changed gears again. 'I hear O'Shannassey spent some time at the seminary last year.'

'That's right,' said Luke. 'He filled in while the rector was away for a few months on sabbatical in the States.'

'Werribee would've suited the Mons, closer to the metro racetracks. I hear he was a punter.'

Luke frowned. 'Not at all. I had more interest in the nags than Dennis. I know he spent a lot of time with his sister in Ascot Vale while he was down there.'

'That would've been when young Travis Brody was at the seminary,' said Vince.

'It was.' Luke paused. 'Poor Travis lost his vocation.'

'His father reckons he lost a lot more than that,' said Vince.

Annie came in with a platter of dips, cheeses, and olives. 'Let's hope those kids have all gone off to sleep,' she said.

Charlie was close behind, bearing the pizzas, a salad, and a bottle of red. 'Tuck in, gents,' he said, passing some plates around.

Twenty minutes later, Vince and Charlie picked up their guitars, tuned up, and started the session. Luke chugged and soared on his blues harp and Annie added some vocals. Vince was rusty and just strummed the chords, with Charlie adding the colour. After a few songs, it all started to come together. Vince lost himself in the music and became truly in the moment for the first time for months. They finished with 'The Tennessee Waltz', with Charlie providing a cowboy-style 'yee-hah!' after the last note.

'Too country for my liking,' said Luke. 'But it's a killer melody.'

'That song always gets me,' said Vince, grabbing a tissue.

'With me,' said Annie, 'it's cellos.'

Charlie and Vince gathered up the empties and plates and took them through to the kitchen, leaving Annie and Father Luke deep in conversation about the recent same-sex marriage plebiscite.

'Mate,' said Vince, loading up the dishwasher, 'do you still run that antenatal drugs and alcohol program?'

'Sure do. Sorry to say it's a rapidly growing part of my work.'

Charlie ran a range of programs from educational sessions, needle exchange, the detox unit, and lots more besides.

'He's a saint, that man,' was how Shirley put it. 'Pope Frank should cannibalise him.'

'Do you usually send information about those girls back to their GPs?'

'Unless the patient declares otherwise. They can request for their WRAD file to be withheld from other agencies. Some of them think there's still a bit of a stigma and are more likely to engage with us if they know it won't go any further.'

'But surely the treating clinician should have access to that information,' said Vince, rinsing out the glasses at the sink. 'It could have ramifications for the management of the pregnancy.'

'If they're HIV positive or hep B or C, then of course we'd have to share that with you guys.'

'We always test for those at the first antenatal visit anyway,' said Vince. 'It's the drinkers that we don't hear about.'

Charlie shrugged and turned on the dishwasher.

Vince headed home with a heavy heart. He loved the cosy domestic vibe at Charlie's house. His own family life was arid and spasmodic by comparison.

'And whose fault's that, you idiot?' he asked his reflection in the rearview mirror as he slowed and crossed the bridge.

31

'Good swell, mate,' Vince said after consulting his surf conditions app. He pulled on his wetsuit, grabbed his board, and he and Deefer trotted off to the beach. The temperature of the Southern Ocean in June was a strong disincentive, but they got there to find several other surfers braving the cold. The icy shock of the water crashing against him as he paddled out took Vince's breath away. He sat out the back to recover and wait his turn, watching the sun come up, then spun around, got onto a two-metre wave, and rode it all the way to the shore—even did a couple of slow cutbacks. *What a start to the day!*

When they got back home, Vince fed Deefer, had a long warming shower and a quick bowl of muesli and fruit, then boarded Benny, pulled out his phone, and punched in Elena's number.

'Morning, Doc. You're up and about early.'

'I'm after that worm.'

'Aren't we all?'

'I'm scratching for tonight. Going to *Hamlet* at the PAC.'

Elena whistled. 'Part of your culture feast with the good Dr Bell, I'm guessing.'

'Correct. Sorry about the late notice.'

'No problem,' said Elena. 'You really are an all-rounder, Doc—Shakespeare, football, opera, guitar, surfing, poetry, cricket, literature …'

'I'm a dilettante,' replied Vince, 'into a very *wide* range of stuff, but only about a micron deep.'

She laughed.

'Except for Obs and Gynae,' he added. 'I reckon I know a bit about that.'

'Pleased to hear it,' she said. 'You'll see Will and his mother at the PAC.'

'You didn't get a guernsey?'

'Not my thing.' She paused, then added in her trademark deadpan voice, 'He's asked me to marry him, though.'

Vince almost dropped his phone. 'Awesome! Congratulations!'

'Whoa, Doc, I haven't accepted. Still thinking.'

'Good-looking rooster with a big house and farm. *And* a nice bloke too,' exclaimed Vince. 'What's not to like?' *Plus that biological clock is ticking …*

'I'm not after a *nice* bloke,' Elena responded. 'I want the *right* bloke.'

'Fair comment.'

'By the way,' she went on in her back-to-business voice, 'I've verified you were at the hospital before mass that morning.'

Bloody hell!

'You're nothing if not thorough, Sarge,' said Vince.

'Just doing my job.'

'While I'm talking to you,' he said, 'how do we know Dusty Cartwright was definitely in Melbourne on the Sunday?'

'He was there all right.'

'Have you spoken to his father?' asked Vince.

'Of course.'

'But I hear he's a drinker. He may not be reliable.' *Bit rich, coming from me.*

'We have CCTV footage of Dustin harassing people at the Bring Them Here rally in Federation Square. He was in the lock-up until Monday morning.'

'Fair enough.' *Another theory down the drain.*

'You do the doctoring,' she added. 'I'll do the policing.'

Déjà vu.

'Got it,' he said. 'Anything else in the wind?'

'I'm still looking at the All God's Children financials. The Monsignor didn't withdraw that money after all—someone else hacked the funds out of the account.'

'Who?'

'Don't know,' she said. 'Yet.'

'But he was the only signatory.'

Elena laughed. 'Not hard to get around that for an IT-savvy person, especially if they knew which account. Any ideas?'

Vince had a think. 'Nope.' *Not my problem, anyway.*

'Have a good time at the theatre—'

'Just *one* more thing,' said Vince. 'You know how the front door of the presbytery was always locked?'

'Correct.'

'And that Monsignor O'Shannassey couldn't hear the bell when he was out the back?'

'Uh huh.'

'Did you know there's a side door from the car park leading into the Monsignor's office?'

'A door that can't be opened from the outside,' she replied.

'Listen to this then, smarty,' said Vince. 'The priests used to leave it unlocked on Sundays.'

'That I didn't know.'

'So anyone could've come in that morning and killed the Mons.'

There was a pause. 'Anyone who knew the door was unlocked. And had a motive. And had no alibi.' Another pause. 'Got anyone in mind, Doc? Or are you suggesting it was a random passerby?'

'I'm just saying that just because Jane was let in the front door—'

'*And* had a motive.'

'Doesn't mean that—'

'*And* admits to assaulting the deceased.'

'—she murdered the Mons.'

An even longer pause. 'Okay. Then who *did*?'

'I don't bloody know!' he said. 'What about Travis Brody?'

'He was at his aunt's place. Watertight alibi.'

'Wouldn't be so sure about that one, Sarge.'

'If you have any further information,' Elena said after an audible snort, 'feel free to pass it on.'

'Stay tuned.' *Need to have another crack at Mrs H.*

'Anyone else?'

'How about Frank Doyle? He has a key to the front door of the presbytery.'

'Really, Doc? The chair of the parish council and respected local solicitor?'

'He was bluing with the Mons about the parish's accounts, you see,' said Vince. 'O'Shannassey was a big picture man and Frank's a pedantic bean counter so he might've—'

'Stop right there,' Elena cut in. 'Mr Doyle was at the Finance Committee meeting at the parish hall from nine-thirty till ten-forty-five. Six witnesses.'

Damn!

'Okay.'

'Any other names for me?'

Vince searched in the far recesses of his brain. *Bingo!* 'What about Pauline Murphy? She'd have known the bank account details. And her mother told me she's into the pokies.'

'But why would Pauline tell Frank Doyle about the missing funds if she was the thief?'

'She was trying to put the blame onto the Mons, see,' said Vince, his mind in overdrive. 'And then, then … he realised it must have been her and was going to dob her in to Frank.'

'And then she killed him. Is that your hypothesis?'

'Yes. *Yes!* She lives opposite Sacred Heart. *And* she knows the set up at the presbytery.'

'Hmm. Sounds unlikely but I'll check it out,' said Elena. 'The boss is putting a *lot* of heat on me about this murder,' she added. 'Unless you have some other compelling alternative, I've no choice but to arrest Jane.'

She paused.

'Monday.'

32

'Calling Mr Rick. Come in, Ricky.'

Vince looked around. He was sitting at a table at the Whalers Hotel opposite the performing arts centre, staring at the wall. Sarah, resplendent in a sleek, silvery flapper-style dress with a brightly coloured silk shawl across her shoulders, had just put their drinks on the table and sat down, her question slicing into his tired mental meandering.

'Thanks, Ilsa. Just daydreaming.' He picked up his lemon, lime, and bitters. 'Cheers.'

'Cheers.' She raised her glass of champagne. 'What did you think?'

'Gruelling, but rewarding,' he said, dragging his attention to the present. 'You get no free kicks with *Hamlet*.'

She smiled. 'Even more murders than in that Midsomer village on TV.'

Vince laughed. 'True. There must have been an equally high homicide rate in Denmark back then. Just shows how dangerous it is to get on the wrong side of the king.'

'Same in modern politics,' said Sarah. 'Look at Rudd, Gillard, Rudd, Abbott, Turnbull.'

'Too right.'

'You forget how many phrases from *Hamlet* are still in common usage.'

Vince nodded. 'My therapist reckons "there is nothing either good or bad, but thinking makes it so"—nails all of cognitive behavioural therapy right there.'

'Shakespeare's just as relevant today as he was in Elizabethan England,' said Sarah.

Vince's mobile beeped a message. Elena. *You're half right. Pauline stole the money but she was on a cruise with her mother over Easter.* Wow, he thought, quick detective work!

He shook his head and stared at the table. 'Well, I'm "suffering the slings and arrows of outrageous fortune" right now, that's for sure.'

Sarah raised her eyes. 'How so?'

'You've heard it all before,' said Vince, looking up. 'Kicked down the highway in disgrace by the Board. Rejected by the woman I love. A stranger to my kids.' He paused. 'My brother suicides because of abuse I should have noticed, and the perpetrator is still at large. His widow is facing a murder charge, and I don't know if she did it or not.' Vince slammed his fist down onto the table. 'And I'm this far,' he held up his hand, thumb and index finger almost touching, 'from being struck off.'

* * *

Vince woke the next day to find a message on his phone. *'In Melbourne for w/e. Watching Maisie play netball at school @9 Sat am on way.'*

He replied: *See you there, we need to talk.*

He'd planned a leisurely drive up to Dunkeld in the Grampians for the Fathers and Daughters camp and had texted Jane last night saying he would call in to see her in Horsham on the way home on Sunday.

He glanced at the time: just after seven—should make it. Ballarat was in the wrong direction but best to grab the chance.

Before heading off, he shot around the front fence to next door and rang the bell. Mrs Harrington came to the door in her dressing gown.

'Sorry to annoy you so early, Mrs H. I'm going to be away for the weekend. Can Kieran look after Deefer for me? I've already fed her for today.'

'Course he can.' She pointed back up the hallway. 'He sleeps in of a Saturday.' She stepped out on to the porch. 'He told me you was asking questions about Travis.'

Vince nodded.

'Kieran can't keep anything from me,' she added. 'I can tell by his face.'

'Sorry, Mrs H. I didn't mean to pry.'

Feel like I'm standing at the bar of the last chance saloon.

Mrs Harrington looked around for the usual invisible eavesdropper, then continued in a loud whisper, 'Don't tell anyone I told you this, specially Mark Brody.' She tapped her nose. 'Travis always goes round to his mum's of a Sunday morning while his dad's at footy training. It's the only chance Geraldine has to spend time with him.' She looked around again. 'She lets on to Mark that she's at mass, see.'

So that's where Travis went on the bus.

And that's the end of my list!

* * *

Vince headed north up Mortlake Road and took the Hamilton Highway toward Ballarat. It was a crisp morning, weak sunshine and clear skies. He tuned in to the cheerful inanities of the Coodabeen Champions on the radio and two hours later skirted the western side of Lake Wendouree and pulled into the Ballarat Grammar visitor's car park. He could see a few games of netball underway on the nearby courts and wandered over. The early winter iciness cut straight through him. Jane was standing in a puffer jacket amongst a group of parents at the side of one of the courts and Vince could see Maisie out there—a small, determined figure, darting in and out of the play.

'Hi Janey,' he said, kissing her on the cheek. 'How are they doing?'

'Okay,' said Jane, 'three goals down, just starting the last quarter. Loreto are the top team.'

Vince pointed out the court. 'Maisie's style looks familiar. Dodges and weaves just like her old man.'

Jane motioned Vince to one side, away from the cheering parents.

'I'm guessing you're not here to talk about my daughter's netball moves.'

'Fair call,' said Vince. 'Just giving you a heads-up, really.' He leant in and dropped his voice. 'You'll be hearing from Elena Genovesi this week.' He paused. 'All the other suspects for O'Shannassey's murder have been ruled out.'

Jane turned to face him. 'So she thinks it was me?'

Vince nodded.

'What about you? Do you agree?'

'*Someone* must've done it,' he said with a shrug. 'The other possibilities have solid alibis.'

Vince had spoken to a nervous Brooke Hay during the week and verified that Aisif was with her that morning and Remy Dauba had confirmed that Father Kelly had brought him Communion at ten o'clock on Easter Sunday, meaning Luke must have continued on his way straight after he let Jane in.

The words of Arthur Conan Doyle, often quoted by Vince's father, rang in his ears. 'Once you eliminate the impossible, whatever remains, no matter how improbable, must be the truth.'

'You had the motive and the opportunity.'

Jane moved her face forward until they were almost touching. 'Listen. I couldn't give a rat's about who killed O'Shannassey and I don't care if you believe me or not.' Her face was white and eyes blazing. 'I've got bigger fish to fry. We've got a lead on Ambrose Dennis. I tracked down his niece in Colac and I'm going to see her next week. And you know what?' She thumped her chest with a clenched fist. 'I'll keep on looking until I find him!'

'You won't be able to do that if they stick you in prison.'

Jane said nothing and looked straight ahead.

She's in denial, thought Vince. *Or guilty*. He glanced at her. *Surely not …*

The full-time whistle blasted through Vince's mental wrestling. Grammar had stormed home in the last quarter and won by two goals. Maisie had starred. Her teammates gathered in a huddle around her, chanted their war cry and high-fived each other.

'Whoo-hoo!' shouted Jane. 'Well played, Grammar!'

Vince clapped and called out. 'Good game, Hanrahan.'

He turned to Jane and embraced her. 'I've got to go.' He dropped his voice. 'Elena is coming after you. Make sure you have a good lawyer.'

Vince congratulated Maisie, said his farewells, headed off with a heavy heart, and drove back into town. Despite himself, he slowed as St Bernard's loomed up ahead. The front gates were festooned with coloured ribbons. Vince had seen on TV that this was part of the 'Loud Fence' movement in support of the victims of child sex abuse.

He looked across at the brothers' house and the chapel and fought to suppress a sudden surge of nausea.

* * *

An hour and a half later, Vince nosed Benny between a Porsche and a sleek E series Mercedes in the car park outside the Dunkeld Hotel.

'Hey, watch the duco!' said a voice from the plush interior of the Merc. 'That rust bucket shouldn't even be on the road.'

'Don't get your knickers in a twist,' said Vince, peering through the tinted window. 'Oh, it's you, Thommo. G'day, mate.'

The two men got out of their respective cars and shook hands. Vince hadn't seen his old anaesthetist since the regatta in Geelong. Vince noticed Andy's ginger hair was turning grey.

'Good to see you, Vince,' said Andy. 'At least I'll have someone to have a few reds with this weekend.'

Vince shook his head. 'I'm on the wagon.' He pointed at the group of men standing in the foyer. 'I'm sure some of those blokes will help you out.'

They grabbed their bags and joined the throng in front of a large noticeboard on an easel in front of the check-in desk.

'Welcome to Canterbury Lady's College Year Twelve Fathers and Daughters Camp,' proclaimed a large poster, bearing the school crest and the words: 'Share, Gain, and Grow'.

'Looks like some of you fellas have grown a bit since I saw you last,' said Vince, shaking numerous hands, patting broadening backs, and receiving a range of jocular replies. When the girls started out at CLC, he'd been too busy being a hero obstetrician to involve himself too much in the fathers group—in fact, he saw more of the *mothers* in those days—but he knew most of the guys with daughters in the twins' year level. Seeing them en masse reminded him of what he'd missed and what he was still missing.

'Hey, Vince,' said one—a small, well-dressed, olive-skinned man, tapping Vince on the belly. 'Speak for yourself.'

'Tony Lamarra,' said Vince, squeezing his hand. 'You still straightening the teeth of all the private-school kids? Can't be many left you haven't done.'

This caused an outbreak of laughter in the group. 'Good old, Vincey,' he heard one man say. 'Hasn't changed a bit.'

'Still the joker, eh?' Andy said as they lined up at the check-in desk.

'Sure,' he answered. 'My life's a laugh a minute.'

Just then a posse of giggling teenaged girls burst into the foyer and fragmented off toward their respective fathers.

'Hi, Dad,' said Georgie, giving Vince a peck on the cheek. 'You growing a beard?'

'Didn't quite have time for a shave this morning, George,' Vince replied, massaging his stubble.

'Those shoes are out of control, Bins,' said Tessa. 'No one wears runners with jeans.'

The twins wandered off with their friends. *Pretty cool welcome,* thought Vince. *Maybe it's just their ages. Time was, they would've given me big crazy hugs.*

* * *

The first activity after lunch was horse riding in the surrounding bushland. Vince found himself trotting along next to Andy while the girls cantered ahead with Andy's daughter, Olivia.

'I hear the Board's still after you,' said Andy. 'Sounds like a vendetta to me.'

Vince raised his eyebrows. 'So much for confidentiality. Where'd you hear about that?'

'I've been doing a few lists with Lachlan McKenzie.'

'That must be a barrel of laughs.'

'I put in an epidural for an elective Caesar he was doing last week. Jim Jobling was there to catch the babe.' He paused and checked that no one was in earshot. 'I heard them chatting afterward, when I was getting changed. They didn't realise I was there.'

'Oh yeah,' said Vince, pulling up his horse. 'And my name came up?'

Andy nodded. 'McKenzie said, "How's your report about The Big Show going?"'

Jobling had conferred this nickname onto Vince, who knew it was predicated on a measure of resentment, a sentiment shared by Little Lachie. Back in his glory days, Vince had trodden on a lot of toes. *It's all coming back to bite me on the bum.*

Andy relayed the rest of the conversation:

'Just about finished,' said Jobs. 'The baby's MRI and clinical features are equivocal, so unless there's definitive evidence of heavy maternal alcohol consumption, I'll be concluding that hypoxia due to a risky forceps rotation is the likely aetiology.'

'Sounds fair,' said McKenzie.

'Meaning we won't see The Show around here again,' added Jobs.

'Won't see him anywhere medical,' said McKenzie. 'Period.'

* * *

After the horse riding, they had a group exercise involving the removal of a beanbag from inside a circle using a stick, some masking tape, and a piece of rope.

'This will require imaginative, collaborative problem-solving within each team,' explained the enthusiastic young teacher, 'and the respectful sharing of strategies.'

Vince loathed these sorts of activities. 'Why don't we just reach in and pick the bloody thing up and then go back in and sit in front of the fire?' he said, which didn't go down well with the year level co-coordinator, the two dads, and the three earnest prefects in his group. The other teams, including the one the twins were in, were all tossing ideas around and seemed to be having a ball.

By the BBQ that evening, Vince had lost his earlier, contrived 'hail fellow, well met' mojo. The twins seemed to be the life of the party and were surrounded by laughing fellow students and fathers. Vince loaded his plate, sat on a large rock off to the side, and gazed up at Mt Sturgeon looming high in the darkening background. He had the feeling he was out of the CLC loop. *Almost out of the twins' loop too.*

'Move over,' Tessa said a few minutes later. She sat down next to him. 'Anna Overingham told us you didn't take the activity seriously and were rude to her father.'

'Come on, Tess, the whole thing was stupid,' replied Vince. 'And that Overingham bloke is tedious.'

Tessa stood and frowned. 'You've got to make more of an effort, Dad.' She looked him up and down. 'You look like you slept in those clothes.' She started to walk off, then stopped and added, 'Even though Ivan The Tool *is* a tool, at least he doesn't embarrass us.'

* * *

Next morning there was a church service and Vince found that he was to do one of the readings. Jolted by Tessa's admonishment, he procured an iron from the front desk, pressed a clean shirt, and took the job seriously. He nodded and smiled his way through the following lunch and did his best not to upset anyone. After that, the formal activities were complete and the large CLC bus pulled around the front to take the girls back to Melbourne.

'Thanks for coming, Bins,' Georgie said in a cold voice.

'Bye, girls, study hard. See you down the 'Bool soon.'

'Goodbye, Dad,' said Tessa, at least giving him a kiss. 'Look after yourself.'

A large, gleaming four-wheel-drive Jaguar pulled up on the opposite side of the circular driveway. Vince was surprised to see it was being piloted by Lydia. She got out and walked over, looking lovely in a close-fitting suede jacket, jeans, and long boots.

'G'day, Lids,' he said. 'Happened to be in the vicinity?'

'Didn't the twins tell you? Ivan and I have been staying at the new Mountain View Lodge in the Victoria Valley. Ivan's playing golf in Hall's Gap, then we're all heading back home.' She looked around. 'Isn't this nice? Have a good time, girls?'

After giving Vince sheepish looks, Georgie and Tessa took their bags over to the big car and hopped in.

'How are you going, Vincent?' Lydia put her hand on his forearm. 'You look a bit run down.'

'Just tickety-boo, Lids,' said Vince, pulling his arm away. 'All good with me. Better make tracks.' He picked up his bag, waved to the girls, walked over to Benny and drove out, almost slamming into Thommo's car on the way.

As the kilometres ticked past, Vince felt he was becoming a waste of space. He slowed as he approached Caramut, and the famous *Hamlet* soliloquy returned, unbidden, into his mind. *To be or not to be …*

He shook his head and punched the steering wheel. *Jesus! I'll lose my mind if I dwell on that stuff!*

As Benny sped up again, Vince turned the radio on, desperate for a distraction. He soon tired of the football commentary, changed channels, and listened for three minutes to a complex discussion about modern Islam before switching to an FM station and drowning in easy-listening schmaltz. He swore and hit the off button.

The next town was Woolsthorpe and, as he eased off the accelerator, Vince tried to invoke Myf's breathing drill, but the intense feeling that it would be better if he just wasn't around sabotaged any attempt at mindfulness. Instead, his pulse rate picked up and his breathing started to tighten. *Maybe it would be best for everyone if I did have a coronary—a fatal one.*

He lowered the windows, turned the radio back on, cranked up the volume, and forced himself to listen to the match between the Brisbane Lions and the Sydney Swans, losing himself in the monotonous minutiae of that struggle. By the time the final siren sounded, he found himself pulling up at the Snapper house.

33

'Have they worked out who killed the poor Monsignor?' Colleen Maloney said as she and Vince walked around the ward the following day.

Although he was banned from the labour ward, Vince liked to look in on his former obstetric patients even though they'd had their babies delivered by someone else. Colleen was a caring midwife but vague on details. He preferred to do his round with Barbara Craig, the Nurse Unit manager, but Pete Paras had gotten in first. *Surprise, surprise.*

''Fraid not,' said Vince. 'It's a mystery.'

'Well, he was still alive at quarter past ten, that's for sure,' Colleen said as they walked into the postnatal area.

Vince spun and put his hand up in front of her. 'Whoa, Col. Back up a little. How the hell do you know that?'

She shrugged, a few strands of curly red hair escaping from her firmly wound bun. 'I went over to his office to ask him about the order of the hymns. I'd left the list at home.'

'How did you get into the presbytery?'

'Well, not everybody's aware of this,' she said with a wink, 'but there's a green door that—'

'Leads into his office from the outside,' finished Vince.

'Anyway, I just knocked on that door.' Colleen seemed surprised Vince was in the know. 'The Monsignor was always in there at that time, going through his homily.'

'How … how was he?'

'Well, he wasn't dead, if that's what you mean. He told me he'd cut himself shaving,' she added, pointing to her cheek, 'and he seemed a bit distracted by that.' She paused, as if a sudden thought had struck her. 'That must've been *just* before he … he was … you know.'

'*Exactly*,' said Vince. 'You hadn't thought of telling this to the police?'

She shook her head. 'Didn't think much about it and no one asked me till now. I was only there for a minute.'

'And you're sure about the time?'

She nodded. 'I looked at my phone as I was walking over. I remember because I almost got cleaned up by a car that was leaving the car park.'

Vince could imagine Colleen wandering along in a daze, phone in hand. 'What sort of car?'

'It was a VW Golf. Same model as mine,' she added, 'but silver. It was flying.'

Ah ha! Jane drives a silver Golf.

'You need to contact the CID stat, Col,' said Vince, 'and tell them you saw the Mons alive and well at ten-fifteen.'

Vince abandoned the ward round, hurried off down the stairs, fumbling for his own mobile, and punched in Elena's number.

'*Detective Sergeant Elena Genovesi's phone. Please leave a message.*'

'Sarge,' he said. 'You're making a big mistake. Give me a ring. ASAP.'

He texted the same message and ran out to his car. When he arrived at the surgery, he tore inside, pulled out his phone again and hit Jane's number.

'Morning, Vinny. Bit busy to talk at the—'

'Listen,' said Vince. 'I've just spoken to someone who saw O'Shannassey right after you left. She saw you drive away. You're off the hook.'

'Don't sound so surprised,' she said with a brief laugh. 'I have an appointment this morning with Detective Sergeant Genovesi at eleven o'clock at the local police station. I guess she won't be coming now.'

Vince glanced at the time—eight-thirty. 'She'll be on the road,' he said. 'I'm trying to get in touch with her to save her the drive.' He noticed a message coming in on his phone. 'I'd better go. You can relax now, Janey.'

'I appreciate your detection work.' She paused. 'But I won't be relaxing any time soon. Bye.'

Vince hit his missed call button.

'Hi Doc, just got your message.'

'Where are you?'

'Sitting in the car with DC Watkins going through—where are we, Doug?—Penshurst.'

'Which way are you facing?'

'Which way do you *think*?' she said.

'Get young Doug to do a U-ey, Sarge. I have a witness who saw O'Shannassey alive after Jane had left him. She's not your murderer.'

Vince heard Elena instruct the constable to stop.

'Are you absolutely sure about that?'

'Yeah, it's rock solid. Jane left a few minutes after ten and this lady talked to the Mons at twenty past.'

'Who *is* this person?' asked Elena. 'And she spoke to him about *what*?'

Vince had seldom heard her so rattled. 'Colleen Maloney, a midwife and the church—'

'Musical director,' said Elena. 'Colleen is from Nullawarre. She was in Luigi's year at school.'

'All them Maloneys are good singers,' PC Watkins added in the background. 'Even young Brendan can—'

'Enough about the Maloneys, Constable,' said Elena.

'She went over to speak to the Mons about the hymns,' said Vince. 'He was alive and kicking.'

There was a long pause, then Vince could hear Elena instructing Watkins to turn the car around.

'See you later.'

'Don't mention it, Sarge.'

'I'm not going to thank you, Dr Hanrahan,' she snapped. 'The boss wants a result—ASAP! I'm right back to square one again. A fifteen-minute window, a bunch of alibis, and an unsnibbed side door are all I've got. And yes, that's correct, *thank* you, Constable—now he'll want to bring the homicide squad down.'

* * *

Vince turned on his computer and started work. He found himself chatting away to the punters as they came and went, enjoying both the repartee and the diagnostic challenges. *This GP caper is not so bad after all.*

At lunchtime, Shirley came to his door with a grim look and a bundle of envelopes.

'You don't usually hand deliver the mail,' said Vince. 'I feel privileged.'

She shoved a letter in front of him. 'Cop a gander at this.'

He scanned down the page. It was from a large personal-injury law firm, which had a branch office in Warrnambool.

Dear Dr Tiang,

This letter is to inform you that Mr and Mrs Cartwright have made a claim on behalf of their daughter, Skylah, against Dr Vincent Hanrahan, who has been employed at your practice for the last two years. The claim relates to alleged brain damage resulting from prolonged birth hypoxia and head trauma following a Kielland's forceps rotation on 7/2/18 at Warrnambool Base Hospital. I understand you have treated the baby and request a copy of your clinical notes including investigations and specialist reports. Enclosed is a signed release from both parents.

Shirley dumped the bundle on Vince's desk. 'Lorraine reckons you haven't opened your mails for over a week.'

Vince shuffled through the envelopes—the usual assortment. At the bottom was a letter from the same firm requesting his files as well. Dated last Monday.

Vince sat back in his chair. 'Did you send them your notes?'

Shirley sniffed. 'Course not. You know the scores. No subpoena, no file.' She pointed at him. 'You a liability, Rooned. You told me this baby Skylah stuff was sorted out.' The door slammed behind her as she marched out.

Vince picked up the phone and speed-dialled the Victorian Medical Defence Association.

'VMDA, Bridget Ryan.'

'Got a letter from Maurice Blackburn. So has Shirley. They are pressing on with the bloody—'

'May I ask who is speaking?'

'Vince, Vince Hanrahan.'

'Aka, my problem child. Shoot the letter through and then we'll discuss it.'

'Will do,' said Vince. 'But this is just a case of "no win, no charge" kite flying, yeah?'

'Not necessarily. They don't take on a matter like this unless they've obtained a supportive opinion from an independent medico-legal specialist. And they don't come cheap.'

'*Independent*,' Vince said with a snort. '"Opinions for sale" more like. I learned that last time.'

He'd been sued three years ago after the maternal death that had precipitated his fall from grace and banishment to Warrnambool.

'Still bitter and twisted, I see.'

Another snort. 'This could be serious, Bridg.'

'Couldn't agree more. But it's hard to prove medical negligence. Just because there's a bad outcome doesn't mean the doctor can be sued. They have to prove that you didn't provide *reasonable* care—not *perfect* care.'

'You know me—always aiming for perfection.'

'Do you mean work or play?'

Vince and Bridget had shared a student house in Carlton decades ago. Back then she and Vince were an item. For a semester. Before Lydia moved in.

'They also have to prove that your failure to take reasonable care was the cause of the alleged injuries that resulted in compensable pain and suffering and ongoing medical costs, etc.'

'Who decides if it was reasonable care?'

'Your care has to be widely accepted by your peers as competent professional practice.'

'The Melbourne obstets bubble is pretty small, Bridg. What if your peers have old scores to settle?'

She paused. 'Just send me the letter. Because the baby was born in a public hospital, I will contact their insurers too and we will obtain a separate medico-legal opinion.'

'Do I respond to the letter?'

'Not until you hear from me, but you *do* need to get in touch with the Medical Board.'

'I'm in almost daily contact with them.'

* * *

Vince brought up his afternoon list and re-entered the fray. His last patient was Max Saunders, the injured Snappers full forward, with the assistant coach Nick Koutolis in tow.

'G'day, Max. G'day, Nick. How are things, gents?'

'What did me latest scan show, Doc?'

Vince highlighted the result on Max's file. 'Improving, but not completely healed.'

'When's he gunna be ready to rock and roll?' said Nick. 'We need him out there kicking goals.'

'Minimum six weeks for a hamstring strain,' said Vince.

'Be close on that now. He did it Easter Sunday morning.'

'Yair,' said Max. 'Just having a practice shot for goal, then twang! Felt like someone had shot me in the back of the leg.'

Vince frowned. 'Brodes told me you did it doing sprints round the boundary.'

Max shook his head. 'Nah, I was just kickin' the footy.'

'Brodes wasn't there when it happened,' said Nick. 'He went off early to cart extra chairs from the clubhouse home for Easter lunch.'

'Is that right?'

'By the time we finished up and put everything away, I was late to me mother-in-law's,' Nick added with a laugh. 'Copped a spray from the missus.'

'Hop up on the couch, Maxxy,' Vince said, then examined the affected muscle. 'Keep on with the physio,' he said. 'Should be ready to go in two weeks.'

After shutting the door behind them, Vince made some notes, shut down his computer, and walked toward the back door to find Lorraine standing in the office, brandishing a phone.

'It's Professor McKenzie,' she said. 'He's *very* insistent.'

'Surprise, surprise.'

Vince took the phone, retraced his steps, and flopped into his seat. 'Evening, Lachie,' he said. 'Nice drop of rain, eh?'

'We've received notification from Maurice Blackburn that they are acting for the Cartwrights who are suing you for medical negligence in relation to birth hypoxia and traumatic brain damage to their baby—'

'*Alleged* birth hypoxia.'

'So you say. We are still awaiting James Jobling's final report—'

'Jobs' *hatchet* job, you mean.'

'Which will be completed by the end of the month—'

'*Fait accompli*, mate.'

'Vincent, this cavalier and reckless attitude is inappropriate. Try to be civil.'

'Scouts honour, Professor.'

McKenzie cleared his throat. 'If this lawsuit proceeds and if Dr Jobling's report is, um, unfavourable, the Board will suspend your medical registration forthwith, pending complete deregistration.'

Vince jumped out of his chair. 'You can't fucking do that!'

'I am merely a mouthpiece of the Board. I have done my best to—'

'To stitch me right up, you—'

Vince managed to clamp his errant tongue and hung up. He sat at his desk, looking around at the examination couch, instrument trolley, foetal stethoscope, and other tools of the trade.

'BASTARD!'

He sent a quick email to Bridget, then jumped in his car and called in at Kermond's, another local institution—rumoured (by Warrnamboolians) to have the best hamburgers in the country—picked up one with the lot, sans chips, and headed off. As he wound through the darkening streets until he pulled up at the Snapper house, he felt an odd sense of familiarity. *Maybe I am home.*

He greeted Deefer, filled up her bowl, sat on his old chair next to the back door, munching his hamburger, and looked up into the sky. He was shivering—not that it was cold—and watched the stars appearing out of the dark grey. The dog finished her dinner and sat next to Vince, content.

'Looks like I'm screwed, old mate,' said Vince, patting her golden head. 'Can't see any way out of this one.' He pointed at the sky. 'Used to think I was born under a lucky star. Dad always maintained I'd been "hit up the arse with a rainbow", but it looks like my luck's run out.'

Vince turned his head; he could hear a tap running. He looked across at his side fence. There was water leaking through from next door. 'Mrs H must have left a tap on.' He and Deefer walked around to the Harringtons' front door and Vince knocked. There was the sound of a baby crying inside.

'Come in, D-d-doctor Vince,' said Kieran. 'We're looking after Skylah while Trace is out. She keeps c-c-crying.'

Vince looped Deefer's lead over the nearest garden gnome and went inside.

'You've got water running in the backyard,' he told Mrs H, who was juggling the distressed infant on her hip.

'Oh yes, of course. I forgot all about it. Just giving them veggies a drink and I got all sidetracked with the little one. Here.' She handed the baby to Vince and ducked out the back.

'There, that's done,' she said, wiping her hands on her apron. 'Could you have a look at her, Dr Vince? I dunno why she won't settle. None of mine screamed like that.'

Won't get this chance again. 'I'll just grab my bag.'

A minute later he stripped off Skylah and sat her on her grand-mother's capacious lap. 'Temp is okay … ears and throat … not dehydrated … chest normal … no odd rashes.'

He looked up at his neighbour. 'Not sure, Mrs H, but it's nothing serious. A virus, or teething maybe.'

Vince said goodbye, collected the dog, and returned to the Snapper house.

'I don't know why she's crying, Deef, but she's got that small head, tiny eyes, and flat skin between her nose and upper lip—typical of Foetal Alcohol Spectrum Disorder.' He went back inside. 'Problem is, how to prove it.'

34

'G'day, Dr Williams.'

'Morning, Vincent. How are things with you?'

Vince rubbed his unshaven jaw and looked at the screen. 'In deep shit, if you really want to know.'

'I understand this legal action is going ahead.'

'That's not the half of it. Your mates on the Board plan to crucify me altogether.'

Myf nodded, seeming uncharacteristically devoid of a response.

'Weird thing is,' he said, looking around his ramshackle kitchen, 'last time around, I'd mucked up. Good and proper. This time I've done the right thing and I'm copping it in the neck.'

'It's crucial that you have appropriate legal representation, Vincent,' said Myf. 'Then you must let them do their jobs. And even if the Board strikes you off, you'll be able to reapply for registration.'

Vince laughed. 'Pigs might fly. If I turned into Mother Theresa, they still wouldn't re-register me.'

Again Myf seemed to have no answer. They locked eyes on their screens for ten seconds until she looked away.

'How did you get on at the fathers and daughters weekend?'

'Disaster. Upset the school, pissed off the fathers, and embarrassed the girls.'

Myf opened her mouth and closed it again. Vince noticed her blue eyes were no longer dancing.

'Have the police discovered who murdered Monsignor O'Shannassey?'

'No, but Jane's off the hook. Someone else saw him after she left.'

'Brilliant! At least you can put that behind you.'

He shook his head. 'I'd still like to find out who did it to help my copper mate. And my sister-in-law is still after the priest who abused Joey. I want to find that bastard too.'

Myf frowned. 'You need to attend to your main game.'

He laughed again. 'You mean the spectre of professional disgrace and unemployment. I'd forgotten about that for a minute there.'

She frowned. 'No laughing matter.'

'Maybe I've got one shot left in the locker.'

'Don't do anything rash, Vincent.'

'Who me? Better go. I have to load that gun.'

* * *

Vince raced off to the hospital and headed for the detox unit. Across the corridor, he could see Charlie McNamee engaged in a deep discussion with the family of a woman in one of the beds. He ducked into the ward office. The computer was on and live. *Beauty!* Vince pulled a memory stick from his pocket and slotted it into the back of the monitor. He found Tracey Cartwright's file and had a quick look. *Like I thought, she's got form.* He saved the file, ejected the device, and closed the screen just as Charlie and his entourage walked out of the patient's room and into the hallway outside the office.

'Morning, Vince,' said Charlie. 'Looking up the footy scores?'

'You must have to be a junkie to get some attention in this joint,' answered Vince. He pulled a piece of paper from his pocket and handed it to Charlie. 'Been looking up some music. Got the harp tab here for that Eric Bibb tune. Probably be a bit beyond you, mate, but have a go.' He looked around the ward. 'Keep up the good work, team. Bye.'

* * *

The atmosphere at the clinic was eerily calm. Shirley, the Prez, and Lorraine seemed to be avoiding him. *I get it*, thought Vince. *I'm yesterday's man; they'll be lining up squeaky clean newly trained GPs for interview. Better than damaged goods like me.*

He marched to his room, shut the door, stuck the memory stick into his computer, and brought up Tracey's file. At her initial hospital visit regarding the new pregnancy, she had filled in the usual antenatal questionnaire to assess family and financial support, screen for depression, and look for substance issues. She had ticked 'more than five units daily' under alcohol, which had triggered the referral to WRAD, who then assessed her as a problem drinker and alcohol dependent. Her initial lab test had shown elevated blood-alcohol and raised levels of liver enzymes. Tracey had attended the clinic sporadically during the pregnancy but then dropped out of the system.

Vince clenched his fist. *Yes!*

He ejected the memory stick and looked at it.

Now, how can I use this information?

* * *

Vince called in his first patient and proceeded through his list on automatic pilot, his mind a million miles away. As soon as he booted the last sheep for the morning down the shute, he made a phone call.

'G'day, Bridg, it's Vince Hanrahan.'

'Morning, Vince. I was about to ring you. Thanks for sending the letter from Maurice Blackburn. I have to tell you that—'

'First, let me ask you something.'

'Shoot.'

'Who owns a patient's medical records?'

'The doctor or hospital that created them. However, the patient also has a right to that information.'

'Can we obtain copies of the hospital medical records of Tracey Cartwright?'

'Only with her written permission,' said Bridget. 'Unless the court issues a subpoena.'

'So if there was incriminating information in her hospital file about her drinking, we could only use that information if the matter goes to court.'

'Correct.'

'Bugger!'

She paused. 'Tell me you haven't accessed any hospital records inappropriately.'

'Hypothetically,' said Vince, ignoring the question, 'if we had such information, could it be used to dissuade Maurice Blackburn from pursuing the case?'

'Not if patient confidentiality was breached in the process. That would place us, I mean *you*, in a much worse position.'

How much worse could it get?

'So,' she went on, 'the good news is that VMDA are willing to act for you in this matter—'

'As they should. I've been paying my sub for twenty-five years.'

'—*unless* our independent medico-legal opinion is that your level of care was not deemed to be reasonable when measured against that of your peers.'

'And then?'

Bridget paused again. 'And then you would be on your own.'

* * *

Vince arrived home to find Deefer licking out her bowl and a note on his kitchen table. 'Crumbed chops + vegies in the fridge. Just needs heating up.'

He nodded with appreciation and popped the dinner in his overworked microwave. The meat was a bit dry and the vegetables mushy, but he wasn't about to complain. His mobile started to sing as he tossed the dishes in the already crowded sink.

'Hi, girls.'

'Hey, Bins,' said Georgie. 'How's life in the 'Bool?'

'Beautiful one day, perfect the next. How are you guys? Demolishing the VCE, I bet.'

'We're trying, Dad,' said Tessa, 'but Ivan says if we don't get into our top preference at Melbourne Uni, the whole year's been a waste of time.'

'What a load of crap,' responded Vince. 'ITT's advice is both incorrect and unwelcome.'

'That's what Mum said,' said Georgie.

'She told him to butt out of it—'

'He went way ballistic—'

'Said he was paying the best tutors—'

'Told Mum she was ungrateful—'

'She said mind your own business—'

'All you care about is golf anyway—'

'At least their father has some common sense—'

'For all his sins—'

'I hear he's about to be struck off—'

'Whoa, girls,' said Vince. 'This is getting out of hand.'

'What does getting struck off even mean?' asked Georgie.

Vince paused. 'I'm in a bit of trouble with the Medical Board.'

'Same old, or new?'

'Newish.'

'You'll be right, Bins,' said Georgie. 'Just hang in.'

I am—by the skin of my teeth.

'I need to sort a few things out.'

The girls have enough going on, they don't need my troubles as well.

'Listen up, enough about me, back to the VCE. I want you to do well, but I'll still love you no matter what happens. So do your best and let Ivan's opinion go through to the keeper.'

They both laughed. 'That's exactly what Mum said,' said Tessa. 'You guys are *so* alike.'

'Yeah,' said Georgie. 'You should get together.'

To paraphrase the Bard of Avon, is there a chink in the wall?

As soon as Vince put his phone down, it started ringing again. This time it was Jane.

'Hello, Vince. I've been trying to get you for ages. You must spend your whole life on the phone.'

'None of it initiated by me,' he replied.

'Just thought I'd let you know that we've made some progress with Ambrose Dennis.'

'Found him?'

'I went to see his niece. Last she heard he was running a bed-and-breakfast somewhere. Maybe in Tasmania.'

Vince laughed. 'Lot of B and Bs in Tassie. You plan to stay in every one till you find him?'

'Just giving you a heads-up,' she replied. 'You said you'd help me.'

'I'm flat out helping myself.'

'I realise you're busy but—'

'I'll help you. Okay? Just got a bit on at the moment. Keep me in the loop.'

'Thanks for that,' she responded. 'When I find him, your detective buddy might have another murder to solve.'

'Don't joke about that stuff. You came very close to being locked up for topping the Mons.'

'Has your girlfriend cracked that one yet?'

Girlfriend! Barely on speaking terms these days.

'Apparently not. Back to the random intruder theory, I guess.'

'One thing I remember now is that when I came out of the presbytery there was another vehicle in that church car park. Over in the back corner.'

'Uh huh.'

'Must've arrived while I was in there.'

'An early bird, I guess. There's some pious old dears in that congregation.'

'Looked more like a ute.'

'Can you remember any details?'

''Fraid not,' she said. 'I was a bit distracted at the time.'

'Thanks, Jane. I'll pass that on.'

'How are the twins?'

'Lots of VCE stress. And I'm no help to them down here.'

'Must be hard for you.'

Everything's bloody hard for me. 'As the old man used to say, "It's all part of life's rich tapestry".'

'Wise man, your dad.'

'You bet,' said Vince.

35

In a flash, it was Friday night and Vince was sitting at Fanny's facing an empty chair. He pulled out his phone and checked his messages—yes, he and Elena definitely had a date. They had not spoken for a week or so and it was close to three weeks since their last rendezvous, but this time neither had cancelled. He loaded up a TED talk and listened to an earnest young woman discussing how growing bonsai plants changed her life—anything to distract him from constant negative ruminating, then flicked to another one talking about the benefits of faecal transplant. *Bloody hell!*

He looked up as Elena arrived and slid into the seat opposite.

'Sorry I'm late, Doc.'

'The life of a copper, eh?'

'No, it wasn't work,' she said. Vince noticed a frown on that inscrutable Mona Lisa face. 'Nonna's had a fall and broken her hip. It was operated on yesterday. She won't eat the hospital food so I just took her up some pasta.'

Elena's grandmother lived on a farm near Timboon with her daughter. She was a frail old dear in her mid-nineties and Vince's patient.

'Why didn't you tell me?' he asked as the waiter came to take their orders.

'Dr Paras was on-call the night she came in,' Elena answered.

'You know I would've been happy to look after her, right? On-call or not.'

'He has been very kind.'

Vince raised his eyebrows. *Course he has.*

'Nonna's going well,' Elena added. 'That's the main thing.'

'Say *bonjourno* for me. I'll go in and make sure Pistol Pete checks her bone density.'

She nodded, then they ordered their food and didn't speak for a few minutes.

'Are we okay, Sarge?' Vince eventually asked.

'I don't know,' she said. 'Are we?'

'Everything seems so complicated.'

Elena paused. 'It doesn't have to be.'

Why did I even go there?

'How's the big investigation going?' he said, changing tack away from the personal.

'Nowhere—like my detective career. Homicide are coming down next week and the boss is ropeable. I've hit a brick wall with this one.'

'Janey told me there was a ute parked down the back of the church-yard when she left the presbytery that day.'

Elena frowned. 'Colour? Make? Signage?'

'She didn't take any notice,' said Vince.

'There's no CCTV at Sacred Heart,' said Elena, 'and there's an awful lot of utes in Warrnambool.'

'Fair comment.'

She grimaced at her wine and took a sip. 'How are things with you?'

'Fair to middling,' said Vince. 'Jane is still chasing Joey's abuser—slowly pulling in the net.'

Elena nodded and they ate in silence for a few minutes, each lost in thought.

'You sorted out your problems with the Medical Board?' *On target. As usual.*

'Far from it,' Vince replied. *Might as well tell her.* He waved up the Cone of Silence and explained about the baby and the associated medico-legal issues.

'Both the Board *and* Maurice Blackburn are on my case now.' He pushed his plate away and gulped down some water. 'Looks like I'll lose my ticket. And wind up in court.' He paused. 'Again.'

* * *

After a weekend of sitting in front of the box watching football and old movies, on Sunday night Vince broke the habit of a lifetime and opened his work email account to find a message from VMDA and another from the Board. His heart started pounding as he opened the first one.

Dear Dr Hanrahan,

We have obtained an opinion from Dr Ravi Das re Skylah Cartwright. Dr Das has reviewed the appropriate clinical information and feels that the aetiology of the baby's delayed development is uncertain. While the baby has some facial features typical of Foetal Alcohol Spectrum Disorder, it's not diagnostic.

The MRI was reviewed by a neonatal radiologist who felt it showed changes consistent with both birth ischaemia and FASD but was not definitive for either, and there was no evidence of brain injury—making forceps trauma or later physical abuse unlikely.

The VMDA is prepared to act for you in this matter, but caution you that the circumstances of this case and your past record make a pre-court settlement advisable.

Those radiologists were just bloody fence-sitters! He clicked on the other email.

Dear Dr Hanrahan,

The Board has received the report from Professor James Jobling regarding Skylah Cartwright, DOB 7/2/18. He has concluded that prolonged birth ischaemia due to instrumental delivery is the most likely cause of the baby's microcephaly, failure to thrive, and delayed development.

Given that your provisional registration excluded you from high-risk obstetrics and the likely outcome of the impending legal suit, the Board hereby suspends your registration to practice medicine from next Monday and intends to cancel your registration completely at our meeting next week. You will then be formally advised by letter.

Yours sincerely,

Simon Rutherford, Chair.

Vince sat motionless on the coach for a few minutes, shaking his head and clenching his fists. Initial white-hot rage gave way to slow burning resignation.

'I'm fucked,' he told the dozing Deefer. 'Might as well have a few reds and be done with it.'

The dog woke, shook herself, and stood. Vince looked at her and pulled himself up too.

'Or else, I can pull that trigger.'

* * *

He grabbed a plastic container off the kitchen table, washed and dried it, and walked around to Mrs Harrington's front door.

'Just bringing this back, Mrs H,' Vince said. 'From that chicken casserole Thursday night. It was delicious, thanks.'

'Come in and have a cuppa,' she responded. 'Kieran's off havin' fish and chips with the family group from the parish.'

Vince walked through to the kitchen, sat down, and glanced around. There was barely a centimetre of wall not covered with family photographs, china plates, and framed prints. There were magazines, newspapers, knitting-in-progress, and folded washing on the kitchen table. It was a bewildering kaleidoscope of clutter. Made the Snapper house look like a monk's cell. Mrs Harrington turned on the kettle and put a plate of freshly baked chocolate brownies in front of him.

'Does he enjoy those outings?'

'Too right.' She poured the boiling water into a large teapot with a mauve nylon cosy and sat down. 'They look after him real good, them church people.'

'You don't go?'

She shook her head. 'Good chance for Kieran to be a bit, you know, independent.' Mrs Harrington gestured at herself. 'I'm not getting any younger.' She poured the tea. 'I was hoping Trace would look after him after I'm gone, but with one thing and another, I don't know if that'll happen.'

Vince nodded. He knew that the parents of disabled children often worried about who would take over that carer's role when they passed away. He took a deep breath—now or never.

'I want to talk to you about Tracey, Mrs H.'

She pursed her lips and frowned.

'You know that she and Dustin are suing me about the baby.'

Mrs H folded her arms. 'Nothing to do with me.'

'Just hear me out,' said Vince. 'I have proof that Tracey was drinking heavily during the pregnancy and I'm sure that's what caused Skylah's problems.'

Mrs Harrington sat stony-faced.

'And if the matter goes to court, regardless of the outcome, that information will come out. And Community Services will get involved in the baby's care.'

And if *it goes to court, my medical career will be over.*

No response.

'If someone was to pass this information onto Tracey and Dustin, it might make them think twice about proceeding.'

She took a swallow of her tea and glanced at a family photograph on the opposite wall: her seven children, partners, and grandchildren, with Kieran beaming at the camera from the back row.

'Thanks for dropping me Tupperware back, Dr Vince.'

36

Shirley was waiting for Vince in his consulting room the next morning. 'Take a seat,' she said, closing the door.

'Problem, boss?'

'You always a problem, bud.' She pointed a long index finger—finished with bright green nail polish—at his chest, then used it to tick off the red-tipped outstretched fingers on her other hand.

'You got your eye off the balls round here, you suspended from labour wards, you being sued, you being castrated by the Board, and Pistols Pete waiting in the wing.'

'Pete Paras! What the hell do you mean?'

'Pistol sick of solo GP, want to join my group. Does babies, give anaesthetics—like recruiting Gazza Dangerfield!'

'You must be joking!'

Shirley again pointed at him. 'So is there a vacancy, Rooned?'

'No, no, NO!' Vince said, then paused. 'Well … maybe.'

Shirley put her head on one side and flapped her upturned palms in a seesawing motion. 'What that even mean?'

'Just give me a few days, Shirley,' said Vince. 'Leave Pete Parras on the interchange bench. Maybe there's a tiny flame at the end of this black tunnel.'

Shirley got up. 'You better get down there and light the bloody thing yourself!'

Vince nodded.

'Or else …' She lifted her head and slashed in front of her neck with a crimson talon.

* * *

Mark Brody was Vince's first patient. He sat down, rolled up his sleeve, and pointed at the blood pressure machine on the desk.

'Check me pressure, Doc.' He grinned. 'Reckon you'll be surprised.'

Vince wrapped the automatic cuff on Mark's muscle-bound upper arm and they both watched as 133/77 came up on the screen.

'That's a whole lot better, Brodes,' said Vince.

'I've given the smokes away. Took your advice.' He pulled a fidget spinner out of his top pocket and placed it in front of Vince. 'Whenever I get the craving, I give this bugger a whirl.' He laughed. 'Like a big kid, eh?'

'Well done,' said Vince.

'You keep that one, I got plenty of 'em.'

'Thanks.' Vince put it in his desk drawer. 'What about we cut the dose of your blood pressure pills by half and check again in two weeks?'

The big man stood up. 'Will do.'

Next on the list was 'Nipper' Flaherty, a local publican who had been two years behind Vince at St Bernard's. Nipper had shared lots of beers with his customers over the years and had the red face and veiny nose to show for it. He'd been a lithe, speedy winger in the school football team but had put on a lot of condition in the intervening thirty-plus years. Most locals regarded the nickname as ironic, but back in the old days it had been accurate.

'I reckon it's time I had the other hip done.'

'Playing up?'

Nipper laughed. 'It used to be my good hip, but since I got the new one, it's become the crook one.'

'Drop your daks and hop up on the couch, mate.'

Vince examined the offending joint and detected the tell-tale reduction in movement, especially outward rotation. 'I think that hip's stuffed, Nipper. Better get it x-rayed and I'll refer you back to Mr Wid-neratne for more carpentry.'

Vince handed over the relevant paperwork and they both stood.

'Remember that priest, Dirty Dennis?'

Vince pricked up his ears. 'Name rings a bell.' *Like Big Ben on steroids!*

'He used to come to St Bernard's and do religious instruction and stuff. Bit of a creep.'

'He was after my time.'

'Well, I was just down at Bruny Island with a few of the boys on a fishing trip.' He pulled out a handkerchief and blew his nose. 'Bruny's down Tassie way.'

'I know where it is,' said Vince. 'And …?'

Vince knew that Nipper not only enjoyed 'huntin, shootin, and fishin', but also spinning out a yarn.

'There was Clarko, Macca, Dyno, and meself.'

Cut to the chase!

'So we're at the Hotel Bruny this night. You know the one at Alonnah, South Bruny?'

'Never been there.'

'Nice pub,' said Nipper. 'Good food.'

'Yep.'

'And I know me pubs.'

Get on with it, Nipper!

'And?'

'I get up to go to the dunny and I walk past this table and this Dennis joker is sitting there with a few local blokes. Looking right at home. So I sez hello to him and tell him who I am.' He paused and chuckled. 'And you know what?'

Vince shook his head.

'Bugger stands up and reckons he's never seen me before and it's a case of, you know …'

'Mistaken identity?'

'That's it.'

'But you're sure it was him?'

'Too right.' Nipper nodded. 'It was Dirty all right. He must be hiding or something.'

'When was this?'

'Weekend before last. We caught a big feed of …'

Vince opened the door. 'Better keep moving, mate.' He pointed out to the packed waiting room. 'Got a few to get through.'

Nipper laughed on his way out. 'You doctors. It's like a bloody sausage factory.'

Vince picked up his mobile and hammered out a message to Jane.

Got a tip that Dennis was seen at the only pub on Bruny Island. Seemed like a regular. Narrows the field a bit.

She replied immediately. *Fancy a trip to Tassie?*

When the smoke clears, Vince answered.

I realise you're flat out down there.

Funnily enough, thought Vince, soon I may have all the time in the world.

* * *

By the end of Friday, there had been no response from Mrs Harrington, no word from the Cartwrights, and nothing further from Maurice Blackburn. Most of his adult life Vince had run his own agenda, been his own boss. Now his whole future was at the mercy of others and there was nothing he could do about it.

He turned off his computer and looked around the room, then panned across to the two certificates on the wall: MBBS, University of Melbourne, 1988 and Fellowship of the Royal Australian College of Obstetricians and Gynaecologists, 1993.

* * *

The town was quiet as he headed along Timor Street and turned left into the main drag. It was dark, and a wild wind was gusting around the streets. His car radio told him they were about to bounce the ball for the Friday night footy—a big Richmond versus Collingwood blockbuster.

'Suppose the locals are all home in front of their TVs,' he told Benny. He found a park down the bottom end of Liebig Street and sat for a few minutes before walking across the road to Fanny's. A vehicle slowed as it cruised past him and Big Brodes wound down the window.

'See you at Koroit Sundy, Doc. Go Snappers!'

A light went on in Vince's brain. A Eureka moment. He walked into the restaurant and saw Elena sitting patiently in the rear. She was side on, her Roman profile, beautiful skin, and cascade of thick black hair contrasting sharply with her glittering earrings and red scarf. *She really is gorgeous.*

Vince greeted her, hung his scarf and old leather jacket on the peg, and sat down.

'I reckon I've solved your murder, Sarge.'

He looked around, waved up the Cone of Silence, leant forward and whispered, 'My mate, Mark Brody. Mark told me he hated the Mons because of what happened to Travis at the seminary.'

'He has an alibi.'

'I'm getting to that.' Vince paused as the waitress filled their drinks and dropped two menus on the table.

'Just in case youse two want something different this week,' she added with a grin.

'Brodes left training early that day on the pretext of dropping some chairs back to his house.'

Elena frowned.

Now I've got your attention. 'But,' Vince leant forward again, 'his wife told me she didn't see him at all that morning.'

'Hmm.'

'And she said they had only six for lunch, so they wouldn't have needed extra chairs.'

'Interesting.'

'*And* Jane saw a ute in the church car park when she left the presbytery.'

She nodded.

'Brodes drives a ute.' Vince winked, sat back, and drained his water glass.

Elena waited while the waitress took their orders and then sat forward. 'Lots of tradies drive utes. All circumstantial, Doc. No proof.'

'You still got the prints from those rosary beads?'

'We do.'

'Why don't you check Brodes's prints?'

She shook her head. 'Can't just pull someone in and fingerprint them.'

Vince stood up. 'Hold that thought, Sarge. Back in a sec.'

He rushed out to his car and shot down to the surgery. Fifteen minutes later he walked back into Fanny's with a specimen bag in his hand.

'That's not some gross sample of someone's body fluid, is it?' Elena asked with a shudder.

Vince upended the bag and dropped a fidget spinner onto a paper napkin on the table.

He pointed at the multicoloured gadget. 'Mark Brody's,' he said. 'Compare the prints on this with the ones from the rosary beads. I bet you a case of Grange they'll match.'

Elena picked up the toy with the napkin, put it back in the plastic pouch and popped it in her bag.

'Wouldn't have seen Mark Brody as a fidget spinner sort of guy,' she said.

'Didn't they teach you about the dangers of stereotyping at Detective School?'

Elena smiled. 'Touché. I'll check it out.' She raised her wine glass in a toast. 'Thanks, Doc, you may have got me off the hook.'

Vince kept his water tumbler on the table. 'Whereas I'm still hanging up there like a dead cow at the abattoir.'

She raised her arched black eyebrows. 'How is that baby going?'

'Just the same—significant developmental problems. And I'm about to be trashed in court,' he added, 'then deregistered by the Board.'

She sat forward. 'But surely—'

Vince pointed at his watch. 'By this time next week I'll be unemployed, unemployable,' he gestured toward Melbourne, 'and couch surfing at Trisha's.'

Unless that shot I fired hits the target by Monday.

They finished their meals in silence and stood outside Fanny's shortly after, the cold wind whipping around their shoulders. Vince leant in to give Elena the usual brotherly peck on the cheek. She wrapped her arms around him, pulled him close, and kissed him on the mouth, her hair draped around his face. He reciprocated the embrace and for an instant they were locked together on that cold Liebig Street pavement. Then a passing car honked and broke the spell.

Vince pulled away, more words of Shakespeare ringing in his head—*that way madness lies*—and stumbled off around the corner to the safety of the waiting Benny.

37

'Popped in to say we aren't going to sue you after all,' Dustin Cartwright said from the kitchen.

'That's right,' added Tracey. 'We realise it wasn't your fault and I was a silly girl to drink so much.'

'Silly girl, silly girl, silly girl,' chanted Mrs H, Little Lachie, and Kieran from the hallway.

The trio's chorus morphed into the sound of Deefer whining at the back door. Vince woke with a start, bathed in sweat. He dragged himself up and looked in the kitchen and up the hall. No one. *Just a weird-arse dream.*

He glanced at the time. 'Shit! Almost nine.' He opened the back door. The hungry dog bounded in and slobbered all over him.

'Sorry Deef, must've slept in.' Well, slept in for the last two hours, that was. Until then he'd been lying there, wide awake, his mind alternating between turpitude and turbulence.

He washed his face, then peered at his image in the cracked bathroom mirror. A lined face with blank eyes, thin lips, and greying stubble looked back. *What would any woman see in that ugly mug?*

Deefer was scratching at the kitchen cupboard. Vince grabbed the dog food and filled up her bowl.

'Time for some exercise therapy,' he told her as she wolfed her breakfast down. He donned his running clothes while she ate and they walked down the drive out onto the street. He peered across to the

Harringtons'—Mrs H's Datsun wasn't in the carport and there was no sign of Dustin's old Commodore wagon.

'So much for that dream coming true, Deef.'

The tide was out when they got to the beach and there was a decent swell, but also a blustery onshore wind and the waves were breaking as soon as they formed. Vince and Deefer trotted down onto the sand. A man in a tinny was leading two racehorses through the water in the shelter of the breakwater, a few fishermen were trying their luck with long surf rods, and many groups of people were promenading along the boardwalk—a typical Saturday morning.

Deefer ran up the beach and barked at the soaring seagulls. Vince trudged behind in the soft sand, the bay curving around in front of him with the see-saw row of Norfolk pines high on his left and the far horizon on his right.

'Morning, Doctor.' A middle-aged woman called out to him from the boardwalk as she walked down onto the beach toward him.

Vince groaned. *Here's trouble.*

'Wanted to thank you for what you done for my Jack,' she said, holding out her hand. 'He's got the pacemaker now. The specialist said you saved his life, sending him to the hospital so quick.'

'Good to hear, Aggie.'

'Hope you don't never go back to Melbourne,' she added. 'We need good doctors like you down here.'

Vince smiled, walked up to the Pavilion Café, and ordered breakfast. He sipped his coffee and looked out to sea, the choppy water heaving under the big sky.

I'll miss this.

* * *

'Evening, Lids.'

'Hello, Vincent.'

Vince had spent the afternoon curled up on the couch, the weekend papers unread on the floor. Judging from the darkness outside, night was falling. His dinner, courtesy of his 'healthy whole foods' app, was waiting in the fridge.

'How are things in Domain Road?'

'Actually, the girls and I are staying with my brother in North Balwyn.'

'Let me guess, renos at the Becker mansion? Cellar need extending?'

There was a heavy sigh. 'The girls and I plan to move back to Canterbury. I've given the tenants notice.' There was a long pause. 'Ivan and I are having some issues.'

'Ah, the trials and tribulations of young love!'

'Lay off, Vincent. I feel humiliated enough as it is.'

'Who, me?'

'Ivan has been very kind, but he works ridiculous hours and I'm a golfing widow.'

'That's odd,' said Vince. 'I thought you were still married to me. And I don't play golf.'

He could hear a muffled sob down the line.

'Okay, Lids. Sorry for being a smartarse, but you're a big girl now and responsible for your own decisions. The twins are my main concern.'

'They're doing fine,' Lydia said after a pause. 'Happy to be away from Ivan's well-intentioned but intense scholastic coaching. Tessa has her head down. Georgie could apply herself more.'

'Say hi from me. I'll ring them next week.'

'I'm concerned that the Canterbury house is too big for me and the two girls.'

'It's smaller than Chez Ivan,' said Vince.

'True,' she said. 'Most houses are. But when the girls finish school at the end of the year I'm thinking of selling and downsizing.'

'Never mind that the house is actually owned by me,' said Vince, 'and the bank.'

'How big is the mortgage?'

'Around a tidy two mill. And they hit me up for around two thousand bucks a week.'

'I see.' She paused. 'I understand that you're in danger of losing your registration.'

Vince shook his head. *The medical grapevine is still alive and well.*

'Will you come back to Melbourne if that happens?'

Vince paused. 'I really don't know what I'll do.'

'I wouldn't be able to keep up those mortgage payments, Vincent. Not on a sessional tutor's pay.'

'Aren't you at the big end of town anymore?'

'Ivan didn't like me working so much so I've taken leave from Mallesons. I'm just teaching part-time at Monash.'

'And being a Lady who Lunches.'

'Being a lady who helps her daughters navigate the VCE. Next year I'll have to go back into corporate law to pay the bills.'

'Way things are going for me,' said Vince, 'I won't be much help on the financial front.'

She sighed. 'I spent over a year with Ivan Becker and I'll never get that time back. How stupid I was.'

'Hey, Lids, I won the stupidest bastard in the world competition, hands down. You didn't even make the semis.'

'You know, Bins,' she added after a pause, 'when I drove away from South Yarra last week I just wanted my world to go back to what it was three years ago.'

Now she says it. And '*Bins!*'

'Remember Daphne du Maurier?' he asked.

'"The past is a different country".'

'That's it.'

Vince stood and looked out the window. Still no sign of life next door. 'Monday's D-day for me, Lids.'

38

Eugene von Guerard's nineteenth-century painting of Tower Hill was Vince's favourite amongst the Warrnambool Art Gallery collection. He loved the majestic perspective and the meticulous detail of the botany. Allan Findlay had told him the picture served as a template for the revegetation of the inactive volcano, which had been denuded over the years by fire, flood, and farming.

Vince had woken just after five, tossed and turned for further twenty minutes, then realised further sleep was a lost cause. So he'd dragged his body out of bed, wrapped himself in his doona, and fallen onto the coach. Groping around in the dark, he'd found the TV remote and loaded up *The Night Manager*. He knew the series off by heart, but found something about that fast-paced thriller comforting. He again lost himself in the story until morning light crept in under the curtains. Deefer started scratching at the door and Vince was shocked to see it was almost eight.

After showering, perusing the paper and eating his breakfast, Vince walked her around the block and spent the morning buying fresh produce at the farmer's market, put on a load of washing, and even gave the floor a cursory mop. Then he grabbed his medical bag, whistled the dog into the back of the car, drove back up through South Warrnambool, and paused at Elliot Street for a stream of cars heading to the golf club.

He headed straight past the hospital—no point going there,

persona non grata—and turned west onto the highway and continued on through Dennington, now full of new house estates, and out into the countryside with the choppy blue sea down to his left. There were potatoes for sale on the side of the road and large windmills whirring in the breeze.

'I feel like Don Quixote, Sancho,' he told Deefer, 'except I'm tilting against real giants—the Medical Board of Australia and the Catholic Church.' He took a right onto Lake View Road and pulled over above Tower Hill to take in the vista.

The ancient crater and lake, with its dark water, cones and spheres, and rich native flora had a timeless but mysterious aura that not even von Guerard had managed to capture on canvas. Vince stared down at the view and shivered as he contemplated the exotic strangeness of what he beheld. After a few minutes, a chime from his phone broke the spell: it was a calendar message reminding him about today's Snappers match.

* * *

By the time he arrived at the Koroit football ground, the reserve game was well underway and the netball courts were buzzing with activity. Families were milling about, laughing and cheering on their teams as the packed cars around the oval broke into bursts of tooting with every goal. *One thing about country people, they know what community means.*

Vince wandered into the Snappers' rooms and spotted Nick Koutolis.

'G'day, Doc. Can you have a look at Simmo? His ankle's a bit wobbly.'

'Sure,' said Vince. 'Where's Brodes?'

'Big fella got a call, then took off and hasn't come back. Musta been an urgent job.'

I bet Detective Sergeant Genovesi was the caller.

'High-five, Dr Vince.'

Vince looked down to the voice, where Nick's little boy, wearing his miniature Snappers' jumper, was looking up and holding high his hand.

Vince obliged.

'Me cough's gone now,' said Sam.

'Sammy reckons you're just the best doctor ever,' added Nick.

Not for much longer.

'I won't be around for the footy next week, Nick,' said Vince.

'Holiday, Doc?'

He nodded. *A really, really long holiday.*

Vince attended to a couple of players, then went out to sit near the fence.

'Thanks for lookin' after Mum, Doctor,' said a passing Koroit supporter. 'She's much better on them new pills.'

Vince sat in the winter sunshine with the sudden feeling he was looking at this whole scene from the outside. Like he was in a different universe and didn't belong to this one at all. His heart rate picked up, his respirations tightened, and he broke out in a cold sweat. *Must be coming down with something.* The palpitations worsened, his breathing became laboured, and the players on the green swathe in front faded to a blur. *What the fuck!*

A constricting pain gripped his chest and he cried out as he struggled to get a breath in at all.

Should've sorted out those palpitations. Now I'm having a bloody heart attack!

'You right, Doc?' said Nick, face up close.

Vince couldn't reply; he slid to the ground, clutching his chest, puffing hard, terror in his pounding heart.

'Get Jimmy!' Nick's voice sounded muffled and distant. 'He's watching young Mardi play in the under fifteens.'

Seconds later another face loomed in: James Sartori, a paramedic. He looped an oxygen mask around Vince's neck, wrapped a cuff on his arm, and ripped his shirt apart, attaching leads to his chest.

'You got pain, Doc? Short of breath?'

Is this how it ends?

Vince felt himself being raised in the air and slid into the back of the ambulance.

'Swallow this tablet and suck on the tube.'

Vince could hear the engine revving, felt his chariot pull away and then, with a blast of sirens and lights, he was flying. He focused on holding onto his out breaths—*slow, slow, slow*—until he felt his respiratory rate drop. *I'm okay, now. Okay.* The pain began to dissolve and he sank into a stupor.

* * *

Vince opened his eyes.

'Well, well, well, if it's not Rip Van Ox.'

He looked around; he was on a gurney, hooked up to a beeping monitor, oxygen prongs in his nose and Danny Nguyen putting an IV line in his wrist.

'How's that pain now?' Danny asked in his usual neat, clipped way.

'Gone.'

Vince glanced at his friend's kind face as it loomed over him amid the familiar surroundings of the hospital's emergency department. *I'm bloody alive!* His eyes filled with tears and he grabbed for Danny's arm.

'Steady, Ox, you'll make me mess this up.' Danny taped the cannula in position and looked up. 'Any past history of heart disease?'

Vince shook his head.

'Family history?'

Another shake.

'Smoking?'

'You *know* I don't smoke, Dan.'

'Just answer the questions.'

'Keep 'em coming, Doctor.'

'Regular meds?'

'Brintellix.'

Danny raised his eyebrows. 'Pharmaceutical name?'

'Vortioxetine,' said Vince. 'A new serotonin modulator antidepressant. Courtesy of my shrink.'

'Any elevated lipids or hypertension?'

Vince shrugged.

'So you don't have your own GP and you wouldn't know. That'd be right.' Danny glanced at the monitor and sat next to the bed. 'No ischaemic changes on your ECG and no sign of heart muscle damage on the first blood test. We'll repeat it in a few hours, but it doesn't look like you're having an infarct, so no need for clot-dissolving meds or flying you off for angiography.'

Thank you, God.

'So, what then?'

Danny pointed at the rapid, regular trace on the ECG monitor. 'You're getting runs of supraventricular tachycardia.' He nodded toward Vince. 'Even Obstetrician-slash-GPs know that's harmless.'

'Doesn't SVT happen in anxious young women?'

'*And* anxious middle-aged men.'

Vince frowned. Such a lame diagnosis; there had to be more to it than that. 'What about the chest pain and shortness of breath?'

'Old-fashioned panic attack, Ox,' said Danny. 'Been stressed lately?'

'Is the Pope a Catholic?' replied Vince, sitting up. 'My brother killed himself, marriage on the rocks, worried about my kids, going to lose my job, and about to be deregistered.' He sank back again. 'Otherwise, mate, it's all good.'

* * *

It was close to eight o'clock when Danny pulled up outside the Snapper house.

'Take it easy, Ox,' he said. 'We'll do a stress echocardiogram next week, just to make sure.'

Vince nodded and opened the car door.

'And get back onto your psychiatrist,' he added as Vince hopped out.

'Thanks, Dan. Sorry for wasting your time.'

'Don't be stupid.'

Vince waved him on. 'I owe you one.'

As Danny pulled away he noticed that there were still no cars or lights next door. *Must have gone away for the weekend*, he thought. *No eleventh hour salvation coming from Number Six.*

Looked like he'd missed the target.

He greeted the hungry Deefer, gave her a feed and went into the house, then put the container of freshly made spring rolls—courtesy of Danny's wife—in the fridge, swallowed the sleeping tablet Danny had given him, lay down in his clothes, and flaked out cold.

39

'In other news this Monday morning, President Trump says unless Kim Jong-un backs off, he will launch a nuclear missile strike on Pyongyang within twenty-four hours, the Queensland floods are receding, and the Giants had a big win over Essendon in Sydney.'

Vince turned off the car radio and cranked up Benny's heating. Even though Warrnambool was bathed in bright sunshine, he was shivering. He parked at the rear of the surgery and walked through the office. Looking straight ahead, he spoke to no one, went into his room, and shut the door. *Dead man walking.*

He finished his notes, checked the current pathology results, and sent out numerous emails, arranging follow-up and hand-over for any punters with pressing issues. *Just like before a holiday, but without the pleasurable sense of anticipation.* After that, he ducked out for a coffee. When he returned, he noticed that during his brief absence, some-one—presumably Lorraine—had placed an empty cardboard box on the floor. *Bloody hell!* He shook his head and started clearing his desk.

Like a man in a dream, Vince removed his degrees from the wall and packed away his medical equipment, then stood in the empty room—his portable ultrasound scanner, which he'd used in countless antenatal visits over three decades, still clasped firmly in his hand. He glanced at the bare desk and looked down at the box. *Is that all that remains of a professional life?*

His work phone jangled and broke the spell.

'Dr Hanrahan, it's Ms Ryan from the VMDA. Shall I say you'll call her back?'

'Put her through, Sharon.'

He sat and took the call with a sense of foreboding. 'G'day, Bridget.'

'Good news, Vince. I received a call from Maurice Blackburn this morning. The plaintiffs have withdrawn their medical negligence action against you.'

Vince stood and punched the air. 'Fantastic, Bridg, that's fan-bloody-tastic!'

'You don't know how lucky you are.' She paused. 'Any idea why they pulled out?'

Because desperate men do desperate things.

'Must've decided they didn't have much of a case.'

'Oh, but they had a good case,' said Bridget. 'The lawyer was furious. She was expecting big damages. And with "no win, no pay", the plaintiffs had nothing to lose.'

Vince paused. 'I may have intimated that—'

'*Stop* right there! I don't want to know.'

'I'm not much worried about the whys and wherefores,' said Vince. 'Now I can move on and try to get the rest of my shit together.'

Bridget laughed. 'I've informed the Board. Don't take this personally, but I don't want to hear from you again.'

'Right back at ya, Bridg. Thanks for your help.'

Vince grabbed his mobile and hit a number on his frequent contact list.

'Professor McKenzie speaking.'

'Behold, the Lord High Executioner!' said Vince.

In the 1987 Melbourne University medical student production of *The Mikado*, Vince had played the title role and McKenzie had been a humble chorus member. *How things had changed.*

'Very droll,' he replied. 'Good afternoon, Vincent. To what do I owe the pleasure?'

'Pleasure's all mine, Koko. I gather you've heard from VMDA?'

'About?'

'I'm in the clear, mate. Exonerated. Despite the best efforts of you and your co-executioner, Monsieur Jobs Defarge.'

'I wouldn't *quite* say that,' McKenzie responded after a lengthy pause. 'I have passed this information onto the Board to consider at the meeting next week. However, I've advised Simon Rutherford that your two-week suspension from all medical practice should still proceed.'

'And then?'

'Your provisional registration to work in general practice in an area of need will continue as before.'

'With only one year left to go.'

'*Two* years.'

Vince jumped up. 'But I've already been here for two bloody years!'

'After this recent, shall we call it, "indiscretion", I'll be recommending a further two years.' He paused. 'And no obstetrics.'

Vince bit down hard on his tongue. *The little bastard holds all the cards.*

He picked up his cardboard box and walked around to Shirley's consulting room. She was sitting at her desk doing paperwork.

Vince upturned the empty box and dropped it on the floor. 'Won't need this after all, Shirl. Dustin and Tracey have withdrawn their legal action. Looks like I'll be round the 'Bool for another couple of years.'

She got up and gave him a big hug, then held him away at arm's length. 'What about delivering sprogs?'

Vince grimaced. 'Still in the sin bin.'

Shirley dropped her arms and stepped away. 'We're going stirs crazy with all these bubs. You not much good to me if you banned from labour ward.' She sat down and pointed at a document on her desk. 'Pistol's VC is shit hot. And he want an answer.'

Vince threw his arms out. 'Just wait till the Board meeting next Monday. Maybe I can talk them around.'

Shirley stood again. 'One week, Rooned. That's all.' She gestured out into the waiting room. 'I got a practice to run.'

Vince went back to his room, sat at his desk, and took a deep breath. He then grabbed his phone and rang Jane.

'G'day, Janey. I've got some clear air and a bit of time off. What about we head down to Tasmania later in the week?'

'Sure, I'm on holidays at present. But I don't know how we'll find him,' she added. 'Broken Rights got a magistrate to issue an arrest warrant, but the Tasmanian Police can't locate Dennis, even with your friend's information.'

'Oh, we'll find the bastard, all right,' said Vince. 'I'll just ask a few questions at the pub.'

'Then what? Citizen's arrest?'

'We'll figure it out. I'll book flights for Sunday.'

* * *

Vince headed off with a lighter heart than during his drive to work that morning. He paused at Merri Street, about to head home, then turned left instead toward the tidy surroundings of North Warrnambool. He parked outside a modern townhouse and knocked on the door.

'Evening, Doc,' said Elena, swinging the door open. 'Come in.'

He followed her through to the kitchen. She was wearing designer jeans with ripped knees and a tight-fitting t-shirt, with a black apron over the top. Dead sexy. There was a delectable smell emanating from the stove.

'Guess what, Sarge? I've got no case to answer about that baby.'

'That's great news!' Elena smiled and moved to embrace him, but backed off just as fast.

'So you'll have to put up with me for another few years.'

She put her head on one side and frowned. 'Hmm, there is *that*.'

'I want to ask you about some copper stuff.'

'Good timing. Just about to serve dinner.'

'I don't want to impose, but—'

'But you did arrive at dinnertime and you look hungry. It's gnocchi with eggplant ragu—lucky I cooked a lot. Take a seat.'

Vince did as he was told and accepted a glass of Italian sparkling water. 'Farmer Will not joining us?'

Elena shook her head. 'We're having a little break.' She flashed her 'don't go there' look.

Vince nodded.

'So what was the cause of the baby's problems?' she asked, tossing the gnocchi into a large pan of boiling water.

'Foetal Alcohol Spectrum Disorder.'

She looked up. 'Will she be okay?'

'Who knows?' replied Vince. 'That nervous system damage can cause lifelong learning and behavioural problems.'

Elena watched the white cubes rise to the surface, her face creased with a frown. 'Poor thing.'

Vince shrugged, his elbows on the table and palms upward. *Not my problem.*

Elena brought over an olive sourdough loaf of freshly baked bread and put it on the table. 'Cut this up, please.'

'The thing is, we know the guy who abused Joey is living in Tassie, almost certainly on Bruny Island. So a magistrate has issued a warrant and Jane and I are heading down there on the weekend to front the prick.'

Elena drained the gnocchi and placed it in the pan with the sauce. 'Why don't the Tasmanian Police arrest him?'

'They can't find him.'

She plated out the food and brought it over to the table. 'But you can?'

'Can't be that hard. Bruny's not very big.'

Elena took off her apron with a flourish, let her hair down, and put a wedge of Parmesan cheese and a grater on the table. She sat and raised her glass of Sangiovese.

'*Buon appetito.*'

Vince smelled the dish in front of him and raised his glass with a smile. '*Grazie, Signorina.*'

'*Prego.*'

After a few minutes of richly flavoursome eating, Vince paused. 'If we find Dennis, can he be extradited back to Melbourne to face the music?'

'Course,' she replied. 'After an application to a magistrate.'

Vince mopped up some of the sauce with a piece of bread. 'Couple more questions,' he said. 'One, can a Victorian copper take him in? Two, are you busy next week?'

Elena laughed and topped up her wine. 'Yes, and no.'

'Fantastico!'

'After the arrest of Mark Brody, the boss is well pleased with me.'

'You were all over the media, Sarge. Front page in the *Observer*—"Local Rookie Detective Solves Mystery Murder of Parish Priest".'

'With a little help from her friends.' Elena raised her glass. 'So no problems spending a few days in Tasmania,' she added. 'On police business.'

Vince cleared the table, rinsed the plates and cutlery, and loaded them into the dishwasher, puzzling thoughts whizzing around in his mind.

'You know, I really liked Brodes,' he said, sitting down again. 'We got on well.' He paused and shook his head. 'I saw him as a gentle giant, but the old guys around the footy club told me he used to get white-line fever when he ran out to play. Then he would turn into an animal.'

'That's football for you, Doc.'

'I know he was upset about the way the Mons had handled Travis's mental illness at the seminary,' Vince went on, 'and he must've also blamed him for his homosexuality.' He drank some of his water. 'Accepting that his son was a gay failed priest with schizophrenia would've been a huge challenge for a macho ocker like Brodes. I *get* all that.' He looked up. 'But to murder a priest in cold blood?' He put his hands up in a quizzical gesture.

'There was more to it,' said Elena. 'Mrs Brody had seen a copy of your sister-in-law's letter on the Monsignor's desk and told her husband about the allegations that he'd sexually abused your brother.'

Vince nodded three times in succession. '*Okay*. So Brodes would've put two and two together and flipped out.'

'Mark told me he took his wife's presbytery key with him to the Snappers recovery session,' Elena continued, 'left training early, drove to Sacred Heart, and went straight to O'Shannessey's office.'

'Would've been breathing fire,' Vince said with a shudder.

'When Brody told him why he was there, the Monsignor laughed and advised him to go over to the church to ask God to heal his son.'

Vince frowned and pursed his lips.

'*That's* when he picked up the rosary beads.'

They sipped their drinks in silence for a minute.

'Did Geraldine know he'd done it?'

'I'm not a hundred percent certain.' Elena stood and turned on her espresso machine. 'Mrs Brody regarded the Monsignor as a saint—until she saw that letter.'

'Did she believe it?'

'She told me she didn't know what to think.' Elena paused as she ground some coffee beans. 'But early Easter Sunday morning she took the presbytery key from her purse'—she looked over at Vince—'and left it on the kitchen bench next to her husband's footy bag.'

<h1 style="text-align:center">40</h1>

'Hobart International Airport,' said Jane. 'Sounds a bit grandiose for such a small operation.'

Vince looked around and nodded. 'At least it's easier to navigate your way around than Tulla.'

'I think it's cute,' said Elena.

'Don't let any locals hear that C word,' he responded. 'The Taswegians are sensitive about that stuff.'

'Tassie's booming, isn't it?' asked Jane. 'Aren't all the mainlanders moving down here, looking for cheap houses and clean air?'

'Clean air all right,' said Vince, pulling his bomber jacket around him. 'Bloody cold air if you ask me.'

Their flight had touched down fifteen minutes ago and they'd already picked up their luggage and were out on the concourse, looking for the car hire depot.

'There's Hertz just over there,' said Elena, pointing to a sign a hundred metres to their right.

They picked up their car and headed off. It was a foggy and chilly evening in the Tasmanian capital and the sun had well and truly set. Vince turned up the heating and demister while Elena drove out of the airport and pulled onto the highway.

By the time they crossed the Tasman Bridge into central Hobart, it was close to eight. They pulled up outside the Customs House Hotel opposite the glistening black water of the harbour, then booked in and found their rooms. After a pub dinner downstairs in the bar, they sat around for a few minutes, but the purpose of their visit dampened any holiday spirit and they soon all retired for the night.

* * *

'Surprised you didn't go with the full fry-up, Vincent,' said Jane, putting her muesli, fruit, and yoghurt next to his on the breakfast table the next morning.

'Usually I do,' responded Vince, looking at the bacon, eggs, hash browns, and mushrooms on offer. 'But I promised the girls I'd lift my game.'

After finishing his breakfast, Vince sipped his coffee and turned on his laptop to work out the route.

'Should be only forty minutes or so down to Kettering. South on the S6.'

He scanned his emails. There was one from Simon Rutherford, sent last night at just after ten. He paused for a few seconds, heart in his mouth, finger poised above the screen, then opened it.

The Medical Board discussed the status of your registration at tonight's meeting. We received advice that the legal proceedings against you have been dropped. In addition, we sought an external medico-legal opinion from Professor Steinberg from Sydney, who advises us that proceeding with a Keilland's rotation in that particular case was consistent with reasonable practice, given the posterior position, foetal distress, and geographical issues.

We have decided that after your temporary suspension, your restricted registration will be reinstated to continue working in General Practice in Warrnambool, supervised by Dr Shirley Tiang.

Dr Felicity Jones, chair of the RANZCOG professional standards committee, has recommended that you be recredentialed to provide obstetric care under her mentorship.

The Board will review the situation in one year.

Yours sincerely

S Rutherford, Chair.

'Woohoo!' shouted Vince. 'Little Lachie's been sidelined!'

'Shoosh, Vinny,' Jane said from across the table, her finger to her lips.

Vince stood and pointed at the screen on his laptop. 'I have to do just *one* more year in Warrnambool. *And* I'm allowed to do deliveries.' He struggled to keep his voice down. 'Then I'll be back in business in Melbourne!'

'That's great,' said Jane, giving him a hug.

'I'm pleased for you, Doc.' Elena stood and shook his hand. 'But that poor little baby is the real victim in all of this,' she said, picking up her key.

Vince opened his mouth to say something and closed it again.

'We better leave by nine-thirty to catch that ferry,' Elena added as she strode to the elevator. 'See you both out the front.'

Vince sent off messages to Shirley and Lydia and the girls, then bounded up the stairs like a young Tasmanian kangaroo.

* * *

Less than an hour later they arrived in the pretty town of Kettering and drove onto the ferry. As the big craft pulled out, Vince reached for the door.

'I'm going up to the top deck to have a look at the view. You can see right along the D'Entrecasteaux channel.'

'I'll join you,' said Jane. 'Coming, Elena?'

She shook her head. 'You guys go for it.'

After twenty minutes of bracing, salty sea air, they clambered back down and re-joined Elena in the car as the ferry pulled into the terminal. They drove onto the island and stopped at an intersection.

'We take Lennon Road off to the right,' said Vince, looking at the GPS, 'then onto the Bruny Island Main Road.'

'An unimaginative but informative name,' said Elena.

Jane nodded and smiled. She had gone quiet since the ferry ride.

They headed southwest for a further fifteen minutes until the road narrowed to a strip with water on either side.

'The Neck,' said Vince, looking at the screen. 'Now we're entering South Bruny.'

They travelled on for another twenty kilometres and pulled up outside the hotel at ten-thirty. Vince got out, steadied himself against the buffeting wind, and walked around. All locked up and no sign of life anywhere.

'Bit early, ladies,' he said, coming back to the car. 'Not even Tasmanians drink before eleven.' He leafed through the tourist guide that came with the hire car. 'There's a winery just down the road. Bet we can get a coffee there.'

'Sure,' responded Elena.

'Can't we wait here until the pub opens?' asked Jane. 'I just want to get on with this.'

'We'll be back before opening time,' said Vince. He pointed at the windswept road, persistent drizzle, and wild sea. 'Nothing to do here.'

Elena headed south down the main road and pulled into the winery car park ten minutes later. They walked past the cellar door and tasting room into a cosy inviting café area with views out onto the vineyard, then sat down and ordered coffees.

'This would be lovely on a nice day,' Elena said as they looked into the gloom.

'Yeah,' Vince replied. 'There are two hectares under vine out there.' He pointed at the wet, grey outside world. 'Apparently.'

Conversation lapsed as the drinks arrived and they sat in silence, the only sound the rain pattering on the windows.

Jane let her coffee sit untouched in front of her and fidgeted with the sugar bowl.

Elena studied the leaflet on the table. 'They seem very proud of their pinot noir.'

'It's an excellent drop,' added Vince. 'I still have a case of the 2007 back in Canterbury. It's one of my favourite Tassie pinots.' He sipped his coffee. 'I mean, it *was*.'

* * *

An hour later they again pulled into the hotel car park. This time it was buzzing with activity. They went inside and chose a table near the fire. Vince did a tour of the bar and the lounge, looking at all the patrons, then returned to the table. He glanced at Jane and shook his head. A waitress gave them water, offered food menus, and placed the wine list in front of Vince.

'Boss in?'

'Yair.' The girl pointed toward the bar. 'Dad's over there.'

Vince wandered up to the man—a tall but rotund fellow with a florid complexion and sandy hair, heavily tattooed arms, a tea towel on his shoulder and a beer on the go.

'Nice place you've got here,' said Vince.

'It's orright.' Laconic, but tight-lipped. Vince knew the type.

He gestured at the busy tables in the dining area. 'I guess you'd know all the locals?'

The man nodded.

Vince brought up a photo on his phone and passed it across the bar. 'What about this bloke?'

He glanced at the image and spent a few seconds polishing an already clean glass. 'Who wants to know?'

'Vince Hanrahan.' Vince put his hand out.

'Jimmy Mason.' They shook across the bar.

'Get yer a beer, Vince?'

'No thanks, don't touch it.'

'Me old man told to me never trust a bloke who doesn't drink.'

Vince laughed. 'So did mine.'

'I get a lot of nosey people comin' in here,' said Mason. 'You're not a copper or a divorce lawyer, are ya?'

Vince shook his head and pointed at the image. 'Used to know this guy back in the day, that's all. Just wanted to say hello.' He took the phone back. 'For old time's sake.'

Mason inspected the photograph and kept on polishing the glass. 'Andre Bannister,' he said after a pause. 'Runs a B and B down yonder. Lanawanna. Name of Primrose Cottage. He helps out at the primary school of a Monday.'

Bet he does! 'Isn't it school holidays?'

'That's right. Another week to go.' He moved off to take an order. 'So he might be down the lighthouse, takin' tours.'

Vince walked back to the table and nodded toward the exit. Jane and Elena got up.

'Sorry, we're not hungry after all,' Elena said to the confused waitress as they followed him out the door.

They got in the car and Vince punched 'Primrose Cottage' into the GPS. 'Got the address,' he told the girls, 'but he mightn't be there.' Jane took a shuddering deep breath and pulled hard on her seatbelt.

They pulled back onto the main road, heading south again, and came to a T intersection, the main road continuing to the left and a smaller one snaking up a steep incline above the water.

'Right, Elena,' said Vince. 'Then straight on for a hundred metres and onto that dirt road up ahead.'

A heavy mist had descended, blanketing everything in a monochrome grey. The choppy water was faintly visible through the trees and Elena sat forward in the driver's seat peering into the murkiness. They climbed onto the bumpy unmade road, and after five minutes Vince pointed up to the left.

'That's the one.'

Elena turned into the drive and parked on a gravel area in front of a large shed behind an empty carport. The house, a pretty timber cottage, surrounded by a thriving native garden, sat high at the end of a meandering stone path. Jane and Vince got out of the car and walked up to the large blue front door. Jane took a deep breath as Vince gave it a vigorous knock. The sound echoed through the house. He walked right around the dwelling, peering in the windows. No sign of life.

He spread his arms palms up and shook his head. 'No one home. Have to try down at the lighthouse.'

'We can't chase him all over the whole damn island,' said Jane. 'I can't take much more of this.'

Vince responded with a rueful shrug and they walked back down to the car. *Not home*, he mouthed at Elena as Jane collapsed into the back seat. Elena entered 'Cape Bruny Lighthouse' as a new destination. She pulled back onto the dirt track and drove to the main road.

'Right hand turn this time,' he said, 'onto Lighthouse Road.'

They continued in silence in a southerly direction into South Bruny National Park, and after twenty minutes the road became rougher and more gravelly and terminated on an elevated headland, choppy water on either side, with the lighthouse rearing up into the clouds in front of them and the heaving ocean stretching to the far horizon. Elena parked in the visitors' area and Jane and Vince went into the adjacent small museum.

'Andre Bannister here today?' he asked a lady wearing a khaki shirt with a picture of a lighthouse on the pocket.

She nodded up the hill. 'He's up yonder doing the kid's tour today.' She glanced at her watch. 'Be finished soon.'

'Okay,' said Jane, zipping up her jacket. 'Let's do this.'

Vince put his arm around her and they set off along the steep path to the lighthouse, a towering majestic tower perched high above them at the very tip of the headland. Velvety green rolling hills flanked the path, seabirds soared overhead, and the sheer rock cliffs fell away to the heaving dark blue water below.

'This place is like the end of the line, Janey,' said Vince.

'In more ways than one,' she replied, shivering and slowing as they drew closer.

Vince and Jane walked around the base of the huge structure; they seemed all alone and the only sounds were harsh cries of seabirds and the howling wind. With a sudden clang, the metal door at the foot of the tower opened and a group of pre-teens filed out and set off down the track.

A tall, stooped, elderly man with a hooked nose, wearing a blue fleece with the lighthouse logo on the front, appeared in the doorway with a clipboard in his hand. Vince stepped forward and blocked his way.

'You're too late,' the man said, pointing at his watch. 'I'm finished.'

'You're finished all right.'

Ambrose Dennis opened his mouth and closed it again. 'Who … who are you?' he uttered in a hoarse voice, his prominent Adam's apple bouncing up and down.

'I'm Joey Hanrahan's brother,' said Vince. He gestured toward Jane. 'And this is his widow.' He moved up close, his face inches away. 'We've been looking for you, Dirty.'

* * *

The trip back to Hobart was a quiet one. Elena stayed behind for an extra day to settle Dennis into the Alonnah Police Station lock-up and liaise with her Tasmanian colleagues regarding his extradition to Victoria. Jane and Vince retraced their steps, caught the four o'clock ferry back to Kettering, and were back in Hobart just after five. They checked back into the hotel, then went for a walk along the waterfront and stopped for a drink at a bar in Salamanca Place.

'Champagne?' said Vince.

'Just tonic water for me, thanks.'

Vince returned with the drinks to find Jane staring into space, tears in her eyes.

'You know, Vinny. I thought I'd be over the moon, but I'm hollowed out and exhausted.' She paused. 'When I came face to face with that man, I didn't feel vindicated. I just felt sick.' She paused again and looked straight at Vince. 'Locking up people like Dennis won't bring Joseph back. It won't bring those other lives back.' She shook her head. 'It won't change anything.'

'It will, Janey, it will,' said Vince, taking her hand. 'Each time a bad priest like Dennis is prosecuted, it further erodes the massive wall of denial put up by the Church. Baby steps, I know, but you and Broken Rights are breaking down that wall.'

He pointed to the rolling news ticker on the TV screen on the wall.

'Catastrophic Institutional Failure. Royal Commission delivers withering criticism of Melbourne Archdiocese. "Inexcusable failures" in Ballarat Catholic Church's treatment of abuse victims. Archbishop to stand trial for concealing the abuse of young boys.'

'It could go all the way to the top,' added Vince. 'Watch this space.'

Jane nodded.

'And the headmaster of St Bernard's has issued an unconditional apology,' he went on. 'Erased the names of the perpetrators from the school honour boards and opened a reflective garden and monument to the sexual abuse victims.'

She nodded again. Face blank and eyes welling up.

Vince reached down to his backpack, pulled out a framed photograph of his brother, and placed it on the table. Joey was in his royal blue footy jumper in front of the goals, ball in his hand, crooked grin on his face, and the flat Wimmera plains in the background. The legend read 'Joseph Hanrahan, Minyip Football Club, Best and Fairest, 1994.'

'Let's drink to Joey,' said Vince. 'Best and Fairest.'

Jane smiled through her tears and raised her glass. 'To Joseph.'

* * *

The next day was bright and crisp. Jane and Vince breakfasted late, both made some calls, then they caught the ferry across the harbour to MONA and marvelled at the extraordinary rock-hewn building and eclectic collection within. They spent the afternoon strolling around the grounds, looking at the sculptures and installations and chatting about Joey, their marriages, their respective children, and life in general. Elena was back in Hobart by mid-afternoon and met them for dinner at a waterfront restaurant.

'My flight leaves at ten-thirty tomorrow,' said Jane, working her way through a sumptuous seafood platter. 'Time I got back to work and caught up with the kids.'

'I'm staying on for a couple of days,' said Elena. 'Got some procedural ends to tie up.'

Vince and Elena exchanged glances.

'I'm on enforced holidays for another week, so I'll hang about,' said Vince. 'Will you be right to get back home, Janey?'

'Absolutely. I'll get the Skybus into the city and catch the Horsham train. Mum will pick me up from the station.' She paused. 'I want to thank you both for holding my hand these last few days. It's been really tough, but I'm glad we did it.'

* * *

Vince dropped Jane at the airport the following morning, while Elena met with some colleagues at the local police headquarters.

'We have the car for another day,' he said when they met up back at the hotel. 'Why don't we go for a drive up to the Freycinet peninsula?'

They took a bush walk en route and had a long, late lunch in Coles

Bay. After a walk on the beach and a visit to a local oyster farm, Vince drove up a steep road onto a nearby mountain.

'We better head back,' said Elena. 'It's nearly seven.'

Vince winked as he glanced at the SatNav, turned off onto a side road, and crested a rise onto a cleared area on a raised plateau. There was a sign saying 'Eco Resort' at the front and half a dozen timber cabins facing out to sea. A woman emerged from the nearby office to great them.

'Mr Hanrahan?' Vince nodded. 'You're in number three,' she said, giving him a key. 'Everything's there for your breakfast in the morning. Enjoy.'

Elena raised her eyebrows as Vince parked the car. They walked across the grass under the darkening sky to the cabin, a large mountain range to the south and the bay stretching out in front.

She opened the door. It was a simple modern structure with a kitchenette, a small bathroom, and a queen-size bed.

'This was the last one available,' said Vince. 'We'll have to share.'

Elena put her arms out, looking down at her clothes. 'We've got no toiletries or spare undies or PJs.'

'Just have to improvise.'

She walked through to the back and opened the blinds. Large bifold windows revealed a spectacular vista—a huge treed valley with a lagoon on one side and the vast ocean as a backdrop.

'Wow,' she said. 'Check out the view! It's like perching up in a tree hut. I could look at that all day.'

They both sat on the end of the bed and gazed in silence.

'I called Tracey Cartwright yesterday, Sarge,' Vince said after a few minutes. 'Dustin has shot through to Cairns, and she's at her mum's with the kids.'

'Uh huh.'

'I told her "no blame, no shame". Made an appointment for her to see Charlie McNamee.'

Elena nodded.

'Put her in touch with a FAS specialist in Geelong and explained how the National Disability Insurance Scheme can help her baby.'

She continued to stare out the window.

Vince flopped back onto the bed and picked up the in-house brochure.

'We could do the walk up to the summit before dark,' he said, 'then drive back down to that pub for dinner.'

Elena turned to look at him. 'Or we could stay right here ...'

Acknowledgements

Many thanks to Amanda Spedding for helping out with the editing of this novel.

My sincere gratitude to my skilled and dedicated publisher, Michelle Lovi from Odyssey Books, for taking a chance on me for a second time.

Thank you also to my many patients over the years. You fill my head with stories and inspire my writing.

And finally, heartfelt thanks to Zoe and Sally for their advice and support, and Carmel, for her love, forbearance, and forensic second pair of eyes.

About the Author

After practicing medicine for twenty-five years on Victoria's rugged southwest coast, Bill and family relocated to the big smoke and he is now a GP in an inner suburb of Melbourne.

He has always been an avid reader, especially crime and contemporary literary fiction, and a compulsive scribbler. For fifteen years he wrote a fortnightly column in *The Australian Doctor* magazine and his debut novel, *Hard Labour*, was published by Odyssey Books in 2017.

Bill's other interests include family, footy, and music. He is seeking to master surfing, guitar playing, and golf but spends way too much time pouring over a sweaty keyboard. (Not to mention having a busy day job.)

You're Never the Same is a sequel to *Hard Labour* and there are rumours of a third in the series.